KATE VEITCH grew up in Melbourne, Australia, and has traveled widely throughout that country as well as in other parts of the world. Currently she divides her time between Manhattan and Byron Bay in northern New South Wales, where she and her partner are building their home. She has written for the *Sydney Morning Herald* and *Vogue* (Australia). *Without a Backward Glance* is her first novel. You can read more about her and the book at www.kateveitch.com.

"A compelling drama with a lot of heart and humanity. Impossible to put down."
—*Australian Women's Weekly*

"A self-assured, moving, hopeful story about the frailties of one—all—families, and the capacity to rage and to forgive." —Frances Atkinson, *The Age*

"A page-turning, upbeat family story written with clarity and grace."
—Katherine England, *Adelaide Advertiser*

"An original and highly absorbing debut novel." —*Sunday Herald Sun*

"A vivid dissection of a fractured family. Veitch has created an enthralling tale of the private sphere that is all the more effective for its consciously minimalist style." —*Australian Book Review*

"A powerful read . . . Veitch writes with sharp insight into the dynamics of families and the clusters of vulnerabilities, longing and tenderness which define them."
—Christopher Bantick, *Adelaide Advertiser*

"A truthful quality . . . that will engross the reader until the final page."
—*Australian Bookseller & Publisher*

"Kate Veitch's first novel is exceptionally good. She writes smoothly, cleanly, and with care and feeling for her characters. I winced when things went wrong for them, cheered when life was bountiful, and worried how they were going to cope with their problems. Veitch writes as if she listens carefully and observes closely."
—*Courier Mail*

Without a
Backward Glance

kate
VEITCH

A PLUME BOOK

PLUME
Published by Penguin Group
Penguin Group (USA) Inc., 375 Hudson Street, New York, New York 10014, U.S.A. • Penguin
Group (Canada), 90 Eglinton Avenue East, Suite 700, Toronto, Ontario, Canada M4P 2Y3
(a division of Pearson Penguin Canada Inc.) • Penguin Books Ltd., 80 Strand, London WC2R 0RL,
England • Penguin Ireland, 25 St. Stephen's Green, Dublin 2, Ireland (a division of Penguin Books
Ltd.) • Penguin Group (Australia), 250 Camberwell Road, Camberwell, Victoria 3124, Australia
(a division of Pearson Australia Group Pty. Ltd.) • Penguin Books India Pvt. Ltd., 11 Community
Centre, Panchsheel Park, New Delhi – 110 017, India • Penguin Group (NZ), 67 Apollo Drive,
Rosedale, North Shore 0632, New Zealand (a division of Pearson New Zealand Ltd) • Penguin
Books (South Africa) (Pty.) Ltd., 24 Sturdee Avenue, Rosebank, Johannesburg 2196, South Africa

Penguin Books Ltd., Registered Offices: 80 Strand, London WC2R 0RL, England

Published by Plume, a member of Penguin Group (USA) Inc. Previously published in a Viking
Australia edition as *Listen*.

First American Printing, July 2008
10   9   8   7   6   5   4   3   2   1

CIP data is available.
ISBN 978-0-452-228947-5

Printed in the United States of America

for phillip

first, best, always

Acknowledgments

The first draft of this novel was written in 2004, while I was living near Ubud on the beautiful island of Bali. My thanks, affection, and respect to all the people there who looked after me so kindly and so well.

A number of friends visited me over those months, and to each of them my gratitude for their company and encouragement, especially to Phillip Frazer, my first reader, lifelong friend, and now my beloved partner.

I have been very lucky to have my novel championed by two such enthusiastic and supportive agents as Fiona Inglis in Australia, and Faye Bender in the United States. Thank you both, so much.

It's also been my great good fortune to find a publishing home among the Penguins both in Australia and in the United States, with Plume, and I can't imagine that an author could be happier. Editors, publishers, cover designers, publicity, and marketing mavens: so many charming, witty, and hardworking women have guided me and my work. My heartfelt thanks to all of you—is it always this much fun?

Lastly, I'd like to thank the many readers who have made the time to contact me with words of appreciation. It's every author's dream to know that her story, her characters, have truly reached other people, moving them sometimes to laughter and to tears, and have given them enjoyment. Thank you!

Without a
Backward Glance

CHRISTMAS eve, 1967

They were plump, meaty birds, Rosemarie admitted grudgingly, as she shoved in handfuls of stuffing. The rich creamy-yellow color of the plucked skin was testament to their short but happy lives, in a generous yard with good food and plenty of it, and they would be succulent and tender. Her mother would've given her eye teeth to have two chickens like these—fowls, she'd have called them—to roast for Christmas dinner. But the few feathers her husband had missed revolted Rosemarie. Lips curled back, she tried to pull out one of the nubby white shafts but the skin lifted toward her, resisting, and she gave up. Oh, she wished she could give up on the whole damn thing, just go and lie down on her bed with the curtains drawn and a wet flannel on her forehead.

Why, for heaven's sake, must he call them "chooks"? And *why* must she turn the oven on tomorrow morning and heat the whole place up when the temperature was like an oven outside anyway? Cooking a baked dinner made perfect sense back home. On Christmas Day in England the sun barely peeked above the horizon, and both the cooking of the meal and the eating were so welcomely warming, like a red coat in a crowd of gray. Feasting and cheer to keep the dark and the cold at bay. Here, where the sun was still glaring onto the patio at seven o'clock in the evening, slicing at her eyes like a bayonet when she glanced out, a meal like this was just . . . stupid. More stupid work for her.

The back door opened and closed again. She heard Alex toeing his gardening boots off, *thud-thud*, and washing his hands at the laundry sink. Singing, he was! That moronic "Rudolph the red-nosed reindeer."

"That's not even a proper carol!" she shouted, but he only called back, "What's that, love?" over the sound of running water. From farther back in the house she heard Meredith's wail start up, piercing as an air-raid siren, and Deborah's ringing tones of command.

The door from the kitchen to the laundry swung open. Her husband's thinning hair was plastered flat to his head where he'd damped it carelessly as he washed; he was beaming.

"Sweetheart!" he cried, though she was only an arm's length from him. "There's just enough of the new beans for Christmas dinner tomorrow! First thing in the morning I'll get out there and pick 'em. While the dew's still on 'em!"

She snorted. "As if there'll be any dew, in this weather."

"Metaphorically speaking." Alex leaned in to kiss her cheek; he smelled of earth and plants and sweat, and she didn't like it one bit. And he was *stubbly,* it prickled her and he knew she hated that. She turned to admonish him, eyes fixed on his chin, but his face was lit by a shaft of lowering light and she saw for the first time that his reddish beard now had patches of white. His jaw seemed huge, suddenly, and the white stubble stuck out of his skin like the shafts of the fowls' feathers. She stared in dismay. *Oh, what have I done? Why am I here with this old man and his gray beard?*

Alex was staring fixedly, too, at her hands, the chickens, the almost empty bowl.

"You're stuffing the chooks."

"Yes, I am stuffing the chooks," she said, facing him square on with dropped shoulders and an expression that she hoped said, *Talk about state the bleeding obvious!*

"The night before?"

"Yes, Alex, it is the night before. The night before Christmas. That's right."

"You should never stuff a chook till just before you put it in the oven."

"Why not? Why bloody *not?*" Her voice had risen; she sounded like a child, petulant and protesting. He heard it, too, and looked at her with cautious pity, and she hated that even more.

"That's what my mother always said."

"Well, your mother's not here to get woken up at six in the morning and watch the kids squabble over their presents and then slave away in a boiling hot kitchen for the rest of the day, is she? And if I want to stuff the chickens now I'll jolly well stuff them now! *My* mother always stuffed the chickens the night before." Actually, Rosemarie couldn't remember ever having chicken for Christmas dinner at home; it had usually been a joint of rather tough lamb, and never quite enough of it. But Alex wasn't to know that, was he?

"The kids won't squabble, love. Not when they see what we've got them."

"Oh, won't they! They've started already, can't you hear them?"

And Alex could, now that she mentioned it, going at it hammer and tongs, the two eldest shouting at each other and the little one bawling again, poor poppet.

"I tell you what," he said, backing away a little from his wife. "How about I settle those ratbags down and have a quick shower, and then I'll take a couple of 'em with me and go and buy fish and chips for dinner. What do you think? Sweet girl?"

He bent a little, placatingly, to look into her lowered face. She nodded fiercely.

"Yes," she said. "No! *I'll* sort the children out, you have your shower. Quicker."

Because he would coax them into a good mood and that would take half an hour, whereas she—

"I've got the wooden spoon!" Rosemarie yelled, thwacking the closed door of the girls' bedroom with the flat of her hand. On the door was a neatly hand-lettered sign: *PRIVATE. SECRET. NO PARENTS.* Inside, the arguing and crying suddenly stopped.

"Don't come in! You can't come in!"

"I am so coming in! I'm counting to five: one, two, three . . ."

There was a desperate "Wait! WAIT!" on five and then Robert opened the door, eyes darting first to check her hands. No wooden spoon. Deborah and James were standing side by side, guarding the secrecy of whatever was under a very lumpy bedspread. The rolls of wrapping paper, the scissors and ribbon and tape, were all heaped in disarray on the second bed. Meredith, the youngest, came forward to stand beside Robert, her plump six-year-old cheeks flushed and wet with tears. Rosemarie raised one hand like a traffic policeman.

"I don't want to know what you were fighting about, I just want you all to stop."

"I wasn't fighting, Mummy," said James mildly.

"I know, James." He never did.

There they were, aligned as always like two opposing sets of salt and pepper shakers. These two pairs, odds and evens: the first-born with the third child, the second-born with the fourth. Deborah the eldest, almost thirteen now and almost not a child, watchful and well organized, and her dreamy, tractable brother James, four years younger. Both with their mother's willowy build, her glossy jet hair and olive skin, though only James had Rosemarie's blue eyes. Deborah's were her father's odd streaky mix of green and brown. And the other two: Robert, *such* a middle child, doomed to be forever stuck between the eldest and the most likable, ever protesting, *That's not fair!* as Deborah bossed them all around, and little thumb-sucking Meredith his self-appointed charge, like a chick under the hen's wing. This pair looked alike too, with tawny red-brown hair and hazel eyes and scatterings of light brown freckles. It was the foxy Scottish coloring you saw in Alex's extended family.

These parts should go together to form a neat whole: two times two equals four—her children. But Rosemarie had never felt quite convinced that they were *really* hers. Yes, yes, of course she *knew* that they were, she could remember being pregnant and waking up after their births, those strange groggy meetings—though she had been awake for the last birth and that was hardly an improvement. And she'd been with them every unremitting moment since; could describe (if, god forbid, she ever had to) every single unremarkable day of each of their lives.

But . . . how could that be? When she still felt just a girl herself? And that was how she looked, too: the mirror confirmed that she was still more dewy maid than thick-waisted matron. Though turning thirty a few months ago had been an awful jolt.

When other mothers—*real* mothers—discussed their babies and their growing children, their voices, even in complaint, seemed full of a passionate engagement that made Rosemarie feel like someone from another planet. An imposter. Often she felt she was hardly relevant to her own children's lives—well, except as a housekeeper, and anyone could do that. What really engrossed them was this never-ending sibling business. The gothic melodramas over an extra spoonful of ice cream or who sat next to whom on a five-minute trip to the shops.

The all-consuming skirmishes that constantly broke out between them, and their stalwart alliances, so unshakeable, left her baffled and exasperated. She had grown up with two brothers so vastly older than herself—benignly disinterested young giants who came and went their own way—that she was virtually an only child. Why did her kids have to make things so *difficult*? It was ridiculous! Here it was Christmas Eve, and the atmosphere in this suburban bedroom was like Wuthering Heights, turbulent with all their seething rivalries—ah, except for that serenely rosy space surrounding James, like a tiny private cloud on which he floated. James, who always chose the easy path, while the others clambered over rocks and fell into ditches.

Right on cue, Meredith drew a huge sobbing breath.

"Debbie said—"

Rosemarie and her older daughter exchanged a quick, tense glance. The girl was nearly as tall as her mother, and their expressions as they faced each other were remarkably alike. *Will we do battle over this one?* each was asking. *If you start, I'll meet you there!* Rosemarie looked away, back to little whining Meredith.

"I don't care what Debbie said! *I* said I didn't want to know!"

"Debbie said you would hate my present!" the child burst out, and started sobbing again. Almost imperceptibly, Robert moved sideways so that the edge of his shoulder nudged his little sister comfortingly.

And I dare say I will. It's awfully hard to like the cheap little things you've all saved up to buy me. But she sighed in a long-suffering way and said, "Meredith, whatever you give me, I will love it, because you gave it to me. The same goes for all of you. You know that. And the very best present you could give me is a day with no fighting. Starting right now!"

"Yes, Mummy."

"All right, Mum." There were smiles all round. They could tell they were out of danger; they'd got off lightly.

"Now, who wants to go with Daddy to get fish and chips for supper?"

"Me! Me!"

As she went past the bathroom she heard Alex in the shower, not even singing really, just yelling out a wordless accompaniment to some unidentifiable melody in his head. In the kitchen, he'd turned the radio on and tuned it to the ABC. Some Australian with a plummy voice was speculating about what might be in Her Majesty's Christmas Day message tomorrow. Rosemarie's face screwed up. This ghastly fawning! That awful old England of headscarves and stiff upper lips and rigid class divisions was *dead* now, didn't they know that? No one *cared* any more—except here, in stupid Australia, the lapdog of two masters, slobbering over the English queen while sending its sons off to fight for the Americans in this horrible war in Vietnam. Savagely she twisted the dial to 3AK *("Where no wrinklies fly!")* and turned up the volume to drown out the sounds of the children's bickering, which had broken out again as they prepared to depart. The Who was "talkin' 'bout my GENeration," suggesting in a mighty sneer to the older one, "Why don't you all just fffffade away?" Rosemarie danced along with it, jerking her shoulders from side to side. *Yes,* she thought, *good idea! Why don't you all just do that? Ffffff . . . something, anyway!*

Finally the car pulled out of the driveway. Robert came sidling in, stopping just inside the kitchen door, testing the air.

"The others have all gone with Dad." His mother nodded. Robert advanced, cautious yet purposeful, edging around the kitchen table until at last he settled there with his box of Derwent colored pencils and a large spiral-bound project book.

"I'll tidy this up the minute they get back," he offered.

His mother couldn't help a small smile. "As if you'd make a mess!" This nervy, neat boy who never even let a pencil touch the table: each was slotted back into its color-coded place the moment its work on the page was done. She started chopping up the vegetables for tomorrow; they could sit in a basin of cold water in the fridge overnight. Even if Alex's mother wouldn't have.

A Beatles song came on. It was a few years old now. What wouldn't she have given to see the Beatles when they'd come to Melbourne! She'd said that to a woman who seemed friendly at the school Mother's Club as they stood side by side making sandwiches for the children's lunch orders, but the woman looked at her as though she were mad. "What, with all those screaming girls?" she asked, curling her upper lip. But Rosemarie could have been one of those screaming girls, oh, how easily! Screaming and sobbing ecstatically . . .

"*Listen . . .*" sang the warm male voice, tender and confident. Who was that: Paul? Maybe George . . . "*Do you want to know a secret?*"

No! she thought emphatically. *And I don't want anyone to know mine!* She leaned her weight on the big kitchen knife with blind efficiency, slicing through a huge piece of homegrown pumpkin. Beads of moisture formed on the slabs of freshly cut flesh. No one wanted to know the *real* secrets, anyway, not the really big ones. That getting married was like slamming a great big door and living forever in just one tiny room. That babies tore you from the bliss of unbroken sleep as ruthlessly as any torturer and you never got back to that lovely place again. That raising children and running a household was mostly tedious donkey work. That the man you'd once found so thrilling became, over the years, so eye-wateringly boring you could hardly bear for him to lay a hand on you in bed . . .

The Beatles song had finished. Advertisers were yapping now and she turned the radio down. Robert glanced up at her with a tentative smile.

"What is it you're doing there, anyway?" she asked, determinedly putting a note of interest into her voice. The vegetables were all chopped now and she set them in their bowl of water to one side.

"I'm working on a project. 'Christmas in Other Lands.' Or, Mum? Do you think 'Christmas in Foreign Lands' sounds better?"

"Why on earth are you doing a project now? The holidays have barely started, you won't be back at school for weeks." *Weeks of bickering kids all day. And flies. And mosquitoes at night. Never being able to get cool, not for more than a moment.*

"It's not for school. It's for me." Robert's head was bent over the page, coloring in a heading with meticulous care. "Or for you, if you'd like it."

"For me? What would I want with a project about Christmas? I've got Christmas coming out of my ears, Robert."

His head sank lower, his nose now barely an inch from the page. "Christmas in Other Lands. Because you miss England, Mum."

There was no reply. He looked sideways over at his mother, but she was just staring at the empty chopping board. "Don't you, Mum? Miss Christmas in England?"

"Oh, in some ways. There was never much of a Christmas to be had when I was little. During the war." She looked up, talking to him properly now. "And when I was your age, ten, the war had only been over for two years and the rationing made things even worse. It was pretty grim, really, that England. And it stayed grim for a long time. It was still grim when I left."

"But the snow was nice, wasn't it? And singing carols in the snow, with the lanterns and everything. A white Christmas," the boy said swooningly.

"Yes. The snow was nice." Rosemarie started opening cupboards and getting out tomato sauce and pickled onions and vinegar. "We'll eat the fish and chips outside, shall we? On the patio." She got some plates out, and leaned on the kitchen bench with her hands on either side of the stack, elbows locked, staring again. Her son watched her.

"When I left it was gray and dirty and poor, it really was. And now it's changed, and I'm not there. That's what I miss: England now."

"But, Mum . . . if it's changed . . ." Robert hesitated, looking puzzled, trying to get this right. With a rush of conviction he went on, "I think you can only miss what you used to have and it's gone, can't you? Isn't that what 'missing' something means? Like, you know, 'Oh, I used to have a really good pocketknife and now I've lost it. I really *miss* that pocketknife.'"

"No, Robert. Oh no. You can miss something you've never had, too. Something you could've had, and should've had, but then you find you haven't got it after all."

"Rosie? Darl, look who I ran into at the fish and chip shop!" Behind Alex, all smiles, were their neighbors from a few doors down, an older couple. Well, Alex's age. "John and Joyce Grounds!" he cried unnecessarily. Their gangling son Tim, twenty-one now (they'd been to the party just a few weeks ago, a big marquee in the back-yard), loomed in the rear. He and Alex and James were all carrying bulky newspaper-wrapped parcels.

"Oh, how lovely!" said Rosemarie. "I'll just get some more plates. Let's all go through to the patio, shall we?"

Alex's face relaxed. "Good-oh!" he cried. "And I'll pour us all a refreshing ale, how about that?"

"Deborah, make up a jug of orangeade for you kids. Lots of—"

"Ice cubes," Deborah cut in, already at the fridge. "I know."

The sun was finally setting and Rosemarie had asked Robert to hose the patio, so now it was cool and wet underfoot. *Quite pleasant really*, she surprised herself by thinking. *In a sloppy Australian way*. The kids were excited by the unexpected company, and although Robert watched with a hawk's eye as Deborah doled out their servings like a sergeant ("No, Meredith! Just two potato cakes, and you have to eat your flake!"), he didn't challenge her. No bickering, no complaints. The kids sat on the patio steps happily eating with their fingers in the gathering dusk, shy lanky Tim sitting with them, perched on the topmost step with his long legs stretching almost to the path. The evening suddenly had a party feel: the adults were happy and excited, too, loose and chatty around the outdoor table.

Joyce placed a confiding hand on Rosemarie's forearm. "I've been so wanting to see you, dear, and tell you about the Christmas party at John's work. I wore that new cocktail frock you made me."

"The pink one?"

"The pink one," Joyce confirmed. "With the green bolero. Rose-marie, I will never again even *hesitate* over one of your suggestions! I don't think I've ever had so many compliments on a frock in my life. Even more than for the mother-of-the-bride outfit you made me for Leonie's wedding."

"Oh, Joyce, I am *so* pleased to hear that."

"I gave your telephone number to three different ladies, I hope that's all right."

"It certainly is. Of course. You know how I love to sew." *And how I love to tuck the money away in my own little bank account.*

"I don't know how you do it. I mean, I can follow a pattern, but how you make these things up out of your own head, it's just marvelous."

"Do you think so?" said Rosemarie, smiling. *You think that's marvelous? These little outfits? If I'd stayed in London I could be designing for one of the trendsetters now: Mary Quant, or Biba. Even here, if I got just half the backing a local girl like Prue Acton's had—I could have my own label! Like her!*

"She's not just a pretty face, my little wifey," said Alex proudly, opening another bottle of beer and refilling their glasses. "Joyce, would you like some green beans for your dinner tomorrow? I'll be picking some fresh in the morning."

"That's so nice of you to offer, but actually we're going to Leonie's tomorrow."

"Oh! That's something different!"

"She's so proud of the new house she and Dennis have built," said John. "She was keen as mustard to have Christmas dinner there and we thought, well, why not? Do something different!"

How very daring of you, thought Rosemarie, all her discontent flaring up again.

"What about your family, Alex? Got anyone coming?"

"As a matter of fact we do. My brother Bob and his wife Joan are coming over."

"That'll be nice."

"It will be nice," Alex agreed, nodding.

"I'm thinking," said Rosemarie suddenly, "I'm thinking of getting some labels woven, to put in the garments I make."

Joyce stared at her, puzzled. "Labels? With . . . what? To say what?"

"The designer. You know. Me."

"You? Your name?"

"Well," Rosemarie gave a little laugh, trying to sound casual. John Grounds was staring at her, too, now, though Alex, at the end of the table closest to the steps, had twisted sideways in his chair and was looking at the kids. "Rosemarie McDonald' might be a bit long. I was thinking . . . something shorter . . ." Actually she had been thinking that "Rose Red" would be charming, and memorable, but now she didn't want to say that.

"I just don't think . . ." said Joyce uncertainly.

"Listen, pet," said John kindly, leaning toward Rosemarie, "you don't want to look like you're big-noting yourself. Not here. People won't like it." His wife nodded emphatic confirmation. Rosemarie felt herself blush fiercely; from the collarbones up, her throat and face were on fire. She hoped desperately that in the deepening dusk no one would see.

"Did you hear that?" asked Alex, turning back to them. "The kids are trying to guess what we've got 'em for Christmas, but they really haven't got a clue!" He gave a happy chuckle. "God I love Christmas. It's such a great time for the kids!"

"And what have you got 'em?" asked John.

Alex leaned in closer. "New bikes," he said softly. "For all of 'em!"

"Oh, aren't they lucky!" said Joyce. She took a decent swig from her glass of beer and turned to her silent hostess. "What about your own family, Rosemarie?" Her voice was over-bright, like an adult trying to cheer up a grumpy child. "Do you ever have anyone come over from England?"

There was a little pause before Rosemarie could make herself respond. "No. It's so far to come, you know."

"Well, yes, it is. Of course."

Suddenly she wanted to shove a sharp elbow into their coziness, these nice middle-aged people, her husband, their friends. "And I didn't exactly make myself popular, you know, running away with an older man."

"Oh."

The table stilled, but it wasn't enough.

"I was only seventeen, after all. And pregnant. We said some very hard things to each other, my mum and dad and me."

"Oh."

"They'd trusted Alex, you see. He was working with my dad. On a bridge project. That's how they met. How *we* met."

It was almost completely dark now and the silence around the table was profound. Suddenly the outside light snapped on, and they all flinched at the glare. Deborah was standing by the back door, her hand still resting on the wall beside the switch. "It's got too dark," she said loudly.

Did she hear? Rosemarie wondered, but Deborah's expression was giving nothing away. Defiantly Rosemarie glanced from face to face around the table but they were all looking in different directions, no one at her. Joyce reached out and started to gather plates. John made a little coughing noise, a let's-all-get-on-together noise.

"We . . . We're thinking of going to my cousin's holiday place down at Rosebud for a few days around New Year. Ah . . . Maybe you could bring the kids down one day?"

"Oh, that's a top-notch suggestion!" cried Alex gratefully. "Kids! What do you think of this idea?"

The younger children came over and leaned against their father as he and John put to them the enticing prospect of a day at the beach. Deborah collected their messy, abandoned plates from the patio steps and said, as she passed her mother, "There's a brick of neapolitan ice cream in the freezer, Mum. Shall I get it out for dessert?"

"Yes, thank you." Rosemarie followed her daughter into the kitchen, a clutter of bottles in her arms. She felt almost ill with shame and defiance. *Why did I have to say that? What earthly good did it do?* "You're such a help to me, Deborah. Sometimes I think you could run this family on your own." She nudged her daughter's shoulder gratefully, and the girl dipped her head in acknowledgment. They stood side by side for a moment looking through the window at the scene on the patio, the three older people talking animatedly again, Meredith snuggled in her father's lap, James draped over his shoulders. Tim Grounds was slouched comfortably in a chair, Robert leaning forward attentively in the one beside him.

"Robert's fingering again," observed Deborah, and yes, Rosemarie could just make out the tight repetitive patterns of Robert's hands, moving his fingers to and fro, in and out, making cat's cradles out of thin air. His subtle, *so* annoying habit. She clicked her tongue and sighed.

"He'll wear his fingerprints clean off, I swear," she said. "Oh, let him go, Deb, don't say anything." They both turned away.

"What about the stewed apricots, Mum, shall we have those, too?"

The Grounds had gone home, the dishes were done, the children were putting the finishing touches to their presents. Alex hadn't said much. Now he hung the damp teatowel on the rail and turned to his wife. She lifted her chin to take whatever was coming. *Give me a good ticking-off*, she thought, *I deserve it. After all, it was my fault, too, what happened back then. I wanted you, too. And I so wanted you to carry me off to the other side of the world, to the land of sunshine and plenty.*

"I know it's late," her husband said, "but it's the best time for watering, in this weather. I want to give the fruit trees a good soak."

"Oh. All right then." Rosemarie's shoulders sagged as he went out through the laundry. The screen door squeaked and then slammed. She felt like a balloon that had been over-inflated and was now slowly coming down. She could almost hear the soft hiss.

She wandered into the living room, sat down in her usual chair. The children started bringing their presents out, carrying them in a little procession from the bedroom and depositing them fussily around the base of the Christmas tree. The tree was decorated with a mixture of delicate glass ornaments, a fixture of Alex's childhood Christmases, and the children's own handmade decorations, yards and yards of paper chains in alternating red and green, cut-outs of snowflakes and stars and reindeer, and a wonky glittering angel with a tinsel halo perched right at the top. The kids looked at each other and lined up self-consciously in front of the tree, facing her.

"Would you like us to sing you a Christmas carol, Mum?" asked Robert importantly.

"Yes, I would," she answered, folding her hands in her lap. "Very much."

"Where's Daddy?" asked Meredith, glancing about.

"Watering the fruit trees. He'll be a while."

"We'll just start, then." Robert turned slightly to count the others in. "One, two, three!"

"O come all ye faithful, joyful and triumphant,

Come ye, O co-ome ye to Be-eth-lehem . . ."

They were surprisingly good. Even little Meredith kept up pretty well. James's voice was particularly pleasant, Rosemarie thought, and his face was just entrancing, relaxed as always and poised to smile. Already so handsome: the crisp dark hair, the blue eyes raised as he sang, the rosy perfect skin. *The good fairy kissed you on the forehead. You'll have a charmed life and I'll never need to worry about you.*

Robert, on the other hand, had his eyes fixed anxiously on her, the muscles in his skinny neck standing out. He was so tense she could hardly bear to look at him. She felt ashamed and made herself smile, then was stricken anew at the way his face lit up. *What a good kid you are. You're all good kids, really. You try so hard to make me happy, you poor things.* He sang a little louder and Deborah shot him a look, plainly longing to tell him to pipe down. Amazing that she'd let him be in charge for even a moment.

They finished. Robert bowed and the others all raggedly followed. Rosemarie clapped hard, and while she was still clapping a car pulled into the driveway. The motor stopped and the headlights were turned off, but no one got out. The kids hurtled over to kneel on the couch and gaze out the window.

"Who's that?"

"Is it Uncle Bob?"

"No, silly! His car's not like that!"

"I'll go and see," said Rosemarie.

They watched their mother at the driver's window, ducking her head to talk to someone they couldn't see. Suddenly she turned and walked quickly back into the house. They heard her go into her bedroom and close the door. They sat together on the couch, facing the tree now, waiting. A few minutes later Rosemarie reappeared in the doorway of the living room. She had changed from her pretty cotton frock into slacks and a smart top. She was holding her big yellow handbag.

"I'm just going to get some lights for the Christmas tree," she said. Her eyes, bright and hectic, swept across them, then she turned and was gone. The four children turned, too, as one, kneeling on the couch again to watch their mother hurry to the stranger's car. She was carrying the tan suitcase with the dark brown stripe, the one that usually sat on top of the big wardrobe. She heaved the case into the backseat and climbed in after it. The car's headlights came on again, it reversed down the driveway and drove off up the street. The children were still kneeling there after the sound of the motor had well and truly faded away.

Their father came into the room, and slowly they slid down and turned to face him.

"Where's your mother?" Alex asked.

part one

chapter 1

Alex woke up troubled about the roses. It was already spring but he still hadn't pruned the rosebushes, and now it was too late. Or was it? Well, first thing after breakfast he'd have a look at them. He would write himself a note, that's what he'd do. Oh, these notebooks were a jolly good idea! The perfect solution to the little tricks his memory seemed to be playing lately. Now he kept notebooks in the car and the garden shed and every room of the house. He bought them in bundles of ten from the $2 shop—couldn't beat that for a bargain! Sometimes he would come across several of them huddled together like children playing hide-and-seek. Yet despite having so many, all too often he couldn't lay his hands on one when he needed it. Or it would be a different notebook, not the one he needed. But never mind, they were still a marvelous idea, because if he wrote things down then he couldn't forget them, could he? Simple as that!

As he leaned across for the little notebook sitting there on the bedside table he caught his own inner swell of triumph, *like one of those bumptious sports stars these days*, he chided himself wryly. When did athletes start carrying on like that? The upthrust arm and victory snarl. Could you imagine John Landy doing that, or Betty Cuthbert, when they won their gold medals right here in Melbourne at the '56 Olympics? Never! He picked up the notebook and the pen and wrote *Check roses for pruning* on a fresh page. There!

With his feet on the floor now and the little notebook still in his hand, Alex flipped back a page reflexively. No need for glasses, how's that! Nothing wrong with his eyesight! *Phone Jeannie, wish her Happy Birthday.* Jeannie? "Now that rings a bell," he said.

A relative, for sure. But which one, and what birthday, and when should he call? Maybe he had that written down somewhere else. The calendar? Really should date these little notes. Or he could— ah, that's the ticket! He wrote underneath this Jeannie message *Check with Deb*, tapped hard to make a good definite full stop, and with a feeling of satisfaction flipped the page over. *Check roses for pruning.* God, the bloody roses!

He kept the notebook open by him as he made a cup of tea and some toast, and the moment he'd finished he took the pruning shears and the medium-weight gardening gloves and went out to the line of rosebushes along the front fence. He had to shake his head twice. He blinked and blinked again. All pruned, and a beautiful job of it, too, and the pinkish shoots of new spring growth coming along. How could that be? The worry in his mind was still there, the vision of the roses unkempt and straggling . . .

"It must have been a dream," Alex said wonderingly, and even as he said it, yes, so it seemed, a dream he had been having just before he woke. Or just before he fell asleep last night. But how could you dream before you fell asleep, eh? Foolishness!

"Something I just need to check with you, Deb. When's Cousin Jeannie's birthday, do you know?"

"Cousin Jeannie? Whose cousin's that, Dad?"

"Well, she's my cousin, isn't she?"

"Your cousin? Sorry, Dad, I'm drawing a blank on this one."

"Oh. An auntie maybe?"

"An auntie? There was Auntie Margaret, but she's dead now, and there's Uncle Bob's wife Joan over in Perth . . . Is that who you mean? Auntie Joan?"

"No, darl, not Bob's wife. Jeannie. She was . . . she was . . . Well, but I made a note to ring her and wish her happy birthday."

Standing in her kitchen, gazing distractedly at various items on the noticeboard beside her, Deborah could picture her father perfectly, standing in his own kitchen just a few kilometers away, probably with his back door open so he could look out to the garden. This was not the outer suburban home of her early childhood, nor the one closer to her father's work that they'd moved to the year after her mother disappeared. Alex had bought this place fifteen or sixteen years ago, when he retired. He'd bought it not for the house, which was small and unremarkable, but for the land: a quarter acre that had been mostly lawn, a blank canvas he could spend the rest of his life filling in. Which was exactly what he'd done, and was still doing, and good for him—but her life was full of more pressing concerns than what bulbs to order and some forgotten relative's forgotten birthday.

"Sorry, Dad. If anything occurs to me I'll ring you back. But I'm just in the middle of doing something right now. Yes . . . yes, I will. Talk soon, Dad, okay? Bye."

Deborah walked back toward the study. Her lower back ached all the time these days. Here it was, only midmorning, and she'd been sitting at that damn computer too long already. And on a Saturday! Angus, unpacking the shopping from the market, tried to catch her wrist as she went past. She paused, her glance flicking past him to the study.

"Your father?" he asked.

"Who else do I call Dad?" she said, her voice sharp.

"Everything okay?"

Deborah rolled her eyes. "God, I don't know. Some cousin whose birthday he can't remember. Honestly, sometimes I think he's going gaga."

"He's getting on, Dee. Isn't he eighty now? His memory's bound to play up a bit, don't you think?"

"I wish you wouldn't call me Dee. It's not my name, it's not any bloody name at all, it's just an initial for god's sake. What if I started calling you by your initial?"

"It's just a nickname," Angus said mildly. "An affectionate diminutive. You never used to mind."

She flapped her hand at him dismissively, and stalked off. But the stiffness across her lower back made it feel like her bum was sticking out, *like a waddling duck*, she thought disgustedly, and she hated Angus for watching her. She reached the study and closed the door with dignified firmness behind her, then realized she'd left her cup of coffee on the kitchen bench. She hesitated, opened the door. Angus was walking toward her with the cup in his hand. She took it from him silently and closed the door again.

"That's okay, darling," she heard her husband say. She pressed her lips together and sat back down at the computer. As the screen filled with text a voice inside her head said, *God, you're mean! Can't you just be nice to him?* She gave a tiny groan. *I know, I know*, she thought. *I'll make it up to him later. Once I'm finished*—Damn, another error! Deborah swooped the cursor onto it, narrowing her eyes. Her back slumped and she didn't even notice.

Olivia was walking over to her grandfather's house that Saturday morning with Mintie and Fly-by. It was quicker to ride, of course, but then she couldn't take both dogs. Mintie was fine running beside the bike, but Fly-by was an absolute idiot, charging across in front of her and panicking if another bike came up silently behind them.

Every dog has at least one unchangeable quirk, and that was Fly-by's. But walking, they were no problem. And Grandpa would give her a lift back later in the afternoon.

Olivia's route from North Fitzroy to her grandfather's in Alphington was carefully planned, taking advantage of every off-leash area along the way. Through a series of parks, beside the Merri Creek and at one point the Yarra river; there were few roads to cross and when she got to them, she always leashed the dogs. When she was little her mum or dad had walked or ridden with her, but a few years ago she had persuaded her parents to let her make the trip by herself. Well, herself and her border collie.

She'd stood in her prime eavesdropping spot, on the other side of a carefully just-barely-opened living room door, as they discussed it.

"I don't know, Angus. She's only nine. It's quite a way to go on her own," her mother had said.

"Yeah, but she's used to it, and she certainly knows the way," said her dad.

"She'd have to stick to the agreed route."

"We know she'll do that. She hasn't changed her walk to school by as much as a house-block in four years!"

"And only with the dogs. Mintie's so devoted, she wouldn't leave her side for an instant."

"And she'd tear the throat out of anyone who tried to have a go at her," her father said.

"I think we'll have to get her a mobile phone. For emergencies. And she has to ring us as soon as she gets to Dad's."

"Definitely."

"Oh, god!" Olivia heard the muted thud as her mother suddenly slapped both hands down on the leather arms of her chair. "*Why* is she so insistent about doing every darn thing on her own! Do you really think it's okay, Angus?"

"I think so, darling, yes. And the thing is . . . she'll just keep on at us till we agree, we both know that."

On the other side of the door, Olivia had smiled, and she smiled again now as she walked, remembering. Even these days, when her parents argued about a lot of things, they still never argued about her. She put that down to good training. It was just like with the dogs—not that her parents were dogs, of course. But Olivia liked orderly routines, she always had, and she had noticed that just about everyone—humans, plants, animals—was happier that way. Logical, familiar, satisfying routines. They made things so much better.

And even with parents, it's not as though it's hard. Tell them what keeps them happy. Do what you say you're going to do. Treat them like they're reasonable creatures even, no, *especially* when they act unreasonably, and sooner or later they'll respond and treat you the same. There: simple, really. Olivia listened to other kids complaining about their parents and how *insane* they were, how they'd completely lost it over this or that, and asked silently, *Why do you bother? I don't get it.* But there were so many things she didn't get about other kids. *Probably never will,* she thought glumly. She was just hanging in till she got to be an adult herself and could do what she wanted. Get a license to keep reptiles, for instance. And goats, she'd love to have goats one day. Those fantastic eyes, and their hard, nubbly little heads.

She ran through her pets' care schedule in her mind. There had been some disruption. It was her last year in primary school, and Deborah had decided that it might after all be a good thing for her to go to a private secondary school, *given the appalling mess that bunch of crooks left the state education system in,* in which case Olivia should try for a scholarship. So there had been a lot of extra study, and her care schedule had got a bit behind. But nor had she been able to make this Saturday morning trip to her grandfather's for a few weeks, and she missed it. She'd been gardening with Grandpa forever; since she was a baby sitting in her stroller watching him work, listening as he told her every single thing he was doing, and why. She knew Grandpa missed her visits, too. And the animals were all fine, really. She'd got extra pellets in before things got too busy; the latest litters of rabbit and rat babies had all just gone to the usual pet shops, and she would bring home a load of leafy greens from Grandpa's today. Tomorrow she would dust the hens for parasites. Next month, the dogs' vaccinations, and she'd get the vet to look at Fly-by's broken tooth. Yes.

"All good, girls," she told the dogs, and Mintie turned her clever black-and-white face up to her for a moment and nodded. Or the dog equivalent. Fly-by, tearing about in true kelpie fashion, covering a hundred meters for every ten Olivia walked, was too busy to make a response.

Alex was in the kitchen when she came through the back door. He started a little. "Gosh, Olivia, I thought you were your mother for a second! The spitting image of her, you are now. Tea?"

"No thanks, Grandpa. These were out by the roses," she said, putting the shears and gardening gloves on the table as he came over to kiss her hello.

"Thank you, sweetheart. I just thought I'd check the roses for pruning," and indeed, as he said this Olivia was reading the very same words in the little notebook lying there beside the teapot.

"But we pruned them in July," she said.

"Of course we did."

"Is it time to give them a spring feed?"

"Not just yet. Thought we'd tackle the veggie garden today."

"Excellent! My hens really need some fresh greens. So do the bunnies."

"Wish I still had some chooks, Ollie. I really miss those girls."

"Me too."

"Rotten foxes."

"Rotten foxes," Olivia agreed, picking up the phone to let her parents know she had arrived. It went straight to message, so she left one.

"Let's get stuck into it then, shall we?" said Alex. "Gloves?" And like two surgeons eager for the blade, they turned with the same motion, pulling on the gloves as they strode purposefully out the back door and into the green spring morning.

CHAPTER 2

Angus was asleep on the couch, the Saturday papers adrift all around him, when the phone rang. He managed to lurch across and answer it before it went to voice mail, although the sudden movement made his left quad twang threateningly. *Lucky I gave up football when I did,* he thought.

"Angus Hume," he said thickly, rubbing the sore spot in his thigh.

"Dad, it's me. Grandpa's having a rest and I wondered if you might be able to pick me up."

"Uh? Uh-huh."

"If you're not busy. Because I've got these big bags of greens for the chooks and the rabbits."

"Sure, Ollie. Sorry, I was half-asleep. You want me to come and get you now?"

"That'd be excellent. Thanks, Dad. See you soon."

Angus put the phone down and stared at it. *My god, Olivia asked for a lift,* he thought. "Dee!" he called, and quickly corrected himself. "Deborah!" But she wasn't in the study, or the bedroom. Must've gone for a walk. He wanted to tell someone this startling piece of news, but then realized how dopey it would sound. "My daughter asked me for a lift." Yes? And your point is?

My point is, Angus thought, getting into the car, *my point is, this child never asks for anything. You have to* beg *to help her.*

The year she started school, for instance, he and Deborah arranged to flex their work hours on alternating days. The local school was not far away, true, but still a fair walk for a five-year-old. Olivia tolerated being driven to and fro or accompanied on foot by one of her parents for the first term. Then she announced that she was going to walk by herself. And once home she could get her own snack and "do things" till one of them got home at six. They argued, suggested alternatives. But no, she would *not* go to after-school care; she wanted to be by herself. She compromised on the time: they could get home at five, then. Otherwise, she was adamant, and convinced them. Not for the first time. Not the last. Angus, a lawyer with a community legal aid group, told the women in his office with whom he exchanged kid-chat: "That girl of mine! She never loses a case!"

In the first week of this new arrangement, there was a sudden cold snap: a day that had started out fine but turned nasty, with driving rain setting in just on three o'clock. Angus told the others in the office he had to go, and as he drew near the school he recognized his little daughter in her bright yellow raincoat slogging determinedly through the pelting rain, head down. He drew alongside, pleased with his own fatherly thoughtfulness, and wound down the window just enough to call, "Ollie! Hop in!"

She looked toward him. Her expression didn't change a bit, and she kept on walking. *She doesn't recognize the car,* he thought. He drove a few meters on and stopped again, actually got half out of the car.

"It's Daddy, Olivia! Hop in, darling!"

She climbed into the backseat, raincoat streaming, didn't greet him or say a word until they pulled into the drive at home. When Angus had switched off the engine she said accusingly, "You said I could walk by myself."

"It's raining, Olivia! It's *teeming!*"

Her face was implacable. "It's only weather, Daddy," she said in a withering tone. "And I brought my raincoat."

He watched, speechless, as she got out of the car, climbed the steps to the porch and opened the front door with the key secured on a long ribbon in her bag. Then she turned as if she'd forgotten something and waited for her father to join her. She took his hand and stroked it several times, consolingly.

"But thank you for coming to get me, anyway."

He told Deborah about it as they prepared dinner together that evening. She, too, had fretted about Olivia walking home in the rain, and had rung his office just moments after he left. As he finished the story she closed her eyes and shook her head slowly, knife stilled on the chopping board.

"Honestly, Dee," Angus went on (he could still call her Dee, then), "She all but said, 'There there, Daddy, you meant well.'"

Deborah gave a shuddering sigh and her eyes snapped open and held his.

"Do you ever think, when you're looking at her, *She's weird*?"

"Weird? How do you mean?"

"I don't know. Eerie. The way she's so self-contained." Deborah shook her head again, her face clouded. "Why can't she just be a child? Happy, carefree? Isn't that what children are meant to be?"

"I think she is happy, Dee," Angus said, but he felt uneasy now.

His mother was still alive then, and although she and his father had moved to Queensland to be near his sister, her way with children was legend in their family. At a quiet moment the next weekend Angus rang and told her the story.

"It's just her nature," she said. "She hasn't much of the child about her, that's true, but it's nothing to worry about. She was born old."

"But, Mum, for a five-year-old to *want* to walk home in the rain! It wasn't just drizzle, it was really pelting down. Don't you think that's a bit . . . odd?"

His mother laughed. "She's a Scot on both sides, don't forget!"

"Meaning?"

"Two hundred years ago, that girl would've been out on the hills barefoot in weather far worse than anything Melbourne can dish up, bossing around a bunch of cattle with horns the width of your car bonnet. Little and all as she is, Angus."

And indeed, as his mother said this Angus could see it, and it all somehow made sense to him. Olivia was only strange in the context of the cosseted, overprotected modern-day child; put her down in another century, or even today almost anywhere else in the world—in the Third World that is—and her implacable capability would be expected, and welcomed. And Angus decided there and then that he would welcome it, too, since that was just how his daughter happened to be.

All of this—the staunch little girl, his mother's calm assurance, the sharing of concern that happened so effortlessly between him and Deb back then—it was all so vivid in Angus's mind as he drove to his father-in-law's house that it jolted him to see the tall slender girl waiting in the front yard, a dog on either side, bits of black hair escaping from her ponytail. Her serious look, almost a scowl, was just the same, but Olivia was no longer that small child. *My god,* Angus thought, *she's starting to get a figure.* His heart swelled painfully. *I have so few years left to really be with her. And what the hell will Deb and I be, when she's not there?*

He glanced at himself in the mirror as he pulled up. His hair—he could remember Deb running her fingers through his hair, a very long time ago, murmuring, "It's the same color as leatherwood honey." These days his hair was as much gray as any other color, and thinning. As Olivia approached the car he had an urge to ask her, "Do I look old to you?" but knew he wouldn't. One doesn't ask one's daughter such a question. *Besides, it's not her I want the reassurance from.*

Olivia slung the bulging black garbage bags of grass and weeds into the trunk. She held a rear door open and the dogs leapt in, Fly-by thrusting her head out the window the moment Olivia rolled it down, Mintie sitting plumb in the middle and gazing keenly ahead between the two front seats, paws neatly together.

"You'd better leave a note for your grandpa, don't you think?" Angus suggested as his daughter settled into the passenger seat beside him.

"Already have."

"He okay?" he asked as they drove away. "Just tired from all the gardening?"

"Yeah . . . I guess . . ."

Angus glanced at her quickly. Hesitation? Olivia?

"What, Ol?"

"Just . . ." She turned in her seat to face him, but Angus kept his eyes on the road, not to put her off.

"When I got there the shears and gloves were lying on the ground by the roses. And when I brought them in Grandpa said he'd gone to check them for pruning."

"Ye-eah . . ."

"Dad, we pruned them a couple of months ago, in July! But then, when we went inside for lunch, he saw this little note he'd written about the roses and he wanted to check them all over again."

"So . . . What did you do?"

"Well, I reminded him we'd pruned them at the right time already so there was no need to check them. But he was so, kind of, deter-mined. Like, *I have to do this*. It was just a bit weird. Grandpa's usually so . . . nice."

"He wasn't nice about this?"

"He was just so, like, *insisting*. As if I was trying to stop him doing something important."

Angus risked a glance. Olivia was scowling, but not in her usual determined way. Her mouth looked soft and uncertain.

"And usually he only has a little nap, ten minutes, or maybe fifteen minutes, and then he drives me home. Today he'd been asleep for nearly an hour when I rang you."

Maybe he's having a heart attack, Angus worried. Didn't people get disoriented just before they had a heart attack? Or was that a stroke? Maybe his father-in-law had gone to lie down and had a stroke. Had fallen out of bed and couldn't call for help.

"Maybe we should go back there for a tick. I think I should look in on him."

"I already did, Dad, twice. Once before I rang you and then just before you drove up. He was sleeping perfectly normally. Normal breathing and all that. His face was, you know, the right color."

"Good for you, Ol."

"Yeah. I did that first aid course, remember? But I . . . I think Mum should know."

"I'll tell her. You want me to tell her? Or would you rather?"

"No, you can, Dad. If you don't mind, that is?"

"Course not. Happy to."

Olivia turned back to the dogs then, chatting animatedly, admonishing them. Her face relaxed. *That's twice she's asked me to do something!* It seemed his self-contained, resourceful daughter had decided something was happening with her grandfather that she didn't want to tackle alone. She wanted her parents to handle it. Angus had a sudden thought, like a needle-prick: *I hope we're up to the job.*

Deborah didn't get home till nearly dinnertime. Angus poured her a glass of the sauvignon blanc he'd been holding back from opening till she got home, and she perched on the stool at the island bench, sipping, as he chopped vegetables and told her Olivia's story about Alex. But not that Olivia had asked him to tell her. Nor did he describe his own stab of doubt about whether they could manage it. Whatever it was.

"I'll call him," Deborah said. "Make sure he's okay."

"Yeah, good. But don't mention that Ollie said anything, okay?"

"God, Angus, as if I would!"

Alex sounded perfectly chipper, hearty even, telling her there was nothing like a good day's work in the garden, can't beat it. Listening to him, Deborah felt relief wash over her. Her mouth filled with saliva as her throat and jaw relaxed and it startled her to realize how tight they'd been. *God, I'm like this half the bloody time these days*, she thought.

"That's great, Dad. Listen, I was just ringing to tell you that when I was out walking today I remembered who Jeannie is."

"Who?"

"Jeannie. She was one of the ladies who helped look after us. When we were kids. I think," and Deborah gave a quick, light laugh, *no big deal*, "I think she might've been one of your girlfriends."

"Girlfriends? What are you talking about, Deb?"

"Well, never mind that. But Jeannie, that's who she is. Was. Mrs. Thornbury. No, Thornton. Jean Thornton."

"Jean Thornton . . ." Her father repeated slowly, but there was no sound of recognition in his voice.

"You rang me just this morning, Dad. You wanted to know if I knew when her birthday was. Jeannie."

"Did I, love? Oh . . . that's right. Of course. Jeannie, that's right."

"But I don't know when her birthday is."

"Well, that's all right, darling. Don't you worry about it. I'll . . . get in touch with her another time."

They said their good-byes and Deborah hung up. She stood staring at the phone for some time, her back to Angus, then raised the glass to her mouth and finished off the wine in one big gulp. She keyed in another number. It rang and rang and finally went to message.

"James, hi, it's Deb," she said. "Listen . . . um, can you call me when you get in, or first thing tomorrow? I've just been talking to Dad, and . . . I dunno, I just think something's not quite right. Okay, talk soon, Jaffa, see ya."

"Deborah?" said Angus questioningly after a few moments, but she just shook her head in a preoccupied way as she left the room. He watched her go. If she had glanced back at him even for a moment, she would have seen the look of desolation on his face.

He must have slept for a long time. When he finally woke it was with a start, and a sour cottony taste in his mouth, and a bad feeling that he had mucked things up somehow. There was an appointment, wasn't there? Someone . . . Olivia! Alex hurried fuzzy-headed from his bedroom to the kitchen but there, propped against the teapot in big clear handwriting was a cheery note from his granddaughter.

Relieved, he wandered out to the backyard. A soft spring twilight was creeping in. *Oh, good work!* The vegetable garden was completely cleared of weeds. They must've gone like the clappers. No tools lying around, yet he couldn't recall putting them away. Maybe Olivia had. He looked in the shed. Yes, and she'd cleaned the fork and the spade first too, what a dependable girl. A born gardener.

Sardines on toast and a nice cup of tea, that would do for dinner. His old favorite. Just as well he had a cupboard full!

"That's got to be a good couple of shoals worth of sardines there!" he said out loud. Suddenly he wished he had a cat; he could just picture a cat, a black one perhaps, licking the oil out of the bottom of a sardine tin. That tabby pair they'd had when the kids were young, what were their names? Ernie and Tiny Tim, that was it, Ernie the big boofhead puss and Tiny Tim his pop-eyed, nervous brother, streaking from the room at any unexpected noise. Lots of unexpected noises with a house full of kids. Or a dog; you can't beat a dog for company, no question. And maybe he'd get one again, someday, but for the moment he was still not quite over losing Banjo. What a great dog he'd been, that Banjo. As Alex sat at the kitchen table eating, it almost seemed that the dog was there, at his feet. He even glanced under the table to check, and the pang it gave him to see only chair legs was unexpectedly acute.

Just as he finished washing up his plate and cutlery, the phone rang. Debbie, his oldest.

"Hello, darling," he said cheerfully. There was something she wanted to tell him. Alex reached for one of the little notepads as his daughter spoke. *Jean Thornton*, he wrote. And then *Girlfriend!* and then on a third line, *Birthday?*

What on earth was she talking about? After they'd finished their conversation he sat down and stared at what he'd written. It didn't seem to make sense, not to him anyway. But Debbie didn't get much wrong, heaven knows, sharp as a tack that girl, always had been. *Jean Thornton, Jean Thornton.* Suddenly inspired, he went and got his old address book down from the shelf above the phone.

There it was: Jean Thornton, and an address in Balwyn. And a phone number, in fact a couple of phone numbers, one crossed out. Well, why not? See if he couldn't solve this mystery. *Girlfriend*, eh?

"You never know your luck in a big city," he said, and carefully dialed the number. A lady answered the phone all right, but she didn't seem to understand him. Didn't speak English, that seemed to be the problem. He tried to apologize for the wrong number and hang up but suddenly there was someone else on the line, a teenage boy by the sound of it, with just a bit of an accent.

"Hello, can I help you, who is calling?" the youth asked.

"Oh, good evening. Well, I'm Alex McDonald, and I was hoping to speak to a lady named Jean Thornton."

"No, sorry. What number do you call?"

Alex told him the number.

"No, sorry," the boy said again. "That is the number here, but no lady by that name. This is the Lim family residence."

Alex thanked him, and apologized, and said good night. The Lim family residence. Well, well. The mystery remained unsolved. He sat staring at the entry in the address book and then announced decisively, "This is pointless!" and crossed it out, the whole thing, name, address, and phone number. He started going through the address book, starting from "A," crossing out each entry that he didn't recognize. But when he got to "G" he stopped, because he had crossed out almost every single entry up to that point, and he didn't care to go on. He closed the address book and put it back on the shelf.

"I think I'll watch a bit of telly," he said, and left the room, turning the light off behind him as he went.

CHAPTER 3

From the front deck of Uncle James's house, Olivia could see a great swathe of Port Phillip Bay, a good part of the beach, and a sliver of the off-leash area.

"Excellent! There's heaps of other dogs there already. I'm gonna head down with the girls, Mum, okay?"

"Okay. Enjoy."

"See you soon. See ya, Uncle James."

"Be careful crossing the road won't you, Olivia?" said James. "It's really busy."

Olivia didn't reply, just disappeared into the garden where Mintie and Fly-by were eagerly waiting.

"You're okay about her being down there by herself?"

"Oh, James, this is Olivia we're talking about! And the dogs are with her."

"Yeah, I guess. Anyway . . . I'm really glad you came over, Deb. I'd just been thinking that I haven't seen you for a few weeks . . . and then when I got home last night, there's your message."

"Well, good on you for dragging me away from the bloody computer. I *so* needed a break! And Olivia's always keen to take the dogs to the beach." The sunlight sparkled on the granite benchtop where Deborah sat perched on a handsome leather bar stool. She laid her head down, cheek to the stone, and stretched out her long arms luxuriantly.

"Like an egg hidden in the nest," said James.

"Huh?"

"Your head. Hair, rather. The speckled black and gray on the granite."

"You calling me an egghead?" she said. He could see the curve of her face, turned away from him, rise subtly as she smiled. "Cheeky bruv!"

"Yeah," he said, with a soft laugh in his voice. He leaned his fore-arms on the bench. "Have to admit, Deb, there's a reason I wanted you to come over."

"Yeah?" Deborah lifted her head and looked at him alertly.

James led his older sister down the wide, shallow flight of stairs toward his studio. Deborah noticed that the two of them were dressed almost identically, in black T-shirts and blue jeans. These days they looked even more alike, ever since she had taken to wearing her hair cut elegantly close to her head. It looked good, she knew that; her bone structure could handle the severity of it. Even her jawline was still relatively crisp.

At the bottom of the stairs she touched James's shoulder lightly.

"It's a new painting?" she asked, and he nodded. "Oh goodie, I was hoping it would be!" They exchanged a little grin. "It's gotta be something special. You're usually so blasé."

He shrugged. "Oh well, you know, it's not that special."

She gave his shoulder a small shove, pretending annoyance. "Ja-af! Why do you *say* that?"

"Um, habit? The Aussie self-denigration thing? Maybe because my paintings really aren't all that special?"

"Huh!" Deborah snorted.

"But anyway, I wanted you to be the first to see this, apart from Silver, of course. I just finished it the night before last." James walked his sister to the far end of the studio and made a double-handed gesture of presentation—*tah-dah!*—toward the canvas still stapled to the wall. "What d'you reckon? Do you remember?"

"Oh wow! It's fantastic! But . . . remember? What should I be remembering?"

"Look. Look."

The painting was almost two meters wide. An underwater scene; in the foreground, the loosely parted hands of the child swimmer whose perspective the viewer of the painting shared. Light came streaked and dappled through the water, forming lovely patterns on the pale sand below, one area of which was cloudy and disturbed. A stingray was rising from the bottom, its graceful winged body emerging from the camouflage of the seabed. Poised above it were the feet and legs and part of the torso of an adult man standing chest-deep in the water, and behind him the shape of an adolescent girl in a dark-red swimsuit, treading water.

"Hey, that's my old red swimsuit! I loved that one!"

"Yep, yep," James cried, catching his sister's excitement now.

"Oh, I *do* remember!" Deb grabbed his forearm. "It's Mr. Grounds! It's that day we went to Rosebud and he got stung by the stingray. And I was right there!"

"That's right!"

"I remember him *screaming*, boy, that really scared me. He had to go to the hospital, didn't he? But, James, I don't remember you being there when it happened. Not right in the water like that. Because in fact I remember the first thing I did was check that you and Robert and Meredith were all safe on the beach, and you were."

"But I'd *seen* that stingray just before, when I had the face-mask on. It lifted off like that when I swam over the top of it, and I went straight in to the beach to do a sketch of it."

"Oh *yes*, I remember you showing me now. And you didn't want me to tell Dad you'd seen it because you thought you might get in trouble for not having warned anyone."

"Did I? Gee . . . You never know what you're going to get in trouble for as a kid, do you?"

"That's true," said Deborah, nodding as she continued to gaze at the painting. She shook her head wonderingly. "Jesus, that summer. How could so much happen in such a short time?"

"Yeah, I know," said James. "It's weird."

"Just that one summer, from Christmas Eve on." Deborah's head dropped for a moment and James felt her mood shift, her excitement suddenly diminished by something else. "I feel like no matter how much I think about it, I'll never really *get it*."

"Really?" asked James, looking surprised. "Me too, but . . . I thought that was just me."

"And I think I've got it all down and then something new comes up, like you do this painting, and suddenly I'm remembering how all that day down at Rosebud I kept looking over at the beach umbrella to see if Mum had turned up. And the way she used to sit under that red and yellow beach umbrella with just her legs sticking out, because she liked to have brown legs."

"You know, Deb, I've been really wanting to . . . It's kind of strange, I've been thinking about what I *don't* remember. It seems like you can picture Mum perfectly, but I can only remember all this *stuff*: the stingray, the color of your swimsuit . . ."

"Mr. Grounds, he's not stuff. You can picture him. And me," she said, gesturing toward the figures in the painting.

"Yeah, yeah, but not *Mum*. And I do feel weird about it. Because it's, because I can remember all sorts of stuff from when I was really, really little, but I can't actually remember Mum at all." He wasn't looking at Deborah now, he was looking at his work table and the mess of paints and brushes there, and his usual relaxed expression had been replaced by one of troubled puzzlement. "I can only see her outline, sometimes, or I get an impression of her moving, like across a room or something. But if it weren't for the photographs and you talking about her, I wouldn't have any real image of her at all."

"Well, you were only eight," said his sister gently. "That's not very old."

"Oh, come on, Deb!" James looked up with a little incredulous grin. "I remember a stingray, but not my mother? I mean, I can remember the exact spacing between the bars of my cot when I was two. But not her? What's that about?"

"I don't think it's that weird, really," said Deborah, crossing her arms thoughtfully and leaning back against the wall. "I think it's . . . you know, shock. Trauma. That's what it's about. Your mother—*our* mother—walks out on you when you're a little kid without a word of warning and just disappears from your life . . . What do *you* think? No consequences?"

"Yeah, I guess that's right," said James. "That's pretty much what Silver reckons, too."

"Uh-huh. Did Silver say you should talk to me about this?"

"Well, um . . . yeah. She was kind of . . ."

"Worried?"

"Nah, Sil never worries. Just . . . curious."

"Look, it messed us all up, Jaf. I think you've actually coped better than the rest of us, because you've got that fabulous easygoing temperament, you lucky dog. Like Dad. Blocking her out of your memory's probably a very healthy response."

"Right," said James skeptically. "Amnesia as a measure of mental health. How does that work?"

"Why not? A survival mechanism, or something. God, I wish I could do it. I wish I could wipe her clear out of my brain."

"But Dad . . . that's different again. He's never even *mentioned* Mum, except when he absolutely had to. Is *that* healthy?"

"I don't know." Deborah started prowling round the studio. She stood on tiptoe and peered out the high studio window, which was open to the sea breeze. She could just see James's lap pool at the far end of the garden, glinting in the spring sunshine. What she couldn't see was her daughter Olivia sitting directly below the window, back to the sun-warmed wall, listening attentively as the dogs lay dozing at her feet.

Olivia knew that what she did was frowned upon—*snooping*—but she didn't care. She firmly believed that being good was no match for being well informed. Not even in the same league. And the fact was that things at home were not quite right lately: her mother so snappy, and now this stuff with Grandpa. Even her dad seemed a bit . . . fuzzy. Adults never liked kids to know what was really going on, which was just so unfair, since being a kid was bad enough without being kept in the dark. If you didn't find out for yourself, then things could sneak up on you . . .

Deborah turned back to James, who had propped one long thigh on the edge of his work table and was watching her, his head slightly tilted, waiting.

"I think . . . when she left, there was all this gossip, and I think Dad just hated it. The neighbors used to talk about her, whether she had a boyfriend, where she'd gone. Why she left. It was horrible."

"Did they?"

"You bet." Deborah twisted her shoulders and put on a nasty face. *"She must've been seeing someone,"* she hissed. *"Poor Alex! Such a sweet man!"*

James pretended to vomit. "Erk!"

"And then the cops coming, interviewing us . . . I think Dad just figured we had to get on with life and we'd be better off if he never . . . if we all just blocked her out."

"So you think that's what Dad did, really just blocked her out of his memory? Completely?"

"Oh!" Deb cried, her hands flying up. *"That's* the thing I rang you about. God, James, I got such a fright last night . . ."

Deborah told him about the odd phone calls, and Olivia's experience with her grandfather the day before. But James was not concerned by what Deborah described. After all, their father was getting old now, in fact not just *getting* old, already well and truly *old*! And old people often had problems remembering things, didn't they? Not to mention the fact that Alex had always practiced, as Deborah herself had just pointed out, a system of selective amnesia. But he was in as good spirits as ever, wasn't he? And the gardening kept him as fit as a Mallee bull. All things considered, Alex was doing fine. Why worry over something that was probably perfectly normal?

"But I *am* worried," Deborah said, looking strained suddenly. "I'm under such a lot of pressure at work, it's just relentless. And things . . . I don't know, James, things aren't so good between Angus and me right now. I just don't know how I'd manage if there was something else to deal with."

"How do you mean, things aren't so good with Angus? I always thought Angus was Mr. Reliable."

"I don't know what I mean. He's still . . . supportive. He never complains about all my meetings, or the work I bring home. He shops, he cooks; the domestic demigod, as ever. But even when he's right in front of me, he's kind of not *there*. As if he's half-zonked all the time. Like when Dad rang the other day and at the end I say, 'Bye, Dad,' and Angus says, 'Was that your father?' I mean, *No, Angus, it was the Minister for Education, I call her Dad.*"

"Oh, sis. Lighten up! So he vagues out sometimes. Angus's never been, you know, that driven A-type kind of guy. That's why you two work so well together."

"Used to," said Deborah gloomily. "Lately . . . we ain't working so well. And . . . god, this is probably more than you need to know, but . . . Well, it's not happening much in bed, either, and that's where things *always* worked."

"Well, sheesh, what can I . . . But, Deb, *how* long have you guys been married?"

"Seventeen years."

"Holy cow!" James made a cartoon face of amazement. "And you still expect to have the hot sex thing happening? Hey, I hate to be the one to tell you this, but things are bound to slow down after seventeen years. Really. Seventeen *months*, most couples. And like they say, it's not all there is to a good marriage, you know."

"Well, that's not how it's been for us," Deborah said stoutly.

"Okay. So maybe you need to take a holiday. A nice romantic holiday, just the two of you, and leave your mobile phone at home. Don't tell the minister where you're going."

"I wish. Not a chance, unfortunately. Damn it."

"Well, maybe you should do something else then. Take up ballroom dancing together. Swim! It works for me!"

"James, everything works for you. It's just the way you were born. I was born with the weight of the whole damn world on my shoulders."

"Oh, you poor old thing," her brother said with affectionate sarcasm. She made a face at him. "Listen, here's an idea: if you're really worried about Dad and the memory thing, how about we talk to Vesna? She's a nurse, she must know about aging and stuff."

"Vesna? Oh, I don't know about involving . . . other people. Not in family matters."

"De-eb! Vesna's not other people, she's Robert's wife! That's family. She's the same as Silver, or Angus."

"No. Look, of course I talk to Angus. And I know you talk to Silver. But we don't have to make it . . . And Vesna's . . . different."

"Why?"

"Because . . ." She rolled her shoulders impatiently. "Oh, I don't know. Because Robert and Vesna drive me nuts!"

"Come on! Vesna's a professional. She'll be able to put your mind at ease about this, I'm sure."

"Oh, I just *hate* other people knowing our business!"

"Vesna's not—" James started patiently.

"Okay, okay! Maybe you're right, James. But will you call them?

I can't bear to hear the blow-by-blow on how brilliantly the girls are doing with Suzuki violin and all that crap."

"Yeah, sure, I'll call 'em. We'll all be seeing each other right here in a couple of weeks anyway. At Silver's fiftieth birthday party."

"Oh my god, is that so soon?"

"Sure is. Shine up your dancing shoes, sis, 'cause it's gonna be one hell of a party."

"Hooley dooley! What's happening to this year? It's gonna be over before . . . I need a coffee, Jaf, right now! You have to make me a cappuccino from that snazzy coffee machine of yours."

"And since you asked so nicely, I will."

Brother and sister left the studio together. Still sitting beneath the window, Olivia tugged thoughtfully on Mintie's soft black ears, then rolled to her feet and padded quickly across the expansive garden to the path that led down to the beach. "Just a quick run, girls," she told the dogs. "That took a bit longer than I thought."

She didn't feel too good: a little queasy, in fact. It was not an unfamiliar feeling; the price she paid for keeping herself well-informed was that sometimes she got *too much information*, as her cousin Laurence would say. It wasn't exactly news to her that her parents weren't having a great time, but that Mum was actually worried enough to talk to Uncle James about those . . . private things . . . *Ugh*. Olivia shook herself. Adults were so . . . gross sometimes. But after twenty minutes of running and playing with the dogs on the beach, she felt okay again. Restored to herself.

CHAPTER 4

The two cars pulled up outside Deborah's house at almost the same moment, just as she was drawing the curtains in the bay window: Robert's Volvo wagon, James's Saab convertible. Both right on time for the siblings' meeting about their father. She watched them walking up the path together, chatting away, and Deborah heard James laugh his splendid easy laugh. Her diaphragm unclenched and she felt a sense of relief, even pleasure. Bless James, he got on so well with everyone, even anxious do-gooding Robert, who could set her teeth on edge with a couple of earnest sentences. Her anxiety about this meeting abated just a little. *Now*, she thought, *if Meredith could just arrive at something resembling the time arranged, and sober . . .*

"Why don't we all go out to the kitchen till Meredith gets here?" Deb suggested after greeting her brothers. Angus had the kettle boiling, Olivia was putting together a plate of crackers and cheese.

"So, Angus," Robert said. "How are things in the eyrie?"

Angus looked puzzled. "Airy?"

"E-Y-R-I-E, eyrie. Well, you are the legal eagle in the family!"

Deborah made a small groan which James sought to cover by quickly asking Olivia about her animals.

"Oh. Right," said Angus as Robert grinned expectantly. "Well, you know, it's just a small community practice; we don't get to represent axe murderers all that often. Mind you, it's amazing what a dispute over a boundary fence can bring out in an otherwise amiable human being."

"I'm sure!" Robert enthused with a little nervous laugh. "It can get pretty nasty in the halls of learning too, believe it or not!"

"I do, I do believe it. In fact, we mediated a surprisingly fraught dispute between a couple of parents and the head of a local primary school just recently."

"Really?" Robert was immediately rigid with attention. Even his graying ginger beard seemed alert. "The principal? Was it a policy issue then? Or a teaching matter?"

"Sorry, ah, I can't really talk about it," said Angus apologetically. "The confidentiality thing, you know. But I was just meaning, yes, I do know how hard you teachers have it these days."

"Especially after the mess the last bloody government left the education system in," said Deborah. "Honestly, we're working night and day to pick up the pieces, fat lot of credit we get for it. And as for the hospitals!"

"So true. It's been a nightmare for Vesna and her colleagues. A pretty fraught decade all round, the nineties," Robert said. He jammed his hands awkwardly into the pockets of his cardigan. Hand-knitted, Deborah suspected, by the admirable Vesna. "Glad that's over, at least: not knowing where the axe was going to fall next. What miracles you'd be expected to work with fewer staff and less money. For about three years that was all anyone talked about in the staffroom: who'd be the next to go . . ."

"Like Stalinist Russia."

"Oh, Deborah! You can't compare Victoria, even under that lot, to Stalinist Russia!" said Robert. Deborah stiffened.

"But you hung in there," said James. "And thank god for that! If people like you and Vesna had left the schools and the hospitals, we'd all be goners. How could the new government have a hope of rebuilding this state without that backbone? The truly dedicated people like you guys?"

Deborah smiled as Robert nodded his earnest agreement. *James the peacemaker*, she thought. *He's amazing.* The doorbell rang at that moment and Robert cried, "Ah, that'll be our Merry girl! I'll let her in, shall I?"

"Hope she's not *too* bloody merry," said Deborah, raising one eyebrow meaningfully.

Meredith was bubbling with apologies and suspiciously high spirits. As quickly as possible, Deborah got all the siblings settled in the living room and was opening her mouth to speak when Angus came in. She looked at him impatiently.

"Sorry to interrupt," he said. "I'm off to the gym, and you guys will probably be gone by the time I get back, so I hope everything goes well."

"Oh, Angus," cried Meredith, "I've hardly even had a chance to say hello to you! How *are* you? And when are you going to that, um, big school reunion?"

"I'm just fine, Merry, thanks," he said, stooping to kiss his sister-in-law on the cheek. "And the reunion was terrific, but it was months ago."

"Was it? Gosh. Must be that long since I've seen you," she said with a giggle.

"Must be. Bye, Deb." He kissed his wife's cheek, too, which was all she offered. "I'll be a few hours. I need a proper workout."

As Angus was leaving the room, Olivia entered carrying a tray with the plate of crackers and cheese, a bottle of sparkling mineral water and some glasses.

"Mum, I'll be doing my homework. Just call out if you need anything else," she said quietly as she set the tray down.

Her mother nodded, her uncles and aunt all made little complimentary exclamations. Olivia smiled at them and left the room, pulling the door almost closed behind her. Deborah, seated in her favorite green leather chair, was about to call out to Olivia to close it properly when Robert distracted her with an authoritative *attention please* noise.

"Shall we commence the meeting?" he asked, and rose from his seat on the couch next to Meredith to stand at the table nearby, his hands clasped loosely behind his back.

Ladies and gentlemen, boys and girls, thought Deborah.

"Well. Thank you for coming here this evening, and to Deb for having us. I know we'll all be enjoying James and Silver's marvelous hospitality the weekend after next, but I didn't think that would be the right occasion for this discussion." Robert paused to take a notepad from his briefcase. "Now. Thanks to Vesna, I do have some information, albeit somewhat speculative at this stage, about our father's health. I'm afraid it's not looking particularly like good news."

Meredith gave a little moan. "Oh no. I can't bear this. I just can't bear it if anything's the matter with Daddy." Her features, already a little blurry, softened further as tears welled in her large hazel eyes.

"Meredith, for heaven's sake!" said Deborah. "Let Robert start, at least, before you decide to fall to pieces!"

Robert leaned over and gave his younger sister's shoulder a consoling squeeze. "It's all right, Merry. Don't worry." Meredith sniffled but managed a brave little smile.

"Very well then. After I spoke to Vesna—after you rang us, James—she dropped in to Dad's place."

"Oh," said Deborah, a statement of disapproval rather than an exclamation.

"She was in the area, on her way to address a diabetes support group, Deb," said Robert defensively. His voice sharpened. "And as I understand it, you *did* request her input."

"Was he home?" asked James quickly.

"Yes. Yes, he was. And Vesna found him in a surprisingly agitated state. Some mix-up about a bill—his credit card statement, there was something on it he swore he hadn't bought. Vesna had her kit with her, of course, so she took his blood pressure. You know how he's been on medication for his high blood pressure for years?"

Deborah nodded; Meredith looked vague. "Has he?" said James.

"And she was alarmed to find how high it was."

"*How* high?" asked Deborah.

"Um, two hundred something over one-thirty. Through the roof, really. And there's a further cause for concern: he had no idea when he'd last taken his medication, and Vesna says he doesn't seem to know he was even supposed to be taking it. Dad told her he doesn't take any pills, didn't need them."

His siblings all spoke at once.

"Doesn't *need* them?"

"Uh-oh."

"Oh no! Daddy!"

"Yes. It's genuinely alarming. Vesna's spoken to his GP about it."

"About what, though?" asked James.

"Is his blood pressure still high?" asked Meredith.

"Is it . . ." Deborah began, and closed her eyes momentarily. "Could it be Alzheimer's?"

"His blood pressure's down for now, Vesna's seen to that. As to the Alzheimer's, it's hard to say. Apparently we need to get a proper assessment done. But Vesna thinks he may have been suffering . . ." Robert consulted his notes, "TIAs: transient ischaemic attacks. Like tiny mini-strokes, apparently."

James had a sudden bizarre image of his father's head as a mini-golf course, all the little obstacles and bridges, and little balls being tapped into the little holes. "Mini-*strokes*?" he said.

"*Could* be, that's all. He needs this assessment. But apparently, yes, someone can be having these mini-strokes, TIAs, so tiny you could even be in the same room with the person at the time and not notice anything. But each one does a bit more damage."

"Damage? To what?" asked Meredith, looking bewildered.

"To the brain."

"To the *brain*? Is Vesna saying Daddy has *brain damage*?"

"It's possible, Merry. I'm sorry. But it's not definite. We won't really know till we get this assessment done."

"Where? What does it involve, do you know, Robert?" asked James.

"And also, how long will it take to get an appointment, and how long does the assessment itself take?" asked Deborah. "We need to know all that, and my schedule is just *insane* at the moment. No, not at the moment, for the foreseeable future."

"And I'm off overseas with Silver a couple of days after the party," added James. "For three weeks."

"You lucky thing, James!" said Meredith. "You're always going away."

"Okay, everybody, a little more shoosh please," Robert said, holding up one hand. "There are specific clinics, apparently, for aged care assessment. Dad's GP is arranging a referral to the one for his area, and I'll make sure it's for a time I'm able to go with him."

"Well, that's such a help, Robert, it really is," said Deborah, her thanks sounding only slightly forced. "And I *do* appreciate Vesna's input; we all do."

Robert looked pleased. "That's all from me at this point, then," he said, putting his notepad back in his briefcase and sitting back down on the couch. James shifted in his chair a couple of times, stretching his arms, and Deborah looked across at him curiously.

"James? Something?"

"Yes, actually. Um, Silver asked me to say something to you all."

They waited.

"She just wants you to know that she's, um, concerned for Dad— he is her father-in-law, after all—and she wants you—wants *us*—to know that whatever happens over the next few years, you know, if Dad eventually has to move out of his own home or anything, that she's, well, that she wants to offer her support. Financially. You know."

Deborah looked away, the enquiring smile gone from her face. Robert and Meredith shifted slightly closer to each other.

"How kind," said Deborah in a cool tone. James looked at her uneasily.

"It *is*," burst out Meredith. "It's really, *really* kind of her. Because you know I would do anything for Daddy but I just haven't got a cent."

"But we don't need anyone else's help, not like that," Deborah went on forcefully. "We all know Silver's got plenty of money, James, but we're not standing on the street corner with our hands out, you know."

"And, James, the thing is, Daddy couldn't possibly leave his house. And especially his garden. He just couldn't!" Meredith's eyes were full again, her mouth quivering.

"Well. I know, I know. But Silver just wanted me to pass that on . . ." James looked at his older sister unhappily. Deborah was stony-faced. Robert picked up his briefcase and fussed with the clasp.

"Let's not get ahead of ourselves," he said. "I'll find out about the assessment and we'll take it from there. Hopefully any changes in Dad's domestic situation are a long way down the track. Hopefully there won't be any need for any changes at all."

After farewelling the group, Angus had headed purposefully to the car, swung his gym bag onto the backseat and backed out of the drive. As he turned onto the road he saw the faint shadow cast by Robert on the curtains of the bay window as he stood to address his siblings. *If there is something wrong with Alex's health, that'll make Deb even more . . .* But Angus didn't allow himself to finish the thought, fixing his attention on the road, the busy intersection on Queens Parade. Once through that he turned into a side street, parked, and reached awkwardly under his seat. He pulled out a small bag with a

Velcro closure, and from that a mobile phone. He had to turn it on and key in a PIN. There were only two phone numbers in its memory; he pressed one.

"Hi," he said in a soft, warm voice when it answered. "I've just left, I'll be there soon. Under ten minutes. Okay. Me too. Bye."

He was smiling as he tucked the phone back into its hiding place. Then he drove on, pulling up, yes, just under ten minutes later outside a small block of flats in Heidelberg. He took the stairs two at a time up to a flat on the third and topmost floor.

Just about three hours later, he parked the car again back in the driveway at his home.

"Hello-o!" he called out.

"I'm in the study," Deborah called back.

"Hi," Angus said, standing in the doorway. His wife was peering intently at the computer screen. "How did it go?"

"Oh, okay. Considering. I'll tell you about it later. I'm just finishing the agenda for this meeting tomorrow, then I'm coming to bed. Won't be long."

"Want anything?"

"Nup."

Deborah wasn't long, maybe fifteen minutes. But by the time she climbed into bed beside Angus, he was already asleep.

"Angus?" she said, placing the palm of her hand on his shoulder blade. He was wearing a soft old T-shirt, and smelled of the shower gel he always took to the gym. She stroked his back several times. "Darling?" But there was no response. She sighed, and leaned forward to kiss the nape of his neck gently. Then she lay quietly on her back, hands folded behind her head, looking into the darkness. They hardly ever seemed to coordinate their bedtimes any more. And how long was it since they'd had sex in the morning? God, she couldn't even remember. It would have to be months. They used to do that often. She sighed again, a long, sad sigh.

CHAPTER 5

The phone rang in James's studio, and he left off doodling in his sketchbook to answer it.

"Hello, James, Robert here," his brother said heartily. "Just wanted to check a couple of things with you about the party. Is this a good time for you, or are you busy?"

"No, fine, fire away," said James, wandering around the perimeter of his big work table with the phone to his ear. "Hey, thanks for that message, by the way, about Dad's assessment. When is it, next Thursday?"

"Correct. But I very much doubt I'll have anything to report by the weekend; I expect it'll take some time to get the results of whatever tests they do."

"Yeah, I suppose. But thanks for organizing it so soon and everything."

"Well, having made the commitment, I felt I should attend to it promptly. The date actually works very neatly with my timetable. Obviously I'll contact everyone once I have those results."

"Great."

"Now, Silver's party. First, Vesna wants to make absolutely sure that she really doesn't want presents."

"Yep, no presents, definitely. She says fifty's way too old for presents."

"I'm with Silver, but our girls are shocked!" Robert chuckled. "What's a birthday party without presents! So, how about flowers, Vesna asked, can we bring her some flowers?"

"Um, I think she's actually hired someone to do flowers, so the place'll be chock-a-block with them anyway."

"Right-o." There was a little pause, probably, James thought, while Robert made a note on his list. "Now, the girls are thrilled about coming of course, but we don't want them to have *too* late a night. If we bring their sleeping bags, would it be possible to bed them down there? In the upstairs guest room perhaps?"

"Sure, not a problem," James said, idly turning his sketchbook upside down, and then back the right way again.

"Thanks. And lastly, unfortunately Vesna has learned that she has to work that night—some supervisory thing she can't get out of—so she'll be coming later, probably about ten o'clock. Is that too late?"

"Too late? No, not at all, this party'll be going into the small hours. Whenever she gets here. Tell her we're looking forward to seeing her. And the girls."

"That's nice," Robert said. His voice relaxed. "Actually, James, Vesna and I were just saying that it'll be quite fun to meet up with each other at a big party again," he said warmly. "Like the party at that mansion in Toorak where we first met."

"Oh yeah—nice. Kind of romantic."

"You were there that night, do you remember? I took you with me." Robert laughed. "Because I was so nervous about going to such a posh place by myself."

"Is that why? It's funny, I was just thinking about that party the other day. Do you remember when it was?"

"Yes indeed. I had just finished my teacher training, so it was

December 1980. Getting on for twenty-four years: amazing. It'll be our twentieth wedding anniversary soon."

"I'd forgotten that's where you and Vesna met. I was thinking about it because Silver just re-sold a painting I did of . . . something from that night. It was one of my first big water paintings. Maybe the very first."

"Is that so? Let's see: those close-up paintings of swimmers' bodies, their feet and so on, those were the first I saw."

"This is even earlier." James started ambling around the studio. He looked out the high wide window toward the lap pool. *Might go for a swim after this.* "It's of . . . Well, it shows two figures . . . um . . ." *Oh, what the hell!* "Two people making love, actually, in the water. In a swimming pool."

"Two people?" asked Robert. There was an unusual tone in his voice. Mischievous. "Not three?"

James stopped dead. He felt like his brain had just gone on hold. "Hang on a second! How did you know?"

"Vesna and I were on the terrace above the pool. We had perfect balcony seats, you might say." James heard the grin in his brother's voice. "Not that we watched the whole show, I hasten to add! We went indoors when it started getting . . ."

"A bit too hot and heavy? Wow! What did Vesna say? Was she shocked?"

"Well, I think I was more shocked than she was, James, to tell you the truth." Robert laughed. "I was a bit of a prude in those days. And terribly . . . naive. Being married certainly changes things, doesn't it?"

"It sure does. It has for me, anyway," said James.

"Yes, you've certainly left your wild ways behind now."

"Absolutely!" said James. "You know, I was thinking about that night and thinking, 'What the hell was that about? Was that *me*?'"

"It certainly looked like you, my lad!" said Robert, chuckling again. "Well, as I say, times have changed since then. For the better, wouldn't you say, for both of us?"

"Yes. Yes, that's right," James hadn't moved from the window. He caught sight of his face reflected in the glass. *Gobsmacked,* he thought, and closed his mouth. Usually he and Robert talked about sports, or current affairs.

"Vesna and I both think it's wonderful, you know, that you and Silver are so happy together. I really mean that."

"Thanks, Robert. Thanks! And we . . . you know, we're both looking forward to seeing you guys at the party. Yeah. It's great!"

"Yes indeed."

They said their good-byes and hung up. Each brother stood for a long moment, pleasantly startled by what had been said, and remembering the events of that long-ago evening.

DECEMBER 1980

As the afternoon drew closer to evening, Robert's indecision was making him more and more unsettled. Should he go to Justin's party or not? He tried to read a book on classroom management—next year he'd actually be there standing in front of a class, a qualified teacher—but found it impossible to concentrate. He went out to the backyard and asked his father if he needed a hand.

"Not really, lad," Alex said from where he was kneeling by a flower bed, transplanting seedlings. "I've just about finished this lot." He looked up at his oldest son standing there restlessly tapping one foot on the ground. "Well, but since you ask . . . The front lawn could use a mow, if you wouldn't mind."

"No worries, Dad," said Robert gratefully. "Should I do the nature strip, too?"

"That'd be beaut."

As he pushed the roaring lawnmower up and down in meticulously straight lines, Robert tried to consider the party invitation rationally. *Justin's a genuinely nice bloke, even though his family's so rich.*

But I don't really know his friends. They might all be snobs. I don't want to be standing there like a shag on a rock with all these private school types ignoring me. And Justin's the host, he'll be busy. But I'd . . . I'd actually love to see his house; that time I picked him up outside, it looked . . . incredible. I've never been inside a place like that.

If only he had someone he could go with, but his few friends from teachers' college were all busy. Meredith would've been perfect; she was a real social butterfly, mixed with anyone, anywhere—but she was away for the weekend.

"James!" he said out loud. He finished the mowing quickly and put the machine back in the shed. His father was sitting on a canvas chair under the shade of a fruit tree, Toby the Labrador flopped on the grass beside him.

"Do you know what James is doing tonight, Dad?"

Alex shook his head. "I think he's working at the pool till six."

"I'll just run down there. But if I miss him and he comes back here, can you tell him I want to ask him about going to a party tonight?"

"I'll do that. That'll be nice for you, Robbie, a party. You deserve to relax. Don't know whether young James does though!"

"Oh, Dad, don't be hard on him. Architecture just wasn't right for him, you know."

"Well no, I don't know actually," said Alex in a prickly tone. "He would've made a bloody good architect. But there you are, it's not up to me what he does, is it?"

"James'll be okay, Dad."

"Oh, there's no doubt about *that*! Well, off you go. I'll tell him to wait if he comes back here."

Down at the local swimming pool, one of the other attendants confirmed that yes, James had finished his shift but he hadn't left yet. "He's doing laps," the guy said, pointing at the fifty-meter pool.

There he was, his long tanned arms and broad shoulders surging steadily through the water, feet flexing in perfect rhythm. Robert walked to the deep end and squatted at the end of James's lane. As his brother approached, Robert reached down in front of the diving block and waved his hand to and fro under the water. James surged in, grabbed Robert's hand below the surface and gave a little tug, not enough to overbalance him but enough to make him yelp and laugh.

"Hi, Rob," James said, flicking back his shoulder-length black hair. He took hold of the steel bar below the block and propped his feet up, knees bent. "What are you up to?"

"I've been invited to a party tonight at my friend Justin's place. Wondered if you'd like to come."

"Justin?" James asked, flexing his body now as though about to launch off into backstroke. "That guy you met in America, right? At the summer camp."

"Yes, we were both counselors. He's a beaut bloke, I think it'll be a good party."

"Uh-huh," James said. He held a breath and let his head fall back so that his face was under the water, still gazing up at Robert intently. He was thinking about water and painting: how to paint the way people appeared when you were looking at them through water; fellow swimmers in other lanes, or people walking beside the pool, coaches for instance, or like his brother was now, beside the blocks. *Look how the outlines are all wavery but you can still tell that he's asking a question. Or someone on the blocks, that'd be good. Tensed and ready to dive in, or—even better—in mid-dive, seen from below.* James lifted his head and blew a whale spout of air and water. "Sounds good. Yeah, I'll come. Still gotta do eight more laps though."

"That's okay, I'll wait. Give you a lift home."

They had a light meal with their father, did the dishes, watched a bit of TV. They headed off for the party a little after nine. A yellow moon just past full hung low and swollen in the sky.

"So where is Justin's place?" asked James, lounging in the passenger seat of Robert's Datsun.

"Toorak. It's his parents' place, they're away for a while."

"Yeah? You're taking me to a party in some Toorak mansion, eh?" James was grinning at his brother. Robert glanced at him and grinned back.

"That's right. You know me, always hobnobbing with the rich and famous."

James chuckled. Robert felt an unaccustomed sense of relaxation flow through his body. *This is going to be a good night,* he thought, and he took one hand from the steering wheel and patted James's shoulder. "Don't worry, little brother," he said. "If you start to feel out of your depth, I'll look after you." He was rewarded with another chuckle.

They drove on, windows open to the tantalizing breath of early summer.

"I got into art school for next year," said James absently.

"What?" said Robert, startled. "Really? I didn't even know you'd applied!"

"Well, I didn't tell many people. Didn't want to upset Dad if there was no need to."

"You think Dad'll be cranky?" asked Robert carefully.

"You know he will," said James, his voice mild as ever. "But he'll get over it."

"He will," Robert agreed. "He was pretty disappointed when you dropped out of architecture, though. You know. It's almost engineering!"

"Yeah, don't I know it!"

They stopped at a red light. "You know who would've been really thrilled?" Robert asked suddenly. From the corner of his eye he saw James turn toward him, his expression asking *Who?* "Mum," Robert said. "She would've been absolutely delighted to have you going to art school."

"Yeah?" said James. "You reckon?"

"Definitely," said Robert, nodding emphatically.

"Why's that?"

"She just . . . Well, she was always drawing, remember? Designing clothes and things." The traffic light changed; Robert put the car in gear and drove on. "And also . . ." he paused, considering. "She just would've been happy you're doing what you're good at. What you want to do. Wouldn't matter what it is." Another pause. "You were always her favorite, after all."

"I was?" said James. Not denying, nor disbelieving, just a little bemused.

"No question. But we didn't *mind* or anything. It's not like you were obnoxious about it. I mean, you were everybody's favorite. Teachers and everyone."

"I didn't know that," said James. He was intent on something in his lap; looking across, Robert saw that he was rolling a joint. Lighting it, James took a deep drag, and said in a quick thin voice without exhaling, "Not Dad's though, I don't think."

"Mmm," said Robert. "Maybe Meredith, for Dad."

James exhaled the stream of fragrant dope smoke gustily out the open window. "Yeah."

"Doesn't that . . . I mean, I thought that with your swimming . . . lung capacity and so on . . ." Robert faltered. He could hear himself trying not to sound disapproving.

"That's why I don't smoke much," said James easily. "Just special occasions. You want some? Get you in the party mood."

"No. No," said Robert, holding up one hand. "I really don't think it would." *I probably wouldn't even be able to get out of the car!* he thought.

Soon after, they arrived at Justin's parents' home, its grandeur drawing a heartfelt "Wow!" from James. The long driveway curved through grounds the size of several ordinary suburban blocks. Music was pouring from the open front door, and a group of people talking and laughing on the broad steps smiled and nodded as Robert and James walked up. They headed toward the music and found themselves in a ballroom. Neither brother had ever been in a house that had an actual ballroom before. A live band was playing on a stage at one end. Lots of girls were dancing; hardly any guys though. The room was so vast it still looked fairly empty.

Someone called out, "Robert! Hi!" A pleasant-looking guy standing with a knot of others was waving, gesturing them to come over.

"There's Justin! Come and I'll introduce you," said Robert. No sooner had they joined Justin's group than a trio of girls left off dancing together nearby and came over. All three, leggy and frisky as foals, were dressed in skimpy spaghetti-strapped summer dresses, and the blonde one suggested straightaway that it was about time the guys started dancing, too. Her two dark-haired friends exuberantly backed her up; they were giggling and bopping flirtatiously. Robert noticed that though ostensibly their invitation was to the whole group, their attention was clearly focused on James.

Within a few moments most of the group, including James, was on the dance floor. Robert drifted unobtrusively to the perimeter of the room, where he leaned with self-conscious casualness against the frame of a handsome set of doors that led out to a terrace and the back garden.

A girl drifted over and leaned against the opposite doorframe. She was wearing a pretty green dress, and she had a cloud of flame-colored hair, more orange than red, which blazed against the dark wood of the frame. Their eyes met, the girl's magnified by her glasses. "Hi," Robert said. She smiled. *What a beautiful smile,* he thought. *That hair is incredible, too.*

On a sudden impulse, he pushed himself off from his lounging position and moved over to her. "My name's Robert," he said. "I'm a friend of Justin's."

"Hi," the girl said shyly. "I'm Vesna. I'm actually a friend of Sarah's, Justin's sister. I don't know many people here."

"Me either, to tell you the truth."

"I saw you come in, with that guy over there in the white T-shirt." She indicated James, who was dancing away with a dreamy expression on his tanned face. His eyes were half-closed but as they watched he opened them fully and looked around, smiling. Even from across the room they were striking, those eyes, as lovely as sapphires. The three girls who had approached the group earlier had him surrounded now, twining sinuously around him and each other.

"That's my brother," Robert said. They watched him silently for a few moments.

"I wonder what it'd be like," the young woman said quietly, "to be *that* good-looking."

"I don't know, but I think I'd hate it," said Robert honestly. "People always looking at you! But James seems to cope with it okay."

"I guess he's used to it. But I'd hate it, too."

"Your name's . . . Vesna?" Robert asked, turning to her. "Is that right?"

She nodded. "It means 'spring.' It's a Yugoslav name."

"It's beautiful," he said, and she smiled at him again, a pleased, radiant smile. Robert felt a little light-headed, as though he'd been drinking, and something else, too, like goldfish were swimming around in his chest. But it was not unpleasant. Not at all.

Over the next couple of hours he and Vesna parted several times to mingle with other people at the steadily swelling party, neither wanting to make the other feel they *had* to stay together. But their eyes kept meeting, from doorways and across rooms, and they were drawn back to each other again and again, to talk more, to laugh quietly and just to stand together, observing. *I feel so relaxed*, Robert marveled. *She's just so easy to be with*. Sometime after midnight they found themselves back in the same doorway where they had first met. The party was in full swing now, the dance floor seething. It was hard to hear each other over the racket of music and voices and loud laughter.

"Let's go outside for a while," Robert suggested, having almost to shout. Vesna nodded. They found a bench at the far end of the stone-paved terrace; the light from the house and the sounds of the party spilled out in a way that was attractive but not obtrusive. There were enormous pots full of shrubs and flowers placed here and there. The delicious perfume of gardenias drifted on the warm air. From their shadowed nook they could see the dark outlines of trees with the moon glimmering through branches, and a suggestion of other terraces below.

Suddenly they heard a loud splash, and lights came on somewhere below them. Standing now and leaning on the balustrade, they saw a swimming pool on a lower terrace. Someone had dived in and was swimming steadily, covering the length of the pool in half a dozen long strokes and turning. James, of course, stripped to his underpants, his T-shirt and jeans tossed over a bench.

"My brother the water baby," said Robert. "He can't stay away from it."

The same three girls who had been pursuing him all evening appeared by the pool. One slipped her party dress over her head, laughing, and dived in wearing her bra and panties. A second, the blonde, took her dress off, too: she wasn't wearing a bra. Not hesitating for a moment, she pulled her panties down and stepped out of them. Her pale pubic hair caught the light for a moment, like a tiny silvery cloud, and with a shriek she jumped into the water.

"Oh!" gasped Vesna. "Gosh!"

James kept swimming up and down, apparently oblivious. The third girl was darting to and fro beside the pool like a dog who wants to join its master but is nervous of the water. "That's not fair!" she cried. She had an English accent. "You know I can't swim!" Her friends ignored her and after a few moments more she said "Oh, rats! I'm going to get another drink then!" She disappeared.

Robert and Vesna watched as the two girls in the water began to swim on either side of James. They had no hope of keeping pace with him. Every few laps they stopped at one end to catch their breath and then pushed off level with him as he turned. Each time they swam closer to him, like playful porpoises. Suddenly one of the girls ducked beneath him. The pool was lit below the surface, and Robert and Vesna saw her twist her body to face his and take hold of his shoulders from below. The other girl, the naked one, swam above him and pressed herself against James's back. The three of them sank beneath the water and then surfaced a moment later, laughing and spluttering. The girls towed James over to the side of the pool: their prize catch.

There was a chromed steel ladder midway along the pool's edge. The girl still in her underwear hooked one arm around the ladder, facing the water. The naked blonde girl, laughing, her arm around James's neck, darted her face to his and kissed him quickly, triumphantly. Then she leaned in to her dark-haired friend and kissed her, too. James lifted both his hands to the girls' breasts, the right breast of one and the left of the other, reaching inside the bra cup to free the perfect mound of buoyant flesh.

"Oh!" said Vesna again. She turned away. "You know what?"

"Time for us to rejoin the party, I think," said Robert.

"I think we'd better!" she confirmed, and was already moving quickly back toward the ballroom. Robert followed, crackling with anxiety. What if she judged him by his brother's behavior and thought he was going to . . . to try something with her? *As if I would!* Robert thought indignantly. But Vesna had stopped by the door and was waiting for him. She was smiling.

"Still hate to be that good-looking?" she teased.

"I'm not like that, Vesna," Robert said earnestly. "That's not for me."

"I know," she said, laying her soft hand against his cheek for a moment before she stepped back into the tumult of the party.

Down in the pool, James didn't know or care whose hands were on which part of him, or which girl he was touching at any given moment. An image danced in his mind: one of those Indian statues of multi-armed, full-breasted goddesses come to life. Someone ducked beneath the water and stripped off his underpants, freeing his penis to leap upright. The water felt like silk around it. Briefly a mouth enveloped its swollen head, sucking, and then it was surrounded by water again, and then by a hand, and pressed against a thigh, then a taut belly. The girls pressed close against him; he was kissing and fondling one and the other and both. Then he found himself behind the naked blonde, whose hand was inside her friend's panties and clearly knew what it was doing there. The two girls were kissing passionately, and James had his arms around both, stroking and squeezing. The blonde girl wriggled in the water, nestling her rump against him, and with her free hand reached between her legs and positioned him against her slit. She pushed down as he pushed up and suddenly he was inside her, the heat and juiciness in there all the more delicious for the coolness of the surrounding water. He pushed in deeper, harder.

As he rocked back and forth in her the blonde leaned forward, undid her friend's bra and lifted one breast clear of the water as she sucked and tongued the nipple, her other hand still working deep inside those panties. "Oh god," the dark girl cried. "Oh god, oh fuck!" The blonde was moaning and gasping too. James watched the face of the dark-haired girl as she came, and just a moment later the blonde's back arched and her buttocks bucked hard against him, inner muscles gripping him tight as her orgasm surged through.

I really want to paint this! he was thinking. *The way the light from below and behind makes the flesh look almost translucent, the way the water-drops magnify the pores. Her mouth just above the surface, half-open . . . that strange expression, the intensity, like pain almost . . . How can I get that just right?*

CHAPTER 6

Robert was standing in his living room. He was not in a good way. He felt as though his skull belonged to somebody else, like it had been fitted on to his body by accident. He lifted his hands to the back of his neck and rubbed there for a few moments, and then at the temples. Weird, the disparity between the information from his fingertips and the way his skull felt from the inside, like an enormous ball that had been dangerously overinflated. He held his hands apart for a moment in the air on either side of his head. There, that was how big it felt. The size of a basketball? Bit bigger, maybe.

Quickly, quickly. Vesna and the girls were waiting in the car, and heaven knows the weekend was always far too short to fit everything in. Around the kitchen again. All lights, off. Microwave, toaster, blender, off. The fridge, now, that had to stay on. That had to stay on. *Walk away from the fridge*, he told himself, in the mock-cop voice the boys at school used. The clock, well, that was battery operated, so that was okay. He lifted it away from the wall to check. Yes, batteries all right.

The laundry. Washing machine, off, dryer, off. Iron in the cupboard, cord safely wound around itself, as though it was tied up. Irons were one of the worst. The bedrooms, one, two, three: all the lights were off. He bent down to check each outlet in case something had been plugged in and left on by accident. A hairdryer, for instance. Maybe someone had used a hairdryer in the bathroom? He'd better check there again.

Well, that was the whole house then. Twice. But what about the computer, had he checked the computer was turned off? Yes, he had, but maybe he should check again? He was going back into the living room when the front door opened and Vesna walked up to him.

"Robert," she said in her calm, kind voice.

"I was just checking that everything's switched off."

"I know." She stood before him and gently put her hands to his face. "It's all okay. You've taken care of everything. We can go now."

Robert closed his eyes and took several deep, slow breaths, as his doctor had suggested. His head felt so much better with Vesna's hands there, keeping it to the proper size. Finally he nodded.

"Is it this assessment with your father next week?" she asked.

"No, no. Well, maybe. Yes."

"It's pretty routine, my darling. Really. Try not to worry."

He nodded again and took her hands, lowered them from his face, held them a moment. They walked to the front door together.

"You didn't say anything to the girls, did you?" he asked.

"About your father?"

"No, about . . . me checking."

"No, darling," his wife assured him.

But they must know. Surely. He glanced in the rear-view mirror at Bianca and Alexa in the backseat, their identical Coke-bottle-thick glasses and lovely wavy orange-red hair, Alexa's with about a dozen green plastic clips in it and Bianca's in pigtails with blue fluffy bands at both ends. They were leaning toward each other with their heads lowered as they looked at a magazine. *They must know something.* But the only comment they had ever made was an occasional wail of "Come *on*, Daddy!" as he prowled the rooms, checking, checking.

And at school? What did they know? Or suspect? The secretary he shared with the principal had given up urging him to leave his computer on when he went home. Switched on at the powerpoint, at least. *It would save you so much time each morning,* he'd been told a thousand times, *and it uses up virtually no electricity at all,* but he just laughed that off and said *I was brought up not to waste a single watt, I'm afraid!* Which wasn't true at all, of course, but no one at the school knew that, did they?

Vesna turned a little in her seat. "Girls? Your friend Daisy, what's her mother's name? I just can't remember."

The two girls looked at each other blankly and then back at their mother. "Mrs. Lee?" offered the older one, Bianca.

"Mrs. Lee." Vesna and Robert exchanged glances, smiling. "Of course. And you're sure it's okay for us to leave you there, they don't expect the parents to stay?"

"No, Mum. It's okay."

"So we'll pick you up after we've been to Ikea."

"But you don't have to *hurry,* Mummy. It's a party!"

"I do have some work to get through today," remarked Robert in an aside to Vesna.

"Mmm. If we get done in time at Ikea, I'll drop you at home and then go and get the girls. Spend some time with my good friend Mrs. Lee." They both laughed softly.

He'd had the thing about outlets, plugs, and electricity for years, since well before he was married. But it had got so much worse lately, from the very day the head of the school council had taken him aside to tell him that he, Robert, was highly favored to replace Andrea Milne as principal when she retired the following year. And it wasn't just the electricity thing, either. He also found himself beset by the conviction that he had forgotten certain essential items: his watch, for instance; books or papers he had to take home from school, or vice versa. He was forever tapping his breast pocket to make sure he had a pen there. And had he put the correct shoes on? Socks? His underwear, for god's sake! Sometimes, when he was about to slip his coat off, or his jacket, he had a moment of horror that he was wearing nothing underneath, absolutely nothing. It was awful. And this was the man the school council thought would make a good principal. My god! *What if anyone found out?* Robert knew he should go and see his doctor again but he just . . . didn't dare.

"I am so looking forward to getting this new sofa. If we can find the right one," said Vesna, stroking his leg lightly.

"Me too."

"And a rug, maybe?"

"Maybe."

"We'll have fun looking, anyway."

He smiled at his wife. *But that report I have to write, did I bring it home? Is it in my briefcase? Where in my briefcase? The middle section? I think I put it in the middle section, but . . .*

On Thursday morning, Robert went to collect Alex for the appointment with the aged care assessment team. *We could go and have coffee together afterward*, he thought as he turned into his father's street. *And a toasted sandwich, in a cafe. That'll be nice.* There was Alex standing by the rosebushes in his front garden, bony shoulders hunched almost to his ears as he examined them. He called Robert over, gesturing urgently.

"Look at this! When did these little buggers arrive, eh? I checked these roses just yesterday."

"Oh dear. Aphids."

"That's right, bloody aphids!" said Alex, furious. "I need to tackle these right now, Robbie. I'll just give 'em a good blast with the hose to start off with and if needs must I'll spray 'em."

"Dad! We haven't really got time! We're due there in fifteen minutes."

"Due where?" his father asked, frowning distractedly. "Where are we going? Just . . . just remind me?"

"The clinic. It's . . . a doctor's appointment." Robert felt awkward, as if he were trying to con his father into something.

"Oh. That's right. Doctor's appointment. What's it for again?"

"It's just an assessment, Dad. A check-up, really."

"Right. Well, this won't take a minute," he said, moving toward the neatly coiled garden hose.

"Dad, please! I'll give you a hand later, but we really should get going *now!*"

Alex gave his son a disgusted look. "All right then," he said reluctantly. "I'll just make a note to remind myself." He was feeling in his pockets. "Blast! I haven't got a notebook."

"I've got one in the car, Dad," said Robert, inspired, propelling his father out the front gate. "The aphids can't do much damage in a couple of hours."

"Oh, can't they?" said Alex darkly. "Fat lot you'd know about it. Bloody useless, you are."

Stung, Robert didn't talk much on the drive to the clinic. He had intended to go through what he understood of the assessment procedure with his father again, but Alex appeared to be sulking about the aphids, or at any rate not inclined to conversation. It was so unlike his father to be surly. Robert wished Vesna was with them, she always knew the right thing to say. *Maybe I could call her while Dad's having the assessment?* Stopping for a red light, he turned to check that his briefcase was on the backseat. Yes. But was his mobile phone in it? He reached for the case but then stopped himself. The lights would change any second. He felt his pockets hopefully, but it wasn't there. *What if I've come without my phone? How can I call Vesna? What if she needs to call me? Or the school does?* The feeling of panic rose and rose until he was able to check his briefcase at the next red light. Yes, it was there. *Thank heavens!*

At the clinic they only waited a few minutes before a capable-looking middle-aged woman came and introduced herself as Margaret Appleby, a physiotherapist with special training in aged care assessment. She would be conducting part of the assessment, but first, if they would just follow her, she would take them to meet the doctor for a chat.

"Both of us?" asked Robert, feeling suddenly unready.

"Well, I assumed, since you came together . . . It's quite standard, you know, for a family member to sit in. But if you'd rather not . . ."

"Dad? Would you like me to sit in on the assessment?" he asked, turning to Alex, sure from his father's earlier testiness that he would say no. But to his surprise Alex said breezily that he'd be delighted to have the company, and together they set off down the corridor to the office of a tall, thin, surprisingly young-looking doctor who introduced himself as Dr. Alvarez, the resident psychiatric geriatrician, or geriatric psychiatrist, Robert couldn't quite remember. *And if I can't remember, how's Dad going to?* he wondered, looking across at his father, but Alex appeared perfectly unconcerned.

Dr. Alvarez had Alex's file from his GP open on the desk in front of him. "For a man of your age, Mr. McDonald, you seem to be enjoying very good physical health."

"That's right, tip-top condition. It's the gardening keeps me fit. Love the garden."

"Good for you. It's so important, to keep fit and stay active. The most important thing, one might say."

"Couldn't agree more."

"No heart problems, no lung problems. There's just the high blood pressure."

"Oh, that's not really a problem. Nothing serious."

"Well you see, it *can* be a problem. It can lead to *serious* problems. It's very important that we check it regularly and that you continue with your medication."

Alex agreed graciously that he would do so. The young doctor started to ask him about other things: did Alex belong to any clubs or hobby groups, were there friends he saw regularly? Did he ever feel depressed; some days perhaps when it just didn't seem worth getting out of bed in the morning? Alex laughed lightly at the very thought. There were other questions, unremarkable, and Robert's attention started to drift, when suddenly he heard an agitated edge in his father's voice.

"Not at all! I have no problems with my memory whatsoever!"

"Mr. McDonald, it's really a very common aspect of aging."

"Well, not mine! I have no problems with my memory what-soever!" Alex repeated angrily. "And if anyone's been telling you otherwise they're a damn liar!" He cast an angry, suspicious look at Robert, who, taken aback, started to protest.

"That's fine, then, that's fine," said Dr. Alvarez, closing the file on his desk and tapping it decisively, so that Alex's attention was drawn back to him. "Thank you so much for this chat, Mr. McDonald, and now I think Margaret Appleby, who you met earlier, is ready to talk to you. But perhaps we can get you both a cup of something first?"

Alex conceded a little stiffly that that would be nice. Leaving his father in a small sitting room, Robert grabbed his mobile phone and stepped outside to call Vesna, but only reached her voice-mail. Even hearing her recorded voice made him feel more settled. He left a brief message and returned to the sitting room, where his father was now chatting cheerfully with an attractive young woman in a blue uniform. Margaret Appleby was there, too, and the whole atmos-phere seemed perfectly convivial. *This'll be fine after all*, Robert told himself, assuming a hearty smile as he entered the room.

"Let's move along to my office then, shall we?" Margaret Appleby suggested when they finished their tea. Robert recognized the words and tone he had used himself ten thousand times: it was the jolly inclusiveness of institutional authority, and it made his heart sink. He cried with a great show of cheerfulness, "Yes, let's! Dad? Ready?" picked up his briefcase and jumped to his feet. *Oh, this is all such fun,* he told himself disgustedly, *checking out whether the old man's really los-ing it!* and that scathing unvoiced thought made him thankful that he'd had the good sense to stick with primary school teaching. There was no way he could cope with the cynicism and sarcasm of adolescent students; his own inner commentary was bad enough. *Best to know your own limitations, really, before others point them out to you.*

Margaret Appleby explained the four or five short tests she would give Alex to help her get an indication of, variously, his short- and long-term memory function and cognitive ability. As she said "memory function" in her brisk voice, Robert flinched, sure that his father would flare up again, but Alex merely nodded politely as he listened. First, Mrs. Appleby said, she was going to say five words and ask Alex to repeat them, and then to tell her those same five words when they had finished the other tests. These would involve a little mental arithmetic, the arranging and duplicating of geometric patterns, and recall-testing using a number of objects.

"Now then. Are you ready for that list of words, Mr. McDonald?"

"Ready when you are, Margaret," Alex replied with a winning smile.

"Right then. I'd like you to repeat the five words when I've finished saying them, then tell them to me again at the end of our session. Here they are: chicken . . . boy . . . cricket . . . motor-car . . . shoe."

Robert told himself a quick story as she said the words: a chicken fluttered up to a boy playing cricket. As he chased it off the pitch a motor-car drove past and someone threw a shoe out of it. *That'll do,* he thought.

"Could you repeat those words to me now, Mr. McDonald?"

"Chicken . . . cricket . . . motor-car," said Alex. "Wait, there's one more. Chicken, cricket, motor-car . . . No, I can't get it. Sorry."

"That's fine, Mr. McDonald," said Mrs. Appleby smoothly. "We'll move on to the next one then, shall we?"

She asked Alex to count backward in sevens from one hundred, which he managed quite well, Robert thought, down to the sixties, and then he seemed to lose track and was subtracting by various inconsistent numbers, trailing out in the thirties. He looked at her enquiringly, and she smiled brightly back.

"Doing well, Mr. McDonald. Any more?"

"No, no, I don't think so," Alex said. Robert felt like his own brain had stalled too. His father had been an engineer, calculating numbers and equations day in, day out, long before there were calculators to do the donkey work. *I was good at arithmetic, but Dad could do long division in his head faster than I could do it on the page.*

Mrs. Appleby was now showing Alex a wooden tray on which sat an assortment of objects, twelve or fourteen perhaps in all. Alex had two minutes to memorize as many as he could, then she would cover them with a cloth and he was to tell her those he remembered. Robert stared at the objects, too, feeling almost panicky. His father was gazing at the tray keenly but appeared quite untroubled. *Candle . . . scissors . . . pencil . . . little sieve thing, what do you call that? Tea-strainer, of course! . . . button, roll of film, rubber glove . . .* Robert started to memorize the objects in groups of four, connecting the objects in each group with a little story that gave him visual cues, but before he had finished, the two minutes were up and the tray was covered again.

Robert recalled ten of the objects, his father five. Robert felt sweat breaking out under his arms and a familiar tight sensation across his chest. *Where's my briefcase?* he thought wildly. *Did I lock the car? Slow down, slow down.* He took several soft, deep breaths and consciously unclenched his hands, relaxed his throat and jaw. *It's all right. It's all right.*

Alex had pulled his chair right up to the desk to copy a simple geometric diagram. He looked like he was enjoying himself; it was, after all, the sort of thing he could once have done in his sleep. Although Robert forced himself not to crane forward in his chair, still he could see that the diagram his father was drawing in the blank section of the sheet was a very imperfect copy of the one printed beside it.

"There we are!" said Alex, sounding perfectly satisfied, even triumphant. *He can't see that it's a mess,* thought Robert.

While Alex tackled the next test, arranging component shapes within a diagram, Robert silently hummed to himself every violin piece his daughters had ever learned, starting with "Twinkle, Twinkle, Little Star." Finally it was over—but not quite.

"Last thing, Mr. McDonald. Do you remember that when we first came in here I read you a list of five words, and asked if you would repeat them for me at the end of our little get-together?"

Instantly the image of the chicken on the cricket pitch rose in Robert's mind, the boy chasing it, the car driving by, a shoe sailing from the window. Alex looked completely blank.

"A list of words, five words. You repeated them to me before we began doing the other tests, and you were going to repeat them again."

"I do beg your pardon," Alex said charmingly. "It must've slipped my mind. But I don't think we've got time for that now, I'm afraid, Robert needs to get me home. I've got a lot of things to attend to."

"Of course," Mrs. Appleby said. "I'll just get Maureen to give you a glass of water before you go." The attractive young woman in the blue uniform reappeared and, taking Alex's arm as though he were her partner for the next dance, engaged him in chat as she led him from the room. Robert made to follow but Margaret Appleby laid a restraining hand on his arm.

"A moment, please," she said, and led him back to the desk. "Dr. Alvarez will be sending the results of this assessment and a written report to your father's GP. But I can tell you now that your father's dementia is presently in the range of mild to moderate, and will almost inevitably become more severe, though at what rate it's impossible to predict."

"Dementia?" Robert repeated blankly.

"I'm afraid so, yes. What concerns me most immediately is the impairment to his spatial perception. Does he drive a car?"

"Yes."

"Often?"

"Oh, I'm not . . . No, not all that often, I don't think."

"Well, he shouldn't. I'll be writing to his doctor about this, too, recommending that his license be suspended pending a driving test, which I can tell you now he will fail. In the meantime, please discourage him from driving."

Robert gazed at her capable, efficient face. He couldn't think of a single thing to say. His briefcase suddenly felt very heavy; he swung it up to his chest and clutched it in both arms.

Margaret Appleby smiled a conclusive good-bye smile. "Thank you, Mr. McDonald. Can you and your father find your own way out?"

part two

CHapter 7

In Deborah's opinion Silver had taken one hell of a risk, having an outdoor party in September. Melbourne's notoriously unpredictable weather was never more so than in spring; many a public event or private function had been ruined by lashing rain and freezing winds roaring in suddenly off Bass Strait. But no, Silver's fiftieth birthday party turned out to be the warmest September day on record. A cool change was due to blow in the next day, but this was a Saturday night for high heels and party dresses, short sleeves and the giddy illusion that the long gray winter was finally over.

Deborah, Angus and Olivia came early to help with anything last-minute, but it all appeared to be well in hand.

"Jeez, guys," said Angus, looking around with admiration after James and Silver had welcomed them. "The place looks like a million dollars!"

"Angus," said Deborah dryly, "that's because this place *is* a million dollars. Closer to two, wouldn't it be, Jaf?"

"'Bout that," agreed her brother amiably. "It does look fantastic though, doesn't it? Silver hired these installation artists from South

Gippsland. They brought down a truckload of stuff and put it all together here."

"It's pretty wild," said Olivia, checking out the neon stick figures just starting to glow as the daylight dimmed, the towering floral displays, the pretty lights twined through the trees and shrubbery. Garden seats were embraced by papier-mâché dragons and other fanciful beasts, and there was a bar done up like a pirate's treasure cave.

"Understatement," said Silver proudly as she surveyed the scene. "It's a gift." Deborah and Angus laughed.

"I tell you what's a gift, Silver," said Angus. "An American with an ironic sense of humor. And especially, having one in the family."

"And happy birthday, congratulations and all that," added Deborah, kissing her. "It feels weird not to be giving you a present."

"No, no presents! It's a condition of attendance at this party."

"Well, you're going to have to chuck me out then," said Olivia, hauling a wrapped rectangular parcel out of her bag and handing it to her aunt. "Because I went ahead and got you one anyway."

"Olivia!" said Deborah, startled.

"For you, my wicked niece, I will make an exception," said Silver, unwrapping the parcel. It was a book of dog photographs.

"Why am I not surprised?" murmured Deb.

"Wonderful! I will treasure this. But don't tell anyone." Silver made kissy-kissy mouths at her and Olivia smiled.

People started arriving, and in droves; the hot day had put all of Melbourne in the mood for a party, and at least half of Melbourne, it seemed, had been invited to this one. Many guests had a connection to the visual arts, whether making it, selling it, buying it, framing it or writing about it, but plenty of others were simply people Silver had met somewhere, somehow, and liked, and who liked her.

"She's incredibly popular, isn't she?" Deborah commented to Angus when they found themselves standing together at one point, after a hectic couple of hours. "I mean, *genuinely* popular."

"Yep. It ain't just her dough, you know."

"And it's not her looks either," said Deborah. She'd had quite a few drinks already.

"Probably not," agreed Angus cautiously. They observed Silver as she stood amid a cluster of animated people all laughing and talking. *She really is plain,* thought Deb. *But somehow you just don't notice that. Not usually.* Silver was a woman with a generous build; she liked her food and her wine and her figure showed it. She was inclined to be lumpy. *Barge-woman's arms,* thought Deb, remembering a disparaging expression she'd once heard Auntie Joan use. Silver's dirty-blonde hair was inclined to be fly-away, too, and her features were rather . . . coarse. But none of this seemed to bother her, and it didn't seem to bother her remarkably handsome husband either.

"You know what?" said Deborah suddenly. "I've never heard James say a harsh word about Silver. Or to her."

"Ye-es," Angus said, even more cautiously. "And what do you make of that?"

Deborah shrugged. "That they're very lucky, I guess."

"I guess so. I wish I was that lucky," he added, addressing the night air. Deborah swung around and gave him a suspicious look.

"What's that supposed to mean?" she asked.

"Whatever," said Angus. "What's Ollie doing?"

"Helping the caterers, last I saw," said Deborah, moving off. "I'm going to get another drink and mingle some more."

Olivia enjoyed taking the platters of food around; it gave her something to do, and the caterers were pleased to have the extra help. But she was relieved to see Laurence arrive, finally, with Auntie Meredith.

"Hey, Ol," he said, coming over to her immediately. He took some gourmet morsel from the platter she was holding and chucked it in his mouth, then another two in quick succession. "Yum! I think that whole plate's got my name on it, waddaya reckon?"

"Looks like it to me. Let's take it over there," Olivia said, indicating an unoccupied swing seat in a quiet spot. "I'm sick of standing up."

Laurence steadily worked his way through the array of delicious titbits, finally declaring, "Not bad for starters!" as he put the empty platter aside.

"Healthy teenage appetite," commented Olivia.

"Hasn't it hit you yet? The take-no-prisoners food thing?" asked her cousin. She shook her head. "You wait. In another year or so you'll be scarfing it down in your sleep."

"So when are you gonna slow up?"

"Who knows? Mum keeps saying 'Any minute now.' Could be just wishful thinking on her part though."

"Hey, did you guys come with Grandpa?"

"Yep. Mum's not such an idiot she's going to drive home from a party."

"How was he, coming over here?"

"How was he? Grandpa? Fine, why?"

"Oh . . . things have been a bit weird." And she told him what had been happening: the strange incident with Grandpa in the garden, and the meeting of all the aunts and uncles at her house that had followed. Laurence listened, nodding from time to time.

"Okay, now I get it," he said. "Mum was pretty twitchy about it but she said everyone was making a big fuss over nothing. She reckons Grandpa'd just been a bit unwell. I thought he had, like, a cold or something."

"Nuh. He's gonna have some tests, Uncle Robert's organizing it. Hey, here's something I wanted to ask you, too: does your mum talk about *her* mum much?"

"She used to. Not so much lately, maybe. But sometimes when she was drunk she used to crap on about how terrible it was to have a parent who just disappeared when you were a little kid. And I'm like, 'Ma, how about a parent who disappears before you're even *born*?'"

"Yeah, good point. But I thought she didn't talk about him hardly? Your dad?"

"Nah, right. Like, what is there to say? 'I had a one-night stand, can't remember his name or what he looked like but he seemed like a nice guy.' Good work, Ma. Nice one."

"Does it bug you?"

Laurence blew a little *pph* of air between his lips. "What's the point? Nothing much I can do about it. Yeah, sometimes."

They watched the party rock on from their secluded vantage point for a while, swinging companionably back and forth in the seat, which was decorated with a lion's head at one end and a sort of enormous snake tail at the other.

"Have I ever shown you Mum's big journal-type things?" asked Laurence suddenly.

Olivia shook her head. "I don't think so."

"That's where she writes about all that sort of stuff. Family stuff. Not just writes, she draws and pastes things in, too. They're pretty amazing actually. Kinda like huge comic books, in a way, about her life."

"Yeah, really? Your mum does this? Auntie Meredith?"

"Yep, that's the one. You should come over next weekend, my friend Crystal's coming to have a look at them. She's doing Year 12 Art, she's sucking up every idea around for her portfolio." He held his hands out as though grasping a long invisible handle and made vacuum cleaner sound effects.

"Is that okay with your mum? I mean, for other people to look at them?"

"Yeah, sure, she's cool about that. You know what my mum's like, she'll spill her guts to the person sitting next to her on the tram."

Olivia laughed. "Not like *my* mum!"

"Hey, I'll tell her now, if you like," said Laurence as he spotted his mother meandering by not far away. He called out to her and Meredith came straight over.

"Oh, you *two*," she cooed, nudging in between them on the swing seat. "It just makes me so happy that you get on so fabulously together. Poor little lonely-onlies!"

"Yeah, our lives are blighted. Mum, can Ol come over next weekend and look at your journal things, too?"

"Of course she can!" said Meredith, planting a kiss on Olivia's cheek. "But aren't your weekends chock-a-block already? Busy going out with your pals?"

"No," Olivia said simply.

"You couldn't *tear* me away from my friends when I was your age. We did *everything* together!"

"Actually, I don't have any friends," Olivia said in a perfectly matter-of-fact voice.

"Oh, don't *say* that! That can't possibly be true!"

"Hey, I'm your friend aren't I, Ol?" said Laurence.

"Yeah, well, kind of. Sure. But you're my cousin," said Olivia.

"But you have to have *girl*friends your own age! That's what's so much *fun!*" insisted Meredith. "You know, Ollie, sweetheart, maybe if you were just a little less, you know, *serious* all the time . . . Just talked more about, you know, movies and make-up and . . . and . . ."

Olivia was looking at her aunt with her customary scowl on her face. One hundred percent serious.

"Maybe a little makeover," said Meredith almost desperately. She lifted her niece's straight hair up in wings from the sides of her head. Olivia gulped. "You could get a really cute cut, you know. Layers. Maybe some highlights . . ."

Laurence took hold of one of his mother's wrists. "Mum," he said firmly. "That's enough. Leave Ol alone, she's fine the way she is."

"Of course she is!" cried Meredith, dropping Olivia's hair immediately and drawing back. "Of course you are, sweetheart! I didn't . . . Oh dear, I get *everything* wrong, don't I?" She snatched up her empty glass from where it had fallen and peered into it as though more wine might magically appear, then turned back to Olivia. "Do you hate me?" she asked beseechingly.

Olivia shook her head vehemently, speechless. Just then Laurence's mobile beeped loudly; a text message. He read it and told them, "Okay, I'm gonna push off soon. Got another party to go to."

"Oh, Laurence, we only just got here!" cried his mother.

"That's cool, Ma, you don't have to leave yet! And I've talked to Ol, she was the only person I really wanted to see."

"That's not very polite! You have to wish Silver a happy birthday."

"Don't worry, I will. I'll go and do that now."

"I'll . . . I'll go and do something, too," said Olivia, jumping up from the seat at the same moment as Laurence, setting it swinging wildly.

"Whoo!" Meredith sang, laughing as she was rocked back and forth. "Wait for me, I'll come with you. My glass needs attention."

As Meredith ordered a fresh drink from the cheerful young people at the bar, she spotted Robert nearby. He was nursing a light beer and looking a little lost.

"Hello, Bobbit!" she cried, embracing him and only losing the tiniest bit of her wine in the process. "Isn't Vesna here yet?"

"No, her shift only just finished so it'll be another half hour at least. I might just go and check on the girls."

They looked in on the clutch of children who were happily watching videos together in an upstairs room. Robert looked like he wouldn't mind staying there but Meredith persuaded him to come back downstairs. They wandered around the flowing living areas of the big house, admiring this and that, chatting to each other. Through a window Meredith caught sight of their father standing with Olivia. They were examining the pale flowers of a tall shrub.

"Look at Dad and Ollie," she said to Robert, pointing. "You know, I'm a bit worried about that girl. She told me just before that she doesn't have *any friends*! Can you imagine that, Robert? That's just not right, is it?"

"Did she sound upset about it?" asked Robert. Alex was bending a branch of the shrub toward Olivia, and they both leaned forward till they were almost enveloped by the blossoms.

"Well . . . no, actually. And that's strange, too, don't you think?"

"But that's the thing, you see. I've been teaching for a long time now and you know one of the things I've learned, Merry? It's not the kids like Olivia you have to worry about. It's the ones who don't have any friends but are desperately unhappy about it. The kids who'd do anything to be in with the in-crowd, they're the ones to keep an eye on. Especially if they're being bullied or ostracized. Olivia's not like that. I think she'll have plenty of friends in a few years, once the other kids have caught up to her."

"Do you think so? Well, she and Laurence get on fabulously, that's for sure; they always have. And all his friends like her. They seem to, anyway."

"Yes. She just doesn't fit with children her own age. See? Dad treats her almost like another adult and they're . . ."

"Happy as clams," agreed Meredith, smiling as she watched the old man and the tall young girl rubbing leaf-tips between their fingers and conferring. "Oh, I'm glad we talked about this, you *always* know the right way to look at things!" She patted her brother's arm. "And Daddy's looking so well, too, don't you think? How did that assessment thingie go, by the way? Okay?"

"Oh yes, it all went smoothly," said Robert. He had already talked about this with Vesna, that they wouldn't spoil the party by discussing the rather upsetting facts of Alex's assessment on the night. "Results in the next week, I expect. I'll let everyone know what they are, of course."

"I'm sure it'll be okay. I feel so sure of that," said Meredith.

They turned away from the window together, hearing the sound of familiar voices, and followed them to find Deborah and James standing at the long dining table.

"Hi there, you two!" cried Deborah, unusually expansive. "Come and have a look at this!"

On the wall behind the table hung the stingray painting. It had been perfectly lit; the scene seemed real, alive.

"Oh, very nice, James! Very impressive," said Robert. "A new work?"

"Yep. Well, just a couple of weeks. Silver likes to have 'em round the house for a while."

"Do you remember this?" asked Deborah excitedly. "That summer, at Rosebud? When Mr. Grounds got stung by the stingray?"

"Oh, by golly, I do! How amazing! It's an extraordinary talent you have, James."

"*I* don't remember," pouted Meredith. "What summer are you talking about? Was I there?"

"The summer Mum left," said Deborah baldly. She poured herself more champagne from the bottle on the table behind her.

"You were there, Merry, but of course you were only little. We went down to Rosebud to visit some neighbors. I think it might have been New Year's Eve."

"That's right, it was!" agreed Deborah. "We were supposed to stay there and let off fireworks on the beach but because of Mr. Grounds getting stung we went back home and just did the fireworks in the backyard. So that was exactly a week to the day after Mum . . . left."

All four siblings turned and gazed at the painting again. It seemed different now, somehow. More ominous.

"I remember other things from that summer," offered Meredith. "I remember riding home from the pool on my new bike with Deb and how hard it was to reach the pedals. And I remember you teaching me how to swim, Bobbit, that was that summer, wasn't it?"

"Yes, it was."

"I remember watching you standing with her for hours in the learners' pool while she thrashed away," said Deborah. "You were so incredibly patient; I remember thinking: I'd be going mental by now." Robert gave his older sister a slightly startled look; it wasn't like Deb to pay compliments. "And, James, you used to be in the big pool, just steaming up and down, up and down. You must've swum a hundred miles that summer. And you were only eight."

"Yeah, that was my big discovery, all right," said James. "The miracle of swimming. Realizing you could get in the water and swim lap after lap and when you got out an hour or so had gone by and you hadn't thought about *a thing.*"

"I remember those yummy sandwiches you used to make when the boys got home from the pool," said Meredith.

"Were they yummy?" Deborah smiled.

"Mmm, that fresh white bread, soft like a cloud, and the tomatoes smelled so *good.*"

"Dad used to pick them in the morning just before he went off to work."

"And I loved the way you buttered the bread so thick. Why can't we have sandwiches like that any more?"

"That's right. I remember when I was buttering them thinking, Mum would yell at me if she saw how much butter I was putting on. And so I'd put on even more—*So there!*"

They all laughed, the four together, and then sobered.

"It was some summer, all right," said James.

"Do you remember when the police came and talked to us?" asked Robert suddenly.

James nodded forcefully and Deborah said, "Do I ever! We were petrified!"

"Wasn't it strange," said Robert, "the way we had all those theories about how she'd been kidnapped and we were going to get a ransom note, or perhaps she was a spy for the government—all those crazy ideas—and then when the police came we couldn't say a single word."

"Well, you lot didn't say a single word! And I just more or less said yes or no when they asked me questions."

"Did you tell them about that night?" asked Meredith. "Christmas Eve, and the car arriving?"

"We'd already told Dad everything we saw and then the cops asked me to tell it again but I just . . . couldn't. Or wouldn't, maybe," said Deborah. "And Dad wasn't very happy about them talking to us either, I had that distinct impression."

"Daddy's *never* been happy to talk about it," said Meredith petulantly. "Full stop!"

They were all quiet for a few moments and then Robert said with a wry smile, "I remember thinking, *I will never trust Deborah with a letter again!*"

Deborah turned on him with her face full of sudden fury. "What the *hell* do you mean by that?"

"I just, I just," stuttered Robert, taken aback, "I just mean . . . I was just talking about, that summer, you know, you steamed open some letters . . ."

"Uh-oh," said James. "I was your partner in crime there I'm afraid, Deb. We were looking for clues, remember?"

"Oh yeah, yeah," said Deb, still flushed but looking somewhat mollified. "Well, big deal. We were desperate. I remember how you used to check the letterbox fifteen times a day!" she flung at Robert.

"I did," Robert said sadly. "I did. And I filled up all those notebooks with my neatest work, thinking I'd be able to show her when she came home. It was . . . soothing, somehow, doing those projects. You know, I've often thought that's when I decided to become a teacher, that summer."

"And because of teaching me how to swim, too, maybe?" suggested Meredith.

"Hey, yeah!" James gave a brief exclamatory laugh. "That was when I decided to become a swimmer!"

Deborah said, "That's when I decided . . ." She took another swig of champagne. Some spilled down her top, and she swiped at the drops. *Oh shit, I think I'm really drunk.* "No, that's when I *realized* . . ." The other three looked at her enquiringly but she was lost in memory.

It was a night toward the end of that summer, just before they were due to start school again. They were watching TV with their father like they did most nights, all of them in a line on the long green couch, and just as the news ended with the warning of "another day of total fire ban," their dad, still looking at the TV screen, said, "Your mother has had to go back to England for a while."

The children's heads swiveled to face him. Alex blinked and gave them a small uncertain smile.

"How long for?" Deborah had asked.

"Well, it's hard to say. Her father is, ahm, not well, and she has to help look after him."

"Is she all right?" asked Robert anxiously.

"Yes. She's all right. She's perfectly all right. You don't have to worry about that."

The theme music for the next program began. Meredith drew her thumb out of her mouth with a loud wet *pop* and asked in a remarkably strong, urgent voice, "When is Mummy coming home?"

"Oh, sometime soon, sweetheart. It's just a bit hard to say. Sometime. And in the meantime, a very nice lady called Mrs. Hardman will pick Meredith up from school each afternoon and she'll get dinner ready for you all. She'll stay here till I get home. So you don't have to worry."

Meredith started to cry. Deborah looked past her father as he twisted awkwardly to cuddle his youngest child, and her eyes met those of Robert and James. *She's not coming back.* In that instant, they all knew it. Robert's hands flexed convulsively in his lap; she saw his thumbs begin to work their private patterns across his fingertips at lightning speed, like the telegraph operator she had seen in a movie, sending an urgent message. James let his head drop back, resting it on the back of the couch. His eyes, gazing up to a corner of the ceiling, lost focus, and his face took on an odd faraway expression, almost as though he were sleeping with his eyes open.

Deborah looked at them, her father, her brothers, her little sister with her face buried in her daddy's neck, sobbing. *All of you,* she thought. *I've got to look after all of you now.* It seemed that the holidays had ended, not just for the summer, but for the rest of her life.

Standing before the painting that had prompted all this, James asked at last, "So, what did you realize, Deb?"

She shook her head. "Nothing," she said, taking another, careful sip of champagne. "I can't . . . explain it."

"I decided something then, too!" exclaimed Meredith.

"Oh, come on!" Deborah said. "You weren't much more than a baby!"

"And that's what I decided!" her sister said, sounding girlishly delighted. "To stay the baby! I mean, why grow up when you just . . . when you just never know what's going to happen? Why would you want to have to deal with all that?"

"Oh, Merry!" said Robert, and gave her a little hug.

"Too true," said Deborah. "Too bloody true."

chapter 8

James regarded the splendid meal that had been put before him with a sorrowful look.

"What's up, hon?" asked Silver, freeing her cutlery from the enormous linen napkin. "Not what you wanted?"

"No, it looks . . . perfect." James sighed. "I was just picturing what they're eating . . . back there." He inclined his head toward the rear of the aircraft.

Silver chuckled. "Well, you're not catching me out! I ain't gonna say let them eat cake!" That got a small rueful smile from him. "Oh, hon! I know it's not great back there but it's not like they're eating pig food. Or six months of weevily ship's biscuits, like it would've been in the olden days."

"I know," he said. "But, Sil, don't you think first class is a bit . . . over the top?" There was so much space between their magnificently engineered seats, it was tricky to lower his voice enough so as not to be overheard by the hovering attendants. "Don't you think we should fly . . ." He hesitated. Despite his egalitarian principles, James had no desire to be crammed in with the masses in economy. "Business?"

"We *do* fly business, usually!" Silver reminded him. "This is only a points upgrade. And you know, I have to hit the ground running the minute we're in London. This is a really big deal for Tanya, sweetie: her first solo show there. I've got a lot of finessing to do. And a whole lotta business . . ." she nodded at her laptop, "for the foundation, before I go to Chicago."

"Hey, did you think Tanya sounded okay when she rang yesterday? She told me she's sure nobody's going to come."

"Oh, that girl!" Silver made a face of fond exasperation. "What a worry-wart! Her work is so *perfect* for the UK market. There'll be so many red stickers they'll want to put up a quarantine notice!"

"Yeah? That's great, then." James settled back in his seat. He had no doubt at all that if Silver said the show would be a success, then so it would be. She'd never been wrong yet. When it came to business—the art market, or her wealthy family's foundation—she was infallible. And hey, if she wanted to fly first class (and take him with her), well, why not?

"Hon?"

He glanced across. His wife was waving the plastic knife at him cheekily. "First class or cattle class, we all gotta use these dumb things!" He laughed.

Silver was her own person, that was the thing: a wonderfully self-propelled, idiosyncratic person. His best friend, as well as his wife. They'd been friends from the day they met, at a small gallery which was showing a couple of James's paintings in a group exhibition. He didn't even have a dealer back then, and she was new to Australia, just nosing around the art scene. But once she decided to become a player, boy, didn't she learn the ropes fast! Even when they were just friends, they were a couple: together, simpatico. Their decision to marry grew out of a shared sense of humor, mutual admiration for each other's talents, and visa hassles, rather than lust or romance. James thought it was the best thing he'd ever done. Silver was terrific: funny, expansive, savvy, hardworking, generous. And despite her bulky figure and plain features, she carried herself with such style and assurance that heads turned when she came into a room, as though she were a model, or a celebrity.

Heads turned when James came into a room, too, but that was because of one simple thing: his looks. The luck of the draw—and James was well aware that he had drawn an incredible amount of luck. More, probably, than his share. He knew exactly who he resembled: the young Elvis Presley. Of course he wasn't exactly young any more, but the crinkles now permanently at the corners of his eyes, the silver threads appearing in his black hair, only added to his appeal. And he was making darn sure that he didn't age the way poor old Elvis had—no fried peanut butter and banana sandwiches for him! James kept to a balanced diet, drank alcohol only once a week, and swam for a good hour every day. When they were traveling, he usually found a swimming pool, but if he couldn't then he ran, and if the weather didn't allow that then he went to a gym. James had skin that glowed with health, a washboard stomach, and a broad-shouldered, tapering body that men as well as women looked at with admiration and, often, longing.

He knew, too, that his faithfulness to his wife made him even more attractive. Funny, really. Before he met and then married Silver, he'd been rushed constantly by ardent women. James hated to disappoint, and he couldn't bear to argue. So he had gradually become more and more like a performing seal, doing his tricks, going through an ever less satisfying routine. It came to frighten him that he felt so little as he brought yet another panting partner to orgasm and then dutifully went there himself. God, what a relief not to have to do that any longer! To be able to go to a party and just enjoy himself, without that pressure! Because he did like a busy social life; he liked to talk, to laugh, to charm, to flirt even, and Silver looked on with indulgent pride because she knew that he would never take it further.

She had given him so much. Artistic success, sure, but James was not particularly ambitious for his art. What he relished most was the sense of being taken care of. Deborah had done it when he was a kid—still did, in some ways—and Silver did it even better. He admired her so much and he had not the slightest desire to risk what he had. To make her unhappy. He knew what it would do to Silver's pride to have her handsome husband fool around with someone younger, prettier than she was.

It was their choice, James felt, and nobody else's business, that their relationship was companionable, not passionate. They snuggled together in their bed, watched movies on the enormous TV while Silver drank champagne and James sipped his soda, read bits out loud from books and magazines—and talked, talked endlessly, gossiped and confided and argued (though without venom), and sometimes held each other as they drifted off to sleep. In their own way they were sensuous. But actual sex? Almost never. It just wasn't *them*.

After the meal they decided to watch an in-flight movie "together"—though each on their personal screens, of course. It was an English film about a troubled family, and as they watched it their thoughts settled simultaneously on the same subject. When the movie ended they turned to each other, Silver saying, "How did—" just as James spoke.

"I haven't told you about that meeting I had with my family," he said apologetically.

"Yeah. Well, we've been busy: the party, the trip. But how was it?"

"Oh . . ." James looked down, occupied himself putting away the entertainment handset. "As well as could be expected, I guess."

Silver waited.

"Dad has to have some tests, I did mention that? Robert's going to let us know. So really there's nothing more to say till we get those results."

"But . . . there's something else? Did you let 'em know about my offer?"

"Yeah." He looked at her ruefully. "They're a funny lot, my family.

For instance, even though Deb agreed to Vesna's involvement, you could tell she still resented it, even Robert talking about it. And when I told them about your offer, they were . . ."

"Yeah?"

"They just . . . I don't know, Sil. I guess they don't want to think about that yet. Christ, *I* don't want to think about it yet, you know. A time when maybe Dad can't look after himself properly."

"I can understand that. So, we put it on the backburner. That's fine." She smiled at him, genuinely, and James was surprised at how relieved he felt.

"I'm just going to stretch my legs," he said, rising from his seat to walk around the cabin, flex and bend and stretch. Silver watched him. *God, he is so beautiful!* It was a thought she had often. From her teens, Silver had trained herself not to let desire show. Too many good-looking boys had turned from her in embarrassed, unspoken rejection. She'd never really had much of a sex life—even in the seventies, when promiscuity was so fashionable, she had been too plain to be chosen, too proud to beg and too smart to be taken advantage of—but that didn't stop her yearning. Sexual passion wasn't part of her marriage because . . . well, what Silver kept very much to herself was her belief that it was because James was not actually in love with her. That, unbeknown to himself, he wa s waiting for someone else. Some other woman who would set him afire, or perhaps—could it be?—some other man. Maybe he was gay and in deep, deep denial. It was not impossible.

Silver believed that one day her husband would find his real, true love. And then he would, inevitably, leave her. Sometimes she imagined that day, in detail, preparing herself. But meanwhile, she could delay it as long as possible. She kept them both happy—more or less—by not putting even the slightest pressure on him to fulfill the desires she kept so sternly under control. She loved him; she wanted to be with him; and this was the best—the only—way to have him.

———

At the end of their first week in London, Tanya's show having opened
to the predicted acclaim (and sales), Silver and James went to a dinner party in a particularly charming part of Holland Park. Their hosts
were old friends of Silver's: Alice, a Canadian collage artist, and her
Dutch banker husband. Of the other guests, two were an unattached
man and woman in their thirties—a match-making attempt, James
figured, on their hostess's part—and the other pair a well-heeled diplomat couple who, it soon transpired, were looking to expand their
art collection. *Ah, another kind of match-making,* James thought. Alice
suggested, apparently on the spur of the moment, that Silver could
perhaps arrange a private viewing of Tanya's exciting new exhibition. The couple was thrilled at the idea; Silver gracefully agreed, and
James observed with admiration the discreet congratulatory lift of
wineglasses exchanged between his wife and her friend. *Nicely done,
you two,* he thought.

The wine was kept flowing (to encourage the unattached guests,
James suspected) and it was a lively evening, with enough shared
opinions to make for agreeably easy conversation, and enough dif-
ferences to make for equally agreeable argument. After the dessert
course cigarettes came out—their host was Dutch, after all, and his
diplomat pal French—and people were feeling sufficiently liquored
and comfortable to start telling colorful jokes and make mock-insults
about things like national characteristics.

"Heaven's above, people say the Scots are dour," said the single
woman, teasing their host, "but they're positively frivolous compared
to the Dutch!"

"Oh, such brisk English economy, Margot! Insulting two nation-
alities in one sentence!"

"Ah, but I'm not English," the woman declared. James had
gathered that she was one of London's most sought-after interior
designers, and she was certainly a confident, good-looking woman.
He found himself enjoying more and more the musical tones of this
Margot's voice and the fine cleavage revealed by her deep blue silk

dress."I'm Irish!" she said."Irish parents, born in Ireland, spent every summer of my girlhood in Ireland. I vote in the Irish elections. And that, I believe, makes me Irish, not English."

"Ah, but you *live* in England."

"Dear Henk, we all *live* in England."

"For the time being, at least," someone else put in.

"Except our Australian friends."

"One of whom is not Australian, but American," Silver pointed out.

"Are we *all* expatriates, then?" asked the female half of the diplomat couple (Italian), and they all looked around the table at each other."Do none of us live in our country of birth?"

There was a round of confirming nods; only James shook his head and said, "Well, except me, then. And I continue to live not only in the same country I was born in, but the same city. I can only boast an immigrant mother—and a highly unsuccessful one at that."

"What, unsuccessful as a mother? Or an immigrant?" asked Alice.

"Well, both, I suppose." And then suddenly James was telling this roomful of strangers about his mother, and how she had walked out on her family and fled back to England one Christmas Eve, never to be seen again. He was astonished at himself but once started he couldn't just stop, since that would surely make it seem even odder. *Am I very drunk?* he wondered, and took extra care not to slur his words, or ramble, or sound too emotional. Not to sound as though he were suffering from some still-raw wound. Like a victim. *A professional bloody victim*: he could hear Deborah's scathing tone so clearly, sneering at Meredith, the only one of them who talked about their mother's departure to outsiders. He made sure the point of the story was the difficulty of adjusting to another country. Not the abandonment; not the image of the children and their father, unwrapping their presents so joylessly the next morning around the Christmas tree. Which still had no lights.

Silver watched him, chin on her hand and a gently encouraging smile on her face. Once his tale was done she let the silence be for a few moments, then deftly picked up that thread of emigration and added to it and handed it on, so that those around the stilled table, each sensing they'd heard something charged with meaning and previously unrevealed, were able to become animated again, though in a kindlier way than before, and the evening was not brought to a darkened close by James's revelation but allowed a further hour of conviviality.

But one person, the Irishwoman in her low-cut dress, stayed quiet. Several times before they all went home James felt her eyes intently on him, but he didn't feel like flirting any more, and dreaded that she might give him a deep and meaningful look. Or worse, try to engage him with some story of her own childhood damage. But when he did risk a glance, Margot was nibbling at her thumbnail and staring off into space, or more precisely at a point a little to her left. She looked neither flirtatious nor overwhelmed with emotion, he realized, but more like . . . like someone trying to finish a crossword puzzle.

In the cab on the way back to their apartment on the Thames, James and Silver held hands as they exchanged companionably inconsequential remarks. But as they were preparing for bed she said to him, "Hon? You know what's occurred to me?"

James answered with a look of enquiry.

"I was just thinking," Silver said, "that in all the years I've known you, you've hardly ever talked about your mom. Not *really*. I mean, you've told me what happened, and we talked about that memory thing. But I don't know *why* she left. Or what you think about her now . . ."

He pulled back the covers and climbed into bed, not answering. *Do I have to go there?* he asked himself. *I don't even know where there is!*

"I guess I'll never know why she left," he said finally, shrugging. "I can't. Simple as that. I mean, she was English, that's all I really know for sure. Australia must've been too big an adventure for her, you know, too raw or something . . ."

"Do you ever think about what she's like now?" Silver asked, lying on her side with one elbow propped on her pillow, watching him. "Do you wonder about that?"

"No." James made a mildly considering face, lying back and crossing his arms above his head. "If I had to speculate, then . . . I guess she could be one of those hearty landed Englishwomen . . . Burberry and foxhounds . . . or maybe some wispy old lady like a little brown wren, sitting in her bedsit and doing good works for the church . . . but those are just clichés. I don't know. She's just a . . . kind of a *blank* to me. An unknown quantity."

"Does that make you sad?"

"No," he answered definitely. "What would be the point?"

"The point?"

"Yeah. I've got a great life, Sil. I couldn't be happier. What would be the point of turning myself inside out over something I can't change?"

"I don't know, hon. Just to . . . understand, I guess."

"I *can't* understand it, though. That's just how it is. I'm going to turn the light out now, okay?"

Over the next day or so James caught himself thinking not about his mother, but rather about the Irishwoman, Margot. There was something about the way she'd looked at the end of the dinner that made him uneasy. Was it that he'd found her attractive, in her glimmering blue dress? Had he flirted excessively, perhaps, under the unaccustomed influence of alcohol? Given her the wrong signals? He hoped not. But if not that, then what? What was it about her that seemed to be . . . hovering? *Unfinished business.*

Hearing her voice on the answering machine a couple of days later, James jumped guiltily. He had an instant image of her leaning forward across the table—enticingly, it seemed. *Uh-oh,* he thought uncomfortably. Her message was addressed solely to him. There was no fabricated excuse, just the request that he call her. He felt sure she wanted to follow up on the other night. *If she thinks there's something going on between us, I've got to knock that idea on the head straightaway,* he decided. He picked up the phone and dialed the number she'd left. Margot answered almost immediately. Once they'd exchanged greetings, she took a deep, determined breath, and hearing this James winced, anticipating an embarrassment of some kind.

"James," she said, "I wanted to talk to you about that story you told us all the other night. About your mother and how she left Australia so suddenly."

"Yes?" he answered, startled by this tangent, but realizing in the same moment that he was glad she'd said "left Australia" and not "left you" or "left her family." He didn't want anyone to make too big a deal out of the story he'd told the other night. It was just a dinner party anecdote.

"The thing is, James, when you told us about her, I suddenly thought, I know that woman."

"Oh?" he said. *Unlikely. Surely.*

"Actually, she's my mother's best friend. I've known her for, oh, ages." He realized that although the warm tones of her voice disguised it, Margot was nervous. "She's been a huge influence on me, really. In terms of . . . erm, I don't know. *Style.* But that sounds so shallow, and she's not . . . Ah, no matter . . . But the story . . . Rose's story's a bit of a secret."

Rose, James thought, but said nothing.

"I didn't know whether to say something to you the other night. But then I thought I should talk to Rose first."

"Talk to her."

"Yes. Because I thought of those things, like adopted children contacting their parents, the shock, and right to know and so on. Not that you were adopted." Margot gave a soft laugh.

"No, right," James said, and laughed, too, but his laugh sounded foolish, inappropriate, so he cut it short.

"So I talked to my mum first, and she talked to Rose, and now I've talked to her, too. And she's . . . well, if you wanted to, erm, call her, she'd be . . . she'd be happy for you to do that. If you want to. She lives in Somerset, by the way, near Bristol. Between Bristol and Bath. I . . . I've got the phone number here. If you want it."

They didn't talk much longer. James wrote down the phone number and his hand as he did so looked odd, like someone else's. After he and Margot said good-bye he found himself walking to and fro around the flat. *I'm pacing,* he thought. *This is ridiculous.* He wished Silver was with him, not in Chicago. *I'll wait till I've talked to her about it.* But then somehow the phone was in his hand again.

He dialed the number. A man answered. He had a Caribbean accent, and James thought momentarily that it was a mistake, a wrong number. But when he asked to speak to Rose, please, the man said pleasantly that he would just get her for him, she was in the studio, and then James could hear him calling distantly, "Rose! Pick up da phone!" sounding as though he was calling up a flight of stairs, and then a different sound as another phone was picked up, and a woman's voice saying, "Hello?"

He could remember her voice. He had never thought of that. He knew her face only from the photographs, but he had never thought about her voice. His eyes were fixed on the small vase crammed with white roses sitting on the desk beside the telephone, and there was the big window and the brown Thames beyond, but he saw all this without seeing it because his head was completely filled by that one word, *hello?,* in this voice that he knew, that he'd always known and didn't know he knew.

"Mummy?" he said, and the tears burst so violently from his eyes that they splashed onto the desk in a rain of fat drops, blurring the number he had written there, on the little notepad right at his fingertips.

CHAPTER 9

There was no way she could keep still, she was so nervous. Already she'd been for a long brisk walk around the fields and over into the woods at the far side of their neighbor's farm, scuffling through the drifts of autumn leaves and muddying her boots as she crossed the little stream, and back home again, mind still fizzing. There was plenty of work to do in her studio but she was too restless to settle to it. She went out into the garden, tore out the straggling skeletons of last summer's tomato plants from the vegetable beds and wrestled some pots into the greenhouse. She heard a car pull up and her heart started hammering—*Oh no! I look a fright!*—but peeping around the corner Rose saw that it was her husband, Roland, home early from Bristol to be there when her—her *son* arrived.

"Not here yet?" he asked as she came up to him.

Rose shook her head and hugged him tight, wriggling in so that his coat was around her and her face was well hidden. He held her close, stroking the sleek silver helmet of her hair with one big hand.

"Nervous, my queen?" he asked gently.

She moved her face up and down against him, nodding.

Roland started singing softly, an old Bob Marley song: *"Every little thing, is gonna be all right . . ."*

Rose giggled and lifted her face up toward his. "Don't you go telling James those stories about you smoking giant spliffs with the Wailers, now," she said.

"Why not?" Roland teased. "All true, you know."

"Even if they are! You're a respectable businessman now, and my husband, and for all I know this young man could be a . . . a Christian fundamentalist minister!"

"Nah," said Roland comfortably, taking his wife by the hand and leading her in to their stone farmhouse. "Didn't he tell you on the phone he's a painter? And how young is he, this 'young man' so-called?"

"Oh lord," Rose said. "I don't want to think! It makes me so ancient. Younger than you, at any rate."

"By just a little bit, eh? By just a few weeks maybe . . ."

"Don't be so cheeky, you! By ten years!" Rose, halfway up the stairs—she was going to change her clothes and at least put on a bit of lipstick before this scary visitor arrived—turned back toward him for a moment. "Well, nearly ten years."

"You want me to come up there with you?" Roland asked suggestively. "I know something that'll settle you right down, y'know. Make you all serene, and smilin' . . ."

"No!" said Rose, tossing her head, but she had a big smile on her face now.

Roland watched her corduroy-clad backside appreciatively as she continued up the stairs. "If you live to be one hundred," he called, "you still be the sexiest damn woman in England!"

"Huh!" her voice floated down as she disappeared. Roland went into the kitchen, grinning, and while he was still debating whether to put on the kettle or get out the sherry decanter, an unfamiliar car, a nippy black BMW, pulled in at the farmhouse gate and rolled slowly, hesitantly, up to the door.

Roland was curious to meet this stranger, and happy to play the role of icebreaker if needed. But as he saw the man who emerged from the car and approached him, smiling, ducking his head uncertainly even as he extended his hand with apparent confidence, Roland was startled almost into wordlessness. The resemblance was extraordinary! He restrained an exclamation, greeting the visitor warmly, and then Rose was approaching (he smelled her perfume), then beside him, and she gasped. James, on the threshold, looked thunderstruck, too. Rose trod on Roland's foot as she stepped forward, James's shoulder collided with the doorframe. They managed, barely, to shake hands, murmuring indistinct greetings.

It was nearly thirty-seven years since these two, mother and son, had seen each other. It was no wonder, Roland thought, they should be at a loss, especially when faced with this: the height, the build, the features, the coloring and, most strikingly, the eyes, together declaring unequivocally: we are family; we are blood.

They went into Rose's favorite room: small, mostly glass, with a view of the garden. Rose sank down as though pole-axed into her favorite pink-upholstered chair, and James, hesitating, sat in the green one opposite. Roland brought coffee—their visitor's choice, though he'd noticed his wife's desperate glance toward the decanter—and kept up the flow of small talk for a while. Then he announced that he had a bit of work to catch up with, if they would excuse him. *Good luck*, he wished Rose with his eyes, and she gave him a strained smile.

After Roland left there was a long moment's silence in the small, pretty room. James looked out through the tall glass doors.

"Those sheep," he said, indicating the neighbor's small flock peering with their customary moronic curiosity through the fence. "Are they carnivorous?"

Rose gave a snort of laughter, this was so unexpected. James laughed, too.

"They just don't look like Australian sheep," he said.

"Don't they? You know, I think I managed to get through thirteen years in Australia without ever sighting an actual live sheep. I ate plenty though!"

They both laughed again, and James was able to look properly at this woman, so elegant in her mauve and charcoal suit, with her slender upright figure, her sleek silver hair. *She's beautiful. Cripes, she must be getting on for seventy, and she's bloody beautiful!*

"My wife," he began, and broke off. "I did tell you about my wife? Silver?" Rose nodded. "My wife asked me the other night if I ever thought about what you would be like now," he continued. "And I said . . . I said . . ." Suddenly he wished he hadn't started this, it sounded impertinent. But he had to forge on now. "I said I imagined you either huntin' with hounds, or as a little brown wren."

His mother smiled. It was, he registered, his own flirtatious smile. "Wrong on both counts then!" she admonished. "No hounds, no brown. Although I do agree that chocolate is taking over from eggplant . . ." she added thoughtfully, and then waved the notion aside.

He could see Deb in her, too, Deb older of course—and yet somehow more youthful, too, because there was actually less tension in Rose's face and body than in his sister's, even though his mother was clearly nervous. *Well, that's okay, I am, too.* But seeing *himself* mirrored in those bright blue eyes, the skin still lively with its coppery glow: that was *so* strange. Beyond strange. How could he ever have forgotten this woman's . . . presence? He wished again that Silver was with him; she'd be fascinated. And if Silver were here she'd know what to say, which would be terrific because he was having a hell of a lot of trouble just now thinking of anything.

"Roland seems like a really nice guy," he offered.

"He is; awfully nice," said Rose, smiling. *Oh, please! Awfully nice? I sound like the vicar's wife!*

"How long have you been married?"

"Oh, let me . . . Nine years now."

"I didn't . . . I don't think I ever knew that you and Dad actually divorced."

"Really? Oh. So he never remarried?"

"No. He seemed to have plenty of, uh, lady friends though."

There was a little silence. "Well," Rose said, "that stands to reason. Alex was a nice man, too. I wonder why he never remarried?"

"Maybe he didn't want to risk it. You know, happening again."

"Maybe." They were both quiet again. James put his teacup down firmly. He had to do it; he had to ask the question. *Ask it now!*

"Why'd you do it, Rose? Mum?" He laughed awkwardly. "I don't know what to call you!"

"I know, it's strange. Maybe Rose is best. I haven't been 'Mum' or 'Mummy' for nearly forty years."

"So . . . *Why?* Did you have a boyfriend? Is that who was in the car?"

Rose closed her eyes momentarily, gathering herself. *How long have I been waiting for one of them to ask me these things? And didn't even know I was?* "No, no. Not a boyfriend. That was a young woman in the car, a girl I'd met. Brenda Simmons."

"So who was Brenda Simmons?"

"She was the receptionist at the local dentist's. Robert was having some fillings done and I just got talking to her one day. Well, she heard my accent first, that was it. She was mad keen to go to England but she didn't want to go on her own, she was nervous. It was still a big deal in those days. I used to daydream about it . . . but I didn't know she'd come around like that on Christmas Eve. It wasn't *planned*, James, believe me. There was just that one Qantas flight that night and there'd been some cancellations. It seemed like . . . now, or never."

"But if it was just her, how come you got in the backseat?"

"Oh. I see." And she could see it, too, suddenly, through their eyes. There in that suburban living room, peering out . . . "Her brother was driving; it was his car. He worked for Qantas and he could get her a cheap ticket. That's how she knew about the cancellations."

"But how did *you* afford it?" James asked. "Deborah's always wondered that, she said plane tickets were incredibly expensive back then. She used to listen in on people speculating, you know, the neighbors. 'How on earth did she afford it?'"

"Oh, I can imagine!" said his mother tartly. "'Must've had a fancy man.' Or whatever it was they would've said. 'A feller.'" She pulled a wry face. "Oh, it was such a tight, judgmental little world! Great for you kids, but for me . . ."

Their cups were empty. She poured them both more coffee. James saw himself and his mother as though from outside the room: the tasteful setting, the china cups. *It's like we're in some ridiculous English play.*

"Do you remember I used to do dressmaking at home?" Rose asked. He shook his head, but even as he did so the memories were suddenly there: the pieces of flimsy white pattern paper laid out like a puzzle on the dining room table, the hungry sound the big gold scissors made as they ate through the layers of fabric. *Snick, snack.*

"Wait, yes," he said. "I do remember that. The sewing machine, and how your hands sort of spread the material out as it went through . . ."

She was regarding him with an odd expression. Curious, and a little sad. "Yes," she said softly. "That's right. I didn't know what you might—"

"I really liked the way the material kind of pooled on the floor in front of it."

"Yes," she said again, and they were quiet a moment, and then Rose lifted her chin and went on. "So: that was how I earned my own money, making dresses for the women around the neighborhood. Special occasion wear, that was my thing, but I could run up a sundress in half an hour, too. No overheads, and I put every penny away in my own bank account. I paid for the ticket out of that. Well, Brenda's brother paid for it initially, because of course the banks were all shut that evening. But I had some withdrawal slips in my passbook."

James had been listening intently. He smiled at this reference to a bygone age. "Gosh, I'd almost forgotten passbooks. Today you just would've transferred it online."

"My dear James, today I'd just pull out my Gold Visa card!" Rose smiled back at him and he had that giddy sensation again, of looking into a mirror at his own charming smile. *This is me, what I'm made of!* For a moment he felt intoxicated, a champagne-like headiness. But he pulled himself back. *I have to ask. I have to find out.*

"But . . . *why*? Were you just homesick? Robert thinks you were; so homesick you just couldn't bear it."

"Oh, James. I wish that were it; it sounds so much nicer than the truth."

"Well, what *was* the truth?"

"I just—I just wanted to have fun!"

He stared at her. Was it incomprehension? Disgust? *How can I make him understand?* She leaned forward urgently. "I'd left home, pregnant, before I turned eighteen. And by the time I was twenty-five I had four children. Do you see, James? The London I'd left behind was such a gray, dreary city, it was so *grim*—and then it suddenly turned into Swinging London. The grooviest place in the world. While I was on the *other* side of the world, stuck in the suburbs with four kids who seemed to do nothing but squabble all the time—sorry, not you, you never squabbled, but the others all did—and a well-meaning middle-aged husband who didn't have a clue. Making mother-of-the-bride outfits."

"Yes," he agreed dryly. "I can imagine *fun* wasn't very thick on the ground."

"I felt like I was going *mad*. I'd be helping cut sandwiches at the school Mother's Club or sorting out the homework and the school shoes and who had sports practice tomorrow, and all the time I had this vision of myself walking down Carnaby Street wearing white lipstick and a miniskirt and dangly plastic op-art earrings. Tight shiny leather boots. Granny glasses! I wanted to be a teenager again, a young woman at least. I was still only thirty when I left. It sounds so selfish, to leave all of you for . . . that. So immature. But that's what I *was*."

James was silent. She could see him struggling with what she'd said, trying to make sense of it.

"But couldn't you have had fun in Melbourne?" he asked at last. "I don't know, gone to dances and stuff? Dad wouldn't have minded you going out, surely, if he'd known how you felt."

"It just . . . wasn't . . . possible," Rose told him, leaving a weight like a judge's sentence between each word. "You have no idea how conservative Australia was then. I mean, people looked at me sideways when I went into the city without *gloves* on. Respectable married women didn't do that! They certainly didn't go to dances, not the same dances the teenagers were going to. And besides, it wasn't *London*. I used to stand in the newsagent and read that pop paper, what was it, *Go-Set*, and I just *despised* it all for a poor antipodean imitation of the real thing."

"You despised it." Suddenly James felt terribly cooped up. Restless. *I need to go for a swim*, he thought. He wanted to be out of there, away from this pleasant room and this poised older woman. *I'm . . . angry*, he realized, and could hardly bear the unfamiliar sensation. He didn't know what he might do next.

"So you were bored," he said tightly. "And that was a good enough reason to walk out like that? To just . . . *leave* us? Leave Dad to bring up four kids? There has to be more to it than that. Dad wasn't . . . *bad* to you, was he?"

"No no, never!" *Does he think Alex abused me? Surely not!* "He was never anything but kind. That was partly it: he was more like a kind uncle or something. I couldn't believe he was my husband. The . . . the passion had long gone."

"So that was *it*? Lots of marriages do very well without passion, you know." *Like mine*, he thought.

"I know. But lots more don't. You're married; what would your wife feel like if there was no . . . Would she be happy with that?"

"I . . ." *Is she? Silver? Happy? Stick to the point!* "That's not the point." *Ask her, ask her!*

"How come you never got in touch with us? Not even on our *birthdays?*" His voice sounded so plaintive, suddenly, so childlike. *Oh no,* he thought, *don't sound like that. God, don't cry!*

"But I *did!* I wrote to you for years, I *tried* to stay in touch! But there was never any reply."

James looked at her, truly uncomprehending. Disbelieving. *Well, that has to be bullshit.* The thought showed plainly on his face.

"It's *true!*" Rose cried out. "In the end I just had to accept that Alex believed it was for the best if there wasn't any contact. Oh! No matter what I say it can't ever be enough!" She flung her hands up, covering her face. "I am so sorry!" he heard her say. When she took her hands away, her face, for the first time, was not assured or charming. It was anguished. "Oh, James! I know it was wrong. *Wasn't* it? It's not forgivable, what I did, I know that."

James got up and in two steps was at the glass door. His hand was on the doorhandle but he didn't turn it, just stood there facing the garden and the curious sheep but not seeing them. There was a storm coming at him, that's how it felt; he could actually *see* the emotions—not the anger, that wasn't the main thing, it was all that pent-up longing, the years and years of yearning and pretending that he had never acknowledged until now—approaching him, reaching him, sweeping through. He put his arms up on the glass. He didn't try to fight the tears, they just coursed down his face. He let his body go through it, let it buffet him, like pushing through waves in the surf.

And such was his resilient nature that even before this tempest had passed, he could see an intimation of light, a promise of sun. *I've found her now,* that was the thought that came. *She's back; I've got her back.*

From behind him at that moment came his mother's voice, thick with tears but daring to be hopeful. "But, James? Is it possible . . . Now that you've found me, if you could manage to forgive me . . . well, we've got each other back."

Her thought was so like his, it was as though she was a part of him. *She's what I'm made of!* Without warning a laugh bubbled up and burst from his mouth and he turned quickly. She rose from her seat as he came toward her and they held each other. For the first time, they embraced. They were both laughing, both crying, a mess. Together.

CHAPTER 10

Deborah always rang him, Robert had noticed, when it was likely that his mobile phone would be switched off. It offended him: he was sure she did it so that she could avoid actually talking to him. But as he listened to the message she'd left, his indignation was smothered by guilt.

"Hi, Robert," said his sister's cool recorded voice. "Just wondering if you've heard from Dad's GP yet about the assessment. It's been two weeks, hasn't it? Surely he's got the results by now. Could you find out and let me know?"

You can't evade this any longer, he told himself sternly. *You're letting Dad down, you're letting the whole family down.* He rang Deborah back, relieved to get her voice-mail, and then ashamed that he was guilty of the same tactic she'd used.

"Hello, Deborah!" he said. The false heartiness of his voice embarrassed him. "Just spoke with Dad's GP a day or two ago, actually, after he forwarded the assessment results. Best we meet, I think. Shall we, ah, shall we leave it till after James gets back?"

He had been sitting on this information, shamefully he felt. He hadn't even told Vesna yet; telling anyone would make it real. *Please, let Deb put it off for a while,* he thought. But this little prayer went unanswered. By the end of the day Deborah had arranged that both she and Meredith would come to his house the following Saturday.

When Vesna took the girls off to volleyball, Robert had the urge to run after the car and shout, "No! Come back!" But he didn't. Meredith arrived, chattering brightly, and Robert felt a little cheered, but Deborah was flustered and impatient; something had come up at work, she'd have to tear in there shortly. On the table lay several copies of the assessment. Meredith leafed through it and put it aside. Deborah sat in silent concentration, fingers supporting her temples, working her way steadily through the document.

She sat back and placed her hands flat on the topmost sheet, almost covering it. "It says mild to moderate." She sounded defensive. *No, not defensive,* Robert thought: *defiant.* "In fact, most of the results are mild, not even moderate," she added.

"See?" Meredith piped. "I told you there was nothing to worry about!"

"But the . . . but the doctor was quite clear that this isn't going to get any better," said Robert. "It'll only get worse."

"There's drugs now, Robert," Deborah said in an irritatingly superior tone. "Did the doctor mention that?"

"He did. Yes, he did. He wants to get some blood tests back first though." Robert had clung, in fact, to the soothing cadences of the information the GP had given him about the use of medication. He recited it now. "Patients in both mild and moderate stages may benefit, but commencing treatment earlier in the disease predicts better efficacy."

"There you are," said Meredith. "Daddy just needs to take this medicine and he'll be fine."

"I'm sorry, Merry, but I really don't think so. The medication only helps slow it. Plateau, he said, a plateau phase . . ."

"Then they'll come up with something new, Bobbit! Don't *worry*!"

"Yes, the drug companies must be working on this like crazy," said Deborah. "Look at the potential profits! And if we get him on this plateau stuff for now . . ."

"It's not that easy!" Robert said desperately. "Dad has *dementia!*"

"No he doesn't," Meredith shot back. Robert gaped. He couldn't believe his ears.

"Well, mild to moderate, maybe," Deborah allowed. Deborah was being conciliatory. The world was standing on its head.

"But this assessment clearly says—" he began.

"They've assessed him wrong," Meredith interrupted. "Look at this . . ." She snatched up the report and flipped to a page. *So you were actually reading it,* Robert thought.

"Symptoms may include," Meredith read, and she began ticking them off on her fingers. "Difficulty performing familiar tasks: well, Daddy doesn't have that. Problems with language: definitely not. Disorientation to time and place: no. Poor or decreased judgment: no. Problems with abstract thinking: no way. So you see?" She looked at them with a glint of triumph. "They've made a mistake. There's nothing wrong with Daddy!"

Robert stared at her. *Could it be?* he wondered wildly. *Could this all have been an awful mistake?* But he had been there, at the assessment. Surely . . .

"Oh, Bobbit, I'm sorry," cried Meredith contritely. "You've gone to such a lot of trouble, when you're so busy! I didn't mean to sound ungrateful! But you can see, can't you? Daddy doesn't have this . . . thing." *Dementia,* she thought. *Silly name. I'm sure that's the name of a band Laurence likes . . .*

"I have to go!" announced Deborah, pushing back her chair. "Thanks for this, Robert," she said, slipping her copy of the assessment in amongst other papers in her bag. "I don't think we need to tell James about this while he's overseas, do you? I'll show it to him after he gets back."

"What about Dad?" Robert said. "The doctor feels we should

have a family consultation, so he can explain it all to Dad as well as us."

"Oh Robert, *no!*" cried Meredith. "That would just be *cruel!*"

"I've . . . I've made a call to the Alzheimer's Association: apparently they have some excellent literature on this," he faltered. This had seemed such a good idea when Vesna suggested it; he had felt pleased with himself. "You should each receive a package in the mail next week. Including brochures on how to explain to grandchildren what's happening."

Meredith seemed not to have heard. Deborah hesitated, then headed quickly for the door. "Thanks, but I really have to *go!*" she said urgently, as though he'd been trying to stop her.

Deborah's hands were shaking on the steering wheel all the way in to the city. *My father has dementia.* Deborah thought of the other expressions she'd used, about other people's parents. *Gone gaga. Lost her marbles. Off with the pixies.* They sounded cruel, now. And stupid.

She knew that Meredith was wrong, but for once she felt completely in sympathy with her sister. *Let it not be so,* she thought. *Make it go away, Daddy; make it go away.*

CHAPTER 11

Silver came back to London after a few short days in Chicago to find a man transformed. She could hardly take in the news James had been bursting to tell her. Was this her laconic, easygoing husband? *I've never seen him like this!* He couldn't keep still. A thrilling vibrancy lit his face, his voice. He kept putting "Rose" into a sentence just to have the pleasure of saying it. "My mother." And his amazement! The wonder! *He's like a boy who's just been given the best present he could ever have,* she thought. *The thing of his dreams.*

As he described what had happened, James roamed the room, bounding back to Silver like a tethered ball, hugging her, touching her hair, her face, stroking her arms. He grasped her hands and urged her to look at their schedule immediately, so that they could go to Marsh Farm together. By now Silver was catching the excitement, too.

In bed that night he kept talking, and touching her. She loved this, it was so . . . Silver didn't want to say the words even to herself. Exciting. Sexy. *Any moment now, he'll fold his hands on his chest like he usually does,* and she hardly dared breathe in case he . . . stopped. She didn't want him to stop. He was propped up on his elbow, talking ten to the dozen about Rose, Roland, the farmhouse, and stroking her left breast in a half-conscious way, as though it were a cat. And then he felt her nipple harden under his palm, and looked at it.

He quieted. Silver had large breasts but unusually small nipples, pink and dainty. "Hello, little rosebud," he said fondly. She felt quick tears of startled happiness sting her eyes.

Gently he used his fingernails to describe a circle all the way around the outer edges of her breasts, first one, then the other. And again, closer in. Silver thought she'd never been so focused on anything in her life. She felt as though a chain of light was coming on behind his fingernails, until both her breasts were pulsing, illuminated. He shifted and knelt beside her, gazing at her, and he took hold of her nipples and rubbed them incredibly softly, like precious jewels. Silver could feel hot threads like fuses burning all the way from there across into her armpits and right down through her belly, setting the whole of her vulva alight. She breathed in deeply, very deeply. He smiled, that beautiful smile of his. Taking both her nipples between his thumbs and index fingers, he squeezed them gently, then harder, and *shook* her breasts.

"Whoa," Silver said, exhaling with a gusty moan, but she didn't mean stop. Her hips lifted a little of their own accord toward him. He pressed against her thigh and she could feel his erection. He bent and kissed her mouth, pushing his tongue in, and she knew absolutely that they were going to have sex. Make love. *No*, she thought, *he's going to fuck me*, and heard herself moan again. He swept his hand down her ribs and belly, caressing their contours, and cupped it over her pubic mound, pressing firmly, making little circular movements with his palm. She reached down and took hold of his penis, *his cock*, she thought, with a sudden image of those handsome fighting cocks she'd seen in Bali, preening and puffing up their feathers, and she stroked him as she'd seen the men in Bali lovingly hold and stroke their roosters. He slid his index finger between her lips and then into her vagina, releasing the wetness welled up there. She felt his cock leap as his finger swept the moisture around her lips and opening.

"Oh, come inside, come inside me," she said.

"In a minute," he whispered, kissing her mouth, teasing her clitoris with his wet finger. "But I think this pussy needs a little stroking first. He-ey? Sweet pussy?" He pushed two fingers in deeper, then out again to her lips and clitoris. "My sweet pussy cat, huh?" The words were so playful and silly, while the challenge in his eyes was utterly irresistible. Silver giggled, and wriggled beneath his hand. He didn't stop.

And then so suddenly it rushed up on her: her mouth fell open and her eyelids rolled down and a growly noise was sounding from down in her throat, her chest, her belly. Every muscle in her seemed to clench, to spasm, and while she was still coming he pushed her willing legs apart with one knee and swung his body above hers, thrusting his cock deep into her. She just couldn't stay quiet, she was urging him on with her body and voice and he came quickly, too, and then they both fell almost instantly into a heavy sleep, as though they'd been drugged. They woke in the night and fucked again, steadily and generously, and fell again into a moist, manky, deeply contented sleep.

Just before dawn Silver had a beautiful dream. She and James were lying on a bed together, in a large simple room full of dappled light. The window was open on to birdsong and a summer's day. James was giving her something, a box of some kind wrapped in gold tissue so soft that her fingers sank into it. She began to unwrap it but even before she had, she felt a flood of joy because she knew what was in there: the thing she most wanted. The thing of her dreams.

The pretty green of rural Somerset delighted her. "I thought this was just in the *movies*!" Silver crowed as they drove past hedgerows and thatched cottages, through little toy-town villages. James grinned, proud as though he'd created it himself. When their car turned in at the gate to Marsh Farm, Silver immediately noticed the svelte, white-haired woman standing gracefully on the doorstep. *Good lord*, she thought, *that's Deborah—in twenty years!* She saw now what James had been trying to convey to her, the arresting power of the family resemblance.

Suddenly, this elegant older woman jumped up and down, her hands clasped together before her. *Like a little kid!* Behind her appeared a strikingly handsome black man in a crisp indigo cotton shirt. He was smiling broadly, but Silver saw, too, the steadying hand he placed on Rose's shoulder, and the way she responded, moving closer and snuggling her head back to his chest.

There was no mistaking the hungry fervor with which mother and son embraced, their eyes closed in the pure joy of the moment. Silver's eyes met Roland's, and between them passed an almost visible skein of shared pleasure. Pleasure in their spouses' pleasure.

Silver had always relished the company of couples who treated each other well, and in the course of the afternoon she saw, to her pleasure and relief, that this was one such couple. There was a lovely playful courtesy between Rose and Roland, a lively tenderness. Beneath Rose's sleek exterior ran a vivid undercurrent of energy that could, one sensed, fly off into wildness or melodrama, but was balanced by Roland's steadiness. Clearly, he was her anchor. *How old would he be? Mid-fifties?* Silver wondered. She herself was five years older than James, but the gap between these two had to be considerably more. *What, maybe fifteen years?* Yet in some way Roland seemed older than his wife.

Among the many photographs in the house, there was one Silver found particularly delightful: an excited little girl in her party dress, caramel skin glowing and fluffy dark hair sticking out in brightly ribboned bunches on her head, balancing like a little acrobat between the chairs of two elderly women, one black with awesome bone structure, dressed in a magenta suit, the other a sweetly faded English rose in pearls and a pretty blouse. Each had an arm around the joyful gap-toothed little girl.

"That's my daughter Jacinta, with her two grannies," Roland said proudly, coming to stand beside her as she admired it. "Shame it's not the weekend," he added. "You could have met her. But during the week she's with her mum in Bath."

"She sure is one beautiful little girl!"

Roland beamed. "Yeah; she's my princess. But not so little any more. She just turned fifteen." He riffled through a pile of loose photos sitting on the side table, showed her one of a long-limbed teenage beauty in jodhpurs, arm around the neck of a horse, smiling. "Soon I figure I gotta get a big stick, keep all the boys in line," he added. They both laughed. It seemed likely to Silver that a big stick might indeed be necessary.

Shown the girl's bedroom a few minutes later, Silver smiled. Those telltale transitional layers: stuffed toys jostling with piles of make-up, posters of foals side by side with quotes from the Dalai Lama and a collage of sexy Calvin Klein underwear ads.

"Loves riding, our Jacinta; that's her pony you saw in the stables," Rose said, standing beside her in the doorway. "In the summer holidays I just about have to bribe her to get off it."

And how is it for you? Silver wanted to ask. *Being a stepmother, at your age? With your . . . history?* "People say teenage girls can be pretty trying," she ventured. "What's she like, young Jacinta?"

"Oh, a darling," Rose said easily. "I mean, so far. There may be hormone hell just ahead, who knows? But really, a darling. Her mother's very nice, too. I've been awfully lucky."

Awfully lucky. O-kay . . .

They moved on to Rose's studio. It was a wide, attractive room, low ceilinged but spacious. A well-utilized working space, with its long cutting table, two sewing machines and a tailor's dummy. Garments at various stages of completion hung on a rack. There was a bank of deep shelves stacked with folded fabric and, next to that, bolts of cloth arrayed on what appeared to be giant kebab skewers. Against one wall stood a big cubic storage unit, shelves piled with fashion magazines, books on costume and design, and well-thumbed sketchbooks.

"So this is it," said James. "Nerve center of the fashion empire."

"Cheeky boy," said his mother, smiling.

"It's a marvelous space," Silver told her sincerely. "It feels so . . ." she gestured roundly, ". . . productive!"

"Does it?" asked Rose. "That's interesting. And you're right, you know, it is." She was standing back from her tailor's dummy and surveying the complicated outfit taking shape there with a dispassionate, assessing expression. Silver felt a little quiver of recognition: it was exactly that look with which James regarded his paintings. "I feel rather like I've come full circle," Rose said. "Designing and making one-off clothes for special occasions. Funny; after more years in the rag trade than I care to remember." She stepped forward, made an adjustment to a sleeve, stepped back again. "You'd think I'm stuck in a backwater here, but it's amazing how many well-off women are willing to navigate the lanes of deepest Somerset to find me."

"Maybe getting here's part of the attraction?" suggested Silver. "It really is so gorgeous, the countryside around here."

"Maybe." Rose shrugged. "And a good story to tell at a dinner party, perhaps, how they had to back up a hundred yards for some dozy local on his tractor on their way to their eccentric dressmaker."

"Maybe it's the eccentric dressmaker who's the attraction!" James said, and he and his mother simultaneously gave the same light, flirtatious laugh. Silver caught a mental snapshot of mother and son, their heads cocked at an identical coquettish angle, blue eyes flashing. *Ah, this is where he gets it from all right!*

The soft autumn dusk was lowering outside. Roland insisted that they have a drink by the open fire in the sitting room while he prepared the evening meal. Soon Rose turned the conversation to the rest of the family, back in Melbourne, and James tried to retreat but his mother would not be deterred. As her questions about her other children and their father became increasingly searching, Silver knew this would be difficult for James. And she could feel her own temptation to smoothe his way and speak for him. *No! This has to be his,* she thought, and took herself to the kitchen where she leaned against the wall beside the stove and chatted companionably with Roland as he cooked.

They talked about food, naturally, the foods of their respective childhoods, his in Jamaica and hers in the States. She relaxed, listening to him speak, the deep voice with its mixture of Caribbean and English accents so charmingly musical to her ear. From this they drifted naturally to their families, and then of course to their spouses' families, to which they were each now joined.

"Did you know about James and his brother and sisters?" she asked. "Before his phone call, I mean?"

"Oh *yeah!*" Roland said, nodding mightily. "Rose told me just as soon as we got serious that she had children. She told me about the family back in Australia. How she'd split on them and never gone back."

"What did you think?" Silver asked, leaning toward him curiously. "Were you shocked?"

Roland had just swept a pile of chopped herbs into a pot on the stove. He paused, considering, the wooden board suspended in his hand. "Shocked? Yeah. I was. I never knew a woman who had done that. Oh, about a thousand *guys,* sure, but not a mother. And Rose . . . she just didn't seem like that kind of woman, you know." He shook his head. "That kind of woman!" he said dismissively, and Silver understood that he was dismissing his own past ignorance or narrowness.

"So what did you do? Or—or say?"

"I say to Rose she must find them. You know, *comm-u-ni-cate.*" He drew the last word out very long, touching each syllable almost prayerfully. "But she say, that would be *wrong.* Not for her to seek 'em out and interrupt their lives. It was real hard for her to talk about."

They were quiet, each thinking of what their partners hadn't talked about.

"But there was a big piece missing in her heart, you know?" Roland went on suddenly, touching one hand to his broad chest and patting gently. "A big hole there. I know it; I know *I* can't fill it, no matter what. Not her work, nothin'. And now James is here. After he first come the other day, that night I said to myself, her heart is full at last." He looked questioningly at Silver. "You know?"

"Yes!" said Silver with feeling, "I do know!"

"So now," he said, gesturing to her and back to himself, "we are family. Amazin', eh?"

Together over the stove, they exchanged a smile that was more than pleased: almost conspiratorial. They knew they had found in each other some kind of ally—a kindred spirit, even. *But*, thought Silver, *I can't just leave it there. I've gotta . . . warn him.*

"Roland," she said. "You know, it's gonna take a bit of adjusting to. Not for me, I don't mean that. For his family in Australia. His older sister especially, and the others. It might be . . . difficult."

"You think so? They won't be happy?"

"I just think it'll take a bit of getting used to. It might be . . ." Silver pursed her lips uncertainly. "The thing is, James is an easy-going sort of guy, you know? He takes what comes."

"Mmm. But not the others?"

"I wouldn't say so, really. No."

"His family is angry with her? With Rose?"

"It's kind of hard for me to say. They don't talk about it much either."

"Mmm." They both stared into the pot of sauce Roland was stirring. "A'right then," he said, looking up, shrugging. "We'll see what come to pass."

A week later James and Silver were on the plane flying back to Australia. Halfway through the long journey, Silver woke from a doze and looked across to see her husband deep in thought, forefinger stroking his upper lip.

"James? Honey?"

He looked at her, his expression clouded.

"Sil, I had a talk with Rose before we left, about telling Deborah and the others. The thing is, I don't think I should. Not yet. You know these letters she wrote to us, that we never got? I think they're *really* important. Maybe Dad's kept some, and . . . if I could find them . . . I don't know."

"You think that'd make it easier for the others? To accept her?"

"Yeah, I really do. If they know she *did* try to stay in touch with us, it'll really open the door. Don't you think?"

"I get you. So, will you ask your father about 'em, straight out?"

"I'd rather just look first. But would you mind? Not saying anything?"

"Your call, hon. It's your family."

"Thanks."

"But James? You can't leave it too long. You've gotta tell 'em some time."

"Of course."

"I mean, some time soon."

"I *know*. Just . . . not yet."

Rose and Roland were sitting at the kitchen table at Marsh Farm, she nursing a coffee while her husband ate his usual hearty breakfast before going in to his office in Bristol. Rose was unusually silent, and after he'd finished eating Roland pushed his plate aside and extended his hand to her, palm up, across the table. She took it, managing a doleful smile.

"Something troublin' you, my one," he said.

"Oh, darling. I had a horrid dream last night."

He waited, and after a little while Rose went on, "I dreamed I was trying to adopt a child, but I had my real children with me. I was making them do all the, you know, the paperwork and interviews and things. They were just the same age as . . . when I left them."

"Who was the kid you were adoptin', do you know?"

"No," said Rose, shaking her head. "It wasn't a particular child, I don't think, but I was so *determined* to do it. My own kids were terribly unhappy. It was mostly Deborah, that was who I was forcing to do everything. I was so *mean!*" She looked very sad. Roland got up and came around to his wife's side of the table; she hugged him, her arms around his waist and her face pressed against his belly.

"In the end," she said, her voice muffled, "she turned on me and just tore into me. Verbally, I mean."

"What did she say?" asked Roland, stroking Rose's soft silver-white hair.

"She said . . . everything I deserve to hear. That I was horrible and selfish. And *cruel.*" At the last word her voice tore and she sobbed.

He knelt on the floor and held her, let her soak the shoulder of his shirt with tears. "My queen," he murmured, "my beauty." At last she drew back and blew her nose on a napkin and said shakily, "Oh dear."

"Your heart grieves for those children," he said gently. "And your soul is sore about the bad things you've done."

"Yes," Rose agreed.

"That was a long time ago that you were bad."

"It was."

"Maybe now it's forgiveness time."

"Maybe," Rose said, her face clearing a little. "But my darling— I think it'll take a long while. There's a lot to forgive. And the others—James doesn't even want to tell them yet."

He kissed her. "That's okay. Maybe better. Maybe you got to forgive yourself first, you know?"

She nodded. She still looked sad. He kissed her again and said softly, "Just so long as it's begun."

part three

CHapter 12

For months now, Deborah had been waking most mornings around 4 a.m. almost gasping with anxiety. All the things she had to do that day jostled in her mind like runners straining to start a marathon. For moment after horrible moment, she could find no sense of priority, no order. Sitting up in bed, heart thumping and skin prickling with sweat, Deborah struggled to make sense of a chaos in which *Check press release on threatened state-wide teachers' strike* had no more importance, and no less, than *Add toilet paper to shopping list*.

Gradually she would calm down, enough for her breath to come more easily and her temples to stop pounding. It was heresy, but sometimes she wished that the political party to whose advancement she had devoted the whole of her adult life had *not* won the election so unexpectedly. It wasn't only their enemies and detractors who had said they weren't ready, she and her colleagues had whispered it among themselves in those first few months. Scared shitless, they'd been. But then the gritty determination to somehow pull it off kicked in, and the goodwill of ordinary people was so uplifting, and everything seemed to go their way, for a while at least. They were the government now. There was too much work to be done to waste time doubting.

But it wasn't just the sheer volume of work that knotted Deborah's stomach and corded her neck with tension. It was the pressure to get it all right. Knowing that any mistake could be fatal, that the dogs were always circling, sniffing for a weakness, and that they always would be. That it was going to go on, and on. Deborah proudly declared herself to be *a true believer*, and yes, she truly believed that now they were in power her party could make this state great again: a place you were proud to live in because it was governed fairly, with equal concern for all its citizens. She loved her work, it was the thing that gave her life meaning. But there were times when panic stampeded through her and she thought, *I can't cope with this. I'm going nuts.*

Was it menopause, she wondered? Even though she was still taking the contraceptive pill, and her hormones, presumably, were regulated by that daily dose? Her doctor wanted her to go off it, check her hormone levels, then consider hormone replacement therapy if necessary, but Deborah was terrified that the symptoms of menopause, which so many of her contemporaries complained about, would send her over the edge. And besides, there was just no *time* for anything but work; work, and worry.

The feeling was eerily familiar: it reminded her, especially in those wakeful night hours, of early motherhood, how shocked she had been by the avalanche of detail and the relentless sense that she would be held to account for . . . everything. Once upon a time, before Olivia was born, she had been quite confident that since she'd practically brought up her three younger siblings, she knew everything there was to know about looking after babies and small children. But that had turned out to be wishful thinking. In reality, she had felt like she'd been slammed into a wall, a wall that she had spent the next year or so slowly sliding down, like a cartoon character. Like Wile E. Coyote in another foiled attempt to catch Road Runner.

Deborah never admitted to anyone that motherhood had made

her feel so desperate, but the sense that she could easily get that way again never left her. She told everyone, including Angus, that she only wanted the one child because she wanted Olivia to be carefree, not prematurely loaded with chores and responsibility as she had been, but secretly Deborah knew that it was she who dreaded more of that. And then Olivia had turned out to be a child who *demanded* responsibility. Probably would've liked nothing better than a platoon of brothers and sisters to manage, and in lieu of them, no doubt, had set about establishing her menagerie of creatures with their endless bloody requirements. Just thinking about it made Deborah grimace.

She'd developed ways to manage the pre-dawn anxiety about her job. Sometimes she turned on the bedside light (it never disturbed Angus) and read: not work-related material, but poetry, which she found soothing. Or, if she went and heated half a cup of milk in the microwave and checked her diary while she sipped it, made some additional notes and a few more lists, then her brain would slow its agitated fizzing and she could usually settle back to sleep again till the alarm went off.

But these days there was something else to worry about: her father. No list or poem or mug of milk alleviated this new sensation—a gnawing at the base of her throat, as though a question or a cry was struggling to emerge—which had begun that spring day, when she realized her dad had no idea who Jean Thornton was, or that he'd asked about her just the day before.

It had come to have the feel of doom, her memory of that day, that phone call. Yes, *doom:* such a melodramatic word, but that was the sense of crushing inevitability she had. Then came the meeting with her siblings, then the results of the assessment, like the inexorable tramp of boots: she looked back on those events and thought, *Before that, I was still innocent.* Now there seemed to be some reference to her father's . . . problem, everywhere she glanced. And each new piece of information made her feel like she'd taken a wrong turn along the path somewhere and entered a perilous tunnel, with no end in sight.

My father has dementia. She'd said these words to people: colleagues at work, friends. Twice she found herself saying them to complete strangers: a woman she got talking to as they waited to be served in a department store one day, and two others on the tram, women a bit older than herself, talking together about their respective mothers' health problems. She said the words almost shyly, wondering if she sounded desperate for sympathy. But the kind, attentive faces that were turned toward her, open and still, not jumping in with advice or a solution—they soothed her. Allowed her to feel, for a little while at least, that this dilemma and her helplessness in the face of it were . . . normal.

My father is losing his memory. Losing your memory. Once it had just been a phrase; now the enormity of it gaped before her and threatened to swallow her up. Because your memory contained everything, from the names of your grandchildren to how to cook a meal. If her father started to lose those things, who would he be? Who would she be to him?

What will happen? What should I do? How will I know when to do whatever it is I should do?

One Friday afternoon she was in precisely this agitated state, dying to get away from the office but with a tricky report to finish and the minister having a meltdown about some looming scandal, when she was interrupted yet again by an unscheduled phone call. Personal, the switchboard had said, and as always she had that little rush of adrenaline, the fear that some harm had befallen a member of her family. Her brother, her daughter, or . . . her father. *No, no, don't think that. Don't be silly.*

"Deborah McDonald," she said briskly.

"Hello, Debbie!" said an unfamiliar voice, a middle-aged woman's voice. "Guess who this is?"

Immediately Deborah's hackles rose. How she detested that sort of childish idiocy! She wanted to snap *I haven't got time to play fucking guessing games* and slam the phone down, but in her position she couldn't afford to offend anyone, not even a complete moron.

"I'm afraid I don't know," she said pleasantly. "Would you mind telling me?"

"I was at Monash University with you," the woman said. There was something there, something ingratiating and unpleasant, that was perhaps familiar after all. Deborah waited.

"Alison Ramsbottom!" the woman finally burst out. "Remember?" Oh yes, now Deborah remembered; most certainly she did. "I'm doing my PhD now," the woman sang. "I'm writing a thesis!"

"Oh really?" said Deborah coolly. "How interesting."

"And guess what? I'm doing it on feminist consciousness raising groups in the 1970s! So naturally I knew I just had to interview you."

"Indeed. Absolutely. Alison, if you could send something in writing to me at the office here, I'll attend to it immediately." *By putting it through the shredder.*

"Oh yes, yes I will. I'll get the survey off to you first thing and then I'll call you and we can make a date for an interview, how would that be?"

"Fine." While she was speaking, Deborah was writing a note for the switchboard and reception, to add the name Alison Ramsbottom to the Loonie List of time-wasters and grudge-bearers whose calls were *not* to be put through. "And right now I'm afraid I must return to some urgent work. Pressing deadlines, you know."

"I always knew you'd go far, Deb. I always knew you'd end up in—"

"Thanks for your call, Alison. Bye now."

Deborah hung up. She finished the report in record time, seething with the energy of rage, and tore out of the office before anything or anyone else got in her way. On the tram going home she didn't see her fellow commuters, tired and cheerful at the end of the working week. All she could see was the bare modernist campus of Monash University in 1973, lashed by a sudden winter storm, and herself in blue jeans and a denim jacket racing across it, long hair flying like a wet flag behind her.

JuLy 1973

Deborah's mood matched the weather as she tore across the campus, snatching what shelter she could from one glass and concrete building to the next. The cold at least cooled her flaming cheeks, the rain pelting on her face wiped roughly at her angry tears.

"How *dare* she?" she said out loud as she ran. *Bloody Alison Ramsbottom, with a face just like her name!* "It's none of her damn business!"

Finally she made it to the lecture theater and tore in, slamming herself into a seat up the back. A few people turned to look at her but most were concentrating on the slides being projected onto the screen in front of them, madly scribbling notes as the lecturer raved on about something or other. Federation, possibly. Certainly Deborah couldn't focus, or concentrate on anything other than her own roaring thoughts.

At least she didn't say it in front of everyone. At least she waited till afterward. She could still feel the touch of Alison's hand on her arm as all the women left their consciousness-raising group.

"Debbie, hang on a minnie," she'd said, friendly as anything. *The snake! Fat snake!* "Something I need to tell you."

Deborah had stopped, reluctantly because the impassioned argument they'd been having—whether lesbians were treated equally by straight women in consciousness-raising groups, whether they even *could* be or was there, in fact, inherent sexism even within the sisterhood?—had gone on so long and she was already running late for her next lecture.

"My little sister Nicole plays volleyball with your sister Meredith," said Alison, her eyes eager and alight.

"Really?" said Deborah. *Jesus, so what!*

"My mum took them to the match at Ivanhoe last Saturday, and Meredith stayed over at our place."

Suddenly Deborah had an uncomfortable feeling that she knew what was coming. "That's nice, Alison. Look, sorry, I'm late for my lecture, I've gotta run . . ."

Alison's hand on her arm again, restraining her. "Meredith says that your mother just disappeared," she said, leaning in close. "She walked out on Christmas Eve a few years ago. Meredith remembers it."

Five years ago actually. Five and a half. "She was just a little kid. That's what they told her. She doesn't remember properly."

"You think so, Debbie? What if I ask her next time she comes over? What if I tell her what you told all of us: that your mother's *dead*. Died of cancer when your little sister was just a baby." Her smile, her glistening eyes, were gleeful. Deborah pulled free and took a step back.

"I've gotta go," she said, but Alison stepped up too close to her again.

"You'd better tell everyone the truth at the next CR meeting," she hissed. "Or else I will. *Miz* High and Mighty Deborah McDonald!"

But by the end of that next meeting the following week, Deborah had turned it into a victory. Her strategy was to tell the truth, or a version of it at least: her mother had abandoned Deborah and her siblings, and this had so shocked and shamed the family that it was less painful to think of her as dead. It was all so terrible and confusing! Deborah also made a tactical decision to cry, something she hardly ever did, and that turned out to be a very smart move. Interesting, how the circle of women drew in closer to her, protectively. The consoling noises, the hands offering tissues and hankies. The murmurs of, "Let it out, it's good to cry," and, "You don't have to hold anything back here. Not with us."

"I've got Alison to thank for this breakthrough," Deborah said in a wobbly voice, tears damp on her cheeks. "She's been so supportive." Through the curtain of her long straight black hair she could see, *oh yes,* that Alison's boofy face was a study: jealousy and uncertain pride mingled. A hand patted Alison's shoulder in sisterly approval but then she was ignored again, as usual, for she was dumpy and uninteresting, while Deborah was clever and tall and striking. A born leader, a star in the making—not that any of them thought in those sorts of out-dated hierarchical terms any more, of course.

Don't think I've forgiven you, Ramsbottom, Deborah thought savagely. No one would ever know how wonderful it had been for her to say "My mother's dead"; how exhilarating. To say it again and again, all this year, ever since she'd started university. Not for the sympathy it garnered, but for the sheer vengeful pleasure of wiping her mother out. Every time she'd said it Deborah felt that she had triumphed over her mother at last, paid her back for her selfish, thoughtless, cheap desertion. And now this lumpy idiot had taken that triumph away from her.

She straightened in her chair, smoothed her hair back with both hands, and looked around the group.

"Thank you," she said with a sincere but still tremulous smile. The circle of women leaned back too, starting to relax after all the emotion. "You're like my family, my *real* family, all of you."

"The patriarchal family is incapable of supporting a woman's choices," said Linda, who was doing the same course as Deborah, Politics/Law, but a couple of years ahead of her. She pulled out a packet of Drum and began rolling a cigarette. "The patriarchy forbids women from even recognizing their own capacity to *make* choices."

"But isn't that what happened to Debbie's mother?" demanded Louise, who had begun the meeting by announcing that it was time the university put some resources into setting up a new student newspaper, by women for women, and urging them to join her in this struggle. "She was being suffocated by the structure of the patriarchal family and she had to escape. To rescue her own life."

A murmur of thoughtful agreement ran around the circle. *What?* thought Deborah, startled.

"Like a prisoner's desperate bid for freedom," said another young woman. "She was a heroine, really, Debbie's mother."

Louise scowled at her. "That's a sexist term," she said sternly.

"Oh. Sorry," the girl murmured, blushing.

"Female hero?" suggested someone.

"Why not just 'hero'? Why can only men be heroes?"

"Shero!" cried Linda.

"This is exactly why we need our own newspaper," said Deborah quickly. She had heard quite enough about how her mother was not . . . what Deborah knew her to be, *to blame*. "To confront sexism in the very language we speak! To eliminate it!"

"Yes! Exactly!" said Linda. "The personal *is* political, and Deb's story demonstrates that. Here in this group, we have this private space where women's stories can be told in an environment that's not controlled by men. Now we need to move that into a public forum! We need to take *action!*"

Remember this, Deborah told herself as the group moved on to further discussion. *Remember that in every situation there's the potential for strategic advantage.* She intended to make sure, too, that she'd get lots of opportunities to use this insight. *Times are a-changing, especially for us women. The Old Boys' network that's been running this country for so long is on the way out and this new Labor government is on the move.* Free tertiary education was getting people who wouldn't have had a chance before into universities, and there was the pill—hooray for the pill!—so now women had the same sexual freedom as men. It amazed Deborah that less than a year ago she wouldn't have been eligible to vote till she was twenty-one, yet eighteen year olds—the boys, anyway—were being called up and sent to fight in Vietnam. All changed, overnight! Having turned eighteen, she would be able to vote tomorrow, if there was an election, and her male friends no longer had to dread their birthdays and the lottery of war.

And now the Prime Minister had appointed a special adviser on women's issues. Oh yeah, the press called her Supergirl and published sneering articles and idiotic cartoons, and she'd heard Louise deride the woman who'd got the job as a tokenistic career professional who shaved her armpits, but Deborah was fired with possibility. The Whitlam government still didn't have a single woman member of parliament among their elected representatives, not one! Soon they'd be desperate for women candidates to field, both at state and federal level—and why not her, Deborah McDonald? Not at the next election, okay, but in another few years . . . She was young, intelligent, committed, ambitious. Good-looking. Women in the houses of parliament. Women as government ministers. A woman as deputy prime minister. And before too long, *a woman prime minister.* Why not? It had to happen, and happen soon, and she'd be ready.

Later that night, after a day full of lectures and tutorials and avid conversations in the caf, Deborah was invited to go to the pub with a bunch of older students, mostly guys. She was pleased. She didn't really know any of them, but she wanted to: these were some of the movers and shakers on campus.

She had the right jargon and the correct political line, but it was her looks that gave her entree with the guys, she knew that. Her long legs and high bottom looked great in tight jeans and boots. She strode when she walked and knew how to flick back her long silky hair in a way that was sexy but not too girlie, not too cute. She liked her beer and she could hold her own at the bar or in an argument, or both at the same time.

Amid the animated conversation and the cigarette smoke, the laughter and flirtation and the jugs of beer slopping on the tabletops, Deborah was enjoying herself thoroughly until the people seated closest to her started talking about Amnesty International and prisoners of conscience. Suddenly, unwillingly, her mind shifted to the bizarre things the others had said today about her mother. *A desperate bid for freedom. Rescue her own life.* Could that—could there be any truth in that? No! Surely not!

But then, as if she were watching a movie, she saw her mother in the house they'd lived in, saw her doing all those normal mother things: moving from room to room, making beds and picking up clothes, shoes, books, toys. Writing shopping lists. Saw her struggling in from the car with big bags of groceries, yelling for the kids to come and give her a hand. Saw herself, Deborah, kneeling on the floor stacking cans of baked beans and tomato soup in the cupboard and her mother above her saying with such passion, *"I hate shopping!"* Heard herself asking genuinely, "Why? I thought you like getting out of the house?" and looking up to see her mother's expression of helpless exasperation . . . and in that moment she knew it was true.

She didn't feel like being in the pub any longer. She picked up her jacket and leather shoulder-bag from the back of her chair and left. Luckily the rain had stopped, but it was cold and dismal and she felt . . . friendless. While she waited for a bus she thought, *I miss my family.* It was actually the first time she'd had that thought all year: she was living in a flat with a couple of other students now, and what with classes and part-time work she was far too busy to get home much, or even call them. *I'll go over there this weekend,* she thought. James; she missed James. *Maybe I'll take him to a movie.*

She got home at the same time as one of her roommates. They chatted for a while, smoked a little joint, then Deborah got ready for bed. From the drawer of her bedside table she took out a thick pad of lined paper, about two-thirds of which was already full. She folded the pages back to the next blank sheet, propped it on her raised knees and began to write.

Dear Mum,

Something happened today that has kind of changed everything. Everything i.e. about my understanding of you, and if my understanding of you has changed, then that means everything I understand has changed.

She went on to describe what the women in the consciousness-raising group had said, and the memories she herself had experienced while sitting in the pub.

What does this mean, she wrote, *about why you abandoned us? Why you deserted us? Why you left me to deal with Robert and James and Meredith? Because you must've known Dad was never going to understand all those things about . . .*

She stopped writing and sat there propped up in bed, staring fixedly ahead. For a long time she didn't move an inch, but a change gradually came over her face: her eyes narrowed, her lips compressed. A cold, angry look returned to her beautifully proportioned, high cheek-boned face, and suddenly she started writing furiously again in large forceful letters: *You got the chance to rescue your own life but what about us? YOU DIDN'T GIVE A FUCK, DID YOU?*

Striding along the street toward home, Deborah rehearsed the Alison Ramsbottom story. She could almost hear the words spilling rapidly from her mouth as she told Angus, almost taste the first glass of white wine from the bottle he'd have waiting, already chilled. But the house was still and quiet. Not even the dogs to greet her. Eventually Deborah had to walk down to the bottle shop and buy some wine herself, since there was no sign of Angus and his phone was going straight to voice mail. Where the hell was he? Olivia had come back with the dogs but now she was out in the shed with Flopsy Mopsy and bloody Cottontail. Deborah poured herself another glass of wine. *Why does everyone always disappear on me? Bugger them!*

She went into her study and wrote for a little while, quick and intent, in longhand on a pad of thick lined paper. When her glass was empty she stopped, tore out the pages. By the linen cupboard in the hallway she knelt down to retrieve a box way at the back. She had to pull out the vacuum cleaner and the old heavy pressure cooker to get at the box she wanted, and then just as she was putting into it the pages she'd written, loosely folded, Olivia materialized beside her.

"Shit!" Deb exclaimed. "You scared the living daylights out of me!"

"Sorry, Mum. Dad home yet?"

"No, he's not. Why?" Deborah was shoving things back into the cupboard all anyhow.

"I want him to look at my English essay."

"Well, *I* could look at it, you know!"

"Okay," said Olivia, sounding surprised. *Now why does she have to sound like that, for heaven's sake?* "Would you like to?"

"Yeah, sure," her mother replied, standing up and closing the door of the linen cupboard firmly.

"Now?"

"Well . . . in a little while. After dinner."

"Okay." Olivia melted away into her room.

The bottle of wine was almost empty by the time Angus's car pulled up in the driveway.

"Hi, darling," he said, breezing in and going to kiss her.

"Where have you *been*?" Deborah asked, fending him off. "I've been home for bloody *hours*. And your mobile's turned off!"

"Is it?" said Angus mildly, fishing it out of the pocket of the jacket he'd dumped on a chair. "Oops!"

"I couldn't reach you!"

"Sorry, Deb. Was there a problem?"

"*Yes,* I—oh, never mind. I just wanted to *talk* to you, for god's sake. Where were you?" She gave him a hard look. "Have you been out drinking?"

"Well, not as much as you, apparently," he said, lifting the almost empty bottle from the wine cooler on the bench. "So I had a meeting after work, and a couple of drinks. So shoot me now, Deb!"

He sounded tetchy, and Deborah's own hostility flared at his tone.

"Can't I rely on *anyone*?" she snarled. "Not even you? God knows you don't have anything *like* the pressure I have, puddling along in your cozy little office doing the same thing you've been doing for twenty years."

Angus had his back to her, getting another wine glass out of the cupboard, and he kept his back to her for quite a long time. Deborah waited for him to turn around, and some of the punch went out of her while she waited, looking at his back in its blue shirt, the sleeves rolled up nearly to his elbow. At the lines on the back of his neck. She liked that neck. When he turned to her again his face was unnaturally still.

"Is there something bothering you?" he asked politely. "Something happen at work?" He picked up a bottle of red wine from the floor beside his jacket. She hadn't noticed it before. They didn't usually drink red.

She told him about the call from Alison Ramsbottom, and even about the upsetting memories it had aroused of her mother's desertion. It all sounded a bit lame now. Like she was . . . playing for sympathy.

"Doesn't sound very pleasant," Angus said, but his voice had none of the plangency of real concern.

"You don't *care*!" flared Deborah accusingly, and in her husband's indifferent expression, in the moment's hesitation before he protested that yes, he did care, sure—she saw that it was so. Angus, who always cared, whom she had always depended on to care, did not. She didn't accuse him again, realizing with a little internal thud that one had that luxury only when it wasn't true.

The argument petered out. They ate dinner with Olivia, everyone seeming a bit flat or preoccupied, and after Angus had read and commented on Olivia's essay they watched some TV, read a little and went to bed. They didn't say much, and didn't touch.

Deborah woke again at 4:14, that's what the numbers on the digital clock said. She lay there worrying helplessly about her father, about the looming scandal she hadn't talked to the minister about before she left work. About that look she'd seen on Angus's face. Alison Ramsbottom's phone call seemed as irrelevant as a week-old mosquito bite now. She lay on her back staring at the curtain rod on the wall opposite, barely discernible in the dimness. When her eyes started to water she wiped them and noticed the bunched-up tension in her cheeks. Her whole face, she realized, was contorted with tension. She made herself relax the muscles there, and in her throat as well. And her shoulders. *Oh god, I feel like I could just implode. I'm like this all the bloody time.*

She rolled onto her side, toward the middle of the bed and the wall-like protective shape of Angus's back, the steady sound of his breathing as he slept the night away, undisturbed by noises or worries or his wife's nocturnal wakefulness, her restless comings and goings. He had always slept like this, deeply, peacefully. Oh, why did she get so irritable with him, so snappy and terse? Did it matter, after all, that he was absent-minded sometimes, and lacked ambition?

Softly she placed her left hand palm-down on his back, just below his shoulder blades, feeling that solid familiar flesh. Well, a little less of it these days: the steady exercise regime he'd taken up was really starting to pay off, he'd lost almost all of that middle-aged heaviness that had started to thicken his frame. *He's a little bit vain after all*, she thought fondly, and wondered again if he really hadn't minded that she hadn't organized a big party for his fiftieth birthday mid-year. *I should have done that. Maybe he thought I didn't . . . care about him. Love him.* She still felt bad about it, as though she had slipped up. But she just hadn't been up to it. And he'd assured her that a small dinner party was much more what he preferred. Good old Angus.

And there was that school reunion thing. He really wanted me to go with him and I just . . . sneered. Her face twisted in the darkness in a grimace of self-recrimination. *Oh, I should've gone.*

She stroked his back, and inched a little closer so that she could smell him, feel the warmth of his body. Gently she kissed the back of his dear, lined neck. Tears prickled her eyes. *I love him so much.* She stroked his hip, where the old soft T-shirt flopped and fell away. He didn't stir. *He hasn't really stopped caring*, she thought. *He can't have. I'll never snap at him again. And we'll do things together, nice thing*s. Finally she drifted off to sleep again.

But in the morning she woke up with gritty red eyes, feeling unrested and like she might be on the edge of a migraine. She complained sharply to Angus when she had to get up and make her own coffee, and he went off to do the shopping at Victoria Market alone. Shortly after he drove off Deborah pulled on her track pants and trainers, yelling to Olivia that she was going for a run. Off she loped and settled quickly into her stride, hoping that in the steady pacing she would find the right way to handle this stupid crisis the minister was freaking out about. Solutions arose like that sometimes, when she was running.

As soon as her mother left the house, Olivia went to the linen cupboard in the hallway, quickly removing the things at floor level till she found what her mother had been so jumpy about the night before. There it was: a large rectangular box from some extinct department store. Lifting its faded lid Olivia found it crammed with papers, some in bundles held together with perishing rubber bands, some just in layers: a thick sediment of paper, all handwritten. Most seemed to be in her mother's writing, but some wasn't. No, wait, this was her mother's handwriting too, but different. From ages ago, when she was still a kid. Most of it was on lined paper, the cheap stuff you bought in thick notepads, some was on plain white sheets, and some on that nice thin crinkled stuff, airmail paper, made specially for writing letters on. In the days when people used to write actual letters. Snail mail. Yes, these were all letters, heaps of them. Maybe hundreds. But none of them had ever been mailed: there were no envelopes, and no replies. And on every letter the greeting was the same: *Dear Mum*, that's how each one began. *Dear Mum*.

CHAPTER 13

Angus had turned fifty the year of his primary school's one-hundredth anniversary. That was part of the reason he'd gone to the centenary reunion: he just liked the arithmetic, the neat doubling. Generally speaking he was not all that interested in birthdays, reunions, anniversaries, or in meeting up with old friends from school or university just for the sake of it. After his parents retired to Queensland, he'd hardly even been back to the coastal town where he grew up.

He hadn't even particularly wanted a fiftieth birthday party, although he knew Deborah wouldn't allow it to pass without organizing something. Organizing, that was Deb's strong suit: chart the course, instruct the crew, steer the ship. Angus basically just kept rowing, that was all he needed to do.

So he was turning fifty. It wasn't that big a deal. Just a number, really. So he was getting a bit pudgy around the middle: he'd get around to putting in some hours at the gym. Hair a little thinner, not much he could do about that. Work was ticking over; daughter as self-propelled as ever, though everyone was warning him the teenage years would bring a few bumps. Yes, his wife was a bit too busy, a bit tense—but that wouldn't go on forever, surely. Things would settle down whether he got himself into a lather or not, so why bother?

The Lake Booradalla Primary School Centenary Reunion had been held in late March, Angus's favorite time of year. He'd tried to persuade Deborah and Olivia to come with him, make it a family trip, camp out maybe like they used to when Ollie was little and they hardly had any money.

"It'll be so *beautiful* at the coast," he promised them in a stagily honeyed tone, making a game of it. "Daytime it'll be clear and sunny. The ocean'll still be warm enough for swimming. And the nights'll be crisp and we can look at the stars . . . And there won't be any tourists, because it's still school term."

"Except for eight million Booradalla reunioneers," said Deborah, shuddering elaborately. "Sorry, darling, we're issuing a major policy statement that week. I can't possibly get away, it's just too big. But you and Olivia could go, you'd like that, wouldn't you, Ol?"

Olivia looked up from mixing some kind of potion to add to her rabbits' feed. "Sorry. That's the weekend of Laurence's birthday party."

"Oh. How old is he?"

"Dad, really! Your own nephew! He's sixteen."

"He's *my* nephew, actually," said Deborah. "And this is the first I've heard about you going to a sixteen-year-old's birthday party. Since when?"

"Since forever. Since he's my cousin," said Olivia evenly.

"But there's probably going to be drinking! Maybe some kids drinking *too much.*"

"But *I* won't be drinking. And, Mum. It's at Auntie Meredith's house," said Olivia, fixing her mother with her level gaze. "I've been watching *adults* drink too much there for as long as I can remember, and that hasn't exactly been a tempting sight."

Olivia went back to mixing the rabbit feed. Deborah and Angus exchanged what they privately called their "Olivia has spoken" look, a resigned face accompanied by a little shrug of helplessness.

"Looks like I'm going on my own then," said Angus.

"Sorry, darling," said Deborah.

"Sorry, Dad," said Olivia.

But neither of them had sounded particularly regretful.

march 2004

This is terrific! Angus thought, looking around the teeming school-yard on the Saturday morning. It had been a good drive up the day before, at his own pace, singing loudly to the songs *he* liked on the car stereo. The weather was just as he'd foretold, a lovely warm day, blue sky, occasional light breeze. And this: everyone who had ever lived in Lake Booradalla and was still alive, it seemed, was there. Excitement and laughter rose all around him as he collected his name tag—*Angus Hume 1959,* the year he'd started in Bubs' Grade, as they called it then—from one of the tables set up near the entrance. The current lot of Lake Booradalla Primary students were proudly acting as guides and helpers, even the plump-cheeked lit-tlies. There was a good turnout of old-timers who'd started eighty years before in a two-room school in what had then been a tiny fishing village.

Both the town and the school had grown considerably: tourism and the coastal property boom had done great things for the local economy. The scrubby grounds that had surrounded the school were taken up with playing fields, portable classrooms, and a new assem-bly hall that doubled as the gym. The old building he thought of as *my school* had been thoroughly remodeled, *and not a bad job either. Carpet in the classrooms! Bugger me!* He walked around, too excited to stop yet and look at the displays, greeting and being greeted, hearing ex-students of all ages declaring "In my day . . ." and then laughing at themselves.

"Hey! Highway!" boomed a big male voice, and Angus turned to see a bulky bloke with a huge grin bearing down on him, instantly recognizable as his old best mate, David Tindall.

"Tin Man!" he yelled back, and they were hugging and gripping each others' shoulders. "Bloody hell! This is fantastic!" Both laughing incredulously.

"How the hell are ya?" asked Tindall, and they were away, yacking and chiacking as they walked around, people calling out to them heartily, smiling to see them together again. How long had it been since they'd caught up? Have to be twenty-five years, twenty-six maybe! When Angus, fresh out of law school, had driven up the coast road from Melbourne to Sydney and dropped in on the then newly married Dave Tindall, working for a plumber in Eden. And Dave's sister Marion had been there, too, just finished high school. They'd all gone to a party, but Dave and his wife Yvonne had gone home early, and Marion had been in a mood to keep partying. *Gus'll look after me,* she'd assured her brother. It was a memory he'd kept tucked away for years: how drunk they'd got, how they'd slipped away together, and just exactly how well he'd looked after her. *Don't tell my brother, for god's sake,* she'd said afterward. Christ, that was the last thing he was about to do! Dave would've knocked him into the middle of next week. He'd never told anyone, not even Deborah. But he hadn't forgotten either. No.

These days, Dave was telling him cheerfully, Tindall's Plumbing was the biggest and busiest in Eden. His older boy was about to get his plumber's license and become a partner in the business, too. "Then it'll be Tindall and Son," he said proudly. "Yvonne does the books. Runs the whole show really. Terrific manager, she is," he added, tearing into an enormous sausage sandwich dripping with fried onion rings, fresh from the grill.

"Boy, this is good!" Angus said, mouth full. "I told my daughter she'd be missing out."

"Hey, there's my sister! Marion!" Dave yelled. A tall woman with thick auburn hair turned, smiling, and started toward them. "Look who I've found! Bloody Highway!"

"Gosh!" she said, holding out her hand to Angus, her brother's beefy arm around her. "Hello, Gus. Remember me?"

"Marion. Yeah, of course." Angus wiped his hand on his trousers and shook hers. He remembered her, but did he actually recognize her? Yes . . . no . . . The cute but ignorable kid sister of his school-days; the lanky eager teenager of that night in Eden; and this mature, graceful woman. *Yes.* "How are you?"

"I'm fine, thanks. Isn't this wonderful? I'm so glad I came now."

"Me too." Angus was trying to figure out her face. It was worn, careworn he thought, as though she'd been through a lot. A softness to her, but not weak-soft. Kind. *Not often you see a really kind face these days.* "Where did you have to travel from?"

"Oh, just up from Melbourne. Not like Perth or anything. Some people *have* come from Perth, you know. And I got a lift, so I didn't even have to drive."

"I could have given you a lift."

"Could you? You're living in Melbourne too then, Gus?"

"Yeah. I am." No one had called him Gus in a million years. His own family had called him Angus, the teachers had called him that or his surname, and with the other boys it was either Humesy or Highway. It had been mainly Marion, in fact, who'd called him Gus. He liked her saying it; it seemed warm and informal. And suddenly, strangely, as he looked at her the noise of all those people swirling around them seemed to recede, became a background murmur like little gentle waves on a beach. He looked at her and he looked. One part of Angus's mind told him that according to the everyday rules of social engagement, it was time for him to look away, resume his banter with Dave or finish his sanger. But he couldn't seem to shift his gaze from Marion's face.

She was a tall woman, almost the same height as him, and she was looking straight back at him, meeting his eyes with an easy smile. He took in her high forehead framed by the thick waves of coppery hair, the pale fragile skin of the redhead, the observant expression in her widely spaced eyes—gray? green?—and the generous mouth. The white teeth just visible between her lightly parted lips. *I just want to keep looking at her. What is this? This is weird.*

Sunday evening, and he was facing her across a candle-lit table in an over-nautically decorated restaurant, the Yacking Yabbie. It was the first time they had actually been alone together, and Angus knew he was talking too much. He'd just finished a story about Olivia's beloved fancy rabbit Hector, who had won first prize in his section at the Royal Melbourne Show the year Ollie was eight (despite kicking the judge so hard he'd yelled), and the photo of them in the newspaper, Olivia grimly scowling and Hector *like a small deranged flokati rug* gripped firmly in her arms. He drew the shape of the rabbit's enormous floppy ears in the air around his own head and made a cartoon cute face, and Marion laughed. The laugh seemed genuine but Angus was still appalled by his own nervous showing off. Just then, to his relief, the waitress brought the appetizers to their table and topped up their wine glasses.

"Enjoy your meal," the girl chirped as she headed off to greet some new customers. Angus took a healthy slug from his wine glass.

"I'm sorry. I've been gabbling."

"Not at all."

"I have. When what I'd really like is to hear *you* talk."

"Okay," she said. "Sure. But first I need to pay some attention to these scallops."

Her smile was a little lopsided; her bottom lip dipped down a bit more on one side than the other. It made Angus smile, too, to see it; he remembered her brothers teasing her about it and wanted to remind her, but then thought he'd better not. Maybe she minded. He looked down at his plate.

"Gosh, I'm really hungry!" he said with surprise. "These prawns look fantastic!"

"You met Lou, who gave me the lift up? She pointed this place out to me on the way. She said it's the best place for seafood on the whole coast."

While they ate they talked about going prawning in the inlets of the lake as kids, and favorite restaurants in Melbourne, and Angus felt himself settling down. Actually Marion's presence was very steadying, it had just been the process of getting away from Lake Booradalla—working up the courage to offer her a lift back to Melbourne, feeling jumpy after she'd accepted in case someone else asked to come as well or Marion suggested someone else come with them: that's what had thrown him. That, and the effort of stopping himself from contemplating what all this meant.

Between the first and second courses they talked about some of the old schoolmates they'd just seen at the reunion: the predictable paths some had followed, the surprising turns others' lives had taken. And that led to discussion, during the main course (snapper, barramundi), of their respective careers, Angus's in law and Marion as a counselor, a family therapist.

"So," he said once the dinner plates had been cleared away. "We've talked about families in general and a bit about my family in particular. But I still don't know anything much about you, whether you have a family, even whether you have kids, or a partner." Actually this was not quite true. He had asked Dave the day before, casually he hoped, if Marion was married. "Used to be," Dave replied, looking a bit tight around the mouth. "Not any more. Bastard did the dirty on her good and proper." He didn't seem to want to say more and Angus had let it go at that.

"Well, you certainly know my first family. Those enormous brothers of mine and their tribes."

"Yes, but—what about you?" He drew a deeper breath and looked at her directly. "Dave told me you *used to be* married. He didn't sound too happy about . . . whatever happened."

"Ah. Well. They liked to think they could look after me, my big brothers. Most people do, after all. They want to protect the ones they love from pain and from harm." She stopped for a moment and looked down at the white tablecloth. Angus noticed that her hair glowed copper in the candlelight. What would it feel like, if he were to lean forward and touch? She gave a little rueful shrug and glanced up. "But it's just not possible. Things happen in life that no one can protect you from."

"Yes. I'm sure that's true. I wish it weren't; especially as a parent, I wish it weren't. But, Marion, can I ask: what were the things that happened to you? That made Dave look so grim."

"Well, it *is* a bit grim, some of it. Maybe it's better not to put a damper on the evening."

Angus was about to accede, to go back to light and cheerful chat, but some part of him said, *No. Talk to her; really talk.*

"I would like to know. If you can tell me."

She looked at him, not smiling, for a long moment.

"Okay." She nodded several times, gathering herself. "I married a guy I met at university, Kim. We were both studying psychology. I know Dave writes him off now, completely, my whole family does, but he wasn't a terrible person. We just had a run of . . . bad luck, which was more than he could deal with.

"When we'd been married for three years, I got pregnant. It was twins, identical twin boys. But there were complications during the delivery and the second one was stillborn. Joshua. That's what we named him. That was hard. But the other baby was fine. Till he was fifteen months old, and then he developed leukemia. He was just over two when he died. Benjamin. Ben."

"Oh god," Angus breathed. He wanted very much to cover her pale, freckled hand, lying on the tablecloth, with his, but he stopped himself. "I don't know how I'd . . ." He shook his head.

"But wait," said Marion with an ironic raised finger, "there's more! About a year after that, we decided we were ready to have another child. I got pregnant again quite quickly, I was still not much over thirty, but it was an ectopic pregnancy. Have you heard of that?"

"Ah . . ." Angus shook his head uncertainly.

"Sorry. Not really a dinner table topic." Angus made a noise and gestures that said, *No, please, go ahead.* "It's when the egg is fertilized outside the uterus, usually in one of the fallopian tubes. In my case, the left fallopian tube. In the old days an ectopic pregnancy would almost invariably kill the woman outright once it got to a certain stage. These days, if you get to a decent hospital in time and they figure out what's going on—as happened with me, luckily—you survive. But it took me a long time to recover. I was a very sick girl."

Angus sat very still, gazing at her. He held himself away from the thought of this woman in pain, in agony, in danger of her life. She started talking again, speaking clearly but quite fast.

"And while I was recovering, Kim left. Everyone—certainly all my brothers—was convinced he was having an affair, because he took up almost immediately with the woman he later married. But really, he wasn't seeing her before we broke up. I know that. He just . . . couldn't bear to be around me. There had been too much pain. Too much loss."

"But you had to bear it."

"We bear what we can. I don't know that I bore it all that well either. I was a mess, too. For quite a long time."

Angus was drawn by the calmness of her voice as she spoke, the straightforward assurance of her phrases, not unemotional but without bitterness or self-pity. The thing that had become more noticeable as she spoke was the look of patient observation in her eyes. He thought of what had occurred to him when he first saw her at the reunion, that she was careworn, as though she'd been through a lot. Had cared a lot. Kind. And now he added, beautiful. *She is such a beautiful woman.*

The cheerful young waitress came back and offered them the dessert menu. Marion said what she really needed was to stretch her legs. Could they walk in the garden, perhaps, she asked the waitress?

"Oh, yes, sure, it's a lovely garden, you probably noticed when you came in. And just past that pond with the fountain," she indicated the direction, "there's a path to the beach. It's really close, you know, and it's such a nice evening."

Angus and Marion looked at each enquiringly. "Sounds great," said Angus. "And then maybe we can come back in and have a coffee before we head off to Melbourne."

They found the path easily. After just a few paces they could hear the sound of the surf, and a little farther on there was the water, lit silver by the moon's clear white light. Marion was ahead of him, framed against the ocean, and he watched the movement of her hips as she walked. She was wearing a short white cotton jumper and pearly gray stretch pants. When the path ended at the beach and she turned and started walking along the sand near the water's edge, he could see the shape of her buttocks moving under the fabric.

Suddenly Angus had an image of her body as it had been that night of the party in Eden, her girl's body stretched out long and pale beneath him in the moonlight. How he'd turned her over, pulled her hips toward him, and the lovely rhythmic bounce of her buttocks then as he'd thrust steadily into her . . . And here she was again, twenty-five years later, walking before him, and she still had a very nice arse, generous but firm. He wondered what she did, what sport or exercise, to be in such good shape. He felt his penis start to stir and thicken, and felt suddenly self-conscious about the flab he'd allowed to gradually settle around his own belly. *Really got to get fit again,* he thought as he watched her move. He imagined resting his hand on that bottom as she walked, imagined sliding his hand down, between her thighs. Gripping them. His erection was growing. Substantially. *Oh boy,* he thought, but that was all he could think.

They walked on, not saying much beyond agreeing on the beauty of the scene. There were some sand dunes quite close to the beach, and at the end of them a little creek flowing into the sea.

"Guess we'd better head back," Marion said, and they turned but had not gone far before she veered away from the shoreline and into the dunes. Angus followed her. They sat together on one of these breast-shaped hills of sand, side by side, looking out at the ocean. Angus toyed with a strand of the tough dune grass, sliding it between his fingers. She turned to him, he was aware of her pale face so close to him, but he kept looking out. He felt her hand on his face, turning him toward her. She leaned in and kissed him. *This isn't happening,* he thought wildly. *This isn't happening.* Then he was returning the kiss, avidly. His hand was in her thick hair, holding the back of her head.

They kissed and kissed and then drew away from each other, gasping. She pressed her hands to her cheeks while she caught her breath; her eyes were very big. Dropping her hands she asked him, "Do you . . . do you remember that night in Eden?"

"Every minute of it," Angus said. "I've never forgotten it."

He leaned toward her, lifted the hem of her jumper up, up, and peeled back a cup of her bra, uncovering one of her breasts. He put his mouth there and kissed softly, several times, took the nipple in his mouth and flicked his tongue across it. She gasped and drew away from him. Her jumper was caught above her breast and she pulled it down. For a moment he thought she was going to get up, leave, but instead she put her hands on his shoulders and pushed him gently onto his back on the sand. She ran her hands down his chest, stroking from his collarbone to below his ribs. Lower. Stroking his chest and his belly through his clothing. Down, stroking his hipbones, down his thighs to the knees. Again. Touching everywhere but his crotch.

Angus's brain was nowhere, there were no words in his mind, he was all cock and his cock was in a state of utter upright disbelief. Then she half lay, half crouched on the sand beside him and rested the side of her face gently on his crotch, stroked his erection with her cheek through the layers of cloth. Stroking, stroking. He touched her hair, lying there looking up at the near-full moon, hearing the surf so close. He ran one hand down her back, had to close his eyes when his fingers touched the soft bare skin between her pants and her jumper. He traced the contours of her buttocks, firm and taut as she crouched there beside him. *Oh god, oh fuck . . .* How he wanted to be there, holding her hips, gazing down at that gorgeous round arse, naked . . . He cupped his hand over a mound of her flesh and squeezed, and truly felt like he was close to exploding.

She sat up and placed her own hand where her head had been, cupping it over his full balls, his swollen cock. Angus didn't think he'd had an erection like this in years. Twenty-five years. She gave a little squeeze.

"Is that a promise?" she asked.

"If you want it to be," he answered.

"For later."

Not later! begged his cock. *Now! Now!* But some other part of him, brain or heart, had come to life and was saying, *She wants there to be a later. Yes! Yes! Not just a quick rut on the beach and skulk off.*

"For whenever you want."

Simultaneously they each drew in a long, expressive breath, and sighed. Happy sighs.

"What are we going to do?" she asked.

"Drive back to Melbourne. Sing along to whatever music you want to put on the CD player. Not think too much."

"Yes."

"And I'll take you home to your place. And we'll see how much *later* it is then."

She smiled at him. Grinned. Jumped to her feet and ran down the sandhill and along the beach making little whooping cries. He followed her, more slowly, somewhat uncomfortably. He felt like he was floating lightly above the whole scene though his feet were sinking ankle-deep into the cool sand. If he hadn't known better he'd have thought he was as stoned as a cricket.

They had a coffee back at the restaurant and then Marion excused herself to go to the toilet. While she was gone Angus took his mobile out of his pocket and called home.

"Hi there. It's me."

"Hey," said Deborah. "How was the reunion?"

"Great, really good. It's kind of still going on actually, I've offered some people a lift back to Melbourne but it's all taking a bit longer than I expected to get away." He had never lied to Deb before, never imagined that he would, or could. But the words came so easily.

"Oh, well, take your time, Angus, no rush. I'm just finishing off some work stuff. You've eaten, right?"

"Yeah, I've eaten. Thanks. How's Ollie? How did Laurence's party go?"

"Fine, as far as I can tell. I picked her up just after eleven, no dramas. You know Olivia, she told me *all* the gossip and gory details—not!"

"Sounds right. Well, I'm kind of on my way but I don't know how long I'll be. Don't wait up for me, Dee, okay?"

"I won't. Drive carefully. And, Angus?"

"Yeah?"

"Please don't call me Dee. Okay?"

"Oh yeah. Right."

"Bye."

"Bye," he said to the dead line. *I love you too, darling,* he thought.

CHAPTER 14

Sometimes Meredith had dreams in which she was a little girl again, sitting in her father's lap, his arms strong around her. She awoke from these dreams contented, as though she had achieved something for which she'd always longed. She daydreamed of the same thing, too, especially when she was just crossing the line from tipsiness to being properly drunk.

Now that Laurence had shot up and was so much taller, suddenly, than she was, she sometimes had this urge with him, too. She could *see* it, almost: herself snuggled in his lap, protected, safe. She only tried it once, though, when she was pretty darn drunk. Laurence simply stood up and let her fall on the floor. "Too messy, Mum," he said, and left the room. That was something he said sometimes; no particular offense was meant. No offense, actually, was ever meant. But she never tried to do it again, no matter how drunk she was.

Occasionally she did sit, delicately, on her father's knee. It didn't feel inappropriate: he was a tall man, strong even as he advanced into old age, and she was by far the smallest in the family, slightly built and of barely medium height. And he didn't seem to mind. Alex.

Daddy. He seemed perfectly content for her to perch there on his knee as they had a cup of tea and chatted, her elbows propped on the kitchen table. And because she was facing the table, not looking at him, Meredith found herself talking more freely. About boyfriends who had come and gone, for instance, or how she still dreamed sometimes of a proper career, except life was just too difficult as a single mum. And he would sip his tea and listen and say, "There now, poppet, I'm sure everything'll turn out all right. I know you do your best."

She loved them, those moments of childhood intimacy restored. But these occasions were only a small part of the time she spent with her father. In fact, Meredith and Alex did a great deal together, more than anyone else in the family knew. She didn't drink when she visited him, a deal she'd made with herself and stuck to, and she knew that helped—helped *her*, especially, to have that alcohol-free space. And wasn't it amazing how much she could get done without a glass in her hand!

Olivia sometimes marveled at what Grandpa had managed to achieve in the garden since she'd last been there, not knowing that Auntie Meredith had spent a whole morning turning that compost from one bin to the next, or barrowing mulch. Robert would say to Vesna, after getting off the phone from his father, "Gee, it's great Dad's doing so many different things in his retirement. I never even knew he was interested in concerts, or art galleries!" Because even to Robert, Meredith preferred not to reveal the extent of her activities with their father. It was part of the specialness of their relationship, and she didn't want to share it with her siblings. *Daddy takes care of things*, that was the good feeling that being with Alex gave her, *and he takes care of me, too.* How it was that Daddy knew her feelings and said nothing either, she didn't know.

The only person she mentioned it to was Laurence, chatting away about what she and Grandpa had done as she mucked around with her quirky big journals, sticking in ticket stubs and scraps torn from programs and brochures, filling comic-style frames with snippets of overheard conversation, jokes, dreams, asides. But Laurence, though he nodded sweetly and said, "Uh-huh, uh-huh," was clearly only half-listening. He was absorbed in his own teenage life, and rightly so.

Meredith worked nights, at a bar in the city, and the hours allowed her the freedom to go to daytime exhibitions and plays and concerts. Meredith had an enduring sense that she could have been *a creative person* of some kind, if her life had been different. But the closest she had come was working as an artists' model now and again. The gap between who she was and who that other, more creative person would be seemed impossibly wide, like . . . like waking up tomorrow and being Chinese. James was an artist, true, her own brother, but James was *the lucky one*. And she was *the baby*: her role was to entertain and admire, and in return she would be indulged.

Some of the shows they went to were free, but if tickets had to be bought Alex insisted on paying for them, which suited Meredith since she was always broke. And she, for her part, did the driving. One day a couple of months after his assessment, when a tang of summer heat was in the air, she arrived at midday to take him to a matinee performance by a visiting Japanese string quartet. Alex was all dressed up and ready to go—except that his shirt was grubby. There were food stains down the front, and as Meredith looked more closely she noticed that the collar was creased and dirty, too, and his tie had blotchy marks on it.

"Daddy," she said plainly, "that shirt needs a wash."

"Does it, darl?" said Alex, looking down.

"Yep. How about you whip it off and get a new one?"

Nodding agreeably, Alex stripped down to his singlet there and then, in the living room. Meredith was taken aback. Her father had always maintained the proprieties of an earlier generation; it might be acceptable to remove a dirty shirt in the laundry, perhaps, but not in the living room! He handed the shirt to her and she headed to his bedroom, a little nonplussed. At the door she turned back, wanting some further instruction, but her father was simply standing there blankly, waiting. She went on, into the privacy of his bedroom.

There was a wicker laundry basket standing empty in the corner and she dropped her father's warm shirt into it. Opening the door of his wardrobe for the first time in years, Meredith was confronted with a jumble of clothing. Tracksuit tops, jumpers and skivvies, things that should be folded and sitting in drawers were instead hung awkwardly, wire hangers jammed into their necks, with shirts or suit jackets awry over their shoulders. Trousers were threaded by one leg over a hanger, dangling precariously. Some suit pants were still hanging from the proper wooden clamp hangers, but were widely separated from their matching jackets. Nothing, she realized, was paired. Nothing matched. Boots and shoes littered the bottom of the wardrobe, here and there a forlorn tie.

Meredith took out a shirt she knew to be one of her father's favorites, a soft blue cotton. She held it up, examining it. It had been buttoned up, but the buttons didn't match their buttonholes, and it, too, was grubby. She tossed it in the wash basket. Another, white with a pale green stripe. Also dirty. *How come?* she thought, and suddenly had a picture of the washing line in the backyard and how it looked each time she'd visited lately: just two or three items pegged there, underclothing and a pair of socks, or maybe a set of gardening clothes. She had assumed without really thinking about it that her father was simply saving time by washing out the odd thing by hand. *He's not using the washing machine at all,* she realized now, and then hard on the heels of that thought came the revelation, *He's forgotten how to use the washing machine.*

Meredith felt woozy with shock. Although she quickly found a clean shirt and they went off to the matinee, she hardly heard a note the string quartet played. She needed to have a drink very badly. She dropped her father back at his place, drove to her own home and had a gin and tonic so stiff that the first sip made her stomach clench. Even as it did, though, she knew this one drink wouldn't be enough. And she had to leave for work in a couple of hours and she was super-cautious about driving when she might be over the limit . . . well, but if she left a little earlier she could take a tram in, and have a second G&T before she left. Reassured by the alcohol now sprinting through her bloodstream, she felt able to sit down and think.

So this is what dementia means. She had resisted her father's diagnosis till that moment. She'd thought it was all a mistake: just Robert, dear Robert, believing in whatever official people told him, and Deborah being mean, as usual. Her father couldn't get old; especially, he couldn't get sick and need looking after, because his job was to look after *her*.

Meredith looked at her watch: it was getting close to four o'clock. Could she call Robert? She knew he was always busy at the end of the school day but she *had* to talk to him, tell him what she had realized about Daddy. Robert would know how to make her feel better about this.

She was still staring at her watch when something new occurred to her. Slowly, she lowered her forearm. *They'll want to put him in a home.* If Daddy couldn't look after himself, that's what they would think was best, Deborah because she was such a horrible cow, Robert and Vesna because they were always so busy and besides, they were used to schools and hospitals and those places that Meredith never felt okay in, so they would think a nursing home was the best place for him. And James because—well, because he wouldn't think of anything else, that's all, he'd just go along with what the older ones organized because that's what James did, he went along with things.

But Daddy would hate that. I know he would. Images of her father's house and garden rushed through Meredith's mind. The warmth of the unfashionable kitchen, his big daggy chair in front of the telly. The way he knew each tree and shrub and plant, talked to them— he did, she'd heard him! The day they buried old Banjo down in the bottom end of the backyard, and planted a white peach tree on the spot. It had only had its first scanty crop, but this summer it would be bursting with fruit. How could Daddy leave the place where old Banjo was buried? He couldn't! It would kill him!

Then she thought, *If his memory's going, maybe someday he won't remember Banjo.* Another belt of shock, to imagine that. How awful! Well, but that's just it, she argued with herself. If someone's having memory problems, then it's all the more important that they stay in the place that's most familiar to them. Didn't that seem sensible? But the others just wouldn't get it.

It's up to me. It's up to me. Meredith tried to take another big swig of her gin but somehow only the icecubes were left. Should she have that second one now? No, better really if she went in to work early and had one there, before her shift started. But even as she decided this, she was standing at the fridge, taking out the gin and the bottle of tonic water. *But it can't be up to ME!* The notion seemed immense, unreal.

The next morning she rang her father and asked him brightly if she could drop in for a visit. Alex was welcoming as ever; he was always delighted to see his little girl.

Almost the moment she arrived Meredith announced, "You know what I want to do today, Daddy? I want to do a great big spring-clean!"

"Oh, poppet," said Alex, "what on earth for? You don't want to be stuck inside doing housework on a gorgeous day like this."

"I won't be stuck inside all day, don't you worry. I'll just do little bits and I'll come outside and watch you in the garden. And you know, Daddy, it *is* a gorgeous day, a perfect day for drying clothes. That's what I'll start with, spring-cleaning your wardrobe."

"You don't have to do that, darl."

"Oh, Daddy! *Let* me!" she pouted, and her father laughed.

"If that's what you want to do, then you go ahead."

She did. She went ahead, bit by bit, that day and in the weeks that followed. No one who came to visit her father, to *inspect* him, would find a single thing out of place. This was the goal Meredith determinedly reached for. She did it gracefully, in such a way that Alex never suspected for a moment what her larger plan was; never suspected that his standards could have slipped and be found wanting.

She washed his clothes, or took them to the drycleaner. She bought food and put it away in the appropriate places, and returned it to those places again and again, since Alex seemed a little unclear these days about what went where. (Rather a lot of ice-cream was found melted in the fridge, or even in the pantry, and surreptitiously disposed of.) She cooked meals that could be reheated easily. She cleaned every nook and cranny of the kitchen and bathroom till they sparkled.

James came by one afternoon; he was thinking, he said vaguely, of putting together some information for a family tree. As soon as he started pulling things out of the cupboards in the living room, and then dipping in to the mass of stuff in Alex's spare room, Meredith realized what an incredible muddle was lying in wait there, too.

"Boy, it's hard to know where to start," James said, peering warily into a drawer jammed almost shut with paper and bric-a-brac. "What is all this, do you reckon?"

"Haven't got a clue!" Meredith said brightly.

James had worked a couple of sheets free. "Looks like old accounts from Dad's engineering firm. Sheesh."

"Tell you what, I'll see if I can get Daddy onto sorting this stuff out. It's not urgent, this family tree thing, is it, James?"

"No," he said, shoving the drawer more or less closed. "No, I guess not."

Meredith and Alex went through all the cupboards together one by one. As they pulled out unused and neglected objects, Alex might launch into a detailed history of one item, and yet another which Meredith remembered from childhood and exclaimed over he regarded with total indifference, as though he'd never seen it before.

He would happily have thrown a lot out, but Meredith was reluctant. What if one of the others—Deborah, say—went looking for something and it was nowhere to be found? That'd be just the thing to set her on the warpath! Instead, Meredith sorted and rearranged, and stored things carefully in labeled boxes in the spare room or the shed.

It was like a campaign, and it took a lot out of her. She was at Alex's house every second day, and while she was busy there she felt calm and purposeful, but when she got home mid-afternoon she was so desperate for a drink that she would *run* into her kitchen and squirt the wine from its cask into the biggest glass she could lay her hands on, and take the first few gulps just standing there. Her campaign was working, though: it gratified her that these days Daddy was always well dressed, and he had filled out, too. He looked so *well*—and only she knew why.

Meredith kept all this to herself. Even Laurence took a while to tumble to what his mother had taken on. She swore him to secrecy, which he protested was ridiculous. But she insisted. That's how scared she was of what would happen to Daddy if the truth got out.

CHAPTER 15

Near the edge of a pretty dell in the woods of Somerset, James and Rose stood on tiptoes, stretching to gather the last of the sloe berries from their tall straggly bushes. It was getting close to Christmas and they both wore gloves and woolen hats against the cold. Pheasants, elegant and brainless, strutted amongst the trees and occasionally took flight, clapping their wings dramatically.

"I don't think I've ever seen a sloe before," said James, dropping the densely black little berries into the plastic container his mother had given him. "I always thought the drink was called *slow* gin, s-l-o-w. A laid-back cousin of the tequila slammer."

Rose laughed. "Oh, sloe gin is wonderful. We're lucky there are still some berries left, they're usually all gone by now. Delicious, it is! You'll see."

"Good-oh." James kept picking. "Always something new and different to look forward to, here in the wilds of deepest Somerset. Like being on safari really."

"James," said his mother in a serious voice. He glanced at her enquiringly, but she was looking into the branches, not at him.

"Yes?"

"James, why haven't you told the others about me yet?"

He felt a blush prickle along his jawbone. "I—I thought I might find some of your letters first. I thought that would be a good way to, sort of . . . introduce you."

"Yes, you said you wanted to look for them. But you haven't found any?"

"No." After a little silence he added, "Well, I haven't looked properly yet. It was all a bit of a muddle at Dad's place. But when I get back, I will."

Rose nodded. They went on picking. After a while James said, "I'm sorry, Rose. I don't really . . . I don't know why I haven't told them. It's harder than I thought."

She had intended to take this further, tell him it was time for her to talk to her other children, but seeing her son's beautiful face suddenly troubled caught at Rose's heart, and she couldn't bear to push him. Indeed, it was complicated for her, too. Quietly she said, "To tell you the truth, I'm rather enjoying having you to myself. It's been such a big thing. And it will all be different once the others know."

"Yes," he agreed. His voice was also very quiet.

"When we get back to the house, though, I want to show you something."

A few hours later, after the sloe berries and the gin had been put together to work their magic, Rose asked James to come up to her studio. She sat him down at her work table with a big book covered in worn green silk.

"It's not a proper photo album, really," she said quickly, sounding a little apologetic. "It's just an oversized sketchbook that someone gave me. But it suited. I covered it myself. It's the same fabric as that green chair in the garden room. The pink is this silk slub, too."

"I see," James said, nodding reassuringly. He'd already learned that when his mother spoke like this, it meant she was nervous. He opened the album.

Most of the photos were familiar. Copies, or similar shots, were in the photo albums at his father's house back in Melbourne. They were all of the four kids, doing typical kid things over the years: fooling around in the backyard, playing with pets, on holidays, in school plays. The earlier pictures were black and white, then color took over. Growing up: Deborah in a mini-skirt halfway up her thighs and an expression of studied sulkiness; the boys and their pals with soft beards and long hair—even Robert! Deborah and then Robert in their graduation gowns; some that James had sent home from his first overseas trip, to Southeast Asia. The last picture in the album was of Meredith in a volleyball uniform, skinny but athletic, her hair pulled back in a ponytail, triumphantly brandishing a trophy with the other girls from her team. Under each photo there were a few words of description, handwritten. James leafed through the pages, exclaiming here and there while Rose sat by him, watching. When he looked up he saw that she had grown melancholy.

"How did you get all these?" he asked gently.

"Alex sent them to me, usually in a bundle once a year. Around Christmas time. It was part of a . . . deal, I suppose, that we had. Or that I thought we had."

"But he didn't stick to that deal, did he? He didn't give us your letters."

"No. But I never knew that for sure. He *said* he did."

"It's so incredible," said James, starting to flip back through the photos with some agitation, as though he was looking for something. "Why didn't you, I don't know, write directly? To us kids?"

"Well, you'd moved, and he wouldn't give me the new home address. All the correspondence was via his office. The one in North Melbourne. I wrote care of that address for years and then my letters started coming back unopened. *Return to Sender*. So I suppose the office moved, too, and the redirection lapsed. Or just didn't happen. I don't know. And after that I suppose I . . . gave up."

James sat, staring at the open album but not seeing; his forehead was creased in puzzlement. He had forgotten his mother's sadness. *Are these just excuses?* he wondered.

"How come you just . . . *let him do that?*" he burst out. "I don't get it. I never would've thought Dad would *be* like that."

Rose looked even more downcast. "I know. Back then . . . how can I explain? For a mother to do what I did, to leave her children . . . It's still a shocking thing even these days. But *then*! In a way Alex was very civilized, really. I know a lot of people would've been happy to see me hung, drawn and quartered."

"But why didn't he think what it would do to *us*? Never to know *anything*?"

"What can I say, darling? Except that I'm sure he would've thought he was doing it for the best. He loved you, I know that; I knew he would take good care of you. Better than I could, the way I was." Suddenly James realized that Rose was close to tears. "And I had to be punished. Even *I* felt I had to be punished."

"Oh, Rose," cried James, stricken. *See: this is what happens when I push things!* "Don't feel like that! We can all go on from here, can't we? The others'll understand . . ."

"But why *should* they? You've been so wonderful, James, to forgive me as you have. But the others . . . Why would they even believe I tried to stay in touch, if Alex won't admit it?"

"I don't know. I think it must've been 'won't' with Dad for a long time," James said, his voice subdued. "He really did just shut down about you completely. But now, with this memory thing he's got . . ." He looked up at his mother, beseeching almost. "I really think it might be *'can't.'* He's repressed it all so long and now it's . . . gone."

"Well, can't or won't, it's too late now. Water long under the bridge," she said, sounding flat and drained. "At least he sent these photos."

"Yes. So you did know . . . something, at least, of what we were doing?"

"Something, yes. Precisely this much, in fact." Rose drew her fingertips several times over her face. He could see she was trying to control threatening tears. Push away the hurt. "Ah well," she said finally. Helplessly. "Ah well."

She took the album from him and put it back in its place on the shelf.

James went up to London on the train to meet Silver, who'd been busy with her own family in Chicago again. She'd booked them into a new boutique hotel, a small, charming, exquisitely expensive place which boasted "a thousand ways to say very, very special." James and Silver had become adept themselves, lately, at making each other feel like that.

Never, Silver thought, not even on their honeymoon, had they enjoyed this kind of romantic playfulness. And London seemed to share their mood: in its festive pre-Christmas gaiety, the city was more enchanting than she had ever known it. One evening, taking a breather betweens turns on the ice-skating rink in the courtyard of Somerset House, Silver leaned close to James and said, "My mom wanted to know how come I'm looking so, quote unquote, *gosh-darned gorgeous*. She says my Aunt Nancy wants the name of my plastic—sorry, *cosmetic* surgeon!"

James smiled. "Yeah? What'd you tell her?"

"I told her I was having an affair," Silver said, grinning wickedly.

"You *what*?"

"Yep. She nearly had a heart attack! I told her I was having an affair. With my husband!"

"Sil, you demon! Why'd you scare your mum like that? I really like your mum!"

"I know, honey. I just couldn't resist."

"I know the feeling," he said, sliding a hand stealthily inside her jacket and squeezing one of her breasts. Silver yelped, loud enough that several people turned and looked. "Oh," she murmured, butting his shoulder, "Just wait till I get you home!"

The next morning, damp and happy, they were in the bathroom together discussing Christmas gifts. Silver perched on the edge of the enormous bathtub, wrapped in a fluffy white hotel robe, and watched James in the mirror as he shaved. She loved observing this quintessentially masculine grooming ritual, and especially the dispassionate attention her husband paid to his own face as he performed it. He was wearing a pair of close-fitting boxer shorts in the softest white cotton, nothing else, and she thought the view was magnificently distracting. But she was trying to pay attention, because she could hear in his voice how excited James was at spending Christmas Day with his mother.

"I was only seven the last time I gave her a Christmas present, isn't that amazing? I never got to give her that last one, you know, the Christmas she left."

"So what will you give her this time?" asked his wife. *Oh my, don't he look goood!* She rolled the words around inside her mouth, her mind, like a piece of chocolate. There was a sensuous luxury to everything these days.

"I'm giving her . . . two presents, actually," James answered. His sentences were oddly truncated as he attended to his shaving, turning his face this way and that and poking his tongue into a cheek. "Neither very grand though. One's a little tiny . . . pair of scissors, you know, for snipping thread with . . . A German company makes them . . . Roland told me . . . she misplaced her last pair and she's been making do with some others that aren't as good." He rinsed the razor, tapping it against the side of the basin, and glanced at her sideways. "He knows I'm getting them, so there won't be *two* new pairs the same!"

"Sounds perfect. Very practical." Silver waited for James to go on, but he just kept shaving. After a little while she asked, "And the second one?"

"Oh. Well, I'm picking that up today, actually, from the framer who does everything for Goldie's gallery." His eyes met hers in the mirror. "It's a drawing."

"One of yours?"

"Yep," he nodded, and looked down, rinsing his razor again, unnecessarily. Still gazing at the foamy, stubble-flecked water in the basin he said, "It's a drawing I did when I was nine; a self-portrait, actually." He glanced at her again. "I always wanted to give it to her; I used to imagine giving it to her. What she'd say."

It was on the tip of Silver's tongue to ask, *And what did you imagine she'd say?*, but she realized she didn't need to ask. What could that little boy have wanted to hear but words of praise and love, of reassurance? She knew those words already.

"You kept that drawing all this time?"

"Yeah. What do you think, Sil? Is it too . . . I dunno . . . cute, or something? Big-eyed puppy thing?"

She rose, standing behind her husband to put her arms around him, resting the side of her face on the back of his neck.

"No," she told him. "It's not big-eyed puppy. It's wonderful."

"Maybe. Yeah, I reckon Rose'll like it." *What if Deb knew?* he asked himself suddenly. It was a sobering thought. *She'd kill me!*

As if she'd read his mind, Silver raised her head and looked at him in the mirror again. Her voice was serious. "Honey, you have *got* to tell Deborah. And the others. It's getting to be almost . . . dangerous. They'll feel like you've *cheated* on them, you know?"

James turned and put his arms around her, drawing her to him. Just at that moment, he didn't want to meet her gaze. "It's okay, sweetheart," he said with seeming confidence. "Really it is. I've talked to Rose about it. It's better not to rush this. I'll find the right time soon, don't worry."

Silver considered pulling back from his embrace and taking this further, maybe even getting him to make that call to Deborah now, today. *Once upon a time,* she thought, *once upon a time just a few months ago, I wouldn't have let it get to this.* But now things had shifted. Silver let herself relax, her body responding to his caress. Even if this was a mistake . . . well, James could make mistakes, and she could let him, because they were his own mistakes to make. And he was a person of enough substance to handle whatever happened. She rubbed her face like a cat does, satisfied, demanding, proprietorial, against his chest.

James felt his penis stir lazily, thickening against the gentle pressure of his underpants, pressing against Silver's belly. *God, how did we live without this for so long?* He wrapped one finger in a lock of her shoulder-length hair and tugged softly, and she made a soft little growl low in her throat. But even as he started to drift into erotic absorption, James was sideswiped by another unwelcome thought: *You're scared of telling the others: you're scared of Deb. You're a coward; you've always been a coward.* His mind flinched from this, just at the moment Silver tilted her face and touched her lips to his.

All these years, she had known they were compatible. But she had not thought James desired her, loved her for her self. Passionately. Now it was as though a door had opened and they'd walked through it, hand in hand, into this rich and wonderful realm. *How could I have believed that wanting sex would ruin it all!*

She had thought that when he fell in love completely, it would be with someone else. And now he had chosen her. Finally, fully. He drew her plain happy face toward him, this beautiful husband of hers, and kissed her with a searching intensity, parting her lips. *This,* thought Silver, *is my own private miracle.*

When James gave Rose the drawing on Christmas morning, she burst into tears. Happy tears, but plenty of them.

"Oh, James," she sobbed, "you have no idea! How much I *longed* to have one of your drawings!"

"Well, now you've got one," he said, a bit embarrassed. Rose held the picture up and kissed the glass! He laughed, but it felt good to see this little drawing of his, in its innocence, lay a healing touch on the pain that had torn at them both, deep down, where the world couldn't see.

Rose's gift to Silver took everyone by surprise: a floor-length dress with deep sleeves and a swooping neckline, featuring a pattern that was both organic and geometric, in warm earthy tones lifted with medallions of gold embroidery.

"Wow!" Silver exclaimed as she held it up.

"Do you like it?" Rose asked nervously, hands clasped tightly before her as she watched. Silver threw her an awed look.

"It's *amazing*," James said. "Did you make this? When?"

"Nineteen seventy three," his mother answered promptly. "Alhambra. That's what we called that range. I always loved this one."

"But I've *seen* this dress," said Silver, whose visual memory was almost as acute as James's. "Or one incredibly like it. At MoMA in New York, in that big exhibition of contemporary fashion a couple of years ago."

"Yes, I saw the catalogue. And you're right, they had this piece in it," said Rose, very pleased. "In the seventies it would've been called a caftan, but caftans tended to be cut a little meanly for my taste. I felt a robe like this should have fullness and sweep."

"My mother," said James, "has been shown at MoMA." He gazed at her with a cow-eyed expression of adoration, and Rose giggled.

"You designed this here, in England?" Silver asked. "Were you working in London then?"

"Yes," James put in, "tell us what you did after you got here." *The missing years.*

"Oh, where to begin?" Rose said. "Well: jobs weren't hard to come by, that's for sure: there were new boutiques opening every day. I talked my way into one called 'Empress,' which was *the* shop at the time, and from sales I moved into the design and management side. After a couple of years I was Erica Lambden's right-hand girl. Lord, I worked hard though!"

"Was she your, you know, mentor?" James asked.

"Erica? Heavens, no! Erica was a spoiled bitch, frankly, and mean as cat's pee. Once cocaine came in she became completely impossible!" Rose laughed, shaking her head as she remembered. "But I shouldn't speak too badly of her, she did give me a free rein with design—as long as she could take the credit. And she introduced me to Rachel Isaacs. Now Rachel, *she* was my mentor."

"She was a designer, too?" asked Silver.

"Oh, Rachel's family had been in the rag trade for generations. In Europe. We met when Erica and I went to Spain: Erica was there for *inspiration*, I was there to run around after her. But that was how the Alhambra range happened."

"Ibiza," said Roland, who had been listening while his big hands quickly and delicately shelled an enormous quantity of fresh peas.

"Yes," Rose agreed. "Rachel poached me from the Empress Erica and set me up with a fabulous boutique in Ibiza. She had the idea of using antique lingerie to make new things. Sounds almost passé now but she was the first. And she knew Ibiza in the seventies was the perfect place for it."

"I'll bet Erica was sorry to lose you, once she knew you were leaving," Silver said.

Rose snorted. "Hah! Erica didn't have a clue! Rachel came to London for the Alhambra launch and stole me right out from under Erica Lambden's coked-up little nose! I walked away that night, without a backward glance."

Something happened: a subtle change in James's expression, a slight shift in Silver's body language. Rose caught it, and thought, *What's that?*

"So-o," James said, stretching, getting up from his chair. "Can I give you a hand with anything, Roland? When does Jacinta arrive?"

It wasn't only the beautiful fifteen-year-old Jacinta who joined them for Christmas dinner but Jacinta's mother, a good-humored music teacher named Molly, and Molly's partner, and their five-year-old son. Plus Jacinta's riding instructor and her elderly father. Ten of them around the big table, with a whole roast goose and all the trimmings, and plenty of mulled wine. The gathering got noisier as the afternoon went on till by the time the Christmas pudding was brought flaming to the table, the din was enormous. James didn't hear his mobile phone ringing, but he felt the vibration in his pocket and hauled it out.

"Hello!" he shouted into it. "Merry Christmas!"

"Merry Christmas, Jaffa," said Deborah's voice.

He stiffened as though someone had grabbed him by the back of the neck.

"You sound like you're having a good time. Where are you?"

James thrust his chair aside and stumbled to the door. "I—I," he said, and then he was in the relative quiet of the living room, the door firmly closed behind him. "I'm just at some friends'. In the country."

"Silver's there?"

"Yeah, of course," he said. "I guess you've done Christmas, right? What time is it there?"

"About three a-bloody-m. I couldn't sleep, so I thought I'd give you a ring."

"Great, ta," James said. He was talking on auto-pilot. "So, how was yours?"

"Oh, not bad I guess, considering we were at Robert and Vesna's. They gave everyone *handmade* presents."

"Nice," he managed.

"Yeah, just what I needed, a pair of gingham-covered photo frames." Deborah laughed sharply. "With lace."

The door opened suddenly and all the racket of the dining room burst in. Rose appeared, asking loudly, "We're making coffee, James, will you have some?"

"Sure!" he cried, squashing the open mobile to his chest. "Be back in a tick!" Rose nodded, smiling, and the door closed again.

"Sorry, Deb," he said.

"Who was that?" Deborah asked.

"Friend of ours. Ah . . ." *Should I lie?* he thought desperately. *Make up a name?*

"God, that voice sounded familiar. Someone I've met?"

James felt like he might faint. "No, don't think so," he said. "English friends. People we've met here."

They talked a little while longer and said their good-byes. James rejoined the party feeling as though he'd just avoided a nasty car accident.

"Everything okay?" Silver asked him quietly. He nodded and squeezed her hand. Then he took his phone out again and turned it off, just in case.

Lying in bed that night, the house restored to order, Rose murmured to Roland, "I think that was one of the loveliest Christmases we've ever had, don't you?" And Roland sleepily agreed.

But after he'd fallen asleep Rose lay there, thinking about that odd little moment before the meal when she had sensed James's momentary withdrawal from her. *What was it we were talking about?* she asked herself, and rebuilt the conversation. The dress, the MoMA exhibition, Erica nutcase Lambden . . . Had she sounded like she was showing off? Or smug? Oh, if only they knew! She hadn't just worked hard back then, she'd been exploited. Twelve- and fifteen-hour days, hardly a day off, for ridiculous pay, and Erica's terrifying tantrums to deal with . . . And she'd told them about Rachel (*Ah, dear Rachel!* Rose still missed her) and the

Ibiza boutique . . . That was hard work, too, it hadn't just been handed to her on a plate. And she had hit middle age there, surrounded by dewy hippie chicks and glamorous blow-ins spoiled for choice. She remembered with a blush of humiliation even now, thirty years later, that semi-famous musician she'd gone to bed with once who lost his erection after he'd taken her bra off, his contemptuous "I can't screw a bird with floppy tits!" She had never confided that to a soul. How grateful she was that her children would never know of the idiotic things she'd done in the promiscuous, drug-addled seventies. *Carefree? No, we were careless, that's all. We had no idea how to care about anything.*

Then a single sentence from that pre-dinner conversation froze her. *I walked away that night without a backward glance.*

How could she have said that, so blithely! To James, whom she had also walked away from, without a backward glance.

That's what she'd done to her parents, too, when she was seventeen: packed up and moved on forever virtually overnight, and there'd been nothing they could do about it. She'd done it to Alex and the children thirteen years later, when she couldn't bear that life a moment longer. Just walked out. And in London, once she'd taken what she could from Erica Lambden, and got a better offer. And again with that perfectly pleasant Dutch chap Bart she'd been living with (for five years! think of that!) when the whole Ibiza thing became stale and jaded . . .

She put her hands to her face, covering her eyes, as she thought with sudden painful clarity, *That's what I've always done!* She felt overwhelmed with horror. All the ghastly messes she'd left behind, again and again.

But I will never, never leave Roland. This popped unbidden into her mind, this rock of truth. Her rock. Roland.

Every time she'd felt held back, she had blamed other people. Thought they must be discarded, like an old coat. It had taken her such a long time to get beyond that; to grow up. It was Roland who kept her steady in the world now. Not about to fly off! Not any more.

And James. Already he was such a precious part of her life. Would that happen again, more and more perhaps, once she got to know her other children, too? Was she really going to have that chance again?

part four

CHapter 16

Olivia's secondary school was three times the size of her old primary, which meant three times as many kids to deal with. Twelve hundred individual cases of mutual bafflement. On the very first day she stood at the edge of the quadrangle feeling assaulted by the tumult, wondering how on earth she was going to get through even a week of this, let alone six years, when a girl walked up to her. She was a fairly small girl with almost white-blonde hair and an old-fashioned sort of face, not sweet-and-pretty old-fashioned but solemn, long, like a medieval painting, and in a cool self-possessed way, without smiling, she said, "You look interesting. What's your name?"

"Olivia Hume," said Olivia.

"I'm Fleur," the blonde girl said. "Hansen," she added. She tilted her head slightly to one side. "Olivia," she said consideringly. "Oh-liv-ee-ah." She looked up at the sky, and back again. "That's an awful lot of syllables for just six letters. Don't you think?"

"I get called Ol. Or Ollie."

Fleur made a face. "Oh no! You can't go through life as *Ollie*! It makes you sound like a cartoon character. A fat one. Which you are not."

Actually, come to think of it, she was right. It was a crap nick-name, and probably time for a change. "So what do you suggest, Fleur Hansen?"

"Let's see . . ." Fleur clasped her hands in front of her face, rest-ing the bridge of her nose on her interlocked fingers. She looked a bit like a saint praying. Then she lowered her hands and nodded. "As a name for teachers to use, Olivia is fine. To be read out at assembly, or written, or printed, Olivia Hume is perfectly acceptable. It has poise, it has dignity. *Ollie*, on the other hand," and here she held her right hand up at face level and used a pinched thumb and forefinger to pick up the offending diminutive and dump it in an imaginary rubbish bin, "is ugly, goofy, and gone."

"And with those few words," Olivia observed, "the companion of her childhood years was banished from her life forever."

"Correct. And from the chrysalis into which the ugly caterpillar had disappeared there emerged the dazzling butterfly—*Liv*."

"Liv. Liver?"

"Puh-lease! Liv has an upward quality. Leaping." Fleur's small pale hand gracefully indicated this. "Almost weightless. *Liv*. Liv Tyler springs to mind. *Lord of the Rings*: elven princess, valiant and beau-tiful *and* she gets the guy. This is impeccable. You can't complain about Liv."

"Am I complaining? I hardly know her."

"That will come, my friend, that will come."

My friend. The words gave Olivia a little jolt. Had she ever heard them before, applied to her? Not that she could think of. A friend. A new name. *Why not?* She liked this girl, the look of her and the way she talked like she was reading from a book, almost, but not stiff like that. And she was not sarcastic, but . . . *sardonic*, that was it. She'd heard her mum say that approvingly, *a sardonic sense of humor.* Olivia liked all of that. *This could be good,* she thought. *This could be excellent.*

———

To Robert's surprise, being the principal was both easier and more pleasant than being the vice-principal. He'd dreaded saying good-bye completely to classroom teaching, but he found he didn't miss it at all. When Robert had first gone into teaching he'd talked about having "a vocation to imbue children with a love of learning," but over the years he'd come to realize that in fact he'd decided to become a teacher because he loved schoolwork. He'd enjoyed teaching, certainly, but now he found that the work of running the school was just as satisfying; more so, if anything. How odd, that it should be the paperwork he loved.

He had been so anxious about whether he was up to the promotion, but once in the job he found it refreshingly unequivocal to be the acknowledged leader of the school community. As vice principal he'd had to keep a foot in every camp: the students, the parents, his fellow teachers, the various committees and administrating bodies. The first port of call for anyone with a problem. Robert's new role protected him from a great deal of time-consuming petty bickering between factions. It was much easier to just get on with things. Privately he rather wished that the old-fashioned title still stood: he had always been a little in awe of the unabashed arrogance of "head" combined with "master." A little like "Superman." He kept to himself the thought that it was a pity the title had had to change to the non-gender specific "principal," because he knew it was a good thing. Progress!

And it *was* progress, too. Robert was aware that the appointment of a male principal could be seen as a conservative move these days, one which might well cause resentment among the overwhelmingly female staff, and among a number of the parents, too. He had sought the advice of Vesna, who as a senior nurse was adept at handling institutional tension between male and female authority, and that of certain trusted colleagues. Carefully then, he set about the work of consulting and reassuring, making it clear that his awareness of these issues was comprehensive, and that gender equity would be addressed more thoroughly than ever under his leadership. Yes, *his* leadership, that was made clear, too.

A few weeks into the new school year, Robert knew that his appointment was now widely popular. The school community had breathed a collective sigh of relief and patted itself on the back. At last, he told himself, he could relax. *Just relax,* he thought, as he completed his end-of-day tour of the school late on a Friday afternoon, checking each empty classroom and office. *Settle in to the job.*

He re-entered the cluster of offices, checking them one after another. He'd made it a rule never to turn off someone else's computer, no matter how great the urge, but by now most of the administrative staff knew him so well that they humored him and turned their own computers off completely at the end of the day. A last round—and there! In the room which used to be his, the vice-principal's office, a skinny black tail emerging from under a pile of folders, a lead running to . . . a mobile phone! Long since finished recharging. *Hah!* Robert found the VP's home number on his own mobile and rang her.

"Bettina? Robert McDonald here. Yes, everything's fine. Just locking up the offices and spotted your mobile phone here on your desk. Yes, thought you might have. Yes, that's fine, we'll be home, just doing pizza and videos tonight, you know, TGIF and all that. No problem. See you then, Bettina. Bye."

You see? Eternal vigilance! He wished for a jury before whom he could flourish this vindicating piece of evidence. He put Bettina's mobile, with its charging unit, in his briefcase. And while he had it open, best to check the contents again: let's see, his day-to-a-page diary, a few pieces of paperwork, a couple of notes from staff, some curriculum items for consideration. Featherlight, these days, his briefcase! All thanks to technology, there on its cord around his neck, weighing so little you couldn't even be sure it was there without checking (so he checked): the USB key drive to transfer files between computers. *Marvelous gadget!*

The buoyant sense of achievement that finding the mobile phone had given him lasted Robert nearly all the way home. It wasn't until he'd turned into his own street that a sneering internal voice intruded: *So what? So* what *if Bettina's mobile had sat there all weekend? Do you honestly think the sky would've fallen in?* His shoulders actually slumped; he felt physically deflated. *Oh, you are pathetic!*

At home, though, his mood was quickly restored. His daughters leaped on him as though he'd been away for a month. He hugged them happily. He and Vesna often talked about this, how lovely it was to have children who still enjoyed the company of their parents, and how they as parents must relish it, every minute, *now*, before the indifference (or worse) of adolescence changed things! Robert loved his domestic life, loved the way he and Vesna discussed every detail and apportioned the tasks and the responsibilities; he even loved the tasks themselves, right down to the pot-scrubbing and the lawn-mowing. Friday was their traditional relax-at-home night, so now there were Alexa's and Bianca's rival shortlists of preferred DVDs for the evening's viewing to adjudicate on, then he made a simple salad while Vesna went through pizza choices and rang to order them. She came and sat beside him at the living room table, where the girls had put out the plates and cutlery and he was catching up with some stories in the paper.

"Quick run-through of the weekend?" she suggested.

"I think I've got the schedule, darling" he said. "Tomorrow, lunch with your family at Taylor's Lakes, right?"

"Yes, after I take the girls' shopping for a present for Mum. And I'm getting them some new underwear, and socks."

"Jolly good. And they're sleeping over at Joseph and Dana's, that's on the calendar, too. You're on afternoon shift tomorrow," he said, stroking her hand, resting beside his on the newspaper. "Sunday I wouldn't mind going to the nursery. I've been thinking some little white correas would look good in that new section of the rockery, what do you think?"

"I think that would be lovely. And, something for Sunday afternoon."

"Oh? Not on the calendar yet?" Robert's fingertips started rubbing gently on his palms. What a good feeling that was, the dry susurration of clean skin on skin.

"Not yet. I spoke to your father today. I think it would be nice for us all to go and see him. Maybe I could make a cake with the girls, take it over there for afternoon tea. Is that okay with you?"

"Of course!" He looked at her enquiringly, noting for the ten thousandth time how her clear brown eyes were magnified by her thick glasses, so that they seemed to extend beyond the boundaries of her face. He liked that effect, he felt it reflected the openness and generosity of his wife's personality. "How did he sound? Do you think he's all right?"

"Oh yes. He sounded fine." She patted his thigh reassuringly and stood up. "Just thought it'd be nice to see him."

Robert's fingers stopped their movement, he let his hands relax. *Yes, that's it, just relax.* Everything was fine and he was managing perfectly well. There was no need for him to see his doctor, certainly no need for Vesna to know that his little habits had not abated, had become if anything a tad more demanding. *I just need to relax. Settle into the job, that's all. Everything's all right.*

Meredith's old blue Corona was parked in the street outside Alex's house.

"Oh, that's nice, Merry's here!" said Robert. "Did you organize this, darling?"

Vesna shook her head and shrugged her lack of prior knowledge. She was smiling, knowing how much pleasure it gave her husband when they got together with his younger sister, *all my girls,* as he would be bound to say at some point. As they opened the gate into the front garden Robert glanced at the carport and stopped suddenly, dismayed.

"Oh dear—Dad's car. I must follow up with his GP on what's happening with his driver's license. It's been months now, hasn't it?"

But Vesna's attention was on the figures standing in the living room looking out at them through the picture window, waving. She waved back enthusiastically.

"Look, girls, there's Grandpa and Auntie Meredith! Wave!"

In the flurry of greetings Vesna surmised that Alex had completely forgotten the arrangement they had made by phone. He was embarrassed, but smoothing over that little awkwardness was made all the easier by Meredith's happy presence.

"Hello, you gorgeous, gorgeous things!" Meredith said, kissing her young nieces. "Phew! Daddy was determined to clean every window in the place! We've been at it like demons for *hours*."

"Must be years since I last gave 'em a clean!" said Alex jovially. He put his arm around Meredith's shoulders and gave her a little hug. "What would I do without this little girl, eh?"

"Lost without me, you'd be!" she chirped, rising onto her tiptoes to give him a kiss on the cheek.

"Good for you, Merry!" said Robert. "The windows look terrific, like a TV ad for—something. Window cleaner!"

"Mummy made an apple tea cake, and I helped her!" announced Alexa.

"I helped with the sandwiches! Have you still got those chookies, Grandpa?" asked Bianca, taking her grandfather's hand and hauling him toward the back door.

"No, sweetheart, I don't, I'm afraid bad old Mr. Fox saw to that. But I'm thinking of getting some more soon. Why don't you girls come and look at the chook house with me and we'll see how we can make it stronger?"

"I'll put these things in the kitchen and get the kettle on," said Vesna. Meredith and Robert were suddenly the only two in the living room. The stillness seemed to ring. Meredith slumped onto the couch like a dropped doll.

"*Oof.* I'm absolutely knackered. And I've got to go to work in a few hours."

"Huge job. It's so good you could make the time to give him a hand," said Robert. "Gee, he's keeping the place up well though, isn't he? Better than before, almost."

"Almost," agreed Meredith, patting the seat beside her. "Sit down a minnie, Bobbit."

He sat. "Actually, I was just thinking about something as I came in," he said, and his fingertips started touching each other in their quick silent rhythm. "Dad's car. They said he shouldn't be driving, and I've just realized I haven't followed up on that."

"It's okay, he hardly drives at all these days," his sister said, and laid her hand gently on one of his. "You still do that, don't you?"

"Only sometimes," Robert said, sliding his hands under his thighs so that he was almost sitting on them. "Not much."

"Deborah still goes on about it. Why the hell does it bug her so much?"

"I don't know. I guess because it bothered Mum."

"Did it? I didn't know that." Meredith thrust her legs out straight in front of her. "Or maybe because she's just such a bossy cow," she suggested, lips thin.

"That's interesting: did you know that 'Bossy' was a common name for a house cow in the old days? As in, 'Bossy cow bonnie, let down your milk, And I will give you a gown of silk.'"

"What's that, an old nursery rhyme?" asked Meredith. She was resting her head on the back of the couch, smiling at him. She loved having Robert teach her things.

"Yes. It's in a little book of rhymes I used to read to the girls."

"It's sweet. I'll think of it every time I see Deborah now!" she said mischievously. They both laughed, sniggered really.

"Oh, don't be too hard on her, sisterling," said Robert. "She's got a lot on her plate. She can't help it."

"She *could* help it!" burst out Meredith, pouting now. "She could change, couldn't she?"

"Could she, Merry? I don't know. We've all got things we *could* change, and *should* change, but can we? Any of us?"

"Maybe not. I don't know," said Meredith gloomily, and sighed. They were quiet for a moment or two, and then she started in a sing-song voice, "We *could* have . . . We *should* have . . . We *might* have . . ."

"But we didn't!" they chorused together, and laughed.

"Come on," said Robert, using Meredith's knee to lever himself to his feet. "Let's have a nice cup of tea, shall we?"

"Gosh you sound like Daddy sometimes," said Meredith, following him. "A nice cup of tea. It's the answer to everything."

CHAPTER 17

Once he and Silver returned to Melbourne in the new year, James had been determined to really try to find his mother's letters. Yet the days and then the weeks passed by and still he'd made no attempt. He wasn't even sure how to go about it. He could ask Alex about them directly, but what if his father denied they'd ever existed? How could he then persist in looking for them? Better to search first. But since (judging by what he'd seen on his first attempt) everything in his father's house was in such disarray, where should he begin? He was unreasonably nervous. The whole thing felt horribly like prying to him, *snooping,* and James was not by nature a snoop.

Finally he visited, to find that all the mess and muddle was gone. Alex told him proudly that Meredith had done a grand job of spring-cleaning. Meredith happened to be there when he dropped in; she looked rather uncomfortable at Alex's praise but quickly showed James, still feigning interest in their family tree, precisely where she'd stored all the records and correspondence.

"It's all there, I haven't thrown anything out," she assured him a little defensively as he carried the big plastic storage box into the living room and put it on the table. "Not a thing! It's all just been sorted and rearranged."

Meredith, James realized as he looked, really had done a terrific job. There was everything from shipboard journals from an emigrating great-great-grandfather, to title deeds for houses long since sold, to Alex's university graduation certificate, to their own school reports. On that first visit James spent hours looking, getting stalled again and again as he came across some fascinating piece of memorabilia, and he'd still barely gone through the first box of three that his sister had indicated. He would have to come back.

A few more weeks went by before he came again. This time his father volunteered to help, sitting in a chair beside him at the dining table, a second plastic box unlidded before them. Almost the first thing James laid his hand to was an envelope from a law firm in North Melbourne. "Campbell, Auchterlonie and Bridge, Barristers and Solicitors," he read aloud.

Alex leaned forward. "I remember them," he said. He took the envelope from James and opened it. There was a typewritten letter and then the document: the final divorce decree ending his marriage to Rosemarie Anne, nee Bartlett.

"Wow," said James, awestruck. "The actual divorce papers." He craned to look at the document in his father's hands. Familiar only with modern no-fault divorce, he noted with a shock that there were grounds sworn. *Adultery.* Rose's adultery.

Alex was staring at the sheets of paper, shuffling back and forth between the decree, the bland covering letter, the envelope they'd been in. He shook his head. "Terrible steps," he said.

"Yes," James agreed quietly. "It must have been a very hard thing."

"Why do people *do* things like that?" Alex asked. His voice sounded both perplexed and fierce. James shook his head, not knowing what to say, and having no way of knowing that Alex was referring to the actual office of Campbell, Auchterlonie and Bridge.

Oh, Alex could see it now! On his final visit there, he had thought for a moment he must have taken a wrong turn, or walked perhaps a block too far. Then he realized that he was in the right place after all, but the building itself had changed. It was still *there*, yes, but the Victorian facade had completely disappeared! The pair of long sash windows, their handsome timber trims painted and repainted a score of times over the hundred years since the place had been built— gone. The mellow, meticulously laid brickwork had vanished, too, except for a couple of narrow strips. All replaced by an enormous plate-glass window, framed in bright aluminium. Behind it, shielding the people in the office from the gaze of passers-by, hung floor-length venetian blinds, off-white with little bright specks on them that caught the light.

Alex had literally flinched. This sort of thing was happening everywhere, but it grieved him sorely. The replacement of real crafts-manship with things that looked like they'd been knocked together by monkeys, not a shred of skill or aesthetic sensibility. He moved at last, reluctantly, toward the front door. But it, too, with its ornate wood panels, its brass knocker and name-plate, was gone. And to even reach the bland glass sheet that had replaced it he had to navi-gate two steps, dreadful steps, both much too narrow and the lower one far taller than the one above. Alex had been an engineer all his working life, helping to design and build new structures, and he was proud of what he did, but this stuff was just . . . rubbish.

"It was just *rubbish*, son," he said to James now, angrily. "Absolutely criminal!"

"Oh, Dad," James said, feeling overwhelmed. His father had never spoken of the divorce before, let alone of his feelings about it. "I'm sorry!"

Alex seemed to recover himself somewhat. "Not your fault, boy," he said. "No one had any sense back then, that's the thing." He pat-ted James's forearm. "Well, I might make a spot of lunch, what d'you say?"

"Sure, Dad. Sure. Do you want a hand?"

Alex shook his head, levered himself up from the chair. For the first time James saw his father as he now was: old, his long frame stiff and bony, his expression a little lost. His heart clenched, thinking of that unpleasant diagnosis. Then his father grinned and gave James's shoulder a couple of hearty pats. "Don't take it to heart now. Life goes on!"

James nodded hard, but he was too choked up to say anything.

His father didn't come back to look through any more of the papers after lunch. James was quite glad of that: it had made the whole thing even more difficult than he'd anticipated. Easier to look by himself. He got through that box, and the third and final one Meredith had indicated. There were many things of interest, but no letters from Rose. Not a single one. He went outside to where his father was sitting in the shade, leafing through last weekend's paper.

"Still here?" Alex said brightly. "Like to stay for tea?"

"Nah, I should get home. Thanks. But, Dad, there was something I wanted to ask you . . ."

His father raised his eyebrows enquiringly, and James screwed his courage to the sticking place.

"You know after Mum left, when we were kids . . ."

"Yes?"

"Well, I was wondering . . . I thought she might've written us some letters. Do you know where they'd be?"

Alex shook his head. "Meredith's sorted all that out."

"I know, I've looked, but I can't find them. This would've been quite a while ago, Dad. Letters from Mum, from England."

"Oh," his father said. "Letters from your mother . . ." He looked thoughtful, and James felt a sudden little leap of hope, but then he shook his head. "No, I don't know about that. You'd have to ask Deborah. She took care of things when you were kids. She was the oldest, you know."

"Yes, Dad, I know."

And so, finally, having searched everywhere he could think of and having found nothing, James decided that he couldn't put it off any longer. It was time to tell Deborah that he had found their mother. Naturally she must be the first of his siblings to know, he didn't question that for a moment.

chapter 18

When James rang inviting her down to the beach house at Sorrento for the Labor Day long weekend, Deborah's first impulse was to brush his invitation aside. *Too busy, always too busy.* But this time she bit the words back.

"You know, Jaf," she said instead, slowly, "that just might be doable. I'm looking at the diary and there's nothing horrific the week after. And it could be just the thing we . . . hmm. When do you need to know by?"

"Oh, no great rush. Next week, say? Ollie's invited, too, naturally. Any of her little pals, if she wants to bring someone."

"Olivia doesn't have 'little pals,' I can assure you, and there's some school camp thing then, too. But thanks, James, you're a honey. I'll confirm in a day or so."

She put it to Angus that evening, over dinner. She had booked a table at a nearby restaurant, somewhere they used to go fairly often, and then rang him at work to surprise him with the news. "We're having a date tonight, with each other!" It was too long since she'd done this sort of thing, made the effort to get home in time to dress up a bit, to go out not to some political function—just to have a date with her husband.

They were having a good time, too. The food was regional Italian and excellent, and there was lots to talk about, to Deborah's relief; she had realized, getting ready, that she wasn't sure whether Angus was much interested in her work these days, the fine detail of policy, the machinations of life in government. But he asked all the right questions, and she even asked him about *his* work and the people in that little community legal office where he seemed content to while away the years. Her questions didn't sound at all forced, she thought. Over coffee, she told him about James's invitation.

"It's your favorite weekend to get away, I know. I remember how disappointed you were when I couldn't come with you to that school reunion this time last year."

"Actually that was the end of March, not the beginning," said Angus.

"Was it? Whatever. Point is, we'll have a lovely time, darling. The weather will be perfect, and Sorrento's the best place on the Peninsula, don't you think? And we haven't spent time with James and Silver in I don't know how long."

"Maybe. Let me think about it, hey, Deb?" he said, throwing her a placating smile.

"*Think about it?* For heaven's sake, Angus!" Her voice, although she didn't know it, was rising. "You're *always* on at me about how I'm working too hard! I propose a getaway to a great place at the best time of year, and you want to *think about it?* What's there to think about? It's perfect! Isn't it?"

"Sure!" he said, holding up both hands. "It's a terrific idea, of course. It's just that some guys I caught up with last year at the reunion are going to be in town, and we had plans to get together, you know, have a few drinks. We might even check out the Grand Prix, you never know."

Deborah reared back in her chair, her eyes exaggeratedly wide to signal her astonishment. "*Check out the Grand Prix?* Angus, what on earth are you talking about? You *hate* the Grand Prix!"

Angus's face went suddenly quite cold. "Do I? Well, thanks for telling me, Deborah. Because otherwise I just wouldn't know what I might like. Or not like."

"Well, you—"

"Look, why don't *you* go down to Sorrento with your brother and his wife? Maybe I just need a bit of space."

Deborah sat back in her chair, too startled to speak. They paid the bill and left the restaurant in silence. In her mind Deborah heard the words spoken by one of the women at a boozy girls' lunch she'd been part of just a couple of weeks before. The conversation had turned to marriages and the difficulty of maintaining them, and this woman had drawled, "When a man says 'I need some space,' it means just one thing: 'I'm having an affair.'" Oh, but not Angus. Never Angus!

In bed that night, the silence continued. Then in a rush Deborah rolled toward him, leaning on one elbow, and said, "Angus, I'm really sorry. I just *assumed* you'd want to come to Sorrento. I should have asked properly, what you wanted and all that. I'm sorry. But I really, *really* would like to do this. I really would like us to . . . get together again. More."

Angus lifted a hand up to her face. He looked sad.

"I'm sorry too, Deb. I didn't mean to snap at you like that. I'll come with you, of course I will. The people from the reunion . . . we'll get together another time."

"Thank you, darling." She leaned down and kissed him. "Thank you. We need this, don't we?"

"Yeah, I guess we do. This. Something."

Olivia went off reluctantly to her school camp, having roped in Laurence to feed the animals. Twice she asked her mother to take Mintie and Fly-by to Sorrento: they would love it so much. But Deborah refused. She said she didn't think dogs were allowed at the house, and besides, they were better value being on duty as burglar deterrents at home. Angus gave Olivia a lift to school on the Friday, since she had a pack full of gear for the camp, and saw her face clench when she caught sight of the bus surrounded by her milling classmates. *Shit, she's not at all happy,* he thought, and realized with a pang that he had hardly paid a moment's attention to his daughter's transition to high school.

"You okay, Ol?" he asked.

"Fleur's grandmother just died. She's not coming," said Olivia shortly, as though that explained everything.

"Oh. That's a shame," said her father, realizing with alarm that he had no idea who she was talking about. *Now she's got two parents who are completely preoccupied, poor kid.* He felt ashamed of his ignorance, but now was not the time to confess it. He swore to himself that when they got back from this long weekend he would spend more time with her, *no matter what.*

On the drive down to Sorrento, Deborah, unusually alert to Angus's mood, asked him tentatively why he was so quiet. He described how Ollie had looked that morning, what she'd said. They talked about their daughter at some length, in the comradely manner that had once been the tone of all their interaction. Now it felt both familiar and yet a little strange, like putting on a once-favorite piece of clothing that hadn't been worn for a long time. Did it still fit? They couldn't tell.

Once they reached Sorrento, though, they started to unwind. The house was no show-off; from the outside it still looked like a beach shack; inside it was well equipped but comfortable. Nestled amid the native coastal shrubs of ti-tree and banksias, it was all the more relaxing for the lack of big views. James and Silver welcomed them ebulliently, and Deborah felt a warm rush of pleasure. That first night they all hung out in the kitchen making dinner together and got through several bottles of wine, even James throwing sobriety to the winds. Then they played poker, increasingly badly, and laughed a lot and teased each other. Deborah kept looking at her brother and sister-in-law. There was definitely something different about them: what was it? There, in the way James and Silver looked at each other, the way they touched, easily and yet with a certain relish. *God, they're . . . hot!* Deborah realized, and at the same moment Angus saw it, too, and thought, *Those two are like new lovers.* It was that plain, if you knew them, and that different. *What were they doing before, then?* they each wondered. And Deborah thought of how her sex life with Angus had dwindled over the past . . . how long? Months, for sure. Years maybe. And Angus thought of Marion. With longing.

The next morning, Saturday, they all got up predictably late and uniformly seedy, and had a slow, quiet brunch. Early in the afternoon Deborah announced she was going for a good long walk. Anyone want to join her? James said he needed to go for a swim; Angus and Silver elected to just lie around and read the papers.

"Okay. Jaf, later this arvo, after you get back, I really want to talk to you about Dad, okay?"

"Sure. Actually there's stuff I need to talk with you about, too, Deb. Don't let me forget, hey?"

"Hint?" she asked, but her brother shook his head, smiling.

Only five minutes after she'd set off on her walk, Deborah realized her new trainers were rubbing badly on one heel, she'd have to go back and change into her old ones. On the sandy track near the house, on a curve shielded by scrub, she paused.

Angus was at their car, squatting down beside the open driver's door, fumbling under the seat. He retrieved something, stood up. A mobile phone. He was keying a number in; he was talking. Her footsteps were noiseless on the sandy soil. He was so intent on his conversation that she came just a couple of meters away from him, and stopped.

"I will, I will," he was saying. And then, fervently, "I love you, too. I love you, too."

Angus pressed the key to end the call, half-turned and saw her. He reared back. "*Fuck!* What are you doing here?"

Deborah had the distinct sensation that an enormous wind had blown up. It was so strong she could barely stand against it, she could hardly hear above its roar.

"Angus!" she cried, "What's happening?" She heard the panic in her voice. He said nothing, only looked at her. The wind died down a little. She made it the last few steps to the car and pressed her right hand on the hood, leaning there. "Who were you talking to?"

Still he said nothing.

"*Who were you talking to?*" Deborah asked again, and this time she was shouting.

"Marion," Angus answered. "Her name is Marion."

"Is she your lover? Are you having an affair? Angus!" she cried. "Are you having an affair?"

"I think you know the answer to that," he said, and turned and walked back inside the house.

Deborah heard a voice rise in a terrible wail, a wordless cry of grief and shock. *That's me,* she realized distantly. *I'm making that noise.* She felt as though the ground in front of her had erupted, as though she'd stepped on a landmine. She couldn't see a thing for the clouds of dust and the confusion.

Now I've completely messed things up, James thought. *It was the perfect opportunity to tell her. And I've blown it.* If only he hadn't drunk too much on the first night. Even though it'd been fun. If only he hadn't gone for that swim to wash out the hangover cobwebs, thinking he'd come back refreshed and in the right frame to tell Deborah everything, before dinner maybe. If only he'd gone for the walk with her instead, and told her then. *If only I wasn't so goddamn gutless.* But instead . . .

Instead he got back from his swim to find that everything had fallen apart. Angus's car was gone. Silver was sitting at the kitchen table looking stricken, the relief on her face when James came in almost palpable. Deborah was sitting there, too, slumped in a chair, her head on her arms. She raised her face to him; already her eyes were swollen almost shut from crying. Fear gripped James's heart so fiercely he actually staggered.

"Oh no, what's *happened*?" he cried. "Is it . . . ?" He was certain, in an instant, of what must've happened: Olivia had been killed in an accident at the school camp. There had been a phone call. Angus had taken the car to go there, to the hospital, the crash site, whatever it was. And in that same instant Deborah, looking at him, could see exactly what he was imagining and how much more frightful it was even than her reality.

"No, no, nothing like that!" she cried. "No one's dead! It's just . . . it's just . . ." She couldn't say it. She looked helplessly across at her sister-in-law. Silver swallowed.

"Angus is having an affair. Maybe a big one."

"Oh Jesus. Oh fuck." James knelt on the floor beside his sister's chair. She turned awkwardly and clung to him, big sobs bursting from her. He held her, stroking her soft, elegantly cut black and silver hair. Her neck looked as slender and vulnerable as a child's. His eyes met Silver's across the table; she let out a long-held breath, shaking her head slowly.

So instead of unburdening himself of one secret that weekend, James ended up with two. Because Deborah was adamant that she didn't want anyone else to know about Angus's affair: no one at work, no one in the family. Not even Olivia. *Not till I know what's going on myself, and I don't really have any idea yet. Do I?* She would stay on with them at Sorrento for the long weekend and *get my head together*.

It seemed to make sense. And it was Deborah's decision. Just as it was Deborah's decision to call suddenly, "Stop, James! Pull over!" when they had only gone a few kilometers on the drive back to Melbourne on the Monday. To insist that they visit the dog breeder whose sign she'd glimpsed. Her decision, to then and there buy the lively little tan and white puppy which was, as far as James knew, the first animal Deborah had ever chosen to acquire.

And when Silver said gently to her sister-in-law, drawing her aside for a moment, "Are you sure this is the right thing to do? I mean, just now, with everything that's happened?" Deborah replied very definitely, almost defiantly, "Yes, I am *absolutely* sure. Why shouldn't I get something that's just for me? *Especially* with everything that's happened!"

How do you argue with that? James thought. *How do you ever argue with Deborah?*

Olivia was dropped off at her home late on the Monday afternoon by the mother of another student, as arranged. She hadn't expected her own parents to be home yet and there was no car in the driveway. But after opening the gate into the front yard she took just a couple of steps and then stopped, her face swiveling to the house, scowling. Something was up with her animals. No one was hurt, she could tell that. Not hungry either. Something new.

Mintie and Fly-by came racing around from the back, full of excitement. She knelt down so they could touch their faces to hers, and let the heavy pack slide off her shoulders, dragging it in one hand as she rose. The dogs moved with her toward the house in a tight little cluster.

"Don't let those dogs in yet!" her mother called from the living room, and Olivia pushed them back with her knee as she sidled through the front door, leaving her pack on the verandah. Her mother sat on the big yellow couch looking keenly toward the door, legs tucked under her and holding a squirming something on her lap.

"Hi!" Deborah said brightly. "Guess what I've got?"

Olivia came closer, peering. A triangular tan and white face with a ridiculously furrowed brow and piercing brown eyes was gazing back at her, its mouth open, showing sharp little white teeth but making no sound, not the smallest yip. The small neat body seemed to have too much skin and not quite enough fur. Its tail curled perkily over its rump.

"Wow, Mum! You got a basenji! Wow! That's *so* amazing!"

The expression on Deborah's face was complicated, pleased and disappointed at the same time. "You *would* know, wouldn't you? These are supposed to be just about the least common dogs in Australia."

"They *are* unusual, I've only ever seen *one*! Well, a pair, actually. But, Mum, they're hard work. Basenjis are notoriously willful. Highly resistant to training."

"Oh, Ol, really, how can you possibly know that? When you've hardly even seen one before? And *must* you talk like some sort of dog association manual?"

Olivia shrugged, sat down on the arm of the couch. The pup's eyes were fixed on her and it was struggling to get free of Deborah's grip.

"What are you going to call him?" she asked.

"Congo. Because basenjis come from the Congo originally," said Deborah.

"Good name."

"Glad you approve," said her mother tartly.

"Well, I can *try* to train him," Olivia offered.

"No!" cried Deborah, pulling the pup back close to her body. "You've got a bloody menagerie as it is. This dog is special and he's *mine*! Everyone else in this house has things that are special, except me. And, and, things that love them, except me. And this dog is mine."

Olivia looked at her mother properly for the first time since she'd walked in. She looked really tense. The muscles in her neck were ropy and her face was sort of too lit up, too eager. The puppy twisted, turning now to face Deborah and pushing at her with all four legs.

"*My* special thing and see, he loves me already."

Congo sank his teeth into the forefinger of Deborah's right hand, a quick, hard efficient nip. She shrieked and jumped to her feet and as she did the puppy flew, it seemed, into Olivia's lap, where he stood with his forepaws on her chest and his little clever face raised to hers, sniffing her intently. He licked her cheek, two licks, a kind of tasting or testing.

Deborah, sucking her knuckle, looked at them furiously. "Don't you go imagining this is *your* dog, young lady!" she cried.

"Mum, honestly . . ."

"And don't roll your eyes at me like that either, I won't stand for it! I found the breeder, I paid for it and he's *mine*."

"Did the breeder warn you about basenjis being hard to train?"

"Of course he did! You're not the only person in the world who knows about animals, Olivia. I chose that dog and he loves me already, I could tell when I picked him, and I'll have him trained in no time. I'll even take him to dog obedience classes if I have to. Puppy kindergarten."

"Fine, Mum. Fine. But love is only a part of successful training, you know. Firmness, patience and constant repetition are the foundation of—"

"Oh, put a bloody sock in it, will you, Olivia? And go and do your homework or something."

Deborah snatched the puppy from her, taking it off into the kitchen. Olivia sat very still on the couch. *That is just too much, even from Mum,* she thought, and followed her out to the kitchen. Deborah was standing over by the fridge, watching the puppy guzzle food from a bowl.

"Mum," said Olivia in a firm voice. It was a statement in itself.

"Sorry, Ol, I'm just really tired," her mother said, not looking at her. Olivia knew that was all the apology she was likely to get.

Little Congo waddled a few steps, dropped his hindquarters a tad and released a flood of yellow pee across the floor. It was amazing how much fluid such a small body could hold. Deborah yelled and snatched up a handful of paper towels. Olivia watched her mopping frantically away.

"Oh, Ollie, can't you give me a hand here? I'm sorry."

Olivia relented. "Have you got a litter tray for him?" Deborah shook her head. "How about a bed?" Again the shake, this time accompanied by a little grimace and then a *Would you?* expression.

"Okay, I'll get 'em together," Olivia said, heading for the back door. She scooped the puppy up as she went by. "And it's time for the others to meet him."

"Okay," Deborah agreed, conciliatory.

As Mintie and Fly-by avidly inspected every centimeter of the new puppy's body, Olivia glanced back toward the house. She saw her mother standing in the middle of the kitchen, unmoving, staring into space. She looked like someone on the TV news, someone who'd been through a disaster, a bushfire maybe. She looked *old*. *Something's happened,* Olivia thought, *and I don't know what it is.*

part five

Olivia felt quite disgusted with her parents. They were being so pathetic, arguing behind closed doors, shutting up suddenly when she came into the room, all that crap. Trying to hide things from her, and worse, imagining they *could* hide it from her. What did they think she was, a child? It was an insult!

"Shows how little they know about me. Or about anything," she said sourly to Mintie, who was snuggled up beside her on the bed. That never used to be allowed, but Olivia figured that if everyone else could toss the rules aside, so could she. And Mintie needed a bit of extra attention; the new puppy was driving her up the wall, though Fly-by was delighted to have a playmate even crazier than herself.

Olivia fondled Mintie's ears absently as she tried to read her book, but it was hard to concentrate over the sound of her parents' voices rising and falling from their bedroom. Every so often one of them would go to the bathroom, or the kitchen, and then back to resume the battle. It was nearly Easter and they were fighting about the holidays: who would go and who would stay, and where and with whom. Olivia wished they'd both just shut up and go away. She had made it clear she wasn't about to go anywhere with either of them; she was staying home with the animals. Her father had wanted to go away somewhere unspecified, refusing to admit "with Marion." Then Deborah was determined to fly to Sydney to stay with her cousin. *Fine. Go!* Olivia silently urged. But now her mother was trying to extract a promise from Angus that he wouldn't see "that woman" while Deborah was away.

Suddenly their door opened and the voices were all too clear.

"Can't you keep your hands off her for five days?" Deborah wailed. "When you're supposed to be looking after your daughter?"

Olivia heard her father in the hallway snarl, "Keep your voice down, for god's sake!" and a house-shaking rattle as he slammed the bedroom door again. Then her mother's muffled sobbing, her father banging things around in the kitchen.

"Charming," Olivia commented to Mintie. *I hate this, I hate this.* How come adults got *away* with this sort of crap? Yelling and fighting, drinking too much, neglecting their responsibilities. Olivia knew for a fact that her mother was way behind schedule with important work stuff: she'd heard her making excuses on the phone. Her dad veered between dazed and frantic; pity the poor person who got *him* as a lawyer right now! And, as parents of an almost-teenager who had just started at secondary school—well, weren't they supposed to show *some* interest? *I could be on drugs for all they know,* she thought darkly. *I could be wagging school every day and . . .* her imagination faltered. What *would* she be doing if she wasn't going to school? *Probably volunteering at the Lost Dogs' Home,* she thought, and even Olivia had to smile at how totally un-wicked she was.

Fleur was the only reason she'd stayed sane these past weeks. Now, as Deborah joined Angus in the kitchen and their voices rose again, Olivia reached across and picked up her mobile from the desk beside her bed. She keyed in a text message: Tonight I may be forced to kill my parents. Within a minute her phone beeped and there was Fleur's response: W8 til they r asleep.

Olivia smiled, pressed the keys rapidly. Will you be my alibi? And Fleur: U've been here since 6.

Heh-heh. Almost made it worth putting up with. And to be fair, the fighting between her parents hadn't been non-stop. Sometimes when her parents were together there was a stiff courtesy between them, or worse, her mother trying to be super-nice to Dad, *flirting* even. That was truly awful. It made her feel so sorry for her mum but at the same time so angry too.

Last night her mum had gone out, and Uncle James rang and asked to speak to Angus. After they'd been talking for a while Olivia overheard her father saying in an incredibly intense voice, "Well I'm not going to end it, James. Don't even ask. I love this woman like I've never loved anyone in my life before." He sounded like someone from a movie, not like her dad. It was scary. Olivia was sure her mum had asked Uncle James to make that call. To plead on her behalf.

"It's all too horrible," she told Mintie, and the dog shifted slightly to plonk her head comfortingly on Olivia's thigh, eyes fixed on her face. "Well, not *all*, Mints. Not you. Dogs aren't horrible—just people."

Deborah flew to Sydney on the Thursday just before Easter, and from the moment Olivia got home from school that day she felt her mother's absence. It was as though the whole house had let out a long-held breath, every piece of furniture, the air itself, everything. There was a huge storm that night; the clamor of rain on the roof woke her up. Like the sky was crying buckets.

The next morning, the storm had blown itself out. Olivia spent Good Friday looking after the animals. She felt exhausted, and these chores and the company of her little critters were the most restful things she knew. Fleur was away, Laurence was busy. She even took a nap mid-afternoon, feeling like a tired little kid.

Toward evening her dad went in to his bedroom; Olivia was pretty sure he was making a phone call. When he'd finished he came into the kitchen where she was making herself some hot chocolate and said super-casually, "I might go out for a while, is that okay with you, Ol?"

Olivia said, "Sure, go ahead," making her voice sound casual, too. For a moment she was tempted to ask, "Are you going to see Marion?" but she didn't. The little kid feeling came over her again; she remembered how she used to be scared of standing too close to her bed in case there was something under there that might get her. But she was too scared to look, too. That night she watched a nature documentary on TV, with all the dogs there in the living room. When Angus came home they made pasta together. She didn't ask him where he'd been.

Olivia woke early to a sparkling morning and took the dogs down to the park while it was still early, wanting to give Congo a big training session, and with Mintie's help she worked the little basenji almost to compliance. Almost, but not quite, and once her pocketful of liver treats was empty he started acting up. "Boy, you're hard work," she told him. But secretly—because she didn't want to make Mintie jealous—she loved this willful creature with a passion. He was so bold and clever, had such a calculating mind of his own. She had never known a dog like him. *Whatever ends up happening with this whole crappy thing with Mum and Dad,* Olivia thought, bringing him to heel for the hundredth time, *at least I got Congo out of it.*

She had some breakfast—Angus was still not up—gave the dogs some bones to chomp on and wrote a note for her dad saying that she was riding her bike over to visit Grandpa. Hey, there was another weird thing: Auntie Meredith being all secretive about the stuff she was doing at Grandpa's. Olivia and Laurence had talked about it. Why was she so paranoid about being sprung for doing something *good*? That was pretty bizarre! Grown-ups. Go figure.

Grandpa was sitting in the old wooden chair down the end of the garden, with an empty teacup and crusts of toast on a tray, and the Saturday paper on his lap.

"Hello there, honeybunch!" he said, looking very pleased. "Well, isn't this wonderful! I was just thinking about you. See here," and he tapped a spot on the newspaper. Olivia came around beside him and read the item—in the gardening pages, of course—aloud over his shoulder.

"'Open for today only: Golden Grove. This fabled garden, never before open to the public, was the life's work of Constance Yule, who died last year aged 91. Miss Yule was a gifted amateur botanist and collected many rare plant specimens in China, Burma and Nepal. An outstanding feature of Golden Grove is the spectacular dahlia garden, at its peak now. The Yule family is opening Golden Grove in honor of their aunt, and to raise money for the orphanage which she supported in a refugee camp on the Thai-Burma border.'"

"Well, Ollie? What do you think?"

"Sounds pretty fabulous, Grandpa. Bet those dahlias took a beating though, in that storm the other night."

"True, true. But you know, I've heard about this garden for years. I've always wanted to have a good look at it."

"Okay. And I haven't brought the dogs with me today, which is good. Where is it?" She looked in the newspaper again. "Oh, that's over near Auntie Meredith's place. How'll we get there?"

"In my car, of course, darling! I can still drive all right you know, I just pick my times when the roads aren't so full of maniacs. But Easter Saturday will be nice and quiet."

Olivia hesitated. Wasn't there some problem she'd heard mentioned, about Grandpa driving? But his car was still there in the carport, so it must be all right. And they hadn't been out on an excursion like this for ages.

"Golden Grove," he said wonderingly, looking again at the little piece in the newspaper.

"Okay, Grandpa," she said. "Let's go!"

It took him a couple of tries to back out of the carport, and somehow the passenger-side mirror got a bit of a bang. Didn't break though. He had used the street directory to pre-plan their route, and

Olivia had it open to the page on her lap as he drove. He gripped the steering wheel hard, staring ahead with utmost concentration, but within minutes there was a blast on the horn from a car which then swept past them. Pretty soon the next car behind was tooting and flashing its lights at them as well.

"Bloody maniacs!" Alex said, clearly flustered. "What's the matter with them?"

"You could go a bit faster, Grandpa," suggested Olivia. "This is a sixty-kilometer zone, I think."

"I'm going fast enough!"

"You're only doing," she leaned across to look at the gauges in front of him, "thirty."

"That's fast enough!" he shouted. "How bloody fast do you want me to go?"

Olivia flinched and said nothing. Grandpa never spoke to her like that. He did drive a little faster for a while, but then slowed right down again and other drivers continued to get cross. She was very pleased to get to Golden Grove, well marked with signs. There were cars already parked for a long way around. As they walked toward the entrance, she noticed that his hands were shaking.

"Grandpa," she said. "Are you all right?"

"Sorry, darl. Just upsets me, all those rude so-and-so's on the road these days. They've got a name for it, too, you know, I just can't think what it is."

"You mean road rage?"

"Could be. Something like that. Never mind," he said, making a visible effort to calm himself, to smile. "That's modern times, eh?"

They paid the entrance fee, Alex graciously accepting the invitation to donate something extra to the orphanage in Burma, and were given a map of the property.

"Devonshire teas being served all day in the gazebo, that's marked there, near the michaelias, d'you see?" said the woman on the gate, indicating the spot on the map.

"Thank you. A cuppa might come in very handy. Thirsty work, this!" said Alex gamely. They went in and strolled around for a while, admiring this and that, but Olivia could tell her grandfather was still unsettled. She spotted a garden seat temptingly located in dappled shade, and there somewhat farther away was the gazebo.

"Grandpa, see that seat over there?" she said. "How about you grab that while I go and get you a cup of tea?"

"That's a good idea, Ollie," he said gratefully, fishing his wallet out from his back pocket. "Here, you get a lemonade or something, too, won't you?"

It took her ages, absolutely ages, to get served. Olivia started to feel anxious. As she made her way back to the garden seat carrying a laden tray, she was relieved to see that her grandfather was still there. Maybe he was dozing: his shoulders appeared to be slumped, and his head was tilted to one side. But as she came closer, she was shocked to see that tears were rolling down his cheeks, his mouth open in unabashed distress.

"Oh, Grandpa," she cried. "What's the matter?" She sat beside him, and he took one of her hands, sobbing. There was a hankie in the pocket of his shirt and she took it out and shook it open, pressing it into his hand. He mopped at his face, still crying. *What should I do?* she asked herself desperately. *Should I get help? But Grandpa would hate that.*

Finally he spoke. "I'm terribly worried about my father," he said. His voice sounded like something had broken inside him, it caught at her heart. "I've been thinking about him and it doesn't seem like I've heard from him for such a long time." He looked at her with a sad, piteous hope. "Do you know where he is?"

"Your father, Grandpa?" she asked. He nodded, gazing at her. *Oh, what should I say? The truth, I suppose; what else can I say?* "I'm afraid your father's . . . dead, Grandpa. He died quite a long time ago, when Mum was just little. She told me. Maybe . . . forty years ago now."

"Dead?" Alex said. He looked down at his lap and gave a long shuddering sigh. "Yes," he agreed sadly. "Yes, I suppose he is."

"I think . . . I think you might have had a dream about him, Grandpa. Maybe you had a little nap here on the bench and had a dream about him."

"Yes. I suppose I did." He sounded completely worn out.

"I went to get us a Devonshire tea. See? How about you drink this cuppa? I think it'll make you feel better."

"Yes, I'll do that," he said. They sat, Alex drinking his tea quietly, Olivia the lemonade. *Auntie Meredith's place is near here,* she thought. *And hopefully Laurence'll be home, too. We just have to get there and then we'll be okay.*

It took Meredith so long to answer the door, Olivia was about to go around the back to see if Laurence was in his bungalow in the back-yard. But there she was, at last, leaning against the doorframe, and the alcohol fumes coming off her were so strong you could practically see them.

"Hello, Daddy!" she said with bleary enthusiasm. "Hello, Ollie, sweetheart! Whadda lovely surprise."

"Hello," said Olivia uncertainly. Her aunt looked shocking, as though she'd slept in her clothes, if she'd slept at all. "Can we come in?"

Meredith bumped into the wall twice as she led the way to the combined kitchen and living area at the back of the tiny house. She sat down heavily at the table. Alex sat beside her. He still hadn't said anything, and Olivia looked at him anxiously. The short drive there from Golden Grove had been alarming; it had seemed as though he barely knew how to drive a car at all.

Now Meredith suddenly burst into tears. "Oh, Daddy!" she wailed. "I've lost my job! I just got into work a lil bit late last night," she held up thumb and forefinger to show just how little it had been, peering at the gap, "and they *sacked* me!"

Oh, wonderful, Olivia said to herself. She went to the sink, filled two glasses with water and carried them back to the table. Her grandfather, to her surprise, seemed to be better. He was looking more alert, patting Meredith's shoulder and making soothing there, there noises.

"Drink this water, please, Grandpa," Olivia told him firmly. "Auntie Meredith, sit up and drink this glass of water." Both of them did so. Meredith was still sobbing and looked even worse than when she'd opened the door, but at least she wasn't actually bawling, and Grandpa was definitely starting to look better.

"Is Laurence home?"

Meredith looked completely baffled. Olivia felt like snapping, *Come on, this is not a hard question!* Instead she just said, "Never mind. I'll go and see."

When she knocked on the door of the bungalow Laurence shouted "Yo!" and she went in. He was slouched on the couch with a couple of other guys, playing a video game. A girl was sprawled on the bed flipping through a magazine. Olivia had met them all before but couldn't think of their names. Wait, the girl was Crystal, the one who'd come to look at Auntie Meredith's journals that time.

"Hey, Ol, how ya doin'? You guys know my cousin Olivia?" They all nodded in a friendly way and said hi. She went over and sat on the arm of the ancient couch. The boys were playing Super Smash Brothers. She smiled; you couldn't help but like those little guys and their little yelping cries as they jumped around.

"Wanna play?" Laurence asked.

She shook her head. "Nuh."

"So what's happening?"

"I've just been out with Grandpa. It was pretty weird."

"Weird? What sort of weird?" Laurence looked over at her now, briefly, his fingers still madly working the controller. He had really changed a lot this past year, he looked like a guy now, not a kid. He was in his last year of secondary school and she was only in her first, but he still treated her the same as he always had, like she was a normal person, not some kind of weirdo or anything. His friends were nice, too. She liked being around them a lot more than being with kids her own age, except for Fleur.

"Weird, like . . . he lost it, kind of. Got really upset."

"So where is he now?"

"In the kitchen, with your mum."

Laurence snorted. "Huh. She's a complete write-off today." He handed the controller to the guy beside him and got up off the couch. "Thrash 'im for me, Tris," he said, putting on a mock-Cockney accent. "Let's get this little lot sorted then, eh?"

In the end, what happened was that Laurence's friend Tristan, who was eighteen and had a license, called his older brother. The brother came around in his car and followed behind while Tristan drove Alex's car back home with Laurence and Olivia and their grandfather. They stayed around for a while to make sure everything was all right. Olivia assured them that it was. Alex just needed to have a nap, and she would ride her bike home.

Back at his own place, Laurence told the other guys casually, "I'm just gonna get some corn chips and stuff together," and went into the house while they headed back to the bungalow. Meredith was passed out at the kitchen table, just as he'd suspected she would be. He got her to her feet, hauled one arm over his shoulders, and half carried, half dragged her to her bedroom. He dumped her on the bed and stood there for a moment.

"Ma," he told her snoring form, "you are a fuckin' mess."

Olivia felt like it had been days since she'd ridden off to her grandpa's, not just that morning. She'd written in her note that she'd be back mid-afternoon, and she wasn't even late. So, she had to remind herself, it was quite natural that when she arrived home Angus was sitting at the outdoor table eating a toasted sandwich, the picture of relaxation. It gave her a strange feeling in her stomach. *This is how it works*, she thought. *People can be perfectly relaxed and happy and meantime someone they love is freaking out. And then they get the news.* She hugged Mintie, then she went over to Angus and hugged him, too.

"Golly, Ollie," he said, startled, hugging her back. "Did you miss me?"

"Dad, something weird happened with Grandpa," she said. Her voice sounded a little bit shaky but she didn't even care.

She told him about everything, Grandpa's terrible driving, the way he got so angry, and then the strange, sad incident on the garden seat at Golden Grove. She even cried a little while she told him that bit. She didn't go into detail about what happened at Meredith's, just that Laurence and his friends had helped get them and the car back to Alex's. Angus listened intently, not interrupting, just nodding.

"Oh boy," he said when she had finished, shaking his head. "Oh boy, oh boy. I wonder if it *was* a dream he had, or one of these ministroke things?"

"What should we do, Dad?"

"Well, umm . . . I think I should call Robert and Vesna. Yeah, that's what I'll do, I'll call them now. And something's got to happen about the car, the sooner the better."

"Dad? Don't call Mum, will you?"

"Well, I'd rather not worry her while she's having this little break in Sydney. Let's see what Robert and Vesna reckon. But I will have to tell her, Ollie. It's her dad, after all. And you're her daughter."

"Well, you're *my* dad, and I'm your daughter, too," Olivia pointed out, her tone suddenly accusatory.

"Absolutely! But meaning?"

"Meaning why don't you tell *me* important stuff? Why are you trying to hide stuff from me?" she said.

Angus sat back. *This is critical*, he told himself. *Don't mess this up.*

"You mean," he said, "about what's going on between your mother and me?"

"Yes!" Tears had filled Olivia's eyes again. "It's not *fair* that you don't talk to me about it. It's not . . . *respectful.*"

"I don't want to be disrespectful of you, Olivia. I really mean that. But your mother thought it was better not to talk to you about it till we know what's going to happen."

"Well, I want you to talk to me about it *now!*"

"Okay," Angus said. "I will."

And he did. He told her about growing up in the same town as Marion, being best friends with her brother. About meeting her again at the reunion a year ago. He fudged a bit, saying that they had been *just friends* for most of that time, but recently they had become *more than friends.* He told her some things about Marion, her job as a therapist, the fact that she was divorced. *No kids,* he said. Not too personal, not yet. He didn't know what more to say.

"Are you and Mum going to get divorced?" asked Olivia. She had been listening with fierce concentration and, even though she felt calmer now, she could hear how strange her voice sounded. Metallic, somehow. Not hard but sort of ringing, like a trumpet.

"I don't know, Ol. I really don't. It's pretty hard to know right now just what's going to happen. But, whatever happens, I want you to know that . . ." Angus hesitated. *Is this going to sound like a dumb cliche?* "To know that my feelings for you won't ever change. I love you, Ollie, you mean the world to me. To both of us, your mum, too. I'm sorry, I hope that doesn't sound like just empty words. Because it's really, really true."

Olivia nodded, acknowledging. Her head stayed down for a moment and when she raised it she fixed her father with a gaze that warned, *Don't try to get away.* "So. Do you love Marion?"

There was a small, profound silence, then Angus gave a nervous laugh. "Gosh, kiddo, ask the hard questions!" He looked away and then looked back at her. "Yes, Ollie, I do."

Olivia regarded him steadily. "Okay, so when do I get to meet her?"

Angus looked shocked. "You want to meet her?"

"Yeah. I do. But, Dad, just because I want to meet her doesn't mean I think you and Mum should split up. I don't *want* you to split up!"

"I know. I understand. I'm sorry, I wish I could say what's going to happen but I just can't. None of us knows what's going to happen, even though we're grown-ups and we probably should."

"Huh!" Olivia snorted. "Yeah, well, even though you're grown-ups . . . I think I should meet Marion and make up my own mind, that's what I think." She looked at him severely. For a moment her young face in its frame of black hair looked far older. Timeless.

"God, Ollie, sometimes you . . ." But Angus didn't finish the thought, not out loud. *Sometimes you scare me.* There was a pause, a moment that seemed to Angus very solemn. Tentatively, he lifted his arms, open, offering, and to his vast relief and gratitude his daughter rose from her seat, jumped toward him as a young child does. Her sudden movement rocked the table, and the dregs of his coffee were upended into the remains of his toasted sandwich, but they ignored the mess, hugging each other hard.

CHAPTER 20

On Easter Sunday Meredith woke late, with a shocking hangover. Everything hurt, her head, her stomach, everything. She was hungry and she managed to make a big pot of veggie soup, but within minutes of eating she was on the toilet. The soup went straight through her like water through a hose. She leaned her sweating forehead on the wall as she sat there and closed her eyes. *I'm wrecking myself*, she thought. She had a sudden vivid image of her body smashed up, literally wrecked, as in a car smash. She saw Laurence left alone. *What am I doing?*

Back in the kitchen, Laurence was on his second bowl of soup, but he was looking grim.

"Mum," he said, "we need to talk about yesterday."

Meredith winced. Her last memory of the day before was of her niece Olivia standing at the front door looking frightened and shocked, and Daddy beside her looking . . . how had he looked? *Not well*, she thought now. Definitely not well. But after that, nothing until she woke up with a bursting bladder and a mouth like old cotton balls.

"You were a mess," Laurence said. "You were worse than a mess, you were a disgrace. Too wrecked at, what was it, one o'clock or something, to help your own dad when he needed you. You don't even know what happened, do you?"

Meredith shook her head. For once she didn't change the subject or flounce out of the room. She sat back down at the table. "Okay," she said. "Lemme have it." He told her what had happened, and she felt ill, actually nauseated with shame.

"I've had it, Mum." There was an angry tone of finality in Laurence's voice that she'd never heard before.

"I know," Meredith said humbly. She was still for a while, staring at her folded hands resting on the table. There was a sign in her mind that she was reading; it was hanging there, lit up like neon. *The end of the line.* Finally she looked up at him. "I can't keep doing this. I don't *want* to keep doing this."

"So what are you going to do about it?"

"AA, I guess."

"No!" Laurence yelled. "You've tried AA before and you always fuck it up!"

"I know I've *tried*—but I wasn't really trying. This time I've got to get real. Not skip meetings. Call them if I feel like I'm gonna backslide. The real deal."

"*No.* I think you've got to go into rehab."

Meredith felt panicky. *Who'll keep things up for Daddy if I'm not there?* But if she didn't get on top of the booze, who was going to look after him anyway?

"Laurence, I'm sorry, I'm really sorry. I'm sorry about yesterday and I'm sorry about—everything. Let me try AA first. If I fall off the wagon I'll go into a rehab clinic. I promise. I swear."

"I'm *serious*, Mum, I want you to know that. I'm deadly serious. This is my final year of school and it's *important*. I have to get a really high score to get into Marketing at RMIT schools. I need some support here, you know!" Her son's voice quavered and Meredith felt tears sting her eyes. "I don't want to live with you being a drunk any more."

"Fair enough. You shouldn't have to," she said.

"Okay then, start by ditching it," said Laurence, his eyes not shifting from hers as he jerked his head from the fridge to the sink. Meredith took a deep breath, got up, and did it: poured every bit of alcohol in the place down the sink. She even got her emergency bottle of vodka from the bedroom and poured that out, too. Laurence came and stood beside her at the sink as she rinsed the last of it away.

"Good one, Ma," he said.

"Easter Sunday." She looked up at him, risking a cheeky little grin. "I'm reborn. Resurrected."

"No need to go all religious on me." He dropped a kiss on the top of her head. "Just get with the program, okay? And stay with it."

Meredith got a new job, four days a week as a kitchen hand in a cafe quite close to home. The pay wasn't nearly as good as bar work, especially without the tips, but it was just enough, and it kept her away from alcohol. She went in there at twelve each day and washed dishes from the lunch crowd, then cleaned the whole kitchen top to bottom and prepared the salads and vegetables for dinner. She finished at six o'clock, when the night shift started. Six o'clock: a dangerous time for a drinker.

Twice a week she went straight from work to a yoga class held in a hall across the road. A friend had talked her into trying it, and Meredith found that yoga suited her. There was no peppy music or bouncing around, just a quiet, thoughtful sort of concentration. She'd always been naturally flexible and the physical work she did had kept her fit. But this was different: she could feel and then actually *see* how her body was toning and strengthening. And she soon realized that it wasn't only her body that benefitted: she left each yoga class feeling more settled, somehow, in herself. That was encouraging.

She did join AA. Two meetings a week, one straight after a yoga class. Some of the people irritated the crap out of her, *but hey*, she thought, *I'm probably just a teensy bit irritating myself at times.* She knew she'd do better this time if she had a sponsor, and at the end of the first meeting she approached a woman named Carmen, a bit older than herself, smart and unpretentious and funny. Carmen agreed; they talked seriously and exchanged phone numbers, but still Meredith felt she shouldn't bother her. Should be able to do this on her own. Carmen usually phoned her a couple of times a week, mostly to have a chat and a laugh but she would always ask, with that meaningful edge, "How are you getting on?"

"You know why I want to talk with you regularly, don't you, Meredith?" Carmen asked her one day.

"Um, because I'm such a great gal?" Meredith ventured.

"As well as that. Because I want you to be in the habit of talking to me. Because if there's an emergency, I want to be the first person you think of to call. Before you buy a bottle. Before you lift a glass to your mouth. Call me. I want my phone number engraved on your brain. That's how it's gotta be. Get it?"

"Got it."

She didn't see her old friends much: they were all drinkers so it wasn't safe. She had dinner with Alex a couple of times a week, and spent more time at home, fiddling around with her journals, making things. She saw more of Laurence. They talked more often, and more deeply. Mothering him had always seemed like the easy bit of her life; sometimes the only bit that made sense. She'd never been much of an authority figure, but then Laurence had never seemed to need much authority. No matter how shitfaced she'd been, she'd always got up for him in the night, always made his school lunch and sat with him while he ate his cereal in the morning, even if her head was pounding and she felt like she was going to throw up. And no matter how much of a mess she was, he'd always been sweet to her. Tolerant. *How lucky I've been*, she thought now, fervently glad that she had come to her senses before all of that got lost forever in the alcoholic swill.

Every day before work, Meredith went over to her father's. He didn't seem any worse after that incident at Easter time. She made sure he took an aspirin each day, along with the tablet to keep his blood pressure down, and the new medication that was supposed to help his memory get better, or stop it getting worse.

She kept his house looking good. Though the big clean-up had been done, there was plenty of maintenance. Plenty! Besides, Alex didn't have his own car any more—Robert had spirited it away—so anywhere he needed to go, for errands or outings, Meredith took him. A couple of times her father asked where his car was and Meredith said airily, "Oh, it's in at the garage for a service," an explanation that seemed to satisfy him.

"I don't miss driving one bit you know, darling," he told her as they were heading off in her car one day. "A lot of maniacs on the road these days. It was getting so bad I hated it."

"Is that so, Daddy? Better off without it then!"

"Yes, that's what I think. In fact, I've been thinking, when they've finished fixing my car up, why don't you have it? I know you love this old Corona of yours, but I do think—no offense—that mine's a much better car."

"Oh, Daddy, that's so kind of you!" She turned to him, delighted. "Are you sure?"

"Yes. Better you make use of it," he said. "Especially since you spend half your time driving your old dad around anyway."

"I don't mind!" she said. "You know I don't mind a bit."

"I know you don't, poppet. Bless your little cotton socks," her father said, settling back contentedly in the passenger seat.

She told Robert about Alex's offer. He said that it sounded sensible but that the others would have to agree, too, *of course*. The next day he cc'd her a copy of an e-mail he'd sent to Deborah and James.

Reading it gave her an unexpected prickly feeling. She knew Robert had to do the right thing, but she still felt put out.

Why did they have to complicate things? After all, Daddy had always helped her in little special ways. She was the youngest, don't forget; she needed more help than the others. But as she was making this internal complaint another voice countered it, quite unbidden. *So what?* it sneered. *So what if you're the youngest?* Well, of course the youngest one needs more help, she answered, astonished. Everyone knows that! *What crap!* said the voice. *You just wanted more help because you were a little sniveller, and then a hopeless drunk.* But . . . but don't I deserve some reward for giving up drinking, at least? *What, for not killing yourself? A reward, for being a normal adult human being? Get over yourself!*

That set her back on her heels. And then she realized, too, that since she had never actually admitted to anyone in the family that she was an alcoholic, she couldn't very well now start claiming special privileges for the fact that she was trying hard *not* to be, could she?

Meredith tried to think differently about why she was entitled to have Alex's car. She wished she could tell the others that she deserved it for other reasons, good reasons: that she was helping Daddy with all his shopping and housework, taking him to appointments. She had an urge to fling her secret at them, cry out, *See! See everything I'm doing for Daddy!* Especially when she saw the snotty e-mail from Deborah suggesting *Meredith could make more use of this city's public transport system, as I do.* But Deb's response also renewed Meredith's fear that her sister (bossy cow!) would never understand the need to keep Alex in his own home. No, she must keep her efforts on her father's behalf secret. James didn't care what happened to the car, of course, and in the end Deborah agreed it was better put to use within the family than to have it sit there idly. No one talked about selling it; that would be admitting something none of them was prepared to face.

Just as Meredith was feeling like she was out of the woods, she caught herself speculating that one little drink wouldn't be such a bad idea. *Fuck off!* she told such notions ferociously, and rang Carmen. Carmen was brilliant at talking her through it, strengthening her resolve. But it got harder. A lot harder. The craving came daily. It would start about 4 o'clock, the time she finished wiping down the last benchtop in the cafe kitchen. She wanted it so much she could just about *see* that glass of wine sitting there, a reward for all her hard work, ready for her to take a little sip from every now and then while she did the food prep, chopping and dicing and slicing.

Some days she just ignored the craving, kept herself busy and it went away. Other days it wasn't going anywhere: it stuck around, and stuck around some more. Then one morning Meredith woke up feeling like she would kill for a drink. She got on with things, tried to keep her mind off it, but by the time she was nearing the end of her shift at the cafe her hands were shaking. *This is really bad*, she thought. *Time to call Carmen.* But she couldn't reach her. Not at her home, not on her mobile. She left messages on both and kept working, but by the time she finished at six o'clock Carmen still had not phoned her back.

It was not a yoga class evening, or an AA meeting. Meredith could see in her mind's eye the drive-through liquor store she passed on her way to and from work. It was *all* she could see. She imagined herself pulling in there. A bottle of wine? A cask! No, a bottle of vodka, much better, harder for anyone to smell it. *No, no!* She rang home, but there was no answer. Then she remembered Laurence had hockey training after school tonight, and wouldn't be home till eight.

She felt so desperate she actually moaned out loud. She thought of Robert, how steady and sensible he was. *I wish I could ask him for help,* she thought, and suddenly it hit her. *I can! I can at least ask!* She keyed in his mobile number, fingers trembling, and he answered straight away. "Robert McDonald speaking."

"Hello, Bobbit, it's Merry," she said, trying to sound upbeat.

"Merry, what's wrong?" her brother said, his voice urgent. Oops, clearly the upbeat thing wasn't quite happening. "Are you okay?"

"Yes. But I just wondered . . . what are you doing now?"

"Right now? I've just finished a meeting here at the school, I'm locking up my office. Has something happened? You sound . . . stressed."

"Can—can I come and see you?" she asked, her voice shaky now. For once, she wanted *not* to cry; she was holding back the tears, trying to keep the whimper out of her voice. What could she say? How could she tell him? *Oh, just spit it out!* "Robert, I haven't had a drink for three and a half months and I think I'm about to fall off the wagon. I can't reach my AA sponsor. I need help."

There was a silence on the other end of the phone, then, "Are you all right to drive? Or shall I come and get you?"

"No, I'm okay," she said. She felt dizzy with relief. *He's going to help me! Thank heavens!* "Maybe . . . do you think we could meet at, um, that Lebanese place, Habibi? That's about halfway. And I could use some baklava, I think I need a sugar hit." Meredith gave a little shaky laugh.

"Yes, that's fine, I'm getting in the car now. Merry, just don't panic, okay? Take some deep breaths, long slow deep breaths, that's what I do. That helps."

"Okay. And I know what I should do, I should drink a boatload of water. Why haven't I done that already? I'll go and do that now."

"Good girl. I'll see you in half an hour then, at Habibi's. Don't rush, drive carefully, sisterling. Take it easy."

"I will. I will."

It was strange, telling Robert. At the AA meetings Meredith often felt a chorus-like, theatrical quality in the telling of her story. With Robert, it suddenly seemed more . . . real. And although people at AA cared, he cared in a different way: about her, about Laurence. She realized she'd expected him to be hurt by it, disappointed in her for sure—*My little sister! How could she!*—but he didn't seem to be. Not at all. What surprised her most was that instead of trying to gloss over or evade the grim details, Robert was genuinely curious. He asked amazingly penetrating questions: about exactly what the craving for a drink felt like, precisely how she handled the urgent desire to give way to it, how AA helped and what other help she might need.

While they were talking her mobile rang. It was Carmen, anxious and apologetic, explaining that one of her kids had been hurt skateboarding, broken an arm it seemed, and she'd had to switch off her mobile while she was with him at the hospital.

"But, Meredith, are you okay?" she asked urgently. "Where are you? What's happening?"

"Yes, yes, I'm fine. Really I am. I'm with my brother Robert. I've told him about the booze, AA, about you, everything!"

"Good for you! I'm so sorry, I have to go again now. But if you need me later, call me, won't you? Please, Meredith! Promise me."

"I will," she said. "I promise."

She ended the call. Robert was looking at her solemnly. "Merry," he said, "I am so glad you called me. I really mean that. That you trusted me and believed I could help."

They smiled at each other gratefully, both understanding that the closeness they'd always shared had become even deeper. And something else occurred to Meredith then. "When I rang you before," she said, leaning forward on her elbows amid the empty coffee cups, the crumbed syrupy plates, "you said I should do some deep breathing, right?"

"Yes."

"You said, 'that's what I do.' What did you mean by that?"

Robert looked away. His left hand touched his chest, a gesture he'd made every now and again the whole time they'd been talking. His mouth opened as though to speak but then he closed it again.

"Robert, *you* don't have a secret drinking problem too, do you?"

"Oh, no. No, no, no. Nothing like that."

"Like what, then? Is it a health problem? Have you got a heart condition you haven't told Vesna about?"

"A heart condition?" Robert looked shocked. "Why on earth do you say that?"

"Because you keep patting your chest, like there's something there you're worried about."

"Do I? Oh." He raised a hand to his shirt collar and drew out a thin black cord. A slender little silver object about the size of Meredith's thumb was attached to the end. She peered at it doubtfully, lying there in the palm of his hand.

"There," Robert said proudly. "It's my USB key drive. A tiny little separate hard disk for my computer. Isn't it amazing?"

Meredith had a computer at home but was completely reliant on Laurence's help to use it, and any new technology usually made her feel somewhat panicky. "Um, I guess so," she said dubiously. "Is it?"

"Oh, it certainly is! I save everything on my computer to this now, all the files I need. It's changed my work life overnight! To think of everything I had to lug about before, great stacks of paper I used to cart back and forth and have to worry about losing, and now—" he clicked his fingers in the air—"disappeared! Into this," and he flourished the silver gizmo on its tether. "School to home, home to school—just this!"

"And now . . . *This* is what you have to worry about losing, right?"

"Yes." Robert frowned now at the tiny little device and tucked it away again, inside his shirt.

"And what else?"

"What else?" Robert frowned distractedly. He started patting his pockets.

"Yes. What else do you worry about?" Meredith leaned across the table and gently tapped her brother's hand. When he looked at her, she gave him her most winning, teasing smile. "Come on, Bobbit, I've told you my secret, now you've gotta tell me yours."

Robert hesitated for a long moment, closed his eyes like a man about to take his first bungee jump, and started to talk. He told her about the fear of losing things, the fear about appliances left on, the constant checking. The way he'd be hit by a wave of anxiety when he thought he'd forgotten something: the pounding heart and shortness of breath. What helped: Vesna's calm presence, the deep breathing, the fingering. Yes, the fingering, he told her what that was really about. He even showed her some of the patterns, how they varied and progressed like music or an equation. Distracting; soothing.

Meredith listened and tried to ask questions as useful as his had been. When did it start? How often does it happen? What sets it off? What does it feel like? Why do you think the fingering makes it better? What makes it worse? And finally they sat there, brother and sister, both exhausted and exhilarated by their mutual revelations.

"What it comes down to, I reckon," said Meredith, "is this: you have to be ready."

"Ready?" Robert gave her a quizzical look.

"Yes. You have to be alert to the moment when you're ready to change. And when you are, and the right person magically steps up who'll help you make that change, don't hold back. You *have* to go with it, Robert! Be ready. And don't—hold—back."

Robert looked at her, his baby sister who had never given him a word of advice in her life. Her face was lit with an eager certainty that made him feel uncomfortable, though he wasn't sure why. And then he realized. *She looks like one of those born-again Christians,* he thought. *Oh, dear!*

"What are we talking about here, Merry?" he asked. "Are we talking about some kind of . . . *faith?*"

"Yep, I guess so," she admitted. They were not and never had been a family for faith. "But not, you know, *goddie*-type faith."

"But doesn't AA have this thing about 'a higher power'?"

"Yeah," Meredith said. "But for me that's . . . I don't know, it's *me!*"

"What's you?"

"The higher power thingie. Well, and you, and Laurence, and Carmen even . . . But mostly I guess I see it as part of me. The best part of me. That's what's gonna get me through the tough bits."

Robert nodded. "I'd like to say, 'Let's drink to that!'" he said. "But on second thoughts . . ."

"Noooo!!" they agreed simultaneously, wagging their heads from side to side. Meredith giggled.

"But I guess it still *is* faith, all the same," she added, momentarily serious again. "You should bear that in mind, Bobbity bro."

CHAPTER 21

In the fields around Marsh Farm, men and machines were busy, their noise drifting with the dust they raised into the brilliant blue of the sky.

"Zummer in Zomerzet," said James, watching from the upstairs window of his mother's studio. "What do you call what they're doing, Rose? Reaping? Mowing?"

"Something like that," his mother said, glancing up from her sketchbook. "I'm not a real countrywoman, I'm afraid. Completely faux."

"How come even the dust is pretty here?" James wondered. "It never looks like that in Australia." He went back to his chair at the big work table and started doodling again.

This was his third visit to Somerset and he was staying with Rose and Roland for a full month while Silver was in Europe and the States on business. He felt a bit unsettled. He thought there might be a painting coming on; he always got restless before a new painting. James drew and sketched wherever he was, of course, that was as natural as breathing, and something he and Rose often did together, sitting at the kitchen table or up in her workroom. They found it easy, companionable. Almost as though they'd been doing it all their lives. But these last few days James could hardly settle to the simplest sketch. He felt like his fingers were going to fly away.

A memory surfaced, clear as a jewel: his mother, younger, opposite him at the dining room table, tapping her brush on the side of a glass of murky colored water, sheets of paper daubed with brilliant colors spread around her. "We used to draw like this when I was a kid, didn't we?" he said.

"When I could get a minute," she answered, smiling. "When I could squeeze a bit of space between you with your drawings and Robert with his blessed schoolwork, beavering away. Those were my favorite times in that house, I think. Actually," she said, sitting back for a moment, "it was Meredith who really amazed me. Do you remember how from the age of about three she used to draw these great sagas, always with the same characters? And she'd dictate what they were saying and make someone write it? It took ages and I'd get fed up. Alex was much more patient."

"Really?" James was mildly intrigued. "I don't remember Meredith doing that."

"Yes. The Penguin and the Horsey, those were her favorite characters. 'The Peng-win,' as she would say. Clearly the Peng-win was her and I think the Horsey was Robert, and she'd turn all their doings into these grand adventures. So detailed. It was quite something." Rose had entirely left off her own drawing now (designs for a range of bed-linen) and was gazing away into space, remembering. "Something I regretted terribly was that I didn't take just one of those drawings of hers when I left. And yours, James." Her eyes moved to the youthful self-portrait James had given her last Christmas, hung now so that it overlooked her as she worked.

"When I got into art school," James said, "Robert told me you would have been really pleased."

"Did he?" Rose smiled. "Dear Robert! And he was right, of

course. But why didn't Meredith go to art school, too? I thought she was bound to become an artist of some kind. An illustrator, perhaps . . ."

"An artist? Meredith?" said James, sounding surprised, almost amused. "No offense, but I . . . I've just never seen that."

"Well, yes," said Rose rather defensively. "I know she was only little, but she had something, I thought. Different to what you had, of course, but . . . What *does* Meredith do now, James? I don't think you've really told me."

"Yes, I have, I'm sure. About the barwork. Although, hmm, I did hear something about her chucking that job. Maybe she's working in a cafe or something now."

"Yes, but surely she does something else besides cafe and barwork?" Rose started tapping her pencil softly on the table. She was looking at him curiously.

"We-ell . . ." James hesitated. "I . . . I guess you'd have to say that Meredith's drinking has probably got in the way of her, um, achieving her full potential."

"So she's a drinker?" Rose's eyebrows went up. "A serious drinker?"

"I don't . . . she's never said anything, not to me anyway. But I think . . . or Deborah thinks she is, anyway."

"I see." Rose looked thoughtful. "Alex's father was a drinker, did you know that?"

"No. He died ages ago, didn't he?"

"Yes, when you were just a baby. He was an exceptionally pleasant drunk, but definitely an alcoholic. He'd served in the First World War, you know. Everyone said that's what did it, the terrible things he'd seen. But I wondered if it didn't run in the family. I think Alex's brother Bob might've had a problem."

"I never knew that. So you think there's a genetic thing happening?"

"Not in *you*, James, clearly! I've never known anyone more circumspect with their alcohol, short of being a teetotaler. But what about the others? Does Robert drink?"

"Oh gosh no, not our Robert! Far too proper. Oh, that's probably unkind of me. It's not like he's a wowser."

"*Wowser,*" Rose smiled. "Now there's an expression I haven't heard in a very long time! What about Deborah?"

"Yeah, Deb likes her wine, but I certainly wouldn't say she's got a problem. She hates Meredith's drinking, though."

"Maybe it scares her?" his mother suggested.

"Scares her? I wouldn't have thought anything scares Deborah!" Again he hesitated. "Maybe it's more that . . . Deb's pretty critical of Meredith all round. Of most people. She's always been incredibly supportive of me, no question, but sometimes I feel like I'm the exception."

"Ah. And is she critical of her husband, too? I'm thinking of the marriage problems you mentioned that she's having."

"I don't know," said James uneasily. "Could be. But her job's very demanding, you know. She sets very high standards for herself. I guess she's a hard person to please."

"This doesn't surprise me, you know. She was like that as a child." Rose was watching him now even more intently. "She's not going to be pleased about *me*, is she?"

"No. Not at first. I'm sorry, Rose. And I'm sure she'll come round. But she's . . . she's pretty, um, bitter, I guess."

"Ah. Yes." Rose sighed. She stopped tapping the pencil. The sudden silence seemed demanding and it made James nervous. Rose asked him in a rush of words, "Is this why you've not told them about me yet? Is it Deborah?"

"No! Not exactly," James said, feeling cornered. "I thought I'd find some of your letters. I've been looking . . ."

Rose raised her eyebrows questioningly, and James shook his head. "I couldn't find a trace. And I looked through everything."

"You asked Alex? What did he say, exactly?"

"He just looked vague and said I should ask Deborah. Because she was the oldest."

"And did you ask her?"

"No, I couldn't see the point. I wanted to tell her about you, letters or no letters, but . . . It's just impossible, the way she is right now, with her marriage and everything. But after this trip . . . I really will tell her. Tell *them*."

Rose nodded consideringly, seeming to withdrawing into herself a little. Then with a decisive movement she picked up her pencil and started drawing again. "You do have tell them, my dear," she said. "You have to stop protecting me some time."

Protecting you? James was taken aback. *Is that what I've been doing: trying to protect Rose? From . . . from what?* He saw again the way, just a few minutes ago, she had swept her gaze up to his little self-portrait, as though to a talisman. Then a sudden image filled his mind: Deborah the last time he'd seen her, curled up like a child in a corner of his big leather couch, weeping with unhappiness. *Everyone needs protecting,* he thought. James had never imagined this was something he could do. He felt a rush of longing for Silver; to lie down with her and hold her, and be held. Imagine if he didn't have Silver . . .

"Aren't we lucky, Rose?" he said softly. His mother looked up quickly, surprised. "Aren't we just incredibly lucky, you and me?"

"Yes," she agreed, almost whispering. "Yes."

James went for a run, to clear his head. As he loped steadily along the little narrow roads the phrase "everyone needs protection" kept pace with his regular footfalls like a heartbeat. He veered off and took a path that led through a small forest, and as he ran between the tall verdant trees he felt piercingly aware of all the life that surrounded him. He ran for almost two hours and when he got back to Marsh Farm he couldn't even stop to take a shower. He sat down dusty and sweating at the kitchen table, snatched up a sketchbook and began to draw.

It came pouring out of him, flowing from the end of his

pencil: landscapes and cloudscapes, trees thick with summer leaf, holed trunks and gnarly branches, buds and leaves, roots poking through the soil. Birds and bunnies, hares tall and alert in the fields under a full moon, sheep clustered by a hedge, mole mounds and badger sets, a goat and a horse grazing together companionably, raspberries on their canes. A trout fisherman casting his fly, a farming woman at her gate, a group of children walking down a lane. Eventually he stopped, not at all exhausted. Satisfied.

"This is exciting!" Rose said, looking through the sketchbook James brought to the dinner table. He had filled it in just those few hours, and he knew he could do it again tomorrow. It was almost like his hands weren't his own. He tried to explain it to Silver on the phone that night, but he didn't feel like he was making much sense.

"You'll just have to see it, Sil," he said. "It's almost got me spooked, you know?"

"Be spooked, hon," she said calmly. "It's okay to be spooked sometimes."

The next day they all walked down to a swimming spot in the nearby river, James and Rose and Roland, with Jacinta and a visiting friend of hers lolloping along near them but not quite with them, full of high spirits, chatting and giggling. As they crossed from one harvested field into the next the two girls raced on ahead. James watched them, their lanky limbs flying as they ran pell-mell across the yellow stubble toward the line of trees marking the river in the distance. It was a scene perilously close to pretty, these two joyous racing figures in the small tamed field, and even in mid-summer the golden English light was soft, so much softer than Australia's. He felt the thrill of challenge: how to capture something so ordinary and innocent, infuse it with a whisper of the sublime, yet not get sentimental? But it was so clear in his mind's eye.

When they came back to the farmhouse he went upstairs to a room next to Rose's studio, one she had suggested had perfect light for painting, stapled a section of primed canvas to the wall, and immediately set to the sketching in. The next day he started painting.

As James worked, something struck him: this was the first painting he'd done in so many years that didn't feature water. This time there was not a drop in sight. He felt a stir of unease. He was known as a painter of water, famously skilled and imaginative in its depiction. Who was he without that? He pushed these thoughts aside and worked on, quickly, deftly, lovingly.

Normally Silver was the first person to see his new work, but she was still in the States. When his mother asked if they could have a look at the work-in-progress, James was nervous. This was the first of his paintings they'd seen; what if it disappointed them? But what he got was a domino effect of delight. Jacinta was clearly thrilled: she had never been the subject of *a proper painting* before, by *a real artist*, and at the age of sixteen this was quite a thing. Roland was delighted by his daughter's pleasure, and this in turn made Rose happy and proud, quite apart from her estimation of the work itself. James felt that familiar sensation of good luck resting its hand lightly on his shoulder. *I don't deserve this*, he thought, but there was no guilt in it. All gratitude.

By the time Silver arrived, the painting was very near completion. He showed her the sketchbooks first, the half dozen he had filled by now, and then led her to the new painting.

"Ah," she said, smiling enigmatically as she took it in. Enigma was not Silver's way, not usually. Again James felt a nervous prickle; Silver wasn't only his wife, she was his agent. And she was also his voice, in a way: she'd always had more to say about his work than he had himself. He didn't care for this silence.

"Well, what do you reckon?" he asked finally. "Is it a load of hooey? Am I any good without the water?"

Silver laughed and kissed him, rapidly, several times. "Oh, it's good, my darling! It's very good. By which I also mean: I can sell this, don't you worry. But that's not the best thing. The best thing is where this is coming from."

"What do you mean?" James asked, rattled. "Where *is* this stuff coming from, Sil?"

"From in here, baby," she said, placing her hand on his chest, just above his heart. "It means you're—what is it? You're *earthed*. At last. Like—you're not—" Silver's hands moved fluidly in the air making the shapes of waves.

"I'm not wishy-washy any more?" he asked, pretending to be offended—and maybe even truly so, a little.

Silver laughed again. *She looks so happy!* he thought, and that made him glad. "I didn't say that!" she exclaimed. "But it's like you're . . . grounded. Home. You know what I'm saying?"

James was staring at her, trying to get a handle on it all; now he turned to look again at the sketchbooks spilled across the table, the large near-completed painting on the wall. He pulled a loose sheet lying on the table toward him. It was a drawing of half-a-dozen fat full-blown roses in a vase, dropped petals forming a soft carpet at its base. In one corner he'd written "Rose's roses" and the date. James smiled. "Home," he said wonderingly. "Yeah."

CHAPTER 22

The first thing Olivia became aware of after she fainted was the sound of a voice, a voice she knew she liked. It was calling, *Liv! Liv!* Calling her back from the darkness, the coolness. She was lying on something that felt wonderfully hard and smooth against her cheek. Reassuringly solid. She remembered a sensation of things whirling, then a flood of heat through her whole body; she could feel the sweat prickling as it cooled on her back. The voice. Fleur. Of course. She was at school. There had been gym first up, then maths. The room had felt so hot. And this coolness now was the concrete floor of the girls' toilets. She knew she'd made it to the girls' toilets, but wasn't sure why. She opened her eyes and there was the familiar scuffed, dark green concrete, and there, too, in alarming close-up was a number of *enormous* drops of extraordinarily bright red blood. Slowly she levered herself up onto one elbow. More blood poured down her nose and dripped onto the floor beside her hand.

"Wow!" said Fleur, who was kneeling next to her. "That's impressive. Say something."

"What happened?"

"Not very original, Liv. Maybe you'd better lie down again."

"No, I'm okay," said Olivia, lying down again.

"I'll be back in just a tick," said Fleur, and she was, in a couple of ticks anyway, with the teacher of the math class they'd both been in and which Olivia had suddenly walked out of without a word, feeling too peculiar to speak. The math teacher, outraged by the rudeness of Olivia's departure, had ordered Fleur not to follow, and told her disobediently departing back that they would *both have a week's detention*. Now she was looking very chagrined: Fleur noted the chagrin with interest, and similarly, once they had got Olivia to sick bay and the vice-principal had come to assess the situation, the teacher's fawning and protestations of concern.

"So does that mean we won't have the week's detention?" she asked earnestly. The vice-principal threw the hapless teacher an appalled look.

"Oh, Fleur!" flustered the teacher. "I never . . . That wasn't . . ."

Fleur murmured, "Ha ha! Got you!" Her voice was so soft that only Olivia could hear her, and she managed a wobbly, appreciative smile.

The blood was coming from a cut on the bridge of Olivia's nose. Antiseptic and a dressing were applied to the nose, and the bleeding soon stopped. But the severe menstrual cramps, which had caused Olivia to faint in the first place, continued. She lay on her side in the sick-bay bed, white and still speechless through the stabbing spasms and the constant pain low in her tummy and groin. Her tailbone ached, and the tops of her legs. It was definitely not nice. She had been given some aspirin but that seemed to make no difference. Fleur sat beside her, silent when any adults were in the room, making quiet, droll comments when there were none. Amid all the unpleasantness Olivia was distantly aware of two things: one, that if she were capable of laughter then Fleur would have her laughing right now, and two, that as word spread through the school of some drama having befallen her, other kids would be saying *It's okay, her friend's with her.* This thought amazed her.

"I'm sorry this is taking so long, Olivia," said the vice-principal, coming back into the room. "Your mother's coming to pick you up shortly."

Olivia wondered why it was her mother who was coming, when her dad worked close by and was listed as the first person to contact. But, whoever. All she wanted was to be in her own bed, with Mintie beside her.

Deborah came. Fleur walked with them out to the car, accompanied by the vice-principal who was explaining that perhaps it hadn't been such a good idea for Olivia to do gym first thing that day, *given the circumstances*, and that it was school policy that girls could be excused from gym or sports *if it's a problem day*. Olivia and Fleur managed to exchange an eye-roll. *Yeah, right!* You'd have to be hemorrhaging and get carted off in an ambulance before the PE teacher would let you out of gym.

She lay down on the backseat and her mum didn't even tell her to put her seatbelt on. They stopped at the drugstore on the way home and Deborah bought some painkillers, strong ones. She turned to Olivia as she got back in the driver's seat.

"We'll be home in just a second, darling," she said. "How are you doing?"

"Mmm," said Olivia, opening her eyes to give her mother what she hoped was a reassuring smile. Deborah had her sunglasses on, even though it was an overcast day. Olivia suddenly registered that she'd had them on the whole time, even when she came into the sick bay. *This isn't a good sign.* Another stabbing pain clutched hard and low inside her pelvis, and she closed her eyes again.

She'd never been so glad to be in her own bed. She didn't even have to ask for Mintie; Deborah called her in there herself, and didn't say a word when Mintie jumped straight up on the bed and snuggled down.

"Here, darling. These will help a lot," Deborah said, offering her two of the painkillers with a glass of water. "And put this hot water

bottle against your tummy, or the small of your back if that's hurting." Olivia got the pills down, took the bottle, lay back again with
her arm resting on Mintie. It was strange being looked after like this,
especially by her mother. But it was okay. Anyway, what choice did
she have?

She drifted off to sleep for a while and when she woke up her
mother was still sitting there in the old armchair on the other side of
the room. She was just staring into space.

"Mum, you don't have to stay here with me, you know."

Deborah started. "Oh! Darling!" She came over to the bed. Now
Olivia could see why her mum had been wearing the sunglasses: her
eyes were swollen to little slits, like a bull terrier's. She must have
been crying for hours before she came to the school.

"How are you feeling now?" Deborah asked gently.

"Really a lot better. It doesn't hurt nearly so much."

"That's good. Are you hungry?"

"Not yet, thanks, Mum. Maybe in a while. But you don't have to
sit here, honestly. I might just read for a while now."

"Are you sure, Ollie?"

Olivia nodded. Plainly something had happened, but she didn't
have the strength to think about it right now.

Deborah said, "Well, if you're sure, I'll go to the study and do
some work. Just call out if you need anything."

She heard her mother stop at the linen cupboard. *Maybe she thinks
I'd like clean sheets,* she thought, and wondered if she should call out
not to bother, she'd just changed her sheets a day or so ago. Then she
remembered the old box full of letters that she'd found in the bottom of that cupboard, the letters never sent. *She's been writing to her
phantom again.*

A little later Olivia got up to go to the bathroom and change her
pad. There were some huge clots amid the blood on the used one.
Gross! No wonder it damn hurt, she thought. Her mother was hovering outside the bathroom door, looking anxious.

"I'm fine, Mum, really. Heaps better."

"My poor girl," Deborah said, stepping closer to her, smoothing the sweaty hair back from her daughter's forehead. "I know, I had some *awful* periods in the first couple of years, too. But the body adjusts, trust me."

Olivia nodded awkwardly. She and her mother had never been up for much girlie chat.

"Are you hungry now?" Deb asked. "Soup? That tinned tomato soup you like? I'll go down to the shop and get some fresh bread."

"Okay. Thanks."

Deborah brought the soup and thick buttered bread in on a tray. There was a glass of flavored milk, too, and a Kit-Kat. Olivia smiled. "Oh boy! Chocolate Quik *and* a Kit-Kat. This makes it almost worth it!" she said kindly, even though she didn't really feel like either.

"I got you these, too." Deborah handed her two sticker books, the old-fashioned kind with all the stickers on perforated pages at the back. You were supposed to match them up with the text on the appropriate page. For little kids, they were, trying to be educational, and you could color in a drawing, too. There was one on whales and dolphins and one, shop-soiled and scruffy, on the rodent family. *World of Rodents*, it was called.

"Fantastic!" said Olivia, snatching it up.

"It's a bit ancient and battered. I don't think it was their top seller."

"It's great! Thanks, Mum. But where's my pencils for the coloring in, huh?"

Deborah smiled. "I'll get them for you, if you like."

"Nah, only kidding. Well . . . maybe."

So Olivia actually did spend the afternoon sitting up in bed, pasting in the stickers like an eight-year-old and coloring in the drawings of rats, rabbits, cavies, beavers, and the exotic ones like jerboas and capybaras. She had seen capybaras, at the zoo. Like giant guinea pigs. She drifted off for a while on a pleasant fantasy of running a capybara farm in the country. They liked water, she would have a dam and streams, and maybe she could have some beavers, too. How would they get on? Though what if they got away, went feral, what could a bunch of out-of-control beavers do to the bush? Scary thought. She'd just have to make sure they *didn't* get away, that's all.

As she amused herself like this, and read, and suffered through a couple more stomach cramps but not nearly so bad, just a general ache now, Olivia could hear her mother moving around the house, talking to people on her phone in the study, doing things in the kitchen. She wondered where her father was. Quietly she tried to call him on his mobile but she could only reach his voice-mail. The day was drawing to a close and she started to feel a bit stale and restless, took herself off to the bathroom where she had an outrageously long hot shower. When she got out she could smell something cooking, and once dressed in her comfortable old track pants she went out to the kitchen.

"Hey, Mum," she said. Deborah was busy at the stove.

"You're up, Ol! How are you feeling now?"

"Pretty good. Normal, really."

"Oh, good. Do you feel up to having Grandpa join us for dinner? I told him you'd been under the weather and he wanted to come around. But only if you're up to it."

"No, that'd be fine. Great."

"All right then, I'll call him back. Meredith'll drop him off and I'll drive him home later."

"Or maybe Dad could?" Olivia ventured, fishing.

"I don't think so," her mother said, keeping her face turned slightly away as she picked up the phone.

I see, Olivia thought. She put on her Ugg boots and thick dressing-gown to go out to the shed. *My own little World of Rodents*, she thought fondly as the rats and bunnies scuttled to their food containers, the rats turning their backs for privacy as they ate but the rabbits regarding her with their mild pretty eyes. Congo and Fly-by were miffed at not having had a walk, but as she fed them she told them they were ungrateful hounds who should think themselves lucky.

There was a *beep, beep* from a car horn as Meredith dropped Alex off. Grandpa didn't make any inquiries other than, *Feeling better now, sweetheart?* Dinner was a beef and veggie stew, rich and hearty and as Grandpa commented several times, *just the ticket for a cold winter's night.* When Grandpa asked where Angus was, Deborah said something vague about him working late or having a meeting, she wasn't sure which. Olivia kept her eyes away from her mother's face. She knew what her mum had said was a fib, and she kind of knew there was something dark and maybe dangerous just beneath the surface. But the truth could wait. It was coming, she felt sure of that.

Grandpa had brought an enormous bunch of daphne, branches of it. The smell was unbelievable, piercing and sweet.

"Gorgeous, Dad," Deborah said as, dinner plates cleared away, she wrestled with the short recalcitrant branches. They were difficult to arrange, kept wanting to slip out of the vase.

"That smell is the loveliest thing about this nasty bit of winter," her father said. "And if you've got a good bush growing, you never want to shift it, you know that, don't you, darl?"

"Yeah, I've heard that," Olivia said. "Daphne doesn't like to be moved."

"Too right," Alex said. "I made that mistake once, you know. I made that mistake with a young lady. I moved her and I thought she was in the right spot, I thought she was happy, but no. She just couldn't adjust to the new place. Roots just didn't take."

Deborah had shot her father one unreadable look, her hands frozen at the vase, and now was staring at the glass doors, at the dark night outside.

"What was her name?" Olivia asked, riveted.

"Daphne," Alex said.

"No, I meant the name of this lady, Grandpa."

He looked puzzled suddenly. "Wasn't it Daphne?" he asked.

"I think it was Rosemarie," Deborah said in a clear, strange voice. She picked up the vase with its fragrant branches and carried it to the living room.

"Rosemary?" said Alex thoughtfully. "No . . . I don't think so. Daphne. Like the flower."

Late that night Olivia surfaced out of sleep, aware that someone was standing beside her bed. She opened her eyes: her dad, outlined against the light from the hallway, was walking away quietly toward the door, which he closed softly behind him. She listened intently. Nothing. Then voices, her parents', quickly becoming raised. Olivia slid out of bed and opened her bedroom door.

She heard her father say forcefully, "There is *no way* Marion is going to have an abortion! Not with her history."

"*Her* history?" Deborah cried, low, heartfelt, penetrating. "What about *our* history? What about us, our family? The family you already *have*!"

"Marion is pregnant and she is going to have a baby, and I am the father. Those are the facts, Deborah, that's what we are going to have to deal with."

So that's it, thought Olivia. Her eyes were open so wide in the darkness they were watering. *There it is.*

CHAPTER 23

James promised Rose, he promised Silver, he promised *himself* that when he got back to Melbourne he would tell the rest of the family about Rose. But somehow, somehow . . . There was his intense engagement with his new artwork; there was Deborah's rage and grief over the breakdown of her marriage . . . There was always some reason to think: not today.

And somehow James had been back in Melbourne for two months and he still hadn't told his siblings about their mother. Almost a year had now gone by since he'd found her, and this in itself made him feel paralyzed. How could he tell them that? Confess that he'd visited Rose three times? The thought shriveled him. With a jolt he realized that the fact of his concealment had become the problem, just as Silver had warned.

And then Rose herself forced the issue. James checked his e-mail one morning and there was one from Rose, with the subject line *Christmas is Coming*.

Hi James—

Christmas is coming and so am I! Well, it's still a few months away but I have decided I absolutely must visit Australia, and soon. Partly to see Alex again while (if?) he can still remember who I am. But mostly to meet my other three children, not to mention my grandchildren! I know this won't be a cakewalk but it seems necessary, doesn't it? And I SO want to.

James closed his e-mail, the backs of his hands tingling the way they did when he'd had a near-miss in the traffic. *No way out of it now, buddy.* He'd always assumed he'd break the news about Rose to Deborah first, but now push had come to shove that didn't seem right. *It has to be Dad.* This thought popped into his mind with the resonance of certainty. *Okay. Now. Right now!*

He got in his car and drove across town to his father's, and all the way there James thought about what he was about to do. How would Alex respond? Apart from those visits when he'd been looking for the letters, he hadn't seen much of his father this past year. Thinking about it now, he realized that out of the four children, he was the one who knew their father least, certainly the one who visited him least. Not that there was any ill-feeling, but just . . . oh, proximity, living on the other side of the city. And they—well, they didn't have much in common. Dad had a technical sort of mind, his was artistic. Dad's private passion had always been gardening, and James was no gardener. And he and Silver had no children, and therefore no grandchildren to create a closer bond.

What's Dad really like now? Deborah was worried about him, he knew that. So was Robert. They both seemed to think it wouldn't be long till he had to be moved to a nursing home. Meredith, he gathered, didn't want that, but what on earth could *she* do? As for James himself, he'd simply avoided thinking about it. In her e-mail Rose had expressed concern that Alex mightn't remember her. Was that possible? Could his father's memory be so damaged that he wouldn't remember the woman he'd once loved, and married, and had four children with?

What will this mean to him, Rose coming back? It hit James that he had not given a moment's consideration to this question throughout the past year's intoxicating reunion with his mother. Who was also, or had been, Alex's wife. What he was about to do seemed preposterous. He was on the brink of turning around and driving home. *No, don't be such a wuss! Grow up, James!*

He knocked at the front door. There was no answer. Bloody hell! He was so keyed up to see his father, and now he wasn't home! A sneaking relief started to seep through him and then he realized that his dad was probably out the back in the garden. But just as James was stepping off the front porch his father's car pulled up. This was confusing: hadn't Robert said his father no longer had the car, that his driving had become too erratic?

Alex got out from the front passenger seat, Meredith from the driver's, and each opened a rear door and retrieved a bulging shopping basket. They were so busy talking to each other they didn't notice James till they were almost upon him.

"Hello, boy!" yelled his father jovially.

"James! How lovely!" cried Meredith. He reached to take the shopping basket from her. "Ta," she said. "We've just been up to High Street and done the weekly shopping. What brings you here?"

"Oh, you know," James said. "Just thought I'd drop in."

"We needed some more cheese," said Alex, unlocking the front door and leading the way through the house.

"I dunno what's with the cheese," said Meredith to her brother in a cheerful aside. "He really has a thing about not running out of cheese. And sardines. Do you think it's because of growing up in the Depression?"

"Could be," said James. He felt completely disoriented: this hadn't been what he was expecting at all. *But what was I expecting?*

"Oh, jolly good!" exclaimed Alex, unpacking the groceries.

"We've got some sardines! Needed them. I'm going to have some sardines on toast, how about you kids?"

"Lovely, Daddy!" said Meredith, winking at James.

Over the next hour James learned two things. One, Alex's memory loss was a very real thing, and two, Meredith was far more on the ball than he had ever given her credit for. She was cagey about just how much she was doing for their father, but it seemed clear to James that it was a lot. There was a cheerful, equitable familiarity between his father and his sister that was . . . well, that was just so unexpected. It was all a bit of a shock, really.

After they'd had their sardines on toast and tea, Alex announced that he was going to put his feet up for a while and went into his bedroom, closing the door behind him.

"Daddy gets up so early these days, he likes to have a nap around now," Meredith said.

"Uh-huh."

"So how does he seem to you?" Meredith asked. "If you haven't seen him for a while . . . Does he seem . . . different?" She pulled some papers and an extra-large envelope out of her bag and was addressing it as she talked.

"Different? Not really, no." James said. He took his time. He wanted to sound positive, but in fact he was starting to doubt his impulse to tell his father about Rose before his other siblings. "Not in like, essence-of-Dad, you know? And I reckon he looks well. Healthy."

"Yeah, he does, doesn't he," Meredith agreed. She was turning over the papers now, three or four large sheets, checking they were all there. Each sheet was covered in drawings in strips and blocks, rather like a comic.

"But his memory's definitely a bit . . . Hey, Merry, what're they?" James asked, curiosity overcoming him. "Can I see?"

"Sure," his sister said, handing the sheets to him. They were on medium weight card, not paper. "It's just something I've done to send Mr. Domasi. He's not well, he's in the hospital. In fact, he's really sick."

"Mr. Domasi? The guy you rent your house from?"

"Yeah, for all this time, nearly twenty years, and he's never put the rent up once and it was ridiculously low to begin with. We used to meet up every month for lunch till a few years ago. Then he moved in with his daughter out in Coburg."

James saw that the four dense sheets told the whole story of his sister's relationship with Mr. Domasi, from the day she helped this old Italian gent off the tram at Kew Junction. Their friendship, the stories he'd told her about village life in Italy, the war, migrating to Australia. The little house he'd rented to her for almost nothing, the handmade cradle that had been his gift when Laurence was born. It was all there in the form of, yes, a kind of comic, or a very detailed sort of storyboard, with collage elements too: an old tram ticket, the rug covering baby Laurence in his cradle made out of a tiny scrap of real cloth, which James guessed was probably a piece from Laurence's actual bunny-rug. It was funny and moving and extraordinarily vivid, and the more he looked, the more he saw.

James heard his mother's voice, telling him about Meredith's story-drawings. *The Penguin and the Horsey.*

"Wow, Merry," he said. "This is amazing! Do you do much of this stuff?"

"Oh yeah," she shrugged. "Always fiddling around with 'em. It's just mucking round, you know."

"This isn't just mucking around," he said. "This is art."

"Art?" cried Meredith, rearing back in her chair. "Oh no, this isn't art! I don't do art, James, *you're* the artist!"

He looked at her sharply. She appeared perfectly sincere and even faintly appalled; her protestations weren't false modesty, they were real. *She's really good and she has no idea*, he thought. Suddenly he longed to be able to tell her what their mother had said: *She was only little, but she had something. I thought she might've become an illustrator, an artist of some kind.*

"Do you have more of these? Would you show them to me?"

"Well, sure, if you want to. I've got heaps of 'em, actually. Laurence calls them my journal things. He quite likes them," she said, looking a bit embarrassed.

"I do too," said James with feeling. He took a deep breath; at last, he had made up his mind. "And, Meredith, I've got some really important news. But I think I should tell everyone at the same time, you and Deb and Robert. What if we organize another family meeting, what d'you reckon?"

"Ooh-ah! Important news!" Meredith goggled theatrically. "Hope it's *good* news! Can I have a tiny weeny hint?"

James shook his head. "Best not."

"Ohhh," she sighed, drawing out the disappointment. "Okay then. Well, just as long as you phone everyone, James, 'cause you know I'm hopeless at organizing things."

James laughed, but he was thinking, *Are you? I'm not so sure that you're hopeless at all.*

CHApteR 24

"Hey, cuz," said Laurence to Olivia, looming behind his mother as they arrived at Deborah's on the Sunday afternoon of the siblings' meeting. "Thought I'd come and hang out with you for the duration."

"Ex-cellent!" she breathed in a Monty Burns gloat. "D'y'wanna come to the park with me and Congo? I'm giving him a solo training sesh."

"Sure."

"Olivia," called Deborah, "Can you take those DVDs by the front door back to the video shop? And take some money, if you want to get something to watch later."

After about fifty meters of Congo trotting decorously at heel, Laurence commented, "Looks like you've got the infamous wild dog tamed. Congratulations."

"Oh no, this is just the good bit. Once we got the 'heel' thing down, he decided he loves being on a lead. But only as long as we keep walking. If we stop, he goes mental. He's hopeless. No, that's not true: he just wants to run everything his way, not mine."

It was true. Even after months of consistent, firm, patient repetition, Olivia couldn't say Congo was trained, not reliably. He exasperated her, challenged her like no other animal she'd ever had, but she loved him with a passion. He had more intelligence and cunning, more strength and agility, more sheer bloody-minded willfulness packed into that tough little tan and white body than any other dog she'd ever known. He'd grown into the too-big skin of his puppyhood but kept the furrowed brow; his mouth was not big but his jaw was incredibly powerful. Most of the time he was eerily silent, but if he was angry or upset he made a frightening, liquid sound from deep in his body; Olivia had read it described as "a bloodcurdling yodel." Having heard it, that description didn't seem melodramatic.

He detested being tied up. Rope or ordinary leads he just tore to pieces. Olivia was walking him today on a new lead, a choke-chain combined with a short, very thick leather strap. She hooked the handle over a post outside the video store, knowing she only had a few minutes before he would get impatient, but they dithered over their selection and she looked up just in time to see Congo step deliberately away from the post to pull the lead taut, then turn his head faster than the eye could follow, sever the leather strap with two deep, jerking bites, and take off.

"Wow," said Laurence, examining the end of the lead now hanging forlornly from the post. "This has got to be a good centimeter thick. More like two."

"I hope I can at least reuse the choker," said Olivia. "This cost a fortune."

"If only he could use these powers for good, hey? What do we do now?"

"He'll be heading for the park, we'll catch up with him there. We'll probably have a really good training session once he's caused his bit of havoc."

As they walked toward the park they could see Congo far ahead, racing along the road, darting joyously in and out of the traffic.

"You know what he's doing, Ol? He's playing chase with the cars. That dog is *insane*, you know that?"

"What dog? I never saw that dog before in my life, okay?"

"Whatever you say."

"Actually, he really isn't my dog. Mintie and Fly-by are mine; Congo is my mum's dog."

Laurence raised one eyebrow.

"No, seriously," she insisted. "Mum bought him, Mum reckons he's hers. Her special dog. You ask her."

"Doesn't matter who *bought* him. You're the one who does everything with him. Takes him to dog obedience school and all that."

"Not any more. He got expelled."

"Shit, I didn't know dogs could get expelled!"

"Nor did I," Olivia said gloomily. "They said he was too disruptive. He scares people. *I* don't think he's scary, but I have to admit he terrifies the other animals. The rats and the rabbits, they're petrified of him, they start literally shaking if he comes anywhere near them."

"Well, gee, Ol, can you blame them? Considering he's probably busy figuring out how to tear them limb from tiny limb."

"Yeah, it's the truth. I just hope he settles down some time before I have a fatal heart attack." They walked on together companionably and then Olivia, glancing sidelong up at her cousin, said, "Hey, Laurence? You know this girl I told you about at school? Fleur? She's kind of changed what the other kids call me."

"Yeah?"

"They all call me Liv these days, that's kind of become my name."

"Like Liv Tyler? Who played Arwen? Smooth! *Liv*."

"Yeah."

"Cool. So, Liv, how's it going at school?" he asked, pushing his hair back from his forehead in a way that reminded Olivia of someone. *Uncle James*, she realized, even though Laurence's hair was blondish, not dark.

"Not bad, actually. Fleur's pretty amazing: she was determined to get us involved in the school play, and wham!" She snapped her fingers. "Now we are! I'm assisting on lights, she's doing stage dressing and wardrobe stuff. It's cool. Almost everyone else is like, Year 10, Year 11. Much better than hanging with the kids my age. They're maggots, most of 'em."

"Hang in there, it'll only get better. Trust me."

"Yeah. How's it going for you?"

"Pretty intense. We just did some more practice exams and I did shithouse."

"Really?"

"Yeah, really. But so did everyone. They make them mad hard just to scare you, I reckon."

"O-kay. So when are the real exams?"

"End of November. Couple of months. Fuck."

"Are you worried?"

"More worried since the other night. I think my mum might've started drinking again."

"Oh, crap! What happened?"

"I got home a couple of nights ago and she was just really spaced. You know how she's been renting our house since forever, before I was born?" Olivia nodded. "Well the old guy who owned it just died. Mr. Domasi. Mum loved him. And now the family's going to sell it, like *soon*. And Mum just freaked. She says she didn't crack, but she sure was acting weird. You'd think no one had ever moved before."

"Oh great. So when will you have to move?"

"Not till after my exams, so I'm okay about that. But if Mum starts getting wasted again, I'm not going to hack it. You know my friend Tristan?"

"Yeah, who drove me and Grandpa home that time, right?"

"Yeah. Well, his older brother's moved out and his parents are sweet for me to live there. I earn enough from watering at the nursery to pay board. They're like this totally sane, together family. And I just can't afford to be stuffed around this next couple of months."

"Have you told your mum that?"

"No, but I will."

"Boy. You know what? Your mum's not the only one acting weird. My mum's lost it too. Looks like my parents are getting a divorce."

"You're shitting me!"

"Nuh. You know I told you about Marion, this woman my dad's on with? She's pregnant."

"Full *on*! Hey, you were going to meet her, right, Ol?" Laurence blinked and corrected himself. "Liv. Not Olive. Just Liv."

She nodded an acknowledgment. "Yeah. And she's actually not a horrible person. But still."

"Still," he agreed. "Man. If I have kids one day and start doing shit like this, slap me, will ya?"

"Count on it. Same for me. Okay, here's the hound from hell. Yeah, you! Maniac! So, Laurence, you wanna hang here while I do the training stuff? Or you could walk around, come back in about half an hour."

"I'll cruise. We need some rope or something, right?"

"Yeah, that'd be excellent."

Just as Olivia had predicted, Congo was now happy to be put through his paces in the training session. Heading out of the park, with a lead cobbled together out of the choker chain and a length of baling twine Laurence had snagged from somewhere, Olivia asked her cousin, "Hey, you know your mum's journal things? Does she do stuff in them about her mum?"

Laurence shrugged. "Maybe. Yeah. Dunno."

"Does she ever like, write to her or anything? Letters?"

"You mean, to England? Nup, how could she? She doesn't know where she lives or anything. Why?"

"'Cause *my* mum's been writing to her, and she doesn't know where she lives either. I found this huge stash of letters."

"Huh?" Laurence frowned at her. "So where does she send 'em?"

"She doesn't," Olivia said. "She just keeps them. Like you said, no address."

"Whoa, pretty weird all right. Are these letters she wrote when she was a kid or something?"

"Some, yeah. Ever since her mum ran off. But off and on the whole time, and *heaps* since Dad's been having this thing with Marion."

"Oh *man*." Laurence made a sorry face, shaking his head in disgust or despair. "That is so sad."

"Deeply," Olivia agreed. "Tragic. When are they gonna grow up? That's what I wonder."

"Dunno, cuz. On the evidence . . . not any time soon." They were nearly back to Olivia's house now. "Hey," he asked, "d'you know what this meeting's about, exactly?"

"More stuff about Grandpa, I think. I'm really getting worried, Mum reckons Grandpa might have to go into a home."

"Uh-oh. That would be horrible. And it'd freak my mum out completely. Shit."

"I know. I think they might be having a big, you know, a big showdown about it."

"Damn." Laurence gripped her shoulder and gave it a small comradely squeeze. "Well, here we are. Assume the brace position."

They put Congo in the backyard and went inside. Heard the sounds coming from the living room, stopped dead, looked at each other. *Not good.* At least three people were talking at once, loudly, and Meredith was crying, also loudly. But maybe she was also one of the people talking?

"Uh-oh," said Laurence.

"We could run away," suggested Olivia hopefully. It was a joke.

Olivia and Laurence pushed open the living room door and stood side by side in the doorway, each with their arms folded in front of them. No one noticed their arrival. Meredith was weeping unrestrainedly, sitting in one corner of the couch, but as they watched she raised her head and cried in a tearful clogged voice, "*How* long, James? *How* long have you known?"

Deborah was crying, too, but less noisily, with both hands covering her face. Uncle Robert, standing by the window, turned and said apparently to the room at large, "This is unconscionable. Utterly unconscionable!" He had his glasses off, and there were tears glistening in his eyes, too, and that was what made Olivia suddenly feel frightened. An awful thought hit her.

"Has something happened to Grandpa?" she cried. "Is he dead?"

Now all the adults fell silent, frozen for a moment in their strange tableau. Then Uncle James took a couple of steps toward them. She had never seen him so upset. His mouth was trembling.

"No, he's fine. It's . . . I've found your *grandmother.*"

"Our grandmother?" said Olivia uncomprehendingly.

Laurence asked, "You mean like, *your* mother? All of yours . . . mother?"

"Who went to England?" Olivia put in.

"Yes. Our mother, yes."

Olivia and Laurence looked at each other in disbelief. *We were just talking about her. This is too weird.*

"She's, what, like, just turned up?"

"Well, yes, kind of," said James unhappily. "Not 'just,' really."

"In England?" *I sound like a moron,* Olivia thought. James nodded. "And is she . . . okay?" she asked. "I mean, is she really sick or something? Or like, *crazy?*"

"No!" said James vehemently. "Oh, no, no, no. She's fine. Completely fine."

"But isn't this," asked Laurence hesitantly, "like, a good thing?"

"Oh *god,*" came loudly from Deborah, a half-moan, half-snarl from behind her hands. "Oh god, *no!*"

Laurence and Olivia jerked and looked at her. They had been so focused on what Uncle James was saying they had almost forgotten the others.

Uncle Robert had a handkerchief out now and was mopping at his eyes ferociously. He held the hankie out in front of him and suddenly yelled at it, "AARRRHHH!" Everyone jumped and stared at him. He shoved the hankie in his pocket and put his glasses back on.

"We've all had . . ." he began, but his voice was reedy and wobbled a bit. He cleared his throat and started again. "We've all just had a bit of a shock. That's all. Olivia, my girl, would you mind putting the kettle on?"

"Good idea," said Olivia, leaving the room with alacrity.

"I'll help!" offered Laurence, hard on her heels. They closed the living room door firmly behind them, leaving the four siblings staring twitchily at each other like a team of spooked horses deciding whether to bolt.

part six

CHapter 25

When Vesna got home from her shift around midnight, Robert was still awake, lying there with the bedside lamp on and his hands linked behind his head.

"Hello, my husband," she said, climbing into bed. It was a little ritual they played sometimes. "What are you thinking about?"

"Hello, my wife. I was just lying here feeling terribly jealous of you."

"Jealous?" said Vesna with amazement. "What d'you mean, darling?"

"Not jealous: envious." Robert had taken his arms from behind his head; he reached for Vesna's hand. "Envious that you have two healthy loving parents, who have been there for you and your brother every step of the way. And wishing I did, too."

"Oh." Vesna's face was soft with sympathy. She hugged him, cuddling close. "I wish you did, too. I *am* lucky, I know it."

"Do you think Dad understood, when we explained to him about—my mother?" Robert asked. "That she's been found?"

"I couldn't tell," said Vesna seriously. "Truly, I just couldn't tell. He seemed to be taking it in, but his lack of interest was so . . . profound. It doesn't seem possible that he could have been so disinterested if he'd really grasped your news."

"I thought exactly that," Robert said. "Is there something more I ought to do, Vesna?"

"I don't think so, darling. Not just now, anyway. But it's odd, I was just talking about your father tonight. Do you remember Bernadette Rooney? Who I worked with at Fairfield?" Robert nodded, a little uncertainly. "She was on the same ward with me this evening. She does agency work now, but she also has a therapeutic massage practice at her home. She works a lot with elderly people. She pointed out something I've never really considered before: that a lot of older people haven't had any physical contact with another person in years. Even decades. Apart from, you know, shaking hands. And medical examinations, perhaps. Isn't that sad?" she said, cuddling her husband even closer.

"It is," said Robert softly.

"And I was wondering, do you think that might be good for your father? A proper massage. He must get stiff from all that gardening. Bernadette's very skilled, she's been studying in China and the States . . ."

"Why not?" said Robert, though he'd never even considered massage before, even for himself, let alone his father. "If you think it's a good idea?" He felt Vesna nodding affirmatively. "Well, if Dad's willing to give it a go . . . Why not?"

A week or so later, Robert took Alex to Bernadette's house. They were shown into a neat, cozy room with a massage table in the center. Robert sat on a chair in the corner while Bernadette talked to his father, filling out an information sheet. She would begin, she explained, by massaging his feet, and they could take it from there. Bernadette put Robert in mind of so many nurses he'd met: unfussed, competent. He particularly appreciated the way she explained things to Alex so directly, without any jargon or condescension.

Alex was chatty and charming while Bernadette slowly massaged his long pale feet. *Has he always been like this?* Robert wondered. He didn't remember his father as such a flirt. Maybe it was a way of handling the memory loss? Or maybe Robert had just never seen his father clearly. Heaven knows, every aspect of his family of origin seemed open to question these days. While he sat there, apparently listening to Bernadette and Alex's conversation, his mind turned restlessly to these recent and almost unbelievable events.

He felt that he was over the initial shock of finding out about his mother, though that had completely unnerved him at first. And he had started to come to terms with James's deliberate concealing of his discovery, distressing and unexpected though such behavior was. Now, furnished with Rose's address, phone and e-mail, Robert was struggling with the idea of contacting her.

He found the prospect utterly daunting. His mind had stalled and blanked a hundred times. *How do I start this? What on earth do I say?* And then his thoughts invariably leapt to how he would sign off. Could he write at the end *love, Robert*? He was shocked to find the idea filled him with unexpected fury. *She doesn't deserve my love!* He thought, of course, of describing his own family, his career—but even then he was again overwhelmed by resentment. *Why should I?* Vesna and his daughters were the most precious things in his life. How could he risk exposing them to the kind of emotional bruising he had suffered as a child? *And what would she care?* Now, as an adult, he could see that Rose must have been desperately unhappy with her own life, her marriage, everything, but since James's news Robert had found himself helplessly reliving the hurt of her prickliness and myriad dissatisfactions which as a boy he had taken terribly personally. His efforts to please her, and the impossibility of doing so—it all seemed so immediate again.

Oh, but he so wanted his mother to know him at last, to know him as a man: successful, respected, a man with a beautiful, happy family. Yes, *he* had achieved that, something she herself had not been capable of! Him, Robert, the nervous nitwit . . . well, still nervous, true. Still riven by anxieties . . .

He felt trapped somewhere, and he didn't want to be. He needed a bridge, a ladder, some way he could approach his mother afresh. So they could meet as equals.

Now Bernadette was suggesting to Alex that he might like to remove his shirt and lie on the massage table for some work on his back and shoulders. Robert rose, intending to leave the room, but Alex cheerfully insisted he stay, and the conversation continued in a somewhat stop-start fashion while Berndadette massaged Alex, gently at first and then with increasing firmness. Alex mentioned he'd been having some knee trouble and she suggested an acupuncture treatment, explaining what that would entail. Alex, completely unfazed, agreed. With fascinated trepidation, Robert watched Bernadette insert the needles. He had imagined it would revolt him, but no. Afterward, Alex walked around the room, experimentally, staring down like someone trying out a new pair of shoes.

"Fixed!" he declared. "Knees like a kid! Like new!" He looked so cheerful, his face such a good color. Could it be that he actually looked younger? The three of them grinned at each other. "Well, aren't I glad to have met you, lass!"

"These things seem to happen at the right time, don't they," Bernadette said, smiling.

In his head Robert heard Meredith's voice: *You have to be alert to the moment when you're ready to change . . . The right person . . .*

"Bernadette," he asked impulsively, "would it be possible for me to make an appointment with you, too?"

"Sure!" she said. "I'll just get my book, we'll make a time."

Two days later Robert was back, face-down on the massage table. Was it the lack of eye contact, partly, that made it so easy for him to talk to Bernadette? The reassuring strength of her hands as she worked on him? Or her matter-of-fact tone as she chatted about the different therapies she had studied, the nervous system and acupuncture, mind/body connection, human responses to stress . . . all sorts of things. Suddenly Robert was telling her about his compulsions: the fingering, the checking. When they had started, how they'd got worse over the past year. His fears, as far as he could voice them, of what would happen if he didn't fulfil each action as he . . . must.

"Have you spoken to your GP about this?" she asked. "First port of call . . ."

"Yes. I know it's obsessive compulsive disorder, that's what they call it."

"And did your GP suggest any treatment?"

"Well, the deep breathing, that was his idea. And that's certainly helped me control the, er, the . . . panic attacks. But he'd like me to go on some kind of tranquilizers, while I prefer to avoid medication."

"Has he ever suggested CBT? Cognitive Behavioral Therapy?"

"I think . . . um, he might've mentioned it . . . But, really. Therapy!" He heard his own voice, how scornful it sounded, and suddenly felt embarrassed. "I just don't think I'm the therapy type," he added lamely. He hoped he hadn't offended her.

"Uh-huh," said Bernadette. She sounded amused. "And a week or two ago, would you have said you weren't the massage type, too?"

"I suppose I would," Robert admitted.

"Well, with your new open outlook . . ." said Bernadette, working away at a knotty bit in his right shoulder. "I know a guy who's had some great results with treating obsessive compulsive disorder. He's a psychologist. Would you consider seeing him?"

Robert took a deep breath. "Can't hurt, I suppose."

"That's right. Can't hurt, good chance it'll help."

At the end of their session, as they sat at Bernadette's little desk and he took out his wallet to pay her, she said, "You know, Robert, I'd like you to come and see me again. You do a lot of desk work and I can help with the consequences of that: just the usual postural problems and muscle tension. The other business, the OCD . . . I've been thinking, before seeing the psychologist I mentioned, there's someone else I think could help you a lot."

"Really? Who?"

"Her name's Theresa Thompson. She's a massage therapist, like me, but she's been working a lot with Bach flowers. Therapeutic use of plant essences, that is. And she's working a great deal these days with Australian native flower essences. Unusual. She's getting some results that I think are—well, let's not pre-empt anything. But I'd love you to see her."

Native flower essences. How . . . "If you think it will help, Bernadette," said Robert with a rush, "then I'll give it a go." *Good heavens, did I just say that?*

With her blue eyes, brown hair and sturdy build, Theresa was so similar in appearance to Bernadette she could be her sister. As they exchanged polite introductory remarks it occurred to Robert that it wasn't only Berndadette and Theresa who were similar. Though Vesna didn't look like the other two women, she radiated the same reassuring qualities: calmness, empathy, capability. *It must be that that makes me trust them.*

The way Theresa massaged him was quite subtle compared to the deep, occasionally somewhat painful work Bernadette had done. From time to time she paused, with her hands lying still on his body. Still, but very much alert. *I should feel self-conscious,* Robert thought, this being only the second massage he'd ever received, other than Vesna rubbing his shoulders sometimes. But instead he felt . . . well, simply relaxed. A state so unfamiliar, it took him a while to identify it.

After he had dressed Theresa talked to him in more detail about his—it was still hard for him to say these words—obsessive compulsive disorder. But it was also becoming easier to talk about, each time. He noticed that every so often Theresa closed her eyes for a little while, almost an extended blink. Finally she said, "I need you to wait here about ten minutes." She went into the adjoining room. When she came back she was carrying two medium-sized brown glass bottles, which she placed on the table in front of him.

"One for home, one to keep at work," she told him. "At moments of stress, when you find yourself starting to do your fingering or wanting to check things—any of those signals—I want you to stop and place three drops of this liquid under your tongue," she withdrew the dropper and squeezed one, two, three drops back into the bottle to demonstrate, "and, if possible, to sit quietly for about a minute while you say the words I've written here. Preferably aloud."

She placed a folded piece of paper beside the bottles. Robert looked at it.

"This is an affirmation," Theresa said, her calm blue eyes holding his. "A declaration about your intent in facing life. You could say it's a mission statement for your soul."

Soul. Hardly a word he was comfortable with. *Are we talking about faith here, Merry?*

"I understand that you may not have said words like this before, or not in this way. But it's very important that you are able to say this affirmation. And that you say it often, especially in these next few weeks. Do you think you can?"

Don't hold back, Robert! Don't hold back. He picked up the piece of paper, opened it. There were just a few handwritten lines.

I honor the universe and my place within it. I trust the universe to ensure that at all times I have with me and within me everything that I need. All is safe; all is well. I require nothing more, and nothing more is required of me.

He felt—what? He felt *attracted* to these words. Even reading them silently had given him a pleasant, expansive sensation. Not weird. *I want to say them,* he thought.

On impulse he asked, "Can I say them now? To you?"

Theresa flashed a sudden smile. "Of course!"

Robert took the dropper from her and placed three drops of the clear, faintly spicy liquid under his tongue. Then he spoke the words of the affirmation aloud in a low voice, taking his time, and as he did so an extraordinarily deep feeling of safety flowed through him. Ease. Warmth. Fullness. Theresa sat and listened attentively with her face perfectly still, and then she beamed at him, and he beamed back.

He looked down at his hands, resting lightly on the tabletop. He turned them palm up, held them before him, touched the palms together, folded the fingers, then parted his hands and rested them again on the wooden surface of the table. *If I can beat this, if I can leave these awful anxious habits behind me—that's what I'll write to my mother about! I'll tell her and she'll understand how much I've changed. How much everything's changed. At last.*

CHAPTER 26

James knew the meeting had gone just about as badly as it could. He'd expected his brother and sisters to be angry with him, but the degree of their outrage had shaken him badly. James was used to being liked, to being approved of and admired; it was terrible to be the cause of such pain and anger. He came away feeling unspeakably miserable.

"I tried to explain that she wrote to us; she tried to stay in touch," he told Silver. "But you know, it didn't even sound convincing to *me*."

"It's early days," said Silver kindly. "They'll come round."

James shook his head. "Go ahead, Sil," he said gloomily, "say, *I told you so*."

"Oh, hon!" she murmured, stroking his arm.

He e-mailed Rose, reporting the bare bones of the meeting and that it hadn't gone well, but sparing the details. He turned his mind away from it with all the slithery skill that a lifetime of avoiding conflict had given him, but it was there, all the time.

It was two or three weeks before Rose reported that she'd had a phone call from Meredith, *very emotional*, but unfortunately Merry had muddled the time difference and called in the middle of the English night. "I was only half awake," Rose said. James got the impression that the conversation had been upsetting, but he didn't want to ask further. A little later she received a letter from Robert, handwritten and delivered by post. "Formal," she told James, "but not entirely frosty."

James got phone calls from both Robert and Meredith, on the same day, and saying much the same thing: "I know this has been hard for you, too." Robert described telling their father about Rose, and Alex's lack of response. He was solemn, James thought, but cordial, and at the end of her call Meredith said, "I've made some pretty big mistakes in my time, too, Jamesey." It wasn't quite forgiveness but it was close, and James nearly wept with gratitude. Still nothing, though, from Deborah, except chilly silence. He felt cowed by it. Then she rang one night, and tore strips off him. She had remembered phoning him on Christmas Day, and figured out who he was with. She called him an "ungrateful rat" and a "sneaking bastard." James wondered if he could possibly feel worse.

He wished he could go back in time. He found himself thinking about the photos in Rose's album, the one with the green silk binding. That other, unsuspected family album. The pictures took on greater and more poignant significance than they'd had when Rose first showed them to him. He kept imagining them being sent across the ocean, bundle by bundle, to his mother, and her trying to piece together her children's lives from these random occasional clues. Documentary evidence, but a documentary without narration.

James found himself drawn by the wish to look again at the photographs in what he thought of as their original form. There was nothing wrong with that, was there? Nothing to be ashamed of—so why did he feel so sneaky when he went to visit Alex early one afternoon, and asked him with studied casualness about getting out the old photo albums?

"Of course, of course," said his father, but he looked a little nonplussed. "The photo albums. You go for your life, lad. I'm just not too sure where they are right now . . ."

"I'm pretty sure they're in the usual place still, Dad," James said, getting up from the kitchen table and heading into the living room, to the big white bookcase. Alex followed him.

"Oh, there they are. Of course," said Alex as James lifted them down from the top of the case, the old black leather album and the second, more recent one with its tan cloth cover. A couple of cardboard shoeboxes beside them contained, James knew, a muddle of unsorted photos, some loose, some in packets with their negatives. He carried the whole lot over to the big dining table.

It was years, decades maybe, since James had opened these albums. How strange it was to see the pictures of his mother as a young woman. As he went through them he put a few aside, intending to get copies made to send to Rose, but he still felt as detached from them as he always had. His *real* mother was not this barely remembered girl; no, she was the vibrant silver-haired older woman he had met just on a year ago. It must be the enormous gap, the long years of absence that made the difference, James decided, since he felt no such disconnection between the photos of his father as a younger man and the interested but slightly baffled eighty-something Dad who was sitting beside him.

Alex reached across and picked up the half dozen photos of Rose that James had put aside. One by one, he gazed at them. "She was a nice girl," he said. His voice sounded regretful. James breathed in hard, almost a gasp. He hadn't said anything yet to his father about Rose, and Robert thought that the news hadn't seemed to really register. But perhaps Alex did understand, after all, that she'd been found? James felt a sudden boldness.

"Would you like to see her again, Dad?" he asked.

"Yes, that'd be nice," Alex said mildly. He put the photos down on the table. *Nice?* That didn't seem right. *As if I asked him if he'd like a cup of tea.*

"That's Rose you know, Dad. Rosemarie. Our mum. Who you were married to."

"That's right," agreed his father.

"And I've found her, and she's going to come out here, at Christmas. And visit us." It all came out in such a rush.

"Jolly good, lad," Alex said, nodding. There was a short silence. "You just let me know about it then, will you?" He pushed his chair back from the table. "You happy to keep on going here, are you? I've just got a few things to do out the back."

James blinked several times. "Okay, Dad." His father left the room and James stared after him. *What the hell was that about? Is this dementia? Or did I just fuck that up, too?*

He might as well continue with the photos, even though it all seemed a bit of an anticlimax now. He started sifting through the shoeboxes. Most of these photos were also well known to him, but then he came across an unfamiliar envelope with a single word written on it in faded copperplate pencil: *Inverness.*

Inside were some very old photographs he'd never seen before. Three children on the seat of a cart: a stern-faced girl of about eight, and a plump toddler hauled onto the lap of a smiling little girl not much bigger than he was. Several pictures of four children lined up on the verandah of a weatherboard house, their bodies in bright sunshine, their heads in deep shadow. The older boy was dressed in a sailor suit, the two girls in long pale dresses with aprons. *Pinafores*, the word popped into James's mind. Here, all standing on the steps in front of the house, squinting into the sun, and a woman had joined them, her hand held slantwise against her forehead to shield her eyes.

A photograph of the same place from farther back, a cottage like a child's drawing with a window on either side of the central front door. A boy was standing on the grass out in front between a pair of spiky trees, date palms, holding a big sloppy-looking horse by its bridle. And here, the family group in a garden: a middle-aged couple, she with steel-rimmed glasses, a deep frown and her hair pulled back, he with his hands in his trouser pockets, his head tilted down shyly, while a young boy on the edge of adolescence leaned against his side, and two teenage girls sat demurely on the grass at their feet. Perhaps the older son had taken the photograph, since he wasn't in the picture. Ah, but here he was, surely it was him again but in a different sort of sailor suit: naval uniform. A studio portrait, with the name of the photographer printed across one corner. James turned the photograph over. On the back was written *Robert, 1939. Age 19.* Uncle Bob. Of course.

There were more. As James looked through them he understood that the older girl was Auntie Isobel, who had died quite young, long before James was born. And Uncle Bob, who'd served in the navy, he'd died not long ago; Robert had gone over to Perth for the funeral. The younger girl was Auntie Margaret, gone too now, and the plump toddler who grew into the sweet-faced boy was Alex himself. The adults were James's own grandparents, before they got old. His grandfather had died when James was just a baby. This shy-looking man was the one Rose had told him was a drinker: *an exceptionally pleasant drunk, but still an alcoholic.* Had it been hard on his wife? His grandmother he remembered from childhood as a rather stern old lady parked in a chair at rare McDonald family gatherings. In the photographs she looked a bit fed up, the way spouses of alcoholics often did. Even the nicest ones. In the art world, James had seen plenty of both.

Alex came back in from the garden. "Cuppa?" he asked brightly, standing in the doorway with his head poked forward enquiringly.

"Thanks, Dad. But, Dad, can you just tell me . . ." James said, beckoning his father over, "what was Inverness? Or where, rather?"

"Inverness? That's in Scotland. The town my mum came from." Alex came over and looked down at the photos spread on the table. "Oh, look at that!" he exclaimed. "That's the house I grew up in!"

"Is it? Maybe Gran called it Inverness after the town, then."

"I suppose she did," Alex agreed, picking up the picture of the boy holding the horse in front of the house. He grinned. "Ah, see . . . that's me and old . . . Benny, that was his name. By golly he was a nice horse. Steady as a rock."

He picked up another. "Oh!" he exclaimed. "Would you look at that!" James craned to see: his father and grandfather sitting side by side on the verandah steps, leaning toward each other with a box of something unidentifiable between them, and a long-legged fox terrier peering anxiously on. "That's when Dora had her first lot of pups. She was a wonderful dog. Champion rabbitter."

"So where was this place, Dad?"

"Up near Castlemaine," said Alex promptly. "Out the back there, past the cemetery. Not the Castlemaine cemetery, another place. Little place."

"How long were you there for?"

"Oh, a long time. Till I went to high school in Ballarat. I boarded there. Then it was Melbourne and the university. Mum wanted me to study. She thought I wouldn't have to fight if I was at Melbourne University. She was right, too."

"To fight in the war, do you mean? The Second World War?"

Alex looked at his son challengingly. "Well, with one son already a POW, she didn't want me going over there, did she?"

"No, absolutely!" said James quickly. "Of course not."

"I'd love to have a foxie again," said his father, gazing at another photo of himself with an arm round the neck of the dog, Dora. "My dad used to say foxies have such long noses because they're always sticking them in where they don't belong."

"So when did your parents leave there? Inverness."

Alex looked up thoughtfully. "Oh, they left there . . . They left there . . ." He grimaced. "Oh, a long time ago. You don't remember?"

"No, Dad, it must've been way before my time. I never went there at all."

"That's a pity. Nice house, that house. I'd love to show it to you, laddie."

"Well," said James, suddenly fired with inspiration, "maybe you could! If it's still there. We could go for a run and see."

"Oh, it's too far to run."

"Drive, I mean, Dad. Not far to drive. It's early—look, not even three o'clock. We could go right now! Have a look around, see what we can see, and still be back in time for dinner."

"I'd want to have a cuppa first."

"Naturally. Cup of tea first. And maybe . . . tell you what, we could take our time and have a counter tea at a pub in Castlemaine. How does that sound?" James could tell by the look on his father's face that it sounded like a grand idea to him.

"Hello, Uncle James," said Olivia, opening the front door to him. "Come in. Mum's in the study."

Hovering in the doorway to her bedroom, Olivia heard him knock at the study door and greet her mother, and Deborah's voice coolly responding. It was the first time Uncle James had been to visit since the big meeting, but Olivia had heard her mother talking to him angrily on the phone, still furious, even crying. *Mind you, she cries about anything these days.* Now they were both going into the kitchen. Good. Olivia joined them there. Her uncle was perched on one of the stools at the bench, Deborah had the fridge door open and her back to them.

"It was amazing, Deb," James was saying. "I wouldn't have believed it if I hadn't been there."

"What was amazing?" asked Olivia, parking herself on the stool beside him.

"I took your grandpa to see if we could find the house he grew up in, up near Castlemaine. Inverness, it was called."

"I'd love a house with its own name," said Olivia.

"Pretentious," Deborah declared, closing the fridge door with her elbow. She had a bottle of white wine, already opened, in one hand, a bottle of soda water in the other. She looked at James questioningly. He pointed at the soda water.

"Inverness was the town in Scotland Dad's mother grew up in," he said.

"Oh?" Deborah said with studied indifference. *Oh, lighten up, Mum,* thought Olivia. *He's your favorite brother!*

James rattled on excitedly, apparently oblivious to the frost. "You could hardly see the road that led to the place, it was so overgrown. But Dad directed me like he'd been there yesterday. All the way out from Castlemaine: *Take this road. Turn left here!* And there it was, sitting under these two huge old date palms, just like in the photos. Well, except the date palms weren't huge then."

"What photos?" asked Deborah, interested despite herself.

"These photos I came across at Dad's earlier today. I can't remember ever seeing them before. They were in an old envelope marked Inverness."

"I bet Auntie Joan gave them to Dad when she came over from Perth a month or so ago. She told me she'd been sorting through things. She probably thought they should come back to Dad, now that he's the last of his lot still kicking."

"Didn't she give you that really pretty bowl?" asked Olivia.

"Yes, she said it used to belong to Dad's mother. You know those Royal Doulton ones with the scenes from Shakespeare?" James made an interested face. "Mine's got Portia making her speech. She gave Meredith one, too, with poor old Ophelia drifting down the stream. All too appropriate, really."

"Me and Robert got some silverware. A carving set, she gave me."

"Mmm, she mentioned that."

"Yeah, Auntie Joan would've brought these photos over, for sure," James said, fired up again. "There's a whole bunch. Dad as a little kid, and his sisters, and Uncle Bob in navy uniform. You'd like them, too,

Olivia," he said, turning to her. "There's some of Grandpa with his first dog."

"What sort of dog?" she asked alertly.

"Fox terrier."

"Oh, I *love* fox terriers!"

"How extraordinary," said her mother dryly. "And you so indifferent to most animals. You know, I'm sure I've heard about this place. I knew Dad grew up near Castlemaine, but he never seemed interested in visiting. No relatives around there or anything."

"Yeah, no," James agreed. "I was trying to figure out when his parents left there. Sometime soon after Dad came to Melbourne to study, but he doesn't seem to know. Or care much."

"That's typical of Dad, though: the past is over and done, for him. No further interest. You know."

"Maybe, yeah," he nodded. "I'm sure you're right, Deb. But gee, he remembers this house all right! And let me tell you the most amazing thing: not only is it still standing, it's got all this stuff in it, almost like people were still living there! Beds, blankets, crockery in the cupboards, everything."

"Well, maybe there *are* people living in it, James! Maybe it's somebody's weekender!"

He shook his head. "If it is, they haven't been there in ages. It's really dusty and it smells of mice and it just has, you know, that uninhabited feeling. I got in through a window."

"God, Jaf!" said Deborah admonishingly, but she was smiling.

Cool, thought Olivia. "Did Grandpa go in, too?" she asked.

"Like a shot!" James said. "Through the back door though, once I'd opened it. He went into all the rooms and described every single stick of furniture that used to be there. Who slept where. Some of the furniture that's still there was actually the same stuff. The bed he slept in, for instance, with those sort of curved iron ends, you know. But it's in a bedroom now, and he says he and Uncle Bob used to sleep out on the back verandah. They had one end sort of closed in, but it's not any more. But when you look on the floor and the wall, you can see where the partition used to be. Dad showed me."

"Wow," said Olivia. "That is *so* amazing."

"And he can't have been there in sixty years," mused Deborah. "The human brain. What a strange thing it is." She shook her head as she spoke.

"Honestly, he could've walked around that place blindfolded. He showed me where the veggie garden used to be. There's still some of the old fruit trees, pretty damn straggly though. But with little apricots forming and stuff. A *huge* almond tree. He got a bit upset that they haven't been looked after. Reckons he'll go back next year and prune them."

"Could we?" asked Olivia. "Could we do that? I'd really like to go there!"

"Well, not without the owner's permission we can't!" said Deborah. "I wonder who *does* own it now? We must be able to find out somehow."

"Would you like me to make some inquiries?" asked James. "I could do that."

"Well ... Why not? But this time, James, *try* to keep the rest of the family informed, will you? Of things that *might* just be of some relevance to all of us?"

"I will, Deb," he said contritely. "I really am so sorry about ... you know ... not telling you about Rose when I should have. I don't know why ... Silver kept telling me I should, I just ..."

Olivia looked away, shifting some fruit around in the fruit bowl, ears pinned back for her mother's response.

"How is Silver, anyway?" Deborah asked, in a perfectly normal tone of voice. *Good, she's letting it go*, Olivia thought. *About time!*

"She's fine. Up in Brisbane this week, hanging a show. I'm flying up for the opening on Thursday."

"Could we maybe do dinner one night before you go?"

"You bet! Tomorrow?"

"Yeah, tomorrow, good." Deborah smiled at her brother, and then her eyes suddenly filled with tears. "I really need to talk to you, Jaf."

Uh-oh, thought Olivia, sliding off the stool and quietly leaving the room. Lately she'd started feeling like there were a stack of things she just didn't want to know.

CHAPTER 27

Olivia paused across the road, her enormous schoolbag weighing down one shoulder, and gazed at her home. *So weird*, she thought. *It still looks exactly the same but inside it feels completely different.* Her dad slept on the fold-out sofa bed in the living room now, when he was there. But he was at Marion's more and more. She missed him. Her mum—you never knew what state she was going to be in, just that it would be a state. Sad and crying one day, furious and bitchy the next. It seemed crazy to Olivia that they couldn't make up their minds and tell her what was going to happen, but at the same time she figured she knew what it was going to be and she could hardly bear the thought.

She'd met Marion half a dozen times now. She knew she was supposed to hate her but it wasn't truly possible: she was too nice, too sensible. And Angus was so happy around her, it was scary. Marion was going to have a baby and . . . and what? What would her family be then? More than ever Olivia felt that only her animals could be relied upon.

One night driving home from one of these dinners with Marion she had said to him, "Dad, if you're going to move out, you have to tell me first."

"I will, Ollie," he said.

"Promise!" she demanded.

"I promise," Angus said.

Fleur invited her to spend a weekend down in the national park at Wilson's Promontory, where her family had rented one of the Tidal River cabins. Olivia had been to the Prom once before when she was about six or seven years old, camping with her parents and another family. She remembered that it was really beautiful and there were lots of birds and animals. Wombats had got into the food tent and there had been scenes of consternation in the middle of the night. Wallabies had hopped casually about the place. And a large goanna had scuttled across the track when they were out walking and sent some foreign hikers into hysterics.

She wanted to go, but as always it was a struggle for her to go anywhere that she couldn't take the dogs. It seemed so unfair for them to miss out, and Congo had been going through another difficult stage, getting out of the yard by hook or by crook and turning up at Olivia's school, prowling the corridors and yodeling eerily until he found her. Then she would have to either leave class to take him home, the basenji running jauntily along beside her bike, or phone her father to come and pick him up. The fact was, Congo scared people. The school's vice-principal called Angus in and told him it was *completely unacceptable* and *simply can't happen again*. It made Olivia nervous. If she went away for a weekend and disrupted his training program, the willful little dog might pay her back with even worse behavior.

"Go, Olivia, for heaven's sake," urged her mother. "It's ridiculous the way you're tied to these animals and their routines. You're thirteen, can't you start acting like a teenager? Have a weekend with your pals! Be irresponsible!"

"But they *need* things! The rabbits—"

"Oh god! Just write it down, I'll take care of your menagerie."

"But what if Congo gets into trouble while I'm away, then what?" fretted Olivia.

Deborah's lips thinned to string. "Excuse me? Congo is *my* dog, remember? And *I'm* going to take care of him."

"Okay, okay. I'll go!" And go she did, and had a really good time. Spring was being truly spring-like that weekend, thrilling with birdsong and the scent of flowers. The nights were thick with stars. They went with Fleur's father and stepmother, and their twin toddlers, and Olivia watched carefully to see how this family configuration worked. It seemed fine, if a little frantic at times. The twins could be pesky but mostly they were pretty cute. On both afternoons the parents sat the wriggling littlies in baby backpacks and took them off on long walks, leaving Fleur and Olivia to wander around and explore and talk. Fleur's dad had a camera, one of the old-fashioned ones with actual film and lots of settings, and he showed them how to use it, explaining about aperture and focus and depth of field, and loaded it with new film and told them they could use the whole roll.

They took close-ups of stones and flowers, and skyscapes and seascapes, and Olivia took two pictures of Fleur sitting on a huge rock at the edge of the river that she just *knew* were going to be special. A breeze came up and swirled Fleur's long white-blonde hair around her head like ghostly streamers. For the first photo Olivia got Fleur to close her eyes. Her face was still and mysterious, and then Olivia said, "Now, open!" and Fleur's enormous eyes, a riveting brilliant blue with a ring almost of indigo around the iris, were fixed on her, *burning*, Olivia thought, and her face exactly as it had been before, still and inward, *like she's in a trance or a vision or something*.

"Wow. That gave me goosebumps. I hope it comes out something like what I just saw."

"It will," said Fleur. "I put a spell on the camera. Every photo will be perfect."

"Mmm. Could you just do that spell on my whole life, please?"

"Sorry. Life's not like that."

"Huh. Limited spell talent, more like it."

"O, ye of little faith," intoned Fleur, shaking her head slowly. "Let's go and eat a whole packet of chocolate biscuits and ruin our appetites for dinner."

"Another excellent idea!"

Really, it was about the best weekend Olivia had ever spent in the company of humans. (Grandpa perhaps excepted.) But still, when she got home she was itching to see her animals, especially the dogs. She dumped her bag in her room, yelled hello to her mother in the study, and raced through to the backyard. Mintie and Fly-by just about turned themselves inside out, whining and lashing their tails and Fly-by trying to climb into her lap. But no Congo prancing up with his wicked little smile. Not chained up, either. Not locked in the shed.

Olivia went back inside to the study. "Mum, where's Congo?" she asked.

"Congo's gone to live on a farm," said Deborah, not turning around from the computer screen.

The words didn't make sense. Did not compute. "What did you say?"

"Congo," said her mother, turning from the screen now and speaking slowly, separating each phrase, "Has gone. To live. On a farm."

It was her mother's tone and the look on her face that convinced Olivia that this was not a joke. The words themselves still didn't make sense. She turned and went to look through the kitchen window at the backyard. Mintie and Fly-by raced over to the back door and barked once, hopefully. Definitely no Congo.

"It's the best thing, Olivia. He was getting to be too much." Deborah had followed her as far as the kitchen and was leaning in the doorway.

"Too much for who?" asked Olivia. She was amazed at how normal her voice sounded.

"Too much for everyone! For you, me, the school, your father, everyone! So I made the decision. He'll be much better off, living on a farm. He was my dog, after all."

"What farm? Where?"

"I'm not going to tell you, you'll only pester them and want to go and see him."

Olivia walked over to the kitchen bench, picked up an orange out of the fruit bowl and started to peel it with her thumbnail. Her eyes were filling hotly with tears but she kept peeling, staring at the piece of fruit, her hands. Suddenly she lifted her head and hurled the orange at the wall of cupboards in front of her. It exploded wetly and fell to the floor, leaving juicy marks on the cupboard door.

"You *bitch*!" she screamed at her mother. "You *bitch*! He was never your dog! He's *my* dog!"

Deborah flinched and straightened up in the doorway. "Olivia—"

"Where's Dad? Where is he? As soon as Dad gets home we're going to go and get Congo!"

"Your father won't be getting home. This isn't his home any more. He moved out on Saturday."

"You *liar*. He wouldn't do that without telling me."

"Well, he has. And don't you *dare* talk to me like that."

Olivia advanced on her mother, right up to her, and snarled in her face, "Oh, that makes sense then. You'd *have* to wait till Dad was gone before you could do this. Because Dad wouldn't have *let* you get rid of Congo. Because Dad's not a completely selfish control freak *bitch*!"

Deborah was millimeters, nanoseconds away from slapping Olivia across the face, like in some bad soap opera, and Olivia was daring her to do it. They both knew that. Slowly, deliberately, Deborah turned her own face away and stared fixedly at the chipped paint on the doorframe right beside her. Olivia waited a moment or two longer then stormed past her mother, down the hall and into her bedroom. She started hauling dirty clothes out of the backpack she'd taken down to the Prom and stuffing clean ones in.

"You needn't make me the baddie here, Olivia. Your father took

Congo to this farm. It was his idea as much as mine," Deborah said, having followed her again.

Olivia ignored her. *Liar*, she thought. She grabbed underwear out of a drawer and hurled it into the pack.

"What do you think you're doing?" Deborah said.

"I'm packing my things. I'm not going to stay here," said Olivia. She was no longer screaming, her voice was low now and filled with furious intensity. "I'm going to live with Dad. Dad and Marion!" She flung that at her mother.

"Oh?" said Deborah, with icy barbs in her voice. "In Marion's flat? And how many animals do you think you'll be able to have there? Not *one*, missie! Not one! A mouse in a cage if you're lucky!"

Olivia froze. It was true. She hadn't thought of that.

"I'm ringing Dad. I'm going to tell him what you've done," she said, straightening.

"I'm not giving you the number at that bloody flat!"

Olivia sneered. It was the first time, Deborah thought with an odd, disconnected clarity, that she had seen her daughter look like a teenager. "A: he does have such a thing as a mobile phone. And B: I happen to know Marion's phone number. I've dialed it plenty of times already, you know."

And yes, *that* made her mother wince. *Ha!* Olivia stalked past her to the phone in the kitchen and dialed the number from triumphant memory. She was trying to look nonchalant but her hands were trembling. Marion answered, and Olivia told her politely who was calling and asked if she could speak to Angus. Her father came on the line.

"Dad, Mum's got rid of Congo," she said urgently. "She's taken him to live on some farm."

There was a silence, and in that silence Olivia knew that what Deborah had said was true. Her father was in this, too, up to his neck.

"Olivia, sweetheart," Angus said. "I know you're unhappy about this. I know it's all a shock. But it's for the best. He was getting to be too much, really he was."

"He wasn't too much *for me!*" Olivia hissed. "And don't you ever, *ever* call me 'sweetheart' again."

She slammed down the phone and without a glance at her mother she called Mintie and Fly-by to her and headed for the park. It was already dark and she didn't have a jacket, but Deborah didn't dare say a word. Instead she went to the fridge, poured herself a glass of white wine and downed a big gulp of it. She leaned her head against the fridge door so that her forehead was resting on the white enamel, between a school notice and a Gary Larson cartoon. The cartoon showed a dog standing flattened against a laundry wall, hiding. A cat was peering curiously, cautiously into the clothes dryer, to the open door of which had been taped a roughly lettered notice saying "CAT FUD." *Oh please*, the dog was praying fervently. *Oh please*.

"Oh, Jesus Christ," said Deborah, eyes closed. "Jesus fucking Christ."

The next morning Olivia waited until her mother had left for work before she emerged from her bedroom. There was a note on the kitchen table: *Olivia, please call me at the office, love Mum*. She dropped it in the bin without even screwing it up.

Fleur was in separate classes until recess, and then she was in the library frantically finishing an essay. "Lunchtime?" she asked, seeing Olivia hovering in the doorway. Olivia nodded. At lunchtime they made their way over to the school hall for a backstage meeting about the end-of-year play.

"What's up?" Fleur asked as they entered the hall. "Were you reading all night again?"

"Nup," said Olivia, but that was all she could manage. She sat through the meeting, trying to look interested, but she barely heard a word that was said. Finally one of the Year 11 girls asked her if she was feeling all right.

"Not really," she admitted. She was staring at the floor and didn't notice everyone turn to look at her.

"What's up?" the same girl asked.

"You know that dog of mine? The basenji?"

"Sure, that one that's been stalking the school, uh?"

"The Hound of the Baskervilles!" said one boy, lifting his chin and howling like a wolf. It was a good wolf howl but it sounded nothing like Congo's strange cry from the jungle depths.

"Yeah," Olivia said, smiling wanly. She looked up then, into a circle of curious faces. "Well . . . my mum got rid of him while I was away at the weekend."

"How do you mean, *got rid of him*?" asked Fleur.

"She's sent him to live on a farm." She saw several of the kids' faces contract. There was an exchange of knowing glances between them, and Fleur, too.

"Ah, right," said one of the boys from Year 10. "The old 'he's gone to live on a farm' routine."

"What do you mean, *routine*?" Olivia asked. She felt strange. There was something happening that she didn't know about.

"That's one of the oldest bits of bullshit in the book," he said carelessly. "Don't you know? It means, *we had him put down*."

Olivia's mouth literally dropped open.

"Oh, great, Bosco," said one of the older guys. "Break it to her gently why don't you?"

"Sorr-y," said the boy Bosco, grimacing. "I thought everyone past fourth grade knew that."

"Put down?" repeated Olivia. No one said anything. She got up. Fleur got up, too, and was one step behind her as she left the hall. The schoolyard was teeming with kids; it stopped Olivia in her tracks. Fleur took her elbow and guided her back into the hall, up the narrow stairs at the side to the lighting booth high in the back wall. It was locked. They slumped together on the narrow piece of floor, against the door.

"*Put down*," Olivia said flatly. "She killed him."

"Not with her own hands," Fleur pointed out.

"No. Not with her own hands. She got someone else to do that. She paid some bloody vet *money* to have him killed. And my dad took him there."

"Your *dad*? No, he wouldn't have!"

"He did. He told me last night. And he's gone to live with Marion. He's left home."

"Oh, Liv." Fleur sounded stricken, too, and Olivia couldn't bear to look at her. It made it all too real. The tan and white body so vibrant with life being held on the steel table, the needle slipped with professional ease into . . . where? His rump? His foreleg? The wrinkles on his permanently questioning forehead suddenly smoothing out and the legs giving way. Slumping. Had anyone spoken? Had her father said, *Good-bye, Congo?* Had he said, *I'm sorry?* Olivia brought her knees up and buried her face in them, wrapping her arms around her head. After a while she muttered, "Could you get me a cheese sandwich?" so that she could have some time completely alone without hurting Fleur's feelings. Then she sobbed.

That night she avoided any contact with her mother, even a glimpse of her. She took Mintie and Fly-by for a long run in the park, aching for Congo's demanding, complicated presence, and went straight to her bedroom after they got back. Deborah tapped on her door and asked her to come and eat dinner, but Olivia ignored her. Later, when she heard the TV go on, she went to the kitchen. There was a meal set out on a plate with a note saying *Microwave me!* but she ignored this, too, opening a can of creamed sweet corn and toasting some bread to go with it instead. She thought she would be sick if she ate the food her mother had cooked. She took the toast and sweet corn back to her room, with a glass of milk, and ate it there.

She heard the phone ring and her mother answer it. After a few minutes of unintelligible murmuring she heard Deborah's voice get louder. *Who's she fighting with now?* Olivia wondered. *Probably Dad. Arguing about who's to blame.* She opened her door quietly to listen in.

"That is *ridiculous,* Robert!" she heard Deborah say. She wasn't talking, she was yelling. "How can Meredith *possibly* look after him? She wouldn't know if her own arse was on fire!"

Oh, great, Olivia thought, *now she's on the warpath about Auntie Meredith.*

"Oh yeah, right," she heard her mother sneer. "AA. On the wagon. Turned over a new leaf. What *crap!* She'll be asking him for money in two seconds flat, if she hasn't already! If she even *bothers* to ask and doesn't just help herself." Her voice went up several notches, wild with complaint. "What is it with you bloody men, always a soft touch for the helpless female with a sob story? Hey? The *poor, poor, pitiful me* line! They are the worst sort of predators, can't you *see* that?"

"You should know about good lines. Like *gone to live on a farm,*" Olivia murmured softly. While Uncle Robert spoke, her mother stood there with shoulders hunched and the phone jammed to her ear, staring at the kitchen floor and tugging hard on a strand of her own hair. Then she erupted again.

"No! No, no, *no!* If Dad can't cook for himself, if he can't remember how to use the bloody washing machine, then he's not safe on his own. He'll be setting fire to things next. He has to go into residential care and that's that! Which means we have to find a nursing home."

Olivia stiffened. *Grandpa.* Now she saw it. Her mother was going to do it to Grandpa, too. Not kill him outright, but she might as well.

"I am *not* upset! I am *not* shouting! A *therapist?* Of course I'm not going to see a therapist, don't be ridiculous! Have you gone mad, Robert? I'd always credited you with common sense at least, until now."

Olivia could feel her mother's anger coming in waves up the hallway, even though she was being quiet again as Robert talked. But not for long.

"This is complete rubbish!" she burst out. "If no one else in this family will make a sensible decision, it's obviously up to me. Again. As usual. *I'll* find a decent nursing home for Dad. There's an agency that handles these things, I've already spoken to them. I'll ring them again tomorrow. Meantime you toddle off to your massages and aromatherapy and whatever else you bloody occupy your time with these days!"

Deborah slammed the phone down and stormed up the hall, Olivia just getting her bedroom door closed before she passed by. *"Affirmations!"* she heard her mother snarl disgustedly. Deborah went into the study and slammed around in there for awhile, then all was quiet and Olivia knew she'd settled in front of the computer.

She sat down on the side of her bed, feeling that her mind had closed in, sharpened to a hard, still point. So much had happened since she got back from the Prom just yesterday evening, and worse, she knew now, was about to come. *No!* she thought fiercely. *She's not going to do this!*

CHAPTER 28

The house was exactly as Uncle James had described it. *Inverness*. It had taken such a long time to get there. First they had to walk with Olivia's bike up to the nearest station and catch a train in to Spencer Street. There, in the dauntingly busy terminal, Olivia found the right place to buy their tickets for the train to Castlemaine. The trip took ages; there were delays, *works on the line* announced a laconic voice over the train's crackling speakers, and apologized unconvincingly. Olivia tried not to think about the look on Mintie's face when she'd hugged her good-bye.

Finally they arrived in Castlemaine and started walking again, wheeling the bike, and Grandpa was quite sure of the way but he started to get tired, and Olivia was exhausted, too. She had hardly slept for the past two nights. She managed to juggle her pack and Grandpa's bag and Grandpa himself onto the bike and actually dinked him, while she stood on the pedals, for several kilometers along the flat country road. Grandpa rested his hands on her shoulders and laughed with delight. Currawongs called to them from the trees *Arrah! Arrah!* as they wobbled by. Only a couple of cars passed them and Olivia was glad of that, she didn't want to attract more attention than she could help.

"Turn off here!" Grandpa said, gesturing excitedly. "This is the track to home!"

They had to dismount, the track was too bumpy for the overloaded bike. As they went on Grandpa started to walk a bit faster. "I used to live down here, you know," he told Olivia.

"I know, Grandpa," she said.

"Oh, I remember one day when I was just a little feller I found a cow standing beside this track, just right about here! She had a rope halter on. She was a Jersey, such a pretty thing, I led her home and I told Mother, 'Look, this is Buttercup!' " He laughed. "I thought we could keep her and she'd be my cow. Such a pretty thing. But she belonged to someone else and I couldn't keep her after all. The farmer gave me tuppence for finding her though."

"Did he?" said Olivia, smiling.

"Tuppence was quite a bit in those days, you know."

The tops of the two big date palms came into view. "Over there! Over there!" he cried. When they actually came in sight of the house Alex stopped and said proudly, "Will you look at that! The old homestead, eh? I feel like I was here yesterday."

Olivia got in through one of the bedroom windows, just like Uncle James had done, and unlocked the back door. The big old-fashioned key was sitting there in the inside lock. It was now late afternoon and Alex set to work immediately gathering kindling wood and getting the old wood stove in the kitchen fired up. It smoked a bit at first but Grandpa soon had it burning beautifully.

"By golly, I'm glad that flue's clear," he said. "I was a bit worried there for a minute. Now let's have a look at the tank."

He went out the back door and sure enough, at the side of the house was a large corrugated-iron water tank on a wooden stand. Alex picked up a long stick and tapped it firmly at various points. There was a heavy, flat sound from within.

"Oh, I think it's full," he said, looking pleased. "Just check the tap in the kitchen would you, lovey?"

At the sink, Olivia turned the tap and out poured the water, no problem. She let it run for a few moments and then filled a glass, which she carried outside to Alex. He took it and held it up to the last rays of sunlight, peering.

"Clear as crystal. Not even any wrigglers," he said with profound satisfaction. "That's good, eh?"

"It's excellent, Grandpa. And look, there's a kettle and a teapot and everything."

"Well, of course there is, darl! What sort of home would it be if I didn't have a teapot!"

She had brought tea, bread, tins of sardines and baked beans from Alex's own pantry, and a small carton of milk, trusting Uncle James's description of a kitchen equipped with utensils and crockery. They cooked their meal as dusk began to settle. There was no electricity, a possibility which hadn't occurred to Olivia, but there were plenty of candles and matches in the kitchen drawers, and a bottle of lamp oil which Grandpa used to top up three lanterns he found in various rooms. There were blankets on the beds, and pillows, and Olivia found sheets in a big old wardrobe in the larger bedroom. They smelled rather musty and dusty and a few silverfish fell out when she shook out the bedding, but they weren't dirty or mouldy so she made up two beds. It was fine.

Alex hadn't questioned the adventure once. As they ate their sardines on toast and drank their second mugs of tea at the kitchen table, he rested his knife and fork upright in his fists beside his plate for a moment and said, "Gosh, it's good to be home. What a grand lass you are, doing all this for me."

Olivia felt her throat swell up inside, her mouth and chin suddenly went wobbly. "That's okay, Grandpa," she said, but her voice was hardly more than a whisper. They smiled at each other in the soft light of the lantern sitting between them on the table. His face looked deeply lined and tired, but happy, so happy. She put another forkful of food into her mouth to stop her bottom lip from trembling.

They both turned in early. Birds or possums scrabbled occasionally in the ceiling, and overhanging branches scratched at the tin roof, but the two travelers just slept, and slept, and slept.

By the time Olivia woke the next morning Alex was already up, exploring what had once, long ago, been a vegetable garden.

"Good morning, Grandpa," she called from the back door.

"Hello there!" he cried, waving enthusiastically. "I'll be right in!"

There was a pot of tea already made, and Grandpa had found a long spindly toasting fork with which he speared a slice of bread and then sat himself down on a chair placed before the wood stove to do the toasting.

"Sorry, darl, I wasn't expecting visitors. There's hardly a thing to eat in the house, I'm afraid."

"Don't worry, Grandpa," Olivia assured him. "Tea and toast is perfect for now, and then I'll hop on my bike and go and get some more supplies in town."

"Oh, would you do that for me? That'd be such a help. I've got a fair bit to do in that veggie garden. Can't believe I've let it go like that."

"Don't wear yourself out though, I'll give you a hand when I get back."

Olivia passed a small local general store, but she didn't want to be asked friendly questions or for talk to start. So instead she rode all the way to Castlemaine and rode around till she found a supermarket there. She dithered over what to get in the unfamiliar aisles. *Do we need cereal? Toilet paper! What about potatoes for dinner? How many?* She wished she'd made a list before she left. Halfway through she remembered her mobile phone, which had been turned off, but when she checked it (half-dreading any messages) she found to her surprise that it was dead. She must've forgotten to recharge it last night. *Damn!* By the time Olivia finished shopping she was ravenous.

She bought a meat pie with sauce from a bakery and wolfed it down, and then felt guilty because Grandpa would be hungry too. But he'd be okay, happily setting the veggie garden to rights.

"Inverness . . . Oh Inverness! You're the best . . . you're the best!" she sang as she rode back, and the bike tires sang along with her on the black tarmac. She had to slow down on the dirt track, she had bought eggs and didn't want to break them. She unloaded her backpack full of goodies in the kitchen and went out to the vegetable garden, but Grandpa wasn't there. *He must've gone back to bed for a rest,* she thought, but he wasn't there either. Nor in any of the other rooms.

"Grandpa," Olivia called, standing at the back door. And again, more loudly, *"Grandpa!"* She listened for his answer, but none came. She went out past the vegetable garden and into what had once been an orchard. There were the apricot trees Uncle James had mentioned, and the huge almond, and apples, too, *full of codlin moth, I'll bet* she thought, and a big pear tree. He wasn't in the orchard. She even peered up into the branches in case he had climbed up to inspect them at close quarters, but no.

At the end of the orchard was a wire fence, almost completely broken down. Beyond that was a clear area and then gum trees, thickening gradually into serious bush. She walked toward it, making sure to keep the house in sight, and called again. *"Grandpa!"* And then *"Alex McDonald!"* Still no answer.

She went back to the kitchen and drank a glass of water, and checked all the rooms again. *Maybe he got sick of waiting for me and went to get some food himself,* she thought. She got on her bike again and rode down the track, stopping several times to call his name and listen, and then on down the road as far as the general store, where she went in and bought a bottle of lemonade just so she could check out whether he was in there, chatting maybe to the woman at the counter. But he wasn't.

She rode back to the house, hoping desperately he would be there.

No. It was now several hours since she'd last seen her grandfather and Olivia was seriously worried. *What do I do now?* she asked herself. She just couldn't think.

For another hour Olivia circled the house, increasingly frantic. The possibility that her grandfather had wandered off into the bush and was getting farther and farther away, maybe more and more lost, was becoming frighteningly strong. *And if* I'm *frightened,* she thought, *then he must be . . .*

She heard the sound of a car approaching, and rushed out to the front verandah. The car came in sight, a big, fancy station wagon that looked a bit familiar, bumping along the track. It stopped in the front yard, the driver's door was flung open and Uncle James leaped out and ran toward her. Silver was behind him, walking at an unhurried pace and smiling broadly.

"Oh Jesus, Olivia!" Uncle James cried and grabbed her in both arms and hugged her really hard. "I am so glad you're here! You're all right!"

"Hey, Olivia," Silver said, stroking her arm just once.

Olivia's mouth and chin were wobbling again. She couldn't seem to speak.

"Where's Dad?" asked James. "Grandpa?"

"I don't know," Olivia said. She scrunched her face up momentarily to keep from crying. "I think he's lost."

After Uncle James called the police on his mobile phone, he said, "I've got to ring your mother and tell her you're safe." Olivia opened her mouth to say *No* and then closed it again.

Silver touched her elbow. "Show me where the orchard is," she suggested. Olivia led her away, and James waited till they were out of earshot before he called Deborah.

Silver asked lots of questions. What sort of trees were in the orchard? Were they still healthy? How old was the house? Olivia answered as best she could, immensely grateful for the kind, distracting chatter. She'd always liked Silver but she couldn't remember ever talking to her like this, just the two of them. Something about her— her Americanness perhaps, or her wealth, or the whole art dealer thing—had always made it seem like Silver wasn't quite part of her ordinary family. It had never been possible to think of her as *Auntie* Silver, and now Olivia felt glad of that.

Suddenly they both heard a car approaching at speed, not slowing for the bumps in the track, and then a little skirl of noise from a siren, more greeting than warning. Olivia jumped, and had taken her first hurried steps toward the house when Silver stopped her with a hand laid gently on her shoulder.

"Olivia," she said, "I just want you to know that whatever happens, you came here with your grandpa for the best of reasons. The very best. I know that, and your Uncle James knows it, too."

Olivia nodded twice and started walking away. After a few steps she turned. "Thanks," she said. "But really, how *can* you know?"

Silver looked taken aback. "I . . . just do," she said. As they came closer to the house they could hear men's voices, James and a couple of others. Silver stopped her again and said in a determined way, "Okay: it's observation, honey, and experience. I've seen you with your grandpa, I *do* know. Sometimes you just have to trust these things."

"Okay," said Olivia, as if allowing her something.

There were two policemen, one a man about her dad's age, one a lot younger. Clearly they assumed James to be the person in charge. They asked Olivia none of the questions she'd been dreading: why she was here or how she'd got into the house. An old man with dementia had gone missing, that was their only concern. They asked Olivia what time she'd last seen him, and where. She led them around the back of the house and pointed out the old vegetable garden. These facts established, the two cops turned as one to face the rise of thickening bush beyond the orchard.

"What d'you reckon?" asked the younger cop.

"Probably," the older one replied gravely, nodding.

"Bugger," said the young one.

"What?" cried James.

The older man sighed heavily. "Mine shafts, from the gold rush days. They're thick as fleas on a dog through there."

"Do you mean they're not covered?" asked Silver. "Someone could . . ."

"'Fraid so. We need to get a proper search underway, quick smart."

"Talking about dogs," said the young cop suddenly, "What about Uncle Col? We could have him here in ten minutes."

The older man nodded. "Yep. I'll radio Tony and get him to swing by Uncle Col's on the way here. Amanda can notify Ballarat and the SES, start getting organized." He headed back to the police car, walking fast but heavily. He was a bulky man, and Olivia couldn't help noticing how his bottom wobbled with each step, though under the circumstances this observation seemed not only irrelevant but disrespectful.

"Uncle Col's got the best nose dog in the district," explained the younger cop. "My name's Mark, by the way." Names were exchanged and hands shaken all around, including Olivia's.

Not long after, a second police car bounced down the track and swung into the drive, and behind it a battered old utility. A brown dog sat in the passenger seat of the ute, looking across at them solemnly as the driver got out and opened the door for it. He was a tall, skinny man in jeans and a checked shirt, with a creased face and thick hair that was mostly gray. He and the dog ambled over to them.

"Curly haired retriever," said Olivia automatically, stooping a little to offer the back of her hand to the dog.

"Dinah," said the man, both an introduction and an instruction, and the dog sniffed her hand politely and wagged its tail. It had yellow eyes, strikingly beautiful against its dark brown fur.

"Hello, Dinah," said Olivia.

"This is Uncle Col," said Mark.

"Tony told me what's up," he said. "Got some of the missing bloke's clothes? Smell."

Olivia hurried inside. Grandpa's jacket was draped over the back of one of the kitchen chairs, and she snatched it up and ran back out to them. Dinah sniffed the jacket thoroughly, thoughtfully, then looked up at Uncle Col as if to say, *Ready*.

"Find 'im, girl," he said laconically. Immediately, the retriever put her nose to the ground and set off, picking up Grandpa's scent in seconds and following it quickly into the vegetable garden, up and down there a couple of times, then into the orchard, and she was racing around each tree so fast she was almost a blur. From the pear tree at the far end to the broken-down fence, through that and off in a fairly straight line to the gum trees beyond.

"Yep. Bugger," said Mark, the young cop.

Uncle Col was not far behind Dinah, walking fast and then breaking into a trot. The rest of them followed in a ragged clumpy line. One of the cops from the second car stayed at the house, the other, a policewoman in her twenties, had joined them. She was carrying a first-aid kit, Olivia noticed, and Mark now had a thick coil of rope over his shoulder.

They heard Uncle Col call out ,"Stay!" and he waited for them to catch up.

"Watch out now," he told them. "Don't want anybody going down a shaft."

"How deep are they?" James asked.

"Varies. Deep," he said. There was a big blank area in Olivia's mind that she was just not going near. *Grandpa, Grandpa, be safe, be safe*, she thought with such intensity it chased all other thoughts away, though she could feel them circling like wolves around a deer.

"You lot follow close behind us. Sandy, keep with 'em," the older cop said, and they all took off again, strung out through the bush like characters in a cartoon chase: first Dinah with her nose to the ground, Uncle Col fast and quiet behind her, then Mark, and the chubby older cop lumbering along, then Sandy the policewoman, with James and Silver and Olivia. They went on and on, deeper into the bush. Sandy pointed out some scrubby mounds.

"Old mullock heaps," she said. "But not all the mine shafts have got 'em. Sometimes they just open up in front of you. You've gotta be really careful."

After a couple of kilometers they heard Mark call, "Over here! Over here!" A few moments later they could see them. Dinah was standing alertly watching their approach; the three men were lying on their stomachs, side by side.

"It's a shaft," said Sandy grimly. Olivia saw Uncle James and Silver exchange an agonized look. Silver reached for Olivia's hand and held it tightly as they approached. The blank space in Olivia's mind was suddenly filled; the wolves were on the deer. *Is he going to be all smashed up?* she thought wildly. *How will we get him out? How will we get him to hospital if he's still alive?*

"Careful, careful," Sandy said. Her voice sounded barely audible to Olivia, as though faintly heard over the booming of ocean waves. She shook off Silver's hand and threw herself down on her stomach, wriggling the final meter till she lay beside Mark. *Let it be just a big dark hole*, she thought at the last moment, before she peered over. *I don't want to see him all smashed up.*

There was a big dark hole. But there was also, on one side of the shaft, a sort of shelf or platform thinly covered with pale sandy soil and spindly grass. It was not much more than three meters below the surface, and not much more than a meter or so wide. And on it stood her grandfather, grubby face upturned and grinning hugely.

"Olivia!" he cried as soon as her face appeared. "How are you, darling girl?"

"I'm fine, Grandpa," she heard herself reply. "What about you? Are you all right?"

"Oh, I'm just beaut. Tripped over and fell in this hole, that's all, darl. What good luck you've come by!"

"Terrific luck, Grandpa," she croaked. Uncle James was now on the ground beside her, and he too pushed himself forward so he could see over the edge of the pit.

"Hello, laddie!" Alex cried. He sounded delighted. "Wonderful! Can you and these other boys give me a hand out, do you reckon?"

"Not a problem, Dad," said James. He heard Mark ask Uncle Col, "You ever seen a shaft with a platform like this before?"

"Yep, seen three of 'em," said Uncle Col. "But them other ones, the timbers rotted out. They just go straight down."

CHAPTER 29

With the help of the rope, they had Alex out of the shaft in just a couple of minutes. He had gravel rash and a few cuts on his hands. His trousers were torn at the knee and his kneecaps were grazed and scuffed. Sandy used the disinfectant in the first-aid kit to clean up his scrapes. He was hungry, but they hadn't brought any food with them, only water. The older cop dug in his pocket and found a packet of Maltesers, which Alex enthusiastically accepted, crunching them up one after another till the packet was empty. Uncle Col offered tobacco but Alex had never been a smoker.

They walked back through the bush, phoning ahead to the policeman waiting at the house that the missing person had been found and was in good condition. Despite this, an ambulance crew came hurrying to meet them. They insisted on carrying Alex the rest of the way on their stretcher, and to Olivia's surprise he didn't object. "My knees are giving me a bit of grief," he confessed, though he'd been keeping up without a word of complaint.

He did object to going into the hospital to be examined, however, and only consented once the ambulance crew agreed—reluctantly, and after an exchange of phone calls with the hospital—that given the circumstances and his apparent lack of injury he could have a meal first. Uncle Col and Silver joined him in a cup of tea at the kitchen table as he ate, while James gave a statement to the police and Olivia packed up her things and Grandpa's bag and put them in Uncle James's car, along with her bike. Then they locked up the house, and the cars peeled out of the front yard one after the other. James followed the ambulance in to Castlemaine.

By the time they got through all the admission procedures it was late afternoon, and the hospital staff insisted Alex stay in overnight for observation. By now he looked absolutely bushed and was happy to settle into the bed with its crisp white sheets and piled-up pillows, in a bright little four-bed ward. His neighbor in the next bed, a man about his own age, leaned toward him.

"They treat ya like a king here, mate," he said confidingly. "You'll never wanna go home."

James, Silver and Olivia booked into a nearby motel. It was just getting dark when they sat down for an early dinner in the dining room. James urged Olivia to order whatever she felt like; Silver ordered a glass of wine and asked Olivia if she'd like one, too. Olivia didn't, but she thought it was very cool of Silver to offer.

Any minute now, she expected, they would start grilling her about what had happened. Pretty soon one of them would tell her (as if she didn't know already) what a dumb thing she'd done. But instead they asked about Inverness, and what Grandpa had said about being there. They were friendly and polite and didn't accuse her of anything. Olivia, still wary, was impressed.

At last James said, "I think I know why you took off like that, Ol. You overheard your mum having that fight with Uncle Robert on the phone, right?"

"Yes. How'd you know?"

"Robert actually rang me that night, after it happened. I spoke to your mum the next day and she was still spitting chips."

"She was saying she was going to put Grandpa in a home, like, *immediately*."

"I know. Everyone got pretty steamed up, Ol; I know. But it wasn't till this morning that Meredith realized Dad was missing, and about the same time your school rang Deb . . ."

I bet Fleur covered for me yesterday, Olivia thought. *I hope she isn't in trouble.* Now that Grandpa was safe, there was room in Olivia's mind to anticipate the trouble she would soon be in. She had freaked out so many people.

"But how did you know to come to Inverness?"

James frowned, trying to recall. "I'm not sure," he shrugged. "A hunch, I guess."

"Oh, you were pretty darn sure," Silver put in.

"Yeah, I s'pose I was, wasn't I? I just . . . put two and two together after your mum called me." He paused, did a little double take. "God, was that really just this morning? Seems like last week! But at first she thought you'd gone over to your friend's house."

"Fleur, right?" asked Silver.

"Yeah. Yeah," Olivia said, but she was no longer really taking part in the conversation. She had withdrawn from them to some other, unhappy place.

"I think there was something more that upset you," said Silver, watching her.

James said gently, "Deborah told me that your dad's moved out."

"Yeah, that's bad, too," said Olivia, nodding dolefully. Then she told them about Congo, about her parents conspiring to have him put down.

"But . . . but, Ollie," said James, looking confused, "I think he really *has* gone to live on a farm."

"No. That's all bullshit."

"How do you know?"

"These kids at school told me. It's just a thing parents say when they want to get rid of a pet. Like Father Christmas in reverse."

"Father Christmas?" asked Silver, lost.

"Just . . . you know, a bullshit thing for kids. But bad instead of good."

James stood up. "I'm going to call Deborah," he said decisively. "I'm going to call her right now and sort this out!"

He walked away from the table, pulling his mobile phone out of his pocket. They could see him through the glass doors that led from the dining room to the motel foyer. He was walking around and around, talking intently. They saw him go over to the reception desk and borrow a paper and pen. He was writing something down.

He came back to the table, walking quickly, holding this piece of paper up in front of him triumphantly.

"Congo *is* on a farm," he said before he'd even sat down again, handing the paper to Olivia. "And this is the name and phone number of the farmer! Deborah says she rang just this afternoon to check that he's all right, and he is. He really is!"

Olivia stared at the note, dumbfounded. *Janine Endicott,* it said, and there were two numbers, a home phone and a mobile.

"Why don't you call now?" suggested Silver.

"Now?" Olivia gaped.

"Yes, why not? Find out for yourself."

Uncle James handed her his mobile. She keyed in the first number.

"Janine Endicott," a woman's firm voice answered.

"H–hello," faltered Olivia. "I—I . . . Do you have a basenji?"

"I have three basenjis, actually," the woman said crisply. "No pups though. Possibly in about a year's time."

"No no, not puppies. Do you . . . Have you got Congo?"

There was a little silence. "Ah," the woman said. "You'll be the daughter. I spoke to your mother a few hours ago. She said you'd be calling me some time."

They talked. Janine explained that she had two female basenjis. "Used to have another male, fantastic animal. Snakebite, damn it. We

all missed him dreadfully, but now Congo's here the two girls are full
of beans again. They're bossing him around something shocking, but
doesn't he love it!"

"My other two dogs are females. He's used to two females bossing
him around," Olivia told her.

"Well, that makes perfect sense then," Janine said. "So they helped
you train him, eh?"

"They did most of the work, really," said Olivia. "Especially my
border collie."

"Oh, a border! No wonder! But really—what's your name again?
Olivia, right. I'm Janine. But you know that. Anyway—Olivia, I have
to say to you, you've done a fantastic job with this dog. Congo is one
of the best-natured and best-behaved basenjis I've ever known. We're
off to a flying start here."

Olivia laughed incredulously. "Thank you!" she said. "Wow!"

"Yep, I mean it. And if you want to come and visit him, you just
call me, okay? You're welcome any time."

There was just one more thing Olivia wanted to know. "Janine,"
she asked, "what sort of farm have you got? I mean, what other animals are there?"

"Aquaculture," said Janine. "Three big dams: yabbies and fresh-
water crayfish." She gave a triumphant sort of chuckle. "Have you
noticed? Basenjis hate the water!"

Olivia said good-bye and ended the call. Her head felt kind of airy,
like it was floating way above her body. The ordinary hotel dining
room looked gorgeous, like the Moulin Rouge or something. Everyone there looked beautiful.

"Thank you!" she said to James and Silver. "Thank you so much!"

They smiled. They looked really pleased with themselves, and
Olivia felt they had every right to. For once, adult smugness was jus-
tified. For a moment.

And then James had to go and say, "But you know, Ol, maybe you
should've trusted your parents a bit more. I mean, Deborah can be

narky I know, but she'd never lie to you. Especially about something as important as that."

Olivia scowled. "That's what you think. Mum lies about stuff. Mum's lied to *you* about important stuff."

James sat back. "How do you mean?"

"Well, she's never told you about the letters, has she?"

"Letters?" James and Silver shot each other a startled look. "What letters, Ol?"

She told them about the box she'd discovered in the linen cupboard, the box chock-a-block full of letters from Deborah to her mother. Secret letters, never sent.

"But there were no letters back the other way, were there?" James asked urgently. "No letters from Rose to Deborah?"

"But there *had* been!" Olivia declared vehemently. "I could tell from the stuff Mum wrote, especially when she was younger, like, a teenager—there were heaps of references to things her mum had written. So I knew she'd got letters from her, but she never told *you* that, did she?" She paused, and Uncle James's silence was profoundly confirming. "So you see?" said Olivia triumphantly. "*She lied!*"

CHAPTER 30

Alex was discharged from the hospital the next morning. The story of his rescue had gone around the hospital overnight, and it seemed like every single person there—nurses, doctors, several patients—was under some sort of compulsion to approach the family to tell them how lucky they were. Olivia started to feel really annoyed. Did they imagine it hadn't occurred to her, to Uncle James and Silver, even to Grandpa himself, just how incredibly lucky they'd been? The fifth or sixth time it happened she was tempted to put on an innocent face and ask "Oh, do you really think so?" But she didn't, she just nodded demurely, thinking to herself, *How come they're so clueless?* Adults, she meant. Then she felt mean, and disloyal. Uncle James and Silver were adults, and look how they'd figured out about Inverness. And been really nice. Everyone who'd helped find Grandpa, the cops, Uncle Col—then again, Uncle Col was a dog person, so of course he *would* be sensible.

They drove straight back to Melbourne, listening to the radio and chatting in a desultory fashion. Alex said a couple of times that he'd be glad to get home, but he seemed well and cheerful. James and

Silver hadn't said another word about the letters, but Olivia knew something was bound to blow. She was sorry she'd said anything now. She'd had all the excitement she could handle, and she wished it would just stop. But she knew it wouldn't.

When they arrived at Alex's house Meredith was waiting, waving cheerily as they pulled into the driveway.

"Hello, Daddy!" she said, opening his car door. "I hear you've been having adventures!"

"I have, darling, I have," he agreed, climbing out and giving her a hug. "Little visit to the old place, very nice. Marvelous people there. You'd have liked them."

"You'll have to tell me all about it," Meredith suggested.

"I will, I will. Just as soon as I'm sitting down with a decent cup of tea. It's true what they say, you know: you can never get a cup of tea as good as the one brewed in your own pot."

"That is so true, Daddy," she agreed. She hugged the others one by one as they got out of the car. Olivia heard her telling James in a fervent undertone, "You *brilliant* brother, you! I didn't even have time to freak out before you had everything sorted."

Then James and Silver took Olivia home. To her surprise Angus was waiting for her, too. This was almost alarming: were her parents about to gang up and yell at her? And if they started fighting with each other again she didn't think she could bear it, not just now. She greeted them both cautiously; the kitchen felt crowded and uncomfortably small. Mintie and Fly-by started whining in the backyard, just by the window; they must've heard her voice. One of them gave a short urgent bark and Olivia muttered something to the adults and went outside to their frantic doggie greeting. The dogs were beside themselves with joy. But no Congo. That still made her feel weird.

"They're not the only ones who are happy to see you, Ollie," her dad said quietly. He must've followed her out. Olivia looked up. Behind him, through the kitchen window, she could see her mum standing talking to James and Silver. Everyone looked calm—so far.

"Can we take these girls down to the park, Dad? They really need it. I can go to school straight after lunch."

"Sweetheart, I think you can have the rest of the day off, you know!"

Suddenly her father stepped closer and put his arms around her, hugging her fiercely. "My darling girl," he said, low and full of feeling. "I've been so afraid of losing you, Ollie. Because of everything I've done. I've been so afraid you won't respect me any more, or . . . love me . . ." His voice wobbled. Olivia felt pretty wobbly, too. She hugged him back hard.

"No, Dad. No," she said into his shoulder. "That would *never* happen."

"I broke my promise to you. It was . . . And I made a terrible mistake, I know, not telling you . . . I'm so sorry I didn't tell you about Congo."

"It's okay, Dad. It's cool. Really."

Mintie gave a short commanding bark. They released each other.

"Okay, Mints, park," Olivia confirmed. "But, Dad, can we just talk about—you know, nothing, for a while? I'm not up to any more big stuff just now."

"Yeah, sure," Angus smiled. His face looked kind of blurry. "Idle chitchat?" he suggested. She nodded. "Idle chitchat it is then. For now. Big stuff whenever."

Inside the house, James sat down at the kitchen table and indicated to Deborah that she take the seat opposite. Quietly Silver slid into the chair at the end.

"Deb, there's something I need to ask you," he said gravely. "And I want a straight answer, okay?"

He told her what Olivia had said about the letters. There was a silence. Deborah said nothing; her face was frozen, expressionless.

"So, Deb," James said. His voice was polite. "What can you tell us?"

Deborah swept one hand to her face and covered it almost completely with the open palm, pressing her fingertips against her forehead. Then she took her hand away and said, "Yes. I need to show you." But she didn't move.

"Show me?" asked James, prompting.

"Should I leave?" asked Silver, half-rising from her chair. "I'll wait in the car, I'm happy to do that."

James lifted one hand and made a patting-down gesture toward her. *Stay.*

"No, don't go," said Deborah. "It's better that I tell you both, I think."

They waited, but still Deborah didn't move. She had covered her face with her hand again and didn't seem able to go on. "So what is it, Deb?" asked James at last.

Deborah got up then and went into her study. She wasn't gone long and when she came back she was carrying a long, sturdily made black cardboard box. James vaguely remembered these boxes from pre-computer days. *Card file*, the name popped up in his brain. Or maybe it was *card index*. Something like that.

"It's this," Deborah said. She opened the box. James expected to see those old stiff lined cards, separated by alphabetical dividers. Instead it was crammed full of envelopes, lined up neat and tight. Most were a uniform size, with red and blue diagonal airmail stripes around their edges, the others, plain white or colored, were larger envelopes for greeting cards.

"What are these?" he asked. He had to hear her say it.

"They're the letters," Deborah said tonelessly, then swallowed hard and closed her eyes for a moment.

"From Rose. From our mother," said James. Deborah nodded, confirming.

His brain was spinning out, like a fishing line racing through the reel. He concentrated on his breathing, trying to slow it down. "She sent these to us?" he said, leaning forward, drawing the box toward him.

"Yes, to us kids."

"But they're addressed to Dad," he said. He'd pushed the first envelope in the box back a little and was reading the name and address. They were packed in so tight.

"That was part of some arrangement they had, she could only write to his office. So he could read them first, I guess. Vet them, or something."

"They really do exist," James said wonderingly. He was running his fingers across the tops of the envelopes. There were so many of them. They were *real.* "But when did you get them? Where were they?" he asked. "Did you pinch them from Dad's office?"

"No. He gave them to me. Not all at once, I don't mean. He gave me each one as it arrived."

"But . . ." James gaped. "You're kidding me! He *gave* them to you? I never saw *any* of these!" He was staring at his sister now, frowning hugely. Nothing made sense.

"No. I was supposed to read them and then pass them on to you younger kids. But . . . I never did." Deborah's voice was unusually light, as though she wanted the words to float away.

"Wait a minute. Dad gave them to you, you read them—and then you . . . what? Just *kept* them?"

"Yes." Again Deborah pressed one hand to her face, covering it. James pulled an envelope from the box at random and drew the letter out. *Darling kidlets*, it began.

"Rose told me she wrote to us," he said. His brain seemed to be working at the wrong speed again; his speeding thoughts could only find words very slowly. "She thought Dad kept them."

"I know. I could tell she thought that. Naturally." Deb, on the other hand, seemed to be talking very fast. "I used to wonder why she didn't accuse him of it. Why he didn't ask me."

"But didn't he?"

"Not once. He never said a word. He just never talked about her, you know that." Suddenly her voice rose in pitch. She looked straight at him, her face contorted with frantic intensity. "Lots of people thought our mother was *dead*, did you realize that?"

James pulled out another envelope, one of the larger ones. Inside was a handmade birthday card, to Robert. His fourteenth birthday. *What it would've meant to him, to get this,* he thought, staring at the whimsical drawing, the fond words.

"All that time," said James slowly, "we thought she never wrote to us, not even a birthday card."

Deborah suddenly put her head down, burrowing into her forearms crossed on the table in front of her.

"I know," her muffled voice said. "She wrote to us for ages. Lots at first, then less and less. They just kind of petered out."

"Did you ever write back?" But he knew the answer to that, and Deb just moved her head from side to side there on her arms, not raising it. "Not to send," she muttered. "I wrote, but I didn't send."

James stared across the table at the top of her head. Suddenly he knew he had to get out of there. Quickly. *I'm gonna lose it if I stick around,* he thought. *I could break things. Cry and not be able to stop.* He stood up so abruptly his chair teetered on its legs. Silver, silent and alert, met his eyes, and that steadied him. He picked up the box and strode with it over to the message book beside the phone and wrote something, quick and short.

"I know I've given you Rose's e-mail address already, but here it is again, so you've got no excuse. You have to write to her and tell her what you've done. Then you have to tell Robert and Meredith. You have to do all that, today."

"Yes," said Deborah humbly. "I will." She had lifted her head now and her face was stricken: he saw that she was sad and ashamed and a lot of other things, but he couldn't bear to look at her a moment longer.

"Tell the others. *Today.* No excuses, Deb."

"I've thought a lot about why I did it," Deborah offered. "I've thought about it so much."

James remembered her voice on the phone to him just a couple of weeks ago, berating him. *Sneaking bastard,* she'd called him, and he'd felt like the worst person in the world. He slapped his hand down on the kitchen bench, hard. "Right now, I don't give a *fuck* why you did it," he said, as close to yelling as he'd ever been in his life. "Jesus! I don't wanna hear it, Deb."

He looked at Silver and she rose immediately from her chair. "Say good-bye to Olivia for us," she said quietly. Deborah nodded. They left the house.

part seven

CHAPTER 31

From: deborah_mcdonald@optusnet.com.au

To: rose_sews@gmail.com

cc: jamesmcd@yahoo.com; vesrob@bigpond.net.au; merry1@hotmail.com

Dear Rose,

James has just left and I have to write to you immediately, before I lose my nerve. It has to be me who tells you, he's right. This is not how I'd imagined our first communication—and yes, I have been imagining it, ever since James dropped his bombshell about you. But I hadn't got very far with making that first contact, had I? Maybe this whole disaster had to happen first.

Today I gave James a box containing every letter and card you ever sent to us. I know you thought Dad never handed them on, but he did, or at least, he handed them to me and then they got no further. James was very angry and upset, and I'm sure Robert and Meredith will be too. Probably more so.

I've thought a lot about why I did what I did. I wanted to explain it to James but he was too angry, and now that I sit down to write this, I'm not sure I can explain it after all. It's like you trying to explain why you dumped us in the first place, I guess. What can you possibly say?

I genuinely believed I was protecting the younger ones by not showing them your letters. I thought it was best for them to make a clean break. That was my job: deciding what was best for them. It's the job you left me with, anyway, and Dad seemed happy to leave things up to me too. But ever since my own daughter was born, I realized I should never have been given that job. You and Dad both failed me, and I failed the younger ones. I seem to have failed at more things than I ever thought possible. Failing is what my life's mostly about these days, it seems.

I don't know why I kept them all. I really don't know. Several times since James told us about you I seriously considered destroying the lot. If we'd had a backyard incinerator like in the old days I think I would have! And in some ways I wish I had, because then no one but me would've known what I'd done. But that's the thing, isn't it: I would've known. I think I literally would not have been able to live with myself if I'd destroyed your letters.

Now James has the whole box-full and he knows what sort of person I really am. I'm sending this e-mail to the others too. I have to. And in a little while you'll be here in Melbourne and we'll all have to face each other. That is, if anyone can bear to see my face again.

Deborah

From: jamesmcd@yahoo.com

To: rose_sews@gmail.com

Hi Rose,

It was great to talk to you on the phone last night. I'm feeling a lot better now. All that stuff I told you about, Olivia and Dad and the mine—I think I was having some kind of delayed reaction. I didn't expect to start crying like that! I guess it's this thing with Deborah too, it's really rocked me. That stuff she wrote about "protecting" us—I am still completely gobsmacked. It's the kind of thing that makes you question, not your sanity exactly, but certainly your judgment—about people, and life and the whole darn thing. And knowing that I've gone along with Deb's notions of "protecting" us for all these years. It's the shattering of trust that's just so—shattering, I guess! Especially for me, because I trusted her totally.

Anyway, I'm just going to take it easy for a couple of days, hanging out at home. I took the letters over to Robert's place this morning so him and Meredith can look at them over the weekend. It's just amazing to read them; I said that on the phone I know. But it is, it's incredible.

I haven't spoken to Deb again yet, and have no plans to.

Thanks for letting me blah all that stuff out to you. Whew!

love, James

From: merry1@hotmail.com

To: rose_sews@gmail.com

Hello dear Mummy!

It seems so STRANGE to write that! But I call Daddy Daddy so it seems like I should call you Mummy. And today you really FEEL like my mummy, now that I've read all your AMAZING letters!

I cried and cried! They are SO BEAUTIFUL!! Me and Robert read them all in one big burst, hours and HOURS we were reading yesterday. And Robert cried too, yes he DID! Twice!!

Mummy, it is SO SAD to think of you writing all those letters and making all those beautiful cards AND NEVER GETTING A SINGLE WORD BACK!! I could KILL Deborah! She is not just bossy and a control freak she is EVIL!! It was an act of pure evil to keep your letters from us.

I am SO SORRY about my phone call to you a couple of weeks ago, or was it longer, I can't remember. I was angry with you, I really was ANGRY! Daddy is such a WONDERFUL person, he is is so KIND and he tried so hard to make a nice life for us kids, I couldn't BELIEVE that you could have just walked out on him like that. I thought you must be a horrible person and you'd just sucked James in.

Oh, if ONLY I'd KNOWN!! Especially that you thought I was artistic! What a HUGE difference that would've made in my life, to know that you SAW something artistic in me when I was just a little girl. If only I had known that you BELIEVED in me! Then I would have believed in MYSELF too, do you know what I mean? Oh, it makes me start crying all over again. I am NEVER going to talk to Deborah again, that's for sure!!

But now I feel like you really ARE my mother again and you can't imagine what that feels like!! SO AMAZING!!! I can't wait till you're here!!

lots and lots of love and kisses

from your little girl (now all grown up!!)

Meredith xxxxxx

From: vesrob@bigpond.net.au

To: rose_sews@gmail.com

Dear Mother,

I have just been re-reading my two previous letters to you. When I wrote them I believed I was being reasonably open in describing my life, family, career, and in particular the therapeutic work I have undertaken recently. However, I now see my caution and indeed distrust as very much in evidence. The revelation of all your past letters has made me look at the whole situation with fresh eyes. Clearly, when James described searching for these letters at Dad's house, he had no doubt whatever that you had written to us. But I couldn't quite believe it, myself. Amazing, the power of the written word. As we read through this veritable treasure trove yesterday, Meredith and I agreed that their existence changes, if not everything, then certainly a great deal.

That Deborah kept your letters from us is profoundly shocking. As someone whose entire professional life has involved the care and guidance of young people, her argument about "protecting" us seems entirely misguided, not to say self-serving. In actuality, it is a kind of theft she has committed, and not just of the material objects i.e. your letters. Deborah robbed us all of the connection we might have had with you. The enormity of this is almost beyond measure.

As a result, I found myself in rather turbulent waters, emotionally speaking. The psychologist I've been seeing pointed out that I may have transferred some of the feelings of abandonment and anger I had held toward you over many years, onto Deborah. But if she had not kept your letters from us, my feelings of anger and abandonment would not have been nearly so great. All in all, it is very difficult at this point to see Deborah's actions as in any way forgiveable. I believe Meredith feels much the same.

Nevertheless, both this therapist and my beloved wife Vesna say it is tremendously important to face things as they are, work through them and move on. Right now I can honestly say that in recent months I have faced a great deal about my past. I will do my best to do that with this situation too.

Vesna asks me to say, Mother, that she is looking forward very much to meeting you and introducing you to your two beautiful granddaughters. I heartily concur!

With warmest regards,

your son, Robert

From: rose_sews@gmail.com

To: vesrob@bigpond.net.au; merry1@hotmail.com; jamesmcd@yahoo.com

Dear Robert, dear Meredith, dear James:

Let me begin by thanking you for all your contact with me: by letter, phone and e-mail. And now, with the e-mail from Deborah, I am in touch with ALL of my children again. Although it has occurred under such difficult circumstances, I want you to know what a joy this is for me. It's been an extraordinary journey, and although the landing is proving, shall we say, a little bumpy, nevertheless it brings a truly great sense of fulfillment to my life. One I had long given up hope of experiencing.

I understand your anger toward Deborah for keeping my letters from you. It would be strange if you were NOT angry! And yet, nervous though it makes me to say this, I feel I must put my hand up and remind you that it is actually ME who deserves your anger. It was me, after all, who left you in the first place. And then out of guilt and fear, I made assumptions that were incorrect, and in doing so I let all of you down for a second time by not taking steps to find out if my letters were getting through, or to be in contact with you in other ways.

Even before I left, I made a lot of assumptions about Deborah: your father and I both did. She was always such a capable, responsible girl, and when I left I knew that Alex would rely on her for a lot of things, as indeed he did. I look back now at what I did, leaving a twelve-year-old with such enormous emotional and practical responsibilities, and I know that only someone as immature and selfish as I was then could possibly have thought that was in any way a good thing. It appalls me. I can't pass the responsibility for this off onto your father; it's my shoulders this must fall on.

I want to say so many things. Thank you from the bottom of my heart for being willing to meet me, and my husband Roland and his daughter—and for talking to me. Don't be afraid to be angry with me: it is right that you should be. I can take it—I hope I can! Try, please try, for everyone's sake, to be kind to Deborah. It would be a very sad thing if by coming back into your lives, I tore a hole in the fabric of your relationships with each other. By the way, I am writing to Deborah too, along these lines.

Thank you all, and I am looking forward so much to meeting you and your families in person, on your home ground, after all this long, long time!

with all my love,

Rose

From: deborah_mcdonald@optusnet.com.au

To: rose_sews@gmail.com

I shouldn't be writing this, I have drunk a whole bottle of wine by msyelf and opened another one so this is stupid but i have to do it. Your letter just gutted me and I didn't expect that to happen, i thought I would be tougher than that but noone has ever admitted what a lot of shit I had to deal with as a kid. Being the eldest and having to look after the younger ones and never being able to just bloody well be myself, just be a kid myself for christs sake. And Dad is such a nice bloke, such a fucking NICE BLokE, god, how can you ever complain about Dad? It was just a water off a duck's back anyway, if I ever got upset about everything I had to do after you left he'd say Fair enough darling. You just leave that for Mrs. Whoever was housekeeping or babysittting or whatever at the time. He never got that I couldn't just laeve it, I just worried and worried and did things and did thing all the bloody time. And now he has dementia and he must be looked after and I don't know how to dael with it but at least I DO know now that I CAN'T FIX IT. I can't fix things and i shouldn't even bloody try. And he will NEVER understand now, he will never understand how he helped make me like this.

And then along comes your e-mail and you do understand. I can't believe it. I can't believe how it makes me fall apart either. Why dos it make me fall apart inside to know thast you understand? And I have to tell you, I reliaze at I have to tell you about the letters, not your letters to us but all the letter I wrote to you over the years. I have to tell you how much I wanted you there and how much I hated you for not being there. So I wrote to you, aall these sad little girl letters and I poured my heart outto you whn I was a teenager, god all these tragic poems! They really are a laugh in a way but it's a pretty sad laugh. I wrote them for yours, then I stopped for a long time and I started again when my marriage started falling apart. Except my marriage was already falling apart exept I didn't kno wit, by the time I knew it was all too late because I wasn't looking, I just wasn't looking, I took him for granted and look what I got. I got what I deserved., God it hurts to say that.

I just have to get this off my chhest and tell you that I never stopped missing you, ven despite the bloody awful thing I did with your letters. but it was bullshit what i said last time about protetcing the younger ones, really I never gave them your letters becusae I hated you so much, you didn't deserve to have the kids love you and write to you. You know that doan't youy. Now I am going to press send because I will never send this if I leave till tomorroiw and i have to.

A couple of nights before she left for Australia, Rose had a dream. It was one of those dreams that is not actually frightening in itself, yet is experienced with such arduous intensity that the dreamer wakes almost trembling with uncertainty and exhaustion.

She dreamed that she had to meet someone urgently, but first she had to find that person's car. She went searching for it through unfamiliar streets and into a crowded shopping center. Now she was searching not for the car itself but for the keys to it. The man she was to meet suddenly appeared amid the crowd and came rushing up to her, saying, "Oh, thank heavens you have my keys!" and looking down she saw that her hands were full of bunches of keys. Then people, strangers, were coming up to her, thanking her and taking their sets of keys and rushing off, until she was left standing there with empty hands and no idea of what to do next.

She described this to Roland as they lay together, the pearly light of an English winter morning just beginning to filter into their bedroom. He listened, sleepy but attentive, stroking her hair, and when she'd finished he said, "I wonder what dreams they having now?"

"Over there?" she asked, tilting her head in a direction they both understood to indicate Australia.

"Yeah. Don't you reckon they dreaming about you coming too?"

"Yes, my love," said Rose softly, after a thoughtful pause. "Yes. I wonder what their dreams are."

CHAPTER 32

James was there to meet them at the airport in Melbourne, just as they had met him at Heathrow before, and since all airports are alike there was something familiar about it. Still, it took Rose by surprise, the little leap her heart made when she spotted him in the crowd, waving. *My son!* The connection was so quick, quicker than a heartbeat. Tears pricked her eyes. *Oh, heavens, why do airports make people so sentimental!* she thought, embarrassed, and then, *Oh, why not?*, and embraced him without wiping those tears away.

James drove Rose, Roland and Jacinta to his home, the big handsome place overlooking the bay they'd seen in photos. It was late morning; the sun shone into the deepest corners of the garden and sparkled on the surface of the lap pool.

"Very nice," complimented Roland, accepting the coffee James handed him with a waiterly flourish. "Is our Silver about?"

"Ah. She'll be back *any* moment, I hope. She's gone to fetch our niece and nephew. Thought it might be nice for Jacinta to meet some family her own age."

"Are they my cousins, then?" asked Jacinta.

"Um . . . I'm not sure what relation they'd be . . ."

"Stepmother's grandchildren . . ." Rose mused. "Doesn't bear thinking about."

"Okay, let's call them cousins, anyway," said James. "They're cousins, too, of each other I mean. You're in between them, age-wise: Laurence is seventeen, I think, he's just finished school, and Olivia is thirteen going on thirty-three. Unusual girl. I think you'll like her, Jacinta, she's really into animals, like you. In fact, I'll bet she brings her dogs with her."

"Cool," said Jacinta.

Silver arrived with Laurence and Olivia soon after, and the three young people went out into the garden with Mintie and Fly-by. The adults could see them wafting to and fro, chatting and laughing together as things loosened up.

"My god, they are *so* beautiful!" said Silver, voicing the thought in all their minds. All three teenagers were tall, even Olivia, but she had the lanky build of a half-grown filly while Jacinta, at sixteen, stood poised in the doorway between girlhood and womanhood. She had skin the color of milky coffee and extraordinary tawny eyes.

"She takes my breath away, that girl of yours," Silver said to Roland.

"She's taken that young man's breath away, for sure," said Roland, and indeed they could see Laurence's attention was focused keenly on Jacinta. And he really *was* a young man, James suddenly realized, with newly broadened shoulders and a wide chest, moving with an easy grace that made his plain T-shirt and jeans look elegant, flicking his thick straight hair back from his eyes from time to time. James smiled. He recognized all of this; wasn't there some element of himself there, after all?

"Oh, dear," said Rose. "Suddenly I feel ancient. I think I'm going to have to sit down."

"Yeah, you the ancient queen," teased Roland, pulling out a chair for her. "The ancient queen who's seen everything."

"Not quite everything, my darling, I hope," she said, taking his hand briefly and kissing it. "Not yet!"

"Dad, Rose!" said Jacinta, bursting in. "Can I go for a walk on the beach? Liv and Laurence are taking the dogs down there!"

Roland looked enquiringly at James and Silver.

"Oh, it's perfectly safe," James said. "Just at the end of the garden, practically."

"Hey, Jass!" called Olivia from just outside the open door, "Can you grab a few apples or something? We're starving!"

Silver gave Jacinta a big handful of apricots from the fruit bowl on the table and they were off, three yearlings sprinting across the grass with the dogs leaping and bounding beside them. Then the garden was empty, though the shimmer of their energy hung in the air awhile. Unexpectedly, Rose felt a sense of certainty welling up: the conviction, quick and sure, that she had done the right thing in coming here, that this visit would be a good one. Good for everyone.

Rose wanted to visit each of her other children by herself, one by one. No one disagreed. James and Silver lent her their spare car, a little Renault. Roland would go sight-seeing with Jacinta—although as it turned out, Jacinta spent a lot of her time with Laurence and Olivia. The further plan was for a gathering of the whole family at Alex's place on Christmas Eve: casual, a barbecue with lots of salads. The big Christmas Day lunch would be at James and Silver's house, and people could walk off their feasting on the beach afterward.

James was preoccupied with a new painting; he apologized for this on their first day, saying (of course) that it was nothing special, but he had just got started and couldn't seem to leave it. When his mother asked if she could see it he actually hesitated for a moment, repeating that he had only just started work on it, and then said, "Yes, yes, of course," and she followed him down the stairs to the studio.

Rose's first glance confused her: the sketched outlines on the canvas suggested something familiar—*Trees, aren't they? Or* . . . but there was a dizzying tilt of planes that threw her eye all out of kilter. Coming closer, she saw that stuck on the wall beside the canvas were detailed drawings, torn from sketchbooks or just on scraps, and by examining these Rose understood where the large painting was going. Yes, trees: it was a forest scene, but from multiple perspectives: there was the root system below the soil, and there again at ground level; the trunks, seen from the eye of an insect or grub and also of the bird zooming in to pluck it up, and similarly with the branches, the twigs and leaves. It was the life of a forest and all the trees within it, from deepest root fiber to slenderest leaf tip, as experienced by the trees themselves and all the creatures who lived there. Simultaneously. No wonder it was dizzying!

"Good heavens! This is amazing!" Rose exclaimed.

"Pretty wacky," said James dryly.

She went back and forth from the small drawings to the outlines on the canvas, peering closely and then stepping back, and close again. Finally she said, "It really is wonderful, James. If you pull this off as you intend, you'll have done something quite extraordinary."

"Thanks," he said matter-of-factly.

"It makes me realize the limits of my own talent. You have this gift of seeing things through completely different eyes. Whole other worlds. I'm in awe."

James shrugged uncomfortably. "And I can't even thread a needle, let alone create clothes from scratch. Different strokes, y'know?"

"Oh, very well, James," she said, smiling. "So. From water to forest. No more people?"

"Maybe the next one. I've been thinking of a family scene."

"Yes?"

"Yeah. All of us, and you. Kind of vicarious—what do you call it? What's the word for getting rid of guilt?"

"Expiation, I think. Absolving? But what do you have to feel guilty about?"

"It's obvious, isn't it? Keeping you to myself for all that time, Rose. Leaving the others out."

"That seems such a little thing to me, James. Relatively."

"Yeah, well, the others didn't think so! But they all stopped being mad at me once it came out about Deb and your letters. That still doesn't mean I wasn't . . . you know, shabby, in a way." He picked up his wide pencil and turned it around in his fingers, then made some inconsequential gestures toward the trees outlined on the canvas. "And a wuss, for sure," he added. Rose smiled tenderly.

"My dear boy. Compared to what *I've* got to feel guilty about! I can hardly believe I'm here now and that . . . It still seems incredible that *any* of you are willing to speak to me, really."

James gave his mother a look that was equal parts knowing and playful. "Well, as Eeyore said: don't settle down to enjoy yourself yet, young Piglet," he teased. "There's still time for you to cop a serve from somebody."

"Cop a serve? Is that the same as being taken to task? I'm rather steeling myself for that."

"Soon find out, won't we? So, who's the first cab off the rank?"

"Robert. Tomorrow morning, eleven o'clock." Rose gave a theatrical shudder to demonstrate the extent of her nervousness.

"Don't worry, Rose, really," James said. "Whatever happens, you can handle it. I'm sure of that."

"I do hope so. I have to. Because there's no running away this time."

CHAPTER 33

Rose, who was a good driver and had an excellent sense of direction, wasn't nervous about driving herself around what was, after all this time, a mostly unfamiliar city. Nevertheless, she somehow made a couple of wrong turns on the way to Robert's house, arriving a little late, a little flustered. *Be calm*, she told herself. *Or at least, pretend to be. Poor Robert will be more nervous than I am.* She pulled up outside the house and noticed a blur of color flash and disappear from the front window. Then the door was flung open and two girls with bright unruly orange hair sprang onto the porch, hesitated, and then hurtled down the steps and across the lawn toward her car. Plainly they were disobeying instructions. A woman with the same remarkable hair, a little less bright perhaps, appeared on the porch, calling them back. The two girls pretended not to hear her, milling instead on the nature strip and peering in excitedly at Rose. The woman looked at Rose, too, and smiled shyly and waved, and Rose waved back and got out of the car.

"I'm Vesna, Robert's wife," the woman said as they met halfway up the front path. She had one hand now on each of the girls' shoulders. *What a shame about the glasses,* Rose thought. All three were dressed in gathered floral cotton skirts and white blouses with lace edging the collars. *Good heavens, homemade mother and daughter outfits! What century am I in?* then chastised herself for being such a fashion snob. *The lace is very good. The real thing.* "Sorry about this rowdy pair! They've been so eager to meet you," said Vesna, and Rose was suddenly in love with that warm, genuine smile. "This is—"

"I'm Bianca," said the taller girl, stepping forward with her hand out. "I'm nearly eleven."

"And I'm Alexa," said her sister, bounding from her mother's gently restraining grip. "Hello, Grandma!" They all shook hands, but clearly the girls were dying to kiss her so Rose bent forward a little and was immediately enveloped in a double hug. When she looked up from their embrace, Robert was walking down the steps toward them, smiling broadly. Rose was reminded powerfully of Alex, the Alex she had last seen almost four decades ago. The thinning brown hair with its trace of red, the long bony limbs. The utter, and completely unselfconscious, lack of style. And as the man came closer she saw traces of the boy, her older son, the good, anxious, disciplined child she'd known back then. And, yes, loved.

"Hello, Mother," he said, and walked straight up and hugged her over the heads of Bianca and Alexa.

"Hello, Robert. Hello, everyone." Rose had the odd but definite sense that this close-knit family group had deliberately expanded its structure to encompass her as though making room for a new dancer in a troupe, a new player on the team. She had not expected this. *How kind,* she thought. *He was always kind. Like Alex.*

Once they were all seated in the living room, the girls stared at their grandmother avidly. No one knew what to say at first, so Rose brought out her presents. First, for Robert and Vesna, a pair of lovely little watercolors of the Somerset countryside, which they exclaimed over admiringly, and then, for each of the girls, a porcelain-headed doll which Rose had dressed herself. She had been worried whether Robert's daughters might not be too old for dolls, but they seemed truly delighted with them. *Can everything really be going so well?*

The resemblance between Vesna and her daughters was even more striking in real life than in the photographs Robert had sent. The extraordinary hair seemed almost to snap and crackle. They were not what you would call beauties, Rose thought, with their round faces and the very thick glasses that magnified their eyes. But the eyes themselves were lovely, brown, well-shaped and clear, and their complexions were creamy, with a sweet dusting of freckles. More, there was such good humor and curiosity in each open face, such readiness to find pleasure in whatever they encountered. *In fact,* Rose realized, *they are remarkably attractive, in the true sense.* Yes: one felt attracted to being with them, being part of their enjoyment. And Robert positively glowed in this setting. *What a good choice he made,* she thought, watching him confer briefly with Vesna on some point. *What a lucky man.*

Bianca and Alexa left the room and quickly returned, each carrying a violin case and a recorder. "The girls are going to give us a little recital before we have lunch," said Robert proudly. "They're both very talented musicians!"

Rose's heart sank. *Oh no, not children's performances!* and quickly admonished herself. *For heaven's sake, these are your granddaughters!* But it was just as bad as she had feared. The girls were not particularly talented, though they clearly loved playing and their parents loved to hear them. Their repertoire was extensive and Rose felt herself going almost cross-eyed with boredom and an eerily familiar irritation. *This is why I ran away,* she realized, appalled. *It was from perfectly ordinary, nice things like this.* She looked across at Robert. *And you, poor thing, you most of all liked to show me what you could do, vibrating with anxiety that I should like it.*

But the Robert she looked at now was not anxious. He sat next to his wife, smiling contentedly at their daughters sawing away on their violins, and then the awful piping of the recorders. Rose looked curiously at his hands: the young Robert's hands had been such a giveaway. But this Robert's hands were perfectly relaxed, one resting on the arm of the couch, the other on his thigh. *So, this therapy he told me about, it must be working?* Who'd have thought it! Sensing his mother's eyes on him, he turned to her and gave a little grin and tipped his head toward the girls as though to say, *Aren't they terrific?* Rose smiled back, nodding her phony agreement with alacrity.

After the girls had finished their recital and received their applause, they put their instruments away carefully in their cases and Vesna said, "Now, you two come and help me in the kitchen and let Daddy talk to Grandma. With no interruptions!"

"Okay, Mum," they said cheerfully, and both bounced over to Rose and gave her a kiss before following their mother out. At the last moment, Alexa turned in the doorway and ran back to her grandmother, leaning in close to whisper, "We think you've got pretty hair!" and raced back again, giggling, ducking under her sister's arm.

"Oh! Thank you!" called Rose, startled and pleased. Bianca closed the door with a flourish.

"So, Mother!" said Robert. "What do you think of my girls?"

"Oh, they are lovely! Ever since I laid eyes on them, I've been thinking what a lucky man you are. Not only your daughters, Vesna too. Just beautiful. I really mean that, Robert."

He nodded, several times, almost too pleased to speak.

"I knew from the moment I met Vesna that she was the right girl for me!" he burst out. "And amazingly, she felt just the same way. It was love at first sight, Mother, even though that's rather a clichéd expression."

"But sometimes a cliché gets it just right, doesn't it? How wonderful! I'm so glad for you. And, Robert? You can call me Rose, you know. I mean, after all these years . . ."

Robert hesitated and then said firmly, "If you don't mind, I'd like to call you Mother. Precisely because of all these years, perhaps."

"Oh. Certainly, of course," agreed Rose, taken aback. She cast about for some new subject. "So, I see you don't do the fingering any more," she said. *Oh, that was hardly tactful!*

"Yes, no," Robert agreed, and laughed suddenly. "I remember it used to drive you up the wall!"

"I'm so sorry," Rose said. "I was such an irritable mother."

Robert shrugged. "Ah well. I'm sure it *was* annoying! It was a hard habit to break though. Well, it was more than that one habit. I told you about all that, didn't I?"

"You did. And I must say again that I was tremendously impressed with your approach. Your openness."

"It took a long time, Mother. I resisted medication, I resisted everything really. I wasn't even completely honest about it with Vesna. I look back now and think, *What was I so ashamed of?*"

"We all have things," said Rose tentatively, "that are difficult to admit to. Don't you think?"

"I do," he nodded firmly. "I do indeed. Almost impossible, I see now, without professional help. Now I regard my therapist as being like . . ." He looked around the room, searching for the right comparison, "My dentist! Go for a check-up regularly or you'll wind up with all sorts of problems! It's as necessary as that, for me anyway."

"Oh, how times have changed! It would've been unthinkable for an Australian man to say that when I lived here. If therapists were even around then, which I doubt."

"It's still difficult for many people even now. Believe me, I was one of them," he said seriously. "I was floundering; I had no idea."

"I'm sure you're being too tough on yourself, Robert," Rose said. "I mean to say, you had a successful career already, a wonderful family."

"True, but at the same time . . ." he paused, thinking, then went on with a rush. "Six months ago, that business with Deborah and the letters would've thrown me into a complete tailspin. I would've brooded on it night and day, in secret of course, and I wouldn't have been able to even contemplate forgiving her. Let alone . . . you."

Rose drew in her breath. *Face it squarely,* she told herself. "I think what I did to you all was far less forgiveable than what Deborah did," she said. Sitting side by side in the still room, they gazed at each other. Their seriousness, the intensity of their concentration, was almost palpable, but there was a calmness, a serenity even, emanating from Robert, and Rose realized, *I'm not nervous any more.* Sounds of Vesna and the girls preparing lunch could be heard distantly from the kitchen.

"I wonder," Robert said gravely, "if you can understand how . . . incomprehensible it was? It tore me up for years, I can tell you. You have no idea how many nights I lay awake going over and over the same questions: *Why did Mum leave like that? Was it us? Was it me?*"

Rose's heart clenched. "I am so sorry, Robert. It's pathetically too little, but I hope not entirely too late. I am *so* sorry."

"But, listen: ever since I married Vesna, and especially since the girls were born . . . Then *I* started to feel sorry for *you.* Everything you were missing out on. I mean, I knew you'd had that first part, our childhood, but it didn't make you *happy*, did it? Not like it's made me."

"No," Rose whispered sadly. "It didn't."

"Vesna would say, when we talked about it, *She must have been so unhappy. More than we can imagine. Poor thing.*"

"You certainly shouldn't feel sorry for me."

"No. And I don't, really, not now. And with my life now, with my family and my work and finally tackling all this anxiousness, this OCD business . . . I ask myself, who does it benefit if I brood and worry? What good does it do to be angry with Deborah? Or you, what purpose would it serve to be angry with you now? It would only make me wretched again. And why deny my lovely girls their grandmother?"

Rose listened intently. This man, this son of hers, was so much more complex than she'd expected. But—what *had* she been expecting? *Children,* she realized with a shock. *I thought they'd still be my children, the ones I left. But they're not, of course they're not. They're all grown up!*

CHAPTER 34

Meredith had moved into Alex's house shortly after the episode at Inverness. This solution, neatly answering two needs—Alex's for greater support, Meredith's for a new home now that hers had been sold—had been arrived at quickly. Deborah wasn't consulted. Rose gathered that the worst of this angry period of shunning Deborah was over, and she was now being included in the extended family's life again, and also that there'd been a fundamental shift. Deb's opinions no longer carried more weight than anyone else's.

Incredibly, Alex had suffered no ill-effects from his adventure, apart from sore knees, and Bernadette's massage and acupuncture treatments soon fixed that. A couple of times he talked about having gone back to the old place, and how the orchard needed attention. Maybe he'd get back there sometime, *give 'em a hand with the pruning, you know.* But then he'd allow that he had his work cut out keeping up with his own garden.

The day after meeting Robert and his family, Rose went to see Meredith. Robert had arranged to take Alex for a massage and lunch afterward, giving Meredith some time alone with her mother. Then a minor complication, when Jacinta asked if she could spend the day with Laurence and his friends, and it was decided that Roland would deliver Rose to the house on their way. There were delays setting out, with missing swimsuits and misplaced car keys. Again—*darn it!*—Rose felt flustered and jumpy.

Meredith greeted them all effusively, with lots of hugs and kisses and exclamations at Jacinta's beauty. Jacinta blushed and laughed; she was curious and rather excited to meet Laurence's mother, but she and Roland were running a bit late and couldn't stay long. Rose took advantage of Meredith's preoccupation to examine her, trying to find some point of recognition. It was much harder to locate than it had been with Robert. Of course, Meredith had been the youngest, only six when Rose last saw her. There was no sign of that plump-cheeked child in this small, fast-moving woman with the soft brown hair heavily laced with gray, and her thin worker's hands. In the hazel eyes, though, her large expressive hazel eyes, perhaps . . .

Once the others had gone on, Meredith, still bubbling, started showing her mother around the house.

"Well, it's only two bedrooms as you can see—this is Daddy's room, gosh, he's had those same old prints up forever but he loves them— so it would've been too small for three of us but it's all worked out okay, Laurence had a standing invite at his friend Tristan's house, Tris was doing his VCE, too, you see, and his parents have been through it all before so that was actually really good. But we told you all that, Rose, didn't we? So, this is *my* room . . . I made those curtains just a couple of weeks ago, the old ones had really had it, though Daddy insists that he wants the ones in his room to stay. That lilac tree out-side the window was *gorgeous* just a while ago, oh, the smell: divine! But of course it's finished flowering now."

Rose was nodding and smiling, wondering if Meredith would ever draw breath. The little Meredith had been a clingy, tearful child. Perhaps she was still there, that sensitive little girl, shielded by this lively chatterbox? And the drinking James had told her about: was that another shielding layer? Though the latest word on that was that Meredith was solidly on the wagon. She looked well, certainly, a little on the thin side but probably that was just her build; her face was a good color and you could see the firm muscles in her arms. And to Rose's surprise, her daughter called her by her name; she had been rather dreading the *Mummy* of the e-mails. Momentarily, she wondered why the shift, especially since Meredith always referred to Alex as Daddy. But it didn't matter.

"It was a bit of a mess a year ago but I've been keeping everything shipshape and now that I'm living here, of course, it's so much easier. And this is what I really wanted to show you; this used to be just the living room but now it's also . . ."

They stood together in the doorway of a large rectangular room, which looked onto the front garden. A comfortable couch, a shabby easy chair, and a television set had been arranged in the back part of the room. At the front, where the light poured in from a big window, two old dining tables stood at right angles to each other, and inside the L they formed was a chair on wheels, one of those modern office chairs adjustable in every direction. On one of the tables was a stack of thick paper, card really, and a plain tumbler full of pencils and pens. On the other, one of those clear plastic multi-drawered containers for bits and pieces full of—well, bits and pieces, and sitting neatly beside it a couple of pairs of scissors of different sizes, a snap-blade cutting knife, and various sorts of glue. And between them, what Rose recognized as a work in progress: one of the "journal things" that James had first described to her in words of astonished praise, and Meredith had mentioned only hesitantly, excited but intimidated by the notion that she might be making . . . *art*!

"It's also your workroom," said Rose to her daughter, who had fallen silent at last. "Isn't it?"

"Yes, this is my workroom," Meredith said quietly. "Well, it's the living room, really."

"And your workroom."

"Am I really allowed to say that?"

"You most certainly are!" Rose exclaimed. "Haven't we moved on from the nineteen sixties, at least? When I always felt I had to clear away my dressmaking things, my sketches and designs, before visitors arrived?"

"Did you work in the living room, too?"

"I did then, my dear: now I don't have to any more. But it doesn't matter where it is. As long as you have the space you need, and the tools, and you're not made to feel that it's something . . . *secondary*. Unimportant."

"Well, I never used to think what I did was important," Meredith said. *Where's that dizzy chatterbox gone?* Rose wondered. This Meredith was a thoughtful woman. "Till James told me what you said."

"But why should that have made such a difference? You'd already been making these pieces, for years, hadn't you?"

"But they were *nothing*! It wasn't until . . . It was like I was—listening out for this voice to tell me it was all right, that they were really . . . That *I* was really real!"

"Don't tell me that was *my* voice you were waiting to hear, Meredith. That would be more, I think, than I could bear."

"All right then!" her daughter said, and beamed cheekily at Rose. "I won't tell you that, since you couldn't bear it!"

"Thank you, you're very considerate!" Rose smiled. "And now, would you show me some of your work, please?"

They examined her "journal things" for almost an hour. Rose was amazed that they had remained unknown, unseen by others all these years. There were so many, on loose sheets of card, mostly, but also in bound volumes of various kinds, books Meredith had picked up here and there. Rose saw throughout a vision that, for all its whimsicality, was acute, original and consistent. The odd comic/collages were a commentary, not only on Meredith's own life, but the world she lived in. They were hard to define, and genuinely unique.

"We *must* come up with the right name for these!" Rose said, carefully replacing a loose sheet in its folder.

"I guess we should," said Meredith, sounding hesitant. She was still shy about them. "Silver says she'll put her thinking cap on."

What will happen to them next? Rose wondered. *She can't still want to keep them private?*

They left off to have a cup of coffee in the kitchen, and immediately Meredith became garrulous again, launching into a detailed explanation of how the household practicalities had been worked out. As Rose listened to her rattle on about part-pensions and a carer's allowance, the other siblings' contribution and the local council's programs, she felt sure that this talkativeness was indeed a screen of some kind, a protective layer. Somehow it was hard to *see* Meredith when she chattered on like this: her lively expressions and constant hand gestures seemed to physically obscure her. It was fascinating, and a little unnerving.

"And as well as the financial help, you know what else Silver's done? Gosh, she is *such* a terrific woman! But you know that already, Rose! She's given me all this incredible professional advice, and she's introduced me to the guy who's now my agent. You know I just signed a book contract, don't you?"

"*No!*" Rose gasped. "A book contract? I had no idea!"

"*Really?* Oh, good old James, I thought he'd have told you, but I guess he thought it should be my news." Meredith was smiling so hard her face looked liable to split in two.

"Oh, congratulations! Who is the publisher? How thrilling!"

So Meredith described all of that, too, and then when she had finished they were both quiet a moment, almost out of puff. Meredith leaned across and put her hand over Rose's.

"One more thing. It wasn't just hearing that you'd always thought I had talent and might be an artist that made all this . . . possible. I'd stopped drinking, too, so I could see my way clear at last. That was what was holding me up, really. I was always full of bullshit excuses but that was really it. You know about my drinking?"

"Something," said Rose cautiously.

"Yeah, well, it was something all right, I can tell you! I was out of control. That's over now, thank god, but I'll be going to AA meetings twice a week till the day I die. For sure."

"So, was it awful? Giving up?"

"Mmm, pretty awful. But I have to say, Robert was fantastic. I'm very lucky to have a brother like him. James, too, of course, but Robert was *incredibly* supportive."

"There was always something special between you and Robert. From the day you were born."

"Yes," Meredith said. "My big bruvver!" She paused, listening. "And that's his car!" Her face lit up with a wicked grin. "*Whoo-hoo!* Come on! Time for you to meet Daddy! The big reunion!" She laughed riotously, as though someone had told a terrific joke.

Well, I wish I thought it was that funny, Rose thought, trailing behind Meredith to the front door. As her daughter's hand was on the door-knob she called, "Meredith, wait!" and caught up to her.

"If he doesn't remember me . . ." she said, her voice suddenly thin and uncertain. "If he doesn't remember that we were married, don't say anything. Please."

"Okay," said Meredith, looking at her searchingly. "If you're sure?"

Rose nodded very definitely. "Please," she said again. Suddenly she was scared, terrified she would break down, lose control somehow. Would she feel sick with regret, with guilt? Revulsion? Overwhelmed by the past rushing in on her? Might there be a shameful surge of relief? Part of her wanted to cry *Don't open it!* and then Meredith opened the door and stepped out onto the verandah, and she followed.

As she watched Robert walking up the path with an old man, she felt . . . nothing. Or a pause perhaps, as though everything in her—body, mind, heart—was holding its breath. Again, she saw her former husband in her son, and realized with a distant shock that Robert was older now by several years than Alex had been when she'd left him. And she'd thought him an old man then!

He was straight-backed and cheerful-looking, a tall man but not a big man, though she had always thought of Alex as big. Alex McDonald. Her first husband.

"Hello, Daddy," called Meredith. "We've got a visitor!"

Alex looked at Rose and stopped in his tracks, gazing at her. A smile spread slowly across his face.

"I know you," he said wonderingly. He came right up to her and took both her hands in his. "We went to school together, didn't we?" he said with warmth and certainty.

Rose laughed lightly, feeling a bubble of delight that could pop and become hysteria, but probably wouldn't. "Something like that," she said, and tilted her head in her charming way.

"Actually, Daddy," said Meredith, and the mischievous tone in her voice alarmed Rose. She glanced quickly at her and yes, her daughter's face was alight with glee. Rose caught her eye and shook her head but Meredith's grin didn't falter. "You used to know this lady very well indeed! This is Rose. She used to be called Rosemarie. This is . . . my mother."

"Well, fancy that!" exclaimed Alex, still holding Rose's hands. "I've always wanted to meet your mother, darl. And to think we used to go to school together, too!" He gave her hands a welcoming squeeze, and Rose's heart, which had choked as Meredith said precisely what she had asked her not to say, galumphed into a thumping beat. *I could smack her bottom!* she thought, and the thought was so absurd she had to laugh again.

"Well, come in, come in," Alex urged. "Let's have a nice cup of tea and I'll show you around my garden. Rose, is it? And you're just as lovely as a rose, too," he declared gallantly.

Rose allowed Alex to lead her down the hallway. Behind her she could hear Meredith and Robert giggling and whispering together like naughty children. *Is this how they cope with it?* she wondered. *By turning it into a kind of game? Or is that just how I'm seeing it now?*

They sat together on a bench in the garden, almost, Rose felt, like an old married couple. Robert was facing them in a big slatted chair, Meredith perched on the arm. *Our children.* Rose felt like she was floating several feet above the scene. *Oh, this is unreal,* she thought. *This is too much!* For an awful moment she had an overwhelming urge to jump up, to run out to the street, ring Roland, get away. And then Meredith made some silly joke that Rose didn't even hear but Robert and Alex both erupted into laughter, and Robert made as if to push his sister off the arm of the chair and she cried "Eek!" and caught her mother's eye and grinned and Rose thought, *No, it's all right, I can do this. I can stay.*

CHAPTER 35

With Deborah it was harder, Rose found. Hardest. Jacinta came with her, because *Liv wants me to meet her friend Fleur,* and the presence of the three girls talking and laughing in Olivia's room warmed the atmosphere of the house. But then they took the dogs to the park, leaving Rose perched at the kitchen bench with an awkward silence. Deborah had offered her mother an assortment of teas and coffee but had not made one for herself, nor had she sat down once since Rose arrived, keeping herself busy with little chores. On the floor beside the bench sat a plastic bucket containing several large bunches of flowers, and now Deborah hoisted it up and stood there meticulously preparing all these flowers and arranging them in the vases she'd got down from a high shelf. Stem by painstaking stem. She was facing her mother but Rose wondered if the activity had been planned precisely so that Deborah could avoid looking at her as much as possible.

They talked about Deborah's work, mostly, and politics. Deborah asked her mother a lot of questions about the British parties, how they were perceived, and especially about the new system of government in Scotland. Rose silently thanked her lucky stars that she had some good friends who lived in the Borders, south of Edinburgh, both ardent nationalists who had regaled her with the workings of the Scottish system over many a boozy dinner, so she was able to sound quite knowledgeable. Deborah became more and more interested, even animated: it was plain where her passions lay. While they talked, Rose observed her eldest daughter. She was striking to look at. Beautiful, in a spare, sculpted sort of way. But she looked tired, too. Sad. A little gaunt.

When the flowers had all finally been arranged, Deborah said abruptly, "Right then. Let's go for a walk and catch up with those girls, shall we? It'll be nice and shady over in the park now."

As they entered the park with its huge elms towering over long avenues and picnicking groups, Deborah said, not looking at her mother, "That e-mail you sent everyone about the letters. Where you asked them to go easy on me. Thanks for that."

"Oh. I . . . I felt it was the only thing to do, really," said Rose, startled. "I mean, I'd caused the whole sorry business in the first place, hadn't I?"

"Yes," said Deborah bluntly. "You had."

They walked on in silence. Just as they caught sight of the three girls sitting under a group of trees, throwing a ball for Mintie and Fly-by, Deborah said, "Did you tell the others about my e-mail? The one I wrote when I was drunk?"

"About your letters to me? No, I didn't. I felt . . . It wasn't my place. It was too . . ."

"Too what? Soppy? Dripping with gooey sentiment?"

"No!" Rose stopped, and Deborah did, too, although still she didn't look at her mother. "Just too private, that's all."

"Okay. Well, thanks. Hi, girls!" Deborah called, lifting one arm in the air to attract their attention and striding ahead. Clearly the subject was closed. Rose followed her slowly. How could Deborah describe her naked confession of such painful emotions as *dripping with gooey sentiment*? How could someone deride their own deep feelings so bitterly? It shocked her. Then, thankfully, the girls enveloped them in their game with the dogs, their talk, their laughter, too delightfully self-absorbed to notice that Deborah and Rose were both a little remote.

As they were leaving the park Rose screwed up her courage and asked Deborah quietly, "Those letters you wrote . . . do you think you might show them to me, one day?"

Deborah gave her a speculative look. "Maybe. I don't know that you'd want to read them, really. There's a hell of a lot of crap in them, you know. Hurt. Anger. Resentment. All sorts of lovely things."

"I'd still like to read them. I should know."

Deborah pursed her mouth and nodded, but it was not necessarily a nod of agreement or consent.

They went to dinner at a local pizza place. The girls were in high spirits, quite silly. It was a fun end to the evening and Rose was much relieved, since the rest of her visit had been so strained.

Rose was in the car outside the house, waiting for the girls nattering on the footpath to finish making their arrangements. Deborah stepped forward and leaned her hip against the driver's door. Arms folded, she said in a considering tone, "It'll take a while, I guess."

"For what? For us to . . . get to know each other again?"

"Mmm. And being on the other side of the world doesn't help."

"I suppose not. But we can be in touch, Deborah, if you want to. We can e-mail. We can phone, if you like."

"Phone. E-mail. Don't you think it'll take more than that?"

"But . . . I *do* live in England, and it *is* on the other side of the world. And you're here, and you have your life and your family here . . ."

"My family!" said Deborah. "You know what? The best thing I could do for my family right now is just to give them a break. A break from me."

"Oh, Deborah. Don't say that."

"Yes! I'm not being melodramatic, it's true!" Deborah turned to face her mother properly for the first time. She gripped the edge of the open car window tightly. "If I came," she said urgently, "If I came and lived in the UK for a while, do you think . . . Would you want to see me? Do you think?"

"Yes, of *course!*" Rose said, placing her hand on top of her daughter's, pressing it. "Could you? Is that possible?"

"Yes. Yes, it is," Deborah said. Just then the girls wound up their farewells and Jacinta clambered into the passenger seat. Deborah released her grip and shoved herself away from the car door with both hands. She stood back in the roadway and gave her mother a wry, enigmatic smile. "Well, see you in a couple of days then, on Christmas Eve. At Dad's place."

"Yes. But can you tell me . . ."

Deborah shook her head. "Later, maybe," she said. "Bye!"

"Bye, Liv! Bye, Fleur! See you soon!" yelled Jacinta from the passenger's window as they drove off. For a few minutes Jacinta chattered ebulliently and then there was silence. Rose glanced across and saw that the girl had fallen fast asleep, like a tired child. She drove on through the summer night, along the sporadically familiar streets. She wiped at her face with the palm of one hand. Tears were coursing down her cheeks and she was glad no one was there to ask, *Rose, why are you crying?* because she wouldn't have known how to answer. She wouldn't know where to begin.

Deb sat at the outside table, drinking her way through most of a bottle of a wine. For the first time since all this had begun, more than a year ago now, she felt outside the storm. At last, a breathing space. A little window to look through, and consider.

The dogs snoozed on the paving at her feet; Olivia had gone to spend the night at Fleur's. Deborah drank slowly and steadily. As her position gradually became clearer, so did her options. And the best and most effective strategy.

In order for my life to move forward, she thought, *I have to take a step sideways. In order not to be diminished, I have to be bigger than I am.*

When the bottle was empty she stood up and stretched. "Yes!" she said in a loud, definite voice. Mintie lifted her head sleepily; a silent cat walking delicately along the top of the fence froze, waiting. "I'm going to do it!"

CHAPTER 36

On the morning of the family gathering, Rose was gripped by spasms of panic. *Christmas Eve!* It was almost macabre! To gather everyone together on the exact anniversary of the night she had walked out on her former life, so eager to grab her own future and so careless of the futures of her husband and children. Oh, what had possessed her to arrange this trip *now*? What had she been *thinking*? She hadn't been thinking, that was it. As usual, she castigated herself, it was a case of act in haste, repent at leisure. But there was no help for it now, the arrangements were all made—and there could be no running away this time.

The day was hot, another reminder of that long-ago Christmas Eve, but a mild change came through in the late afternoon. Rose still felt jittery when she arrived at Alex's house with Roland, James and Silver. Jacinta had spent the afternoon there helping Meredith and Laurence with the preparations. They walked around to the back of the house and Rose took a deep breath and started to relax. Alex's garden was a beautiful oasis, the shadows just starting to creep onto the green lawns, the floral beds a riot of color. Tinsel had been strung here and there through shrubs and branches, even through the wire netting of the chook pen, and fairy lights that would glimmer and twinkle as the evening came on. The laden fruit trees formed a romantic shady backdrop. *Thank heavens he has this still*, Rose thought, watching as Alex picked peaches straight from the tree for Alexa and Bianca. *He will always be a happy man if he has his garden*. She thought of how fiercely she had resented all the time he spent in the garden, when she was an impatient young woman itching for more. *Ah well!*

Trestle tables had been set up in the shade, covered with plain white paper on which Meredith had drawn in crayon the wise men and their star, shepherds and angels, a baby in a low crib, his parents and the barn animals looking on—but the faces of the Nativity characters were the faces of her own family, and the dogs faithfully guarding the crib were Mintie and Fly-by and dear old departed Banjo. Flowers had been scattered here and there amid the drawings; it seemed a shame to cover them with the platters of food.

Robert fired up the barbecue and before too long was calling out for everyone to come and get their steaks, chops, sausages, and a prawn or two if they were quick! For the next few minutes people were occupied loading their plates and finding a place to sit, and while they were settling themselves Deborah approached Olivia, seated in a canvas director's chair with her two dogs behind her.

"I think now's the right time," said Deborah.

"Do you? Okay," Olivia said. "You still want me to, you know, announce you?"

"Yes, please, if you wouldn't mind."

"Okay." Olivia stood up and put her plate on the seat of her chair, shooting a stern *Don't even think about it!* look at the lurking Fly-by. She picked up a glass tumbler and a fork and, stepping to the center of the garden, began tapping the glass to make the sound of a bell.

"Hello! Everybody!" she called. "If I could have your attention please!" *Ding, ding, ding!* "My mum, Deborah that is, has something important that she'd like to tell you all."

The gathering quieted quickly. Olivia sat down and Deborah took her place in the center of the lawn, the eyes of her family on her and every face lit with interest.

"Well, thank you," she began, sounding a little nervous. "Thank you all for coming, and thanks to Dad for having us here, and to Meredith and everyone for making it all look so special. And welcome to our visitors, especially thank *you* for being here!" She raised the glass she was clutching in the direction of Rose and Roland, and there was a general glad acknowledging murmur. "It's Christmas Eve, nearly the end of the year, and it's been a very interesting year for all of us. A big year. And for me it's been a *really* big year!" She stopped a moment and looked around. James smiled at her, curious, encouraging.

"A lot's happened, and I've had to face up to a lot of things," Deborah went on. "A lot of things about this family, and myself. There's a saying, isn't there, about how no one is indispensable? If there isn't, there ought to be! That was my biggest mistake: I forgot that."

Some people frowned, and some smiled. Deborah looked hard at the grass at her feet for a few moments, and then lifted her head.

"Well, I've got over that. No one, *including me*, is indispensable! Life goes on, that's the important thing, and just to prove it, I want to announce that you'll all have to do without me for a while! I've accepted a twelve month position with the government in Scotland. I'll be leaving for Edinburgh in mid-January—just a few weeks."

Amid the general exclamations, Alex could be heard commenting approvingly, "Edinburgh, that's good! My grandfather went to the university in Edinburgh."

"During which time," Deborah continued, "Olivia's father will live in our house with his new partner Marion, so that Olivia's life and schooling won't be interrupted—except of course by the arrival of her new little brother or sister, since Marion and Angus's baby is due at the end of March. And I want you all to know that I wish them all well, I really do. I wish . . . I wish all of them and all of you the very best of good luck and good health. And a merry Christmas!"

She raised her glass a second time, as for a toast, and everyone raised their glasses, too, and called, "Cheers!" and, "Merry Christmas!" and Alex said, "Here here!" and someone called, "Good for you, Deb!" Deborah went over to James, who was smiling and patting the seat beside him in invitation. She made a relieved face as she sat down; he kissed her cheek, and she tilted her head to rest it momentarily on his shoulder. Meredith had put her own dinner aside and brought a laden plate of food over to her sister, squatting next to her and putting a hand on her knee.

"That is such incredible news, Deb," she said. "A year in Scotland! Wow!"

"It *is* pretty amazing, isn't it? When it came up, I just thought . . . you know, the timing, everything . . . I'm very lucky, Meredith, I know I am. I couldn't go away for a year now, for instance, if you weren't here with Dad."

"Well, we're *both* doing what we want, then! Even better!" said Meredith chirpily.

About an hour after that, when everyone had finished eating, and the dogs were chewing quietly on the bones, and the plates had been gathered up and the leftovers taken indoors, just as darkness was creeping into the garden and people were starting to make going-home noises, Olivia noticed Uncle Robert going around to each of his siblings. Judging by his eager look and their attentiveness and then the nods, he was suggesting something. She watched, curious, as they gathered on the lawn and turned to face the rest of the family. Robert took up a glass and a piece of cutlery, just as Olivia had done earlier, to ding like a bell and attract everyone's attention.

When they were all quiet, Robert gestured for his mother to come toward them. She paused a couple of meters away and he said in a ringing voice, "Mother, we'd like to sing you a Christmas carol."

"Oh!" cried Rose, lit by a sudden flash of memory, and her hands flew to her face.

Robert turned slightly to count the others in. "One, two, three!"

"O come all ye faithful, joyful and triumphant,

O come ye, O come ye to Be-ethlehem."

Vesna joined in, hitting the high note in a voice of real loveliness, her daughters quickly following:

"Come and behold him, born the king of angels . . ."

And then the others were all singing, too, even Alex, the garden full of swelling *O come let us adore him*s, and Alex even tried to start the second verse but not many people could remember the words to that one and besides, a couple of voices were wobbling now. Tears were trickling down Rose's face; she hadn't even tried to sing, she was just smiling hugely and crying and saying, "Oh . . . oh . . . ," again and again.

"Welcome back, Mother," said Robert, stepping forward and folding her in a close embrace. The other three surrounded her then, all reaching to stroke her shoulder or hug her, saying, "Welcome back," and, "Merry Christmas, Rose."

"And you'll have noticed," said Robert, stepping back at last, "That there's no Christmas tree here?"

"Yes?"

"So we don't want to hear any rubbish about you going off to get some lights for it, all right?"

"All right. Yes, all right," Rose said, laughing shakily through the tears. Someone handed her a napkin and she blew her nose and mopped at her eyes. "Oh, look at me. You've made a complete mess of me, you rotten kids!"

"Well, *of course* we have!" said Meredith, her hands on her hips. "That's the whole *point*, isn't it?"

The little knot broke up. Alexa and Bianca came running in to hug their father, one on either side. Watching them, Olivia thought, *There's something different about Uncle Robert.* He looked bigger somehow: not like he'd put on weight, quite the opposite, more like he'd taken up swimming maybe. That was it, that open swimmer's chest, like Uncle James, noticeable even though he was bending a little to return his daughters' hugs. And he just seemed . . . less *fussy*, somehow. More relaxed, like her own dad. And at that thought, a pang of missing her father tightened her throat again, and she thought, *I'll e-mail him as soon as I get home.*

As soon as she had fed her other animals and settled the dogs, Olivia went into her bedroom and opened her elegant white laptop. Instantly it sprang to life, displaying her latest screensaver: a photo of Congo with his basenji girlfriend, taken on a recent visit to Janine Endicott's farm.

How Olivia loved her new computer. She had never been much of a one for writing before, not beyond schoolwork, but since Silver had given her this laptop she had been writing more and more. All sorts of things, just as they occurred to her, not trying to keep them in order. It was all too confusing for that, everything that had happened. But as she wrote, it started to seem a bit *less* confusing. That was good.

She opened up her e-mail program and popped Angus's address in the "To" space.

Hi Dad—

Merry Christmas Eve! We just got home from Grandpa's. This was the McDonald family get-together that I told you about for my grandmother. I really wish you could meet her. Maybe next time. She looks incredibly like Mum, except older of course. Well, not surprising, she is her mother! She doesn't seem much like a grandma—I mean that in a nice way! She asked me to call her Rose. Mum and everyone call her Rose too, except Uncle Robert, he calls her Mother, you know how he is. I like her, she seems really sensible. Her husband is here too, he's really nice and his daughter is FANTASTIC, her name's Jacinta and she is 16. You know how Laurence is taking a year off before he starts at RMIT? Well, Jacinta's dad has offered him a job with his company in England and Laurence can work there and stay at their place and everything, and travel in Europe and stuff while he's there too. He is really excited. I think he really, REALLY likes Jacinta too. I'm glad she's so nice.

Mum told everyone about going to Scotland next year, and you and Marion coming to live here. So now it's official! Every single adult except Grandpa came up to me kind of privately afterward and asked me how I felt about having a new baby brother or sister. Oh, Silver didn't ask either, she is pretty cool and I guess she already knows how I feel! I told them all I'm really happy about it and I also said that I really like Marion and they would too. They all looked pleased, it was good. Auntie Meredith gave me a big hug and said how lovely it will be to have a new baby in the family. She got a bit sooky, you know how she is. But nice. Her living at Grandpa's house is working out really well.

Well, I hope you have an excellent Christmas Day and get lots of presents! Please say hello to Marion for me and wish her Merry Christmas too. See you both soon. Have a good time there in Paradise (joke - because it's Eden, right?).

Love you, Dad

Liv (Olivia) xxxx

She clicked on *Send* and the message disappeared, swirled away into cyberspace. Olivia exited her e-mail and opened a new document.

She wrote about the evening just past, and Jacinta meeting Fleur. About the incredible, heady feeling of being someone who had *two* friends, and the relief, the *joy* as those two friends met and liked each other, too.

It was late by the time she finished. Now she saved the document one last time, and instructed the computer to *sleep* and closed its lid. The soft round light on the front of the sleek white box glowed dimmer and brighter, dimmer and brighter. As she settled down to sleep she smiled, feeling that it was watching over her. It would breathe in and out with her through the night, patiently waiting until she was ready to tell it more; to open the lid again on her magic box of words.

In the guest room of his old mate Dave's house in Eden, Angus's laptop registered the newly arrived e-mail, but he'd know nothing of it till next day. He was lying on the bed with Marion; they had just made love. She had gone to bed not long after dinner and Angus had come to join her, quietly nestling against her back and bottom. He stroked her; he lifted her long soft cotton nightie, and one thing led to another. Now they were both drifting contentedly toward sleep. She lifted his hand from where it lay on her hip and snuggled it to the mound of her belly, between navel and pubic hair. Below his hand, their baby, who weighed a little over two pounds now and was six months and millions of cells on from that initial chance meeting of egg and sperm, flexed and stretched its little body against the elastic confines of Marion's uterus, still perfectly comfortable in its watery home.

The baby was a little boy, but his parents didn't know that, having elected through all the various tests and procedures not to be informed of its sex. Embedded in his genes were those for his mother's height, and her stoicism, but not her auburn hair, and in there too was his father's easygoing nature and three unusually long middle toes. This baby was already encoded for a healthy body and a personality inclined to cheerfulness and contentment; destined not for great things, but for good ones. But no one knew that yet. His parents talked about him, and dreamed, but no one knew him at all.

GLOSSARY OF AUSTRALIAN
WORDS AND EXPRESSIONS

p. 12 - **big-noting yourself**
To attempt to inflate your status or achievements, deriving from race-track punters who placed bets using large-denomination bills in order to appear wealthy. (Australian culture tends to frown on self-promotion of any kind.)

p. 42 - **fit as a Mallee bull**
Physically strong; toughened by harsh conditions. (The Mallee is a famously arid agricultural area in southeast Australia, home to tough tree roots and bulls alike.)

p. 57 - **shag on a rock**
Isolated, deserted, exposed. (From the manner in which the seabirds called shags or cormorants stand alone with their wings outstretched.)

p. 56 - **beaut**
Excellent, great. (Originally short for *beautiful*—Australians love to abbreviate.)

p. 135 - **boofy**
Plain of face and not too clever-looking either.

p. 148 - **chiacking**
Teasing banter.

p. 149 - **sanger**
Short for *sandwich*—and a *snag sanger* is a sausage sandwich.

p. 162 - **daggy**
An appearance lacking in style. (Originally, dags were the dirty clumps of wool around a sheep's rear end; now dag [noun] and daggy [adj] are used, often affectionately, to describe someone who is goofy or unfashionable.)

p. 134 - **minnie**
Short for *minute*.

p. 201 - **arvo**
Short for *afternoon*.

p. 212 - **wagging**
Cutting school or class.

p. 239 - **wowser**
A killjoy, especially a person who is prudish and anti-alcohol. Reputedly derived from the acronym of a nineteenth-century temperance group: W(e) O(nly) W(ant) S(ocial) E(vils) R(emoved).

p. 256 - **bunny-rug**
The small, soft blanket in which a new baby is wrapped.

p. 311 - **spitting chips**
Very angry (having shouted so much that the mouth is dry as wood).

p. 315 - **narky**
A scolding, complaining person; one who is always interfering and spoiling the pleasure of others.

p. 366 - **sooky** (rhymes with *cookie*)
Tearful; from sook, a crybaby.

Author's Note: I hope that your enjoyment of my novel has been enhanced by the inclusion of these few examples of Australia's richly idiomatic vocabulary. I didn't set out to write a novel full of slang—if I had, this glossary would be ten times as long. No whinging, now, or I'll do my block! (Don't complain or I'll get really mad!)